POLITICAL ANIMAL

POLITICAL ANIMAL

a novel

DAVID MIZNER

ISBN 1-56947-386-2

Library of Congress Cataloging-in-Publication Data
Mizner, David.
Political animal: a novel/David Mizner.
p. cm.
ISBN 1-56947-386-2 (alk. paper)
1. Political campaigns—Fiction. 2. New York (N.Y.)—Fiction.
3. Speechwriters—Fiction. 4. Young men—Fiction. I. Title.

PS3613.I96P65
813'.6—dc22   2004011250

For John Mizner
who didn't get a chance to read this book.
I think he would have liked it, and I know
he would have edited the hell out of it.
Thanks, Dad. I love you.

Acknowledgments

Without the support of my family, this book would still be a dream, and I'd still be working in an office, dying a slow death. Alison Mizner, the world's greatest mother-editor, helped me every step of the way, and Sarah Marston, with her husband Josh, always encouraged me—and always picked up the check.

I relied on my friends for editorial as well as emotional guidance. Alex Sherwin has given me twenty years of perfect friendship and 86.7 percent of my laughter. (A few of the book's best lines are his; not as many as he'll claim, however.) Julian Rubinstein, my fellow dreamer and chief commiserator, inspired me in many ways, most of all with his bravery. Every writer should have the benefit of Kostya Kennedy's intelligence and generosity.

Finally, there were the people who pushed the book into print. Jane Dystel and Miriam Goderich didn't give up when lesser agents would have. Juris Jurjevics pissed me off to productive purpose and allowed me to alliterate as much as I wanted to. Seriously, man, thanks. You changed my life. And Michael Sowiski who found it and started it all.

1

I'm eating Kung Pao chicken with a spoon and listening to people tell lies. I usually avoid work-related functions, especially going-away parties, but today my hangover hunger clouded my judgment. This is where we have staff meetings, where we make decisions that get overturned by decisions made in smaller rooms. The only window gives you a view of the wall across the hallway. I often imagine that the window is a one-way mirror and that this is a police interrogation room, though in an interrogation room the hostilities are in the open, the indignities obvious. More obvious, that is.

Tod Wilcox, the communications director, is giving a toast. Mona, he tells us, is a "wily veteran." He calls her other things when she's not around: lesbian avenger or Peter, Paul, and Mary, a dig at both her politics and her sexuality. "We've all benefited from your years of experience," he says, raising his plastic glass of Diet Sprite.

"Amen, brother," says Shawn, who talks black when he talks loudly.

Mona Bern has worked for Schecter—Representative Arnie Schecter (D-NY)—since he first ran for Congress in '78. Until last month, she was the legislative director in DC. She's an old-school liberal so her views no longer jibe with Schecter's. They fired her in stages, first sending her up here, to the headquarters of the Schecter for Senate campaign, then nudging her toward the door with all the subtlety of bouncers. The guys who run the campaign have no use for a sixty-eight-year-old woman, especially one who gives you the peace sign when she passes you in the hall. She's leaving to work on a race in Wisconsin.

"I don't know where to begin, sister," says Lisa Karsch, the new legislative director, one of eight Schecterites who came up from DC to say goodbye to Mona—and to check on the campaign. The Man himself isn't here; he's hitting a few black churches in the Bronx. Joining him today is an entourage composed of Danny Cohen, the campaign manager, and seventy-five percent of our black employees. Schecter probably would have brought along all four, but *someone* needs to answer the phones.

As I slop sesame noodles on my plate, a pain pierces my temple, and I imagine blood clotting in an artery like grease in a drain. The last part of last night, I realize, is a blur. Ethan and I went to a bar, where we came up with the idea of making a documentary about the privatization of the prison industry. "There's no reason not to do it," he said, knocking over his drink. After that: a conversation about love, a man who showed us his nipples, a chicken parmesan hero. When my reeling head hit the pillow, I was going to create a muckraking masterwork, but this morning, standing naked in the chill of the refrigerator, water dribbling off my chin and into my chest hair, I had aspirations only of making it through the day. On the subway out to Brooklyn, I devised a plan: kill the morning by reading the papers, eat a long lunch, pretend to work on an op-ed about gun control, leave by eight, go to bed by ten. The problem is, my plan required an uneventful day, unlikely with the Primary Election only three weeks away.

Shawn is guffawing, probably at something he just said, and people are looking at me. They think I should give a toast. Having worked with Mona both here and in DC, I'm supposed to stand up and share a gently mocking memory, some mild humor to balance the semi-sincerity of my "but seriously" ending. What I ought to do, though, is blow up this shindig with a truth-bomb.

Calliope Berkowitz, my best friend in the office, is pointing at her head, telling me to use mine. *She* wants me to tell it like it is and I would, I would goddamnit, if my chest weren't so tight, if a hot thick liquid weren't flowing in behind my sternum and hardening like lava. I breathe in through my nose for eight seconds, but the air's too stale to bring relief; it's a mixture of garlic fumes, body heat, and sleep-deprived breath.

Now Calliope's rubbing her eye and holding back a giggle.

I have a glob of sesame sauce on my eyebrow.

Nobody cares if I speak.

Good.

Mona opens her presents: a bumper sticker that says "Don't Blame Me, I Voted For McGovern," and a gift certificate to Barnes and Noble, which she holds in front of her coke-bottle glasses, examining it as if it were a parking ticket. *This* is my thanks, she's thinking, money given in my name to a corporate villain. Do these people know me at all? Why not a case of Coors and a pair of Nikes?

"Thank you so much," she says.

"Not so fast, girlfriend," says Shawn, the youngest person on staff; at this time last year he was annoying people at Syracuse. "You've got one more gift." He reaches into a bag and pulls out a yellow-green Sytrofoam hat shaped like a wedge of cheese, the sort worn by fans at Green Bay Packer games. "It's to make you feel at home in Wisconsin." He hands it to Mona, who has no choice but to put it on. Cheers, all around.

The room quiets as she stands up from her seat at the head of the table. With the hat concealing her thicket of hair, her nose has taken on a new prominence. She looks like Henry Kissinger—irony she wouldn't appreciate since she doesn't appreciate irony. She adjusts the cheese, pulling it tighter with both hands, then looks down at her notes. I admire Mona—she was on the political frontlines when there *were* political frontlines—but she's not going to be honest for fear of offending Schecter. She still loves him. She still loves him even though he prays to polls, even though he didn't come to her party. There seems to be nothing he could do that she couldn't explain away.

"I got into this business to make the world a better place," she says. "And I still believe that we can help those—"

The ring stops her, an electronic gobble. It's the conference phone in the middle of the table, barely visible amid the white village of food containers. Tod pokes the phone with a chopstick, and Schecter's power-drill voice bores through: "How's the party?"

"Perfect timing!" Mona says, and lunges toward the phone, her glasses sliding to the tip of her nose. "As usual," she adds, and Calliope looks at me.

"As per usual," I say, ever eager to please her. It's one of our favorite asinine sayings, along with "Same difference" and "He's good people."

"Hey there, Mona," Schecter says. "I can't believe we're going to run a campaign without—" His voice is lost beneath crackly static. With a breaststroke, Shawn pushes the containers away from the phone. Calliope smiles at this, the illogic.

I love her.

The static persists. Mona is staring at the phone, which looks oversized and fake, like something out of an old science fiction movie, the past's vision of the future.

"Maybe he's got Lewinsky in the car," I say, getting a few laughs, a few glares. It's shamefully easy, Monica humor, but whatever it takes.

"He'd probably go for a shiksa," Calliope says.

It dawns on me that the static might be on our end only. Which means he heard my joke. If he did, I might be done, Schecter having fired people for less. This isn't the way I want to go out, riding a cheap crack. I picture yelling, righteousness, applause. And music. I've even concocted a not completely crazy scenario in which I march out of the office past a throng of cheering factory workers.

But if he heard me, then he heard Calliope too, and we'd take the fall together. We could leave tonight. Drive to Montana, take off our clothes, jump in a stream.

There are three dumplings left. I've already eaten too much, but I'll enjoy that moment when the dough breaks open, giving way to juicy ginger pork. And when do you ever get to eat as many dumplings as you want? When you have dim sum. But I never have dim sum. I pour sauce over the dumplings and stuff them in my mouth, puffing out my cheeks to make room.

". . . going to miss you," Schecter says, the static partly clearing.

"We couldn't hear you for the last few minutes," Tod says.

"I basically just said thank you."

"Thank *you*," Mona says. "I want to say something I've been meaning to say for a long time. Do you remember what happened at the rally in seventy-eight?"

"What?"

"At the rally in seventy-eight, with the Perleman supporters?"

"Now I can't hear you. I'm going to hang up."

"Wait," Mona says. "Please."

"Don't be a stranger, Mona. Everyone else, we've got a race to win."

"Arnie," she yells. "Don't—"

She's cut off by violent dial tone, which sounds about right. Theme music. "Hang it up," I say, and someone does. Mona falls back into her chair as though pushed. There's motion: men turning away, waiting for women to take charge because that's what men do at times like this.

The volunteers and interns clustered around the table clear a path for Calliope as she makes her way to Mona, who's begun to tremble. I send Calliope a mental message, telling her to take off Mona's hat, but she doesn't hear me. We don't communicate as well as we should.

Callie sits and Mona bites Calliope's shoulder. Mona's tears come in convulsions that seem to shake the room. Twenty years of good work, but she'll be remembered as a sobbing hunk o' cheese.

I spring from my seat as though I have to be somewhere and shuffle sideways through the crowd, bumping elbows and asses. As I escape through the door, I realize that I *do* have to be somewhere: the bathroom, known around the office as my office. The light in the bathroom shuts off after twenty minutes if no one comes in. A few times, it's gone out while I was on the toilet. Shitting till dark is what I call it.

★ ★ ★

By the time I come out of the bathroom, things are back to normal, as though Mona never broke down, as though she never worked here. The show must go on.

The office, which occupies the seventh floor of an eight-story building in downtown Brooklyn, is a web of low-ceilinged rooms, crammed with desks, bookshelves, boxes, filing cabinets, and tables, and littered with campaign literature, newspapers, soda cans, coffee cups, food wrappers, and food containers. The structure of the office, with its nooks, contributes to the fragmentation of the campaign. Danny and Tod are friends from Princeton, but they've clashed in recent weeks, and Lana Knox, the field director, is making a play for power, so the office is divided into rival fiefdoms, and within those there are conflicts too numerous to keep track of, though some people try.

Tod's my boss. My desk used to be in the heart of his territory, but I claimed the noise disturbed me and was granted exile in the research room, which I share with Gerry, the research director, and his assistants, Jenny and Jen. They're not a scintillating trio—they chat about the Earned Income Tax Credit the way most people chat about movies—but they show flashes of humor, and I find their disinterest in office politics refreshing. They're content to sift through documents.

"You left the party in a hurry," Jenny says. She's similar to Jen in more than name: they're both tiny, they both went to Yale, and they both think I'm ridiculous. But Jenny's Korean and Jen's blond. I'm not attracted to either, but out of a sense of workplace camaraderie, I allow them to join forces in my fantasies. Oddly, the midnight kimchi-on-white sandwich that we create doesn't translate into daytime arousal. My stomach hurts.

"He had to get to his office," says Gerry, who's holding a document in front of his glasses. He actually appears to be sniffing it.

"Yeah," Jen says. "He had to take a big meeting."

I am Potty Man. I am Slob Clown. As roles go, it's honest. It's also rebellion of sorts. But I've been trying to clean up my act. For one thing, it's not as funny as it once was. For another, it's holding me back. I have in mind more courageous forms of rebellion. I have ideas. I want to lead, to win hearts and minds, to shape the future of the planet, and it's hard to do all that with pee stains on your pants.

There's one e-mail in my inbox, from Mona, which she sent to everyone: "I'm sorry I got so emotional. Thanks again for a wonderful party. Go Schecter!"

I open up a file that will become the op-ed about gun control. But not today. I won't contribute to an institution that humiliates a fine woman. I turn off my computer, which groans with pleasure as it shuts down. To make my idleness obvious, I swivel my chair so that I'm facing the door.

A meager protest to be sure, a joke compared to the speech I should have delivered in the conference room. Opportunities like that don't present themselves every day. Most of our victims are distant—they're percentages—but today our expediency bloodied one of our own. On the other hand, maybe Mona didn't want anybody to come to her defense; after all, she welcomed the party, if not the cranial attire. I would have been speaking more for me than for her. Well, of course, and so what?

Calliope comes in, her fingers in a bag of peanut M&Ms. She smiles a smile that intrudes on her cheeks. "I'm sorry, Ben. I didn't mean to interrupt you."

The four of us watch her walk toward me. You have to look at her. Even if you don't find her attractive—I didn't at first but now I do—you have to look at her. She's five-ten, with wild auburn hair that falls to the middle of her back and a big-featured face that has a million different looks. Her breasts are large, just how large I'm not sure because they always lurk beneath loose clothing.

She sits down on the brown corduroy couch next to my desk and hangs her right leg over the arm. "They had an election to pick the color of the new M&M." The deepness of her voice still surprises me; first time I heard it, I thought she was joking. "Twenty million people voted. Twenty million people voted for a piece of chocolate."

"What color did you vote for?"

"Silver."

"I take it your candidate didn't win. Too radical."

"No, but he's moving toward the center, toward gray."

This is how we talk sometimes. We think we're clever. We know we are. But I'm tired of being clever.

Her leg looks almost white between her black dress and her black boot. She's swinging it back and forth, and every time it hits the couch, her calf bulges. Her legs and arms are toned from yoga, but I imagine that there's chunkiness under her dress.

"Terrible," she says.

"Terrible."

"*So* bad."

"The worst."

"Getting rid of her wasn't enough so they had to humiliate her."

"The old cheesehead torture."

"Right," she says. "They make you wear cheese and throw bullshit at you."

"Now we get to hear Schechter talk about how cruel the Republicans are."

Contemplating this, she scratches the couch, her thumbnail riding a cordoroy groove, her lips puckered in an oval that bumps up against her nose, which curves down.

She shrugs with only her face. "Stuff like that happened everywhere. I worked at an orchard, rape crisis center, restaurants. Even at the yoga place people got shat on."

"Literally?"

She glares at me, her brown eyes sleepy but intense. Emotions register immediately and unmistakably on her face. I like this about her, and envy her for it.

She unhooks her leg, pushes herself up. "Come visit."

I hear Tod in the hall, his laugh preceding his arrival like music in a horror movie. He greets the researchers: a nod here, a wink there. He's relentlessly friendly—an astounding feat on a campaign, where coworkers become as familiar as family members. I've had to consider the depressing possibility that Tod is a happy person. I tell myself that the kind of happiness I'm going for, in however fucked-up a way, is more profound than his kind—so profound that happiness isn't even the right word.

Tod is blond and balding and sharp-faced. In his charcoal suit and yellow tie, he looks like an investment banker. The Democratic Party is now comfy for people like Tod, who's liberal only insofar as he thinks abortion should be available, especially to women he gets pregnant. In any case, he doesn't care about issues. He cares about getting laid and looking good. And golf. He smokes fat cigars and tells filthy jokes. His political judgments are unsullied by emotion or morality. He's our Machiavelli, our Dick Morris, our dick. I probably don't dislike him as much as I should, although sometimes I lie awake at night, thinking up scenarios that would allow me to justifiably punch him in the face. I like to imagine the skin breaking over his cheekbone.

"Forget the op-ed," Tod says, leaning against my desk but looking at the door; he's always about to bolt. "Stein accused Schec of saying a Palestinian state was inevitable."

Ed Stein, a congressman from Manhattan, is our opponent in the Primary. He's been attacking Schecter from the right on Israel and from the left on welfare. In other words, he's trying to do what politicians try to do during Democratic Primaries in New York: win the Jews and the Blacks. Schecter's Jewish support is solid, our pollster tells us. Their fear is that we'll lose the Blacks. It's my fear too, I suppose. I admit it: I want to win. I want the Blacks and the Jews and the Black Jews too.

"Schec denied it, of course," Tod says, "but Stein's got the transcript, and now I've got rabbis up my ass. So we need a release saying that what Schec meant when he said he didn't say it, is that he didn't say it in the way Stein says he said it. I mean, what he meant was, it was inevitable but bad. And he doesn't think it's inevitable anymore."

"Maybe I could leave that last part out?"

He blows a laugh out his nose and leaves.

Liberalism, I grant, could use a shave and a haircut, if not an enema, and my own politics are a work forever in progress. Or regress. At the moment my philosophy is probably best described as a hybrid of nineteenth-century anarchism, nineteen-thirties socialism, and nineteen-nineties irony. The revolution I'm planning will make fun of itself. But revolution it is. Maybe. Sometimes Bill Clinton seems to make a lot of sense. In any case, it's not so much the rightward thrust of Schecter's positions that makes me want to bite through my tongue. It's the lying and the saying of things that almost no one in the office believes. I say *almost* no one because Paul Teague, the resident devout Christian and the only African-American among the senior staff, seems genuinely conservative. How nice for him.

I write the release and e-mail it away, doing my best not to think about what I'm doing, as though I were stepping on a big crunchy beetle and quickly flushing it down the toilet. I never thought I could get as disillusioned as I am, given that I never had illusions. Not many, anyway. Okay, a few.

2

In the late afternoon I go to the volunteer room, where Democrats of all persuasions make phone calls, put together mailings, and argue. Calliope presides over the room like the camp counselor she once was, offering words of peace and conciliation. Today, most constituencies are represented: a black guy and a white guy in satiny union jackets, two middle-aged women, an old man, and a pale young couple with dreads.

"You're gay?" the white union guy says to one of the women, his Brooklyn accent thick, like his belly. He thumb-points at the guy with dreads. "This boy here, I can tell he's gay, but you, I'd have no idea if you didn't just tell me."

"I'm not gay," the guy says, gently sponging an envelope.

"Don't get me wrong," the man says. "I don't got a problem with it, as long as you don't flaunt it. Me and Molly, we've been married thirty-two years, and not once have we made a public spectacle of ourselves."

"You're making a spectacle of yourself right now," the woman says.

"Easy, everyone," Calliope says, soothing as a hypnotist. "Remember, we're working for the same thing."

"I've been a Democrat my whole life," the union guy says, "and we did a lot better when we didn't talk about sex."

"Then stop talking about it," the woman says as Calliope and I walk out.

When we get to the roof we go to our spot in the corner, from where, on a clearer day, you can see a sliver of lower Manhattan. It's cold for May: good smoking weather, good for sucking in and blowing out.

The government building across the street is spitting people through its double doors like grass out of a lawnmower. Calliope lights a Camel and scratches her boob. I'd like to take this as a sign of her comfort around me, but she'd do the same thing in front of anyone. Shawn claims he once saw her standing at the photocopier, digging her dress out of her ass. Then she reached under, took off her panties, and placed them neatly on a stack of warm copies. It might not be true, but it could be.

"The volunteers are great," I say. "But it's sad."

"What?"

"Them coming in here, thinking they're making a difference."

"There are too many things that are truly sad." She puts her finger on my chest, on my heart, and scrapes a clump of dried something off my shirt. "I don't have enough space in my brain to be sad about that."

The nicotine is setting in, making me yearn for something. I always claim I could quit smoking without a problem, but I haven't gone a day without cigarettes in a year. I like the tug on my throat and the caress on my lips and the nicotine, which has a weirdly strong effect on me. No matter how much I smoke, my first cigarette always gives me a buzz, a slight change of head that makes me more interesting to myself.

"What's sadder than delusion?" I say.

She smiles, probably because I just sounded like myself. "What's wrong?"

"More of the same."

"As per usual."

"The same but more."

"Spin is good," she says, imitating Tod imitating Gordon Gecko. This is her first job in politics, and she's only beginning to learn the rules. Sometimes I like her ignorance. After I explained Schecter's position on welfare, she said, "I don't get it. Shouldn't they get *more* money? I mean, they're poor, right?"

"The very word spin is spin," I say. "It's a euphemism."

"For lying?"

"Right."

"I don't know about that. I mean, we say pro-choice, they say pro-life. Where's the lie? There's not one truth."

"Oy."

"It's true."

"Whatever *that* means."

"Spinning, lying—call it what you want—it seems pretty . . . self-destructive to get all hot and bothered over it. It's like raging against the weather."

I say nothing, the disagreement feeling familiar, an install-ment in a series. Unlike me, unlike most people I'm drawn to, Calliope generally accepts the world as it is, with all its pain and mess and waiting. The result—or cause—is that she's remarkably at ease, especially compared to other people in her Prozac-taking, emotion-analyzing demographic. The air around her hangs loose, like one of her dresses. But that's not to say she's satisfied. She longs for things: love and intimacy and sex with me on this very roof. Well, love and intimacy for sure.

Awaiting my response, she's looking at me unblinkingly, and it's easy to imagine that the smoke is streaming not from her lips but from her eyes. Her stare is aggressive yet self-exposing; like a boxer's reckless punch, it threatens us both. I turn away, using a fake cough as pretext. She's kind enough not to call me on it.

"Let me ask you a question," she says. "You said you didn't mind working for Schecter at first. So who changed, you or him?"

"Good question," I say, doing a quick mental review of my little career. "A few years ago Schecter occasionally broke from the script. He even said 'I was wrong' once. Can you imagine? But then he started preparing for this race and you know, the bigger the office, the bigger the robot. But I guess I've changed, too. I'm sick of the crap. I know you think it comes with the territory, but I've seen politicians do brave things. I'm not looking for perfect, just good. And Schecter ain't no good."

"He's *pretty* good."

It infuriates me when she says things like this. Is she being generous or clueless? Some liberals think any politician who talks tolerance must be kosher. "Tell me again, why is he pretty good?"

"For one thing, he doesn't want to stick his hands in my womb."

"He would if there were votes there."

"He's all right."

"He's a douche bag."

"So quit."

We have some form of this conversation every day. At first it was thrilling letting her in, showing her the depths of my discontent. It made me feel like an adult. Now it makes me feel like a boy, a slacker who can't get off the couch.

"You need to find something else and do it," she says. "No half-assing. You need to give it your full ass." She slaps my ass, hard. I want her to do it again. "One thing, though. You can't leave before the Primary. I couldn't deal."

I put my arm around her, pull her into an embrace. For all

our talking and flirting and tender touching, this is our first hug. It's nice. Her breasts are less mushy than I thought they'd be. I'm getting a hard-on. I have a hard-on.

Her face scrunches up, her features huddling, and then I smell it: burning hair. I forgot about the cigarette in my hand. "You're an idiot," she says, pushing me away.

She turns so I can inspect the damage, unnoticeable in her mound of hair. "You should do it," she says, her back to me. "You should do what you want to do."

What I want to do is lift up her coat and her dress to see exactly what I'm dealing with. I don't like this tendency of mine to break her down into components. It could be that I want a conventionally beautiful woman. What can I say, I'm a white American male. Maybe my taste or my ego (and try drawing a line between the two) requires a beer-commercial beauty. But I don't think so. I hope not. I suspect that any woman would have a difficult time stealing me away from my imaginary lover, whom I've been living with since about the moment I stopped thinking girls were icky. Sometimes Ms. Fantasy takes on specific characteristics—a woman, say, with the smoothest of skin, who's political but not earnest, neurotic but not nuts, who loves sex but who shockingly never had an orgasm until she met me. Other times she remains unformed, beautiful and blank, a soothing presence with limitless potential who helps me sleep at night. In fact she's lying next to me. Ms. Fantasy is my life's great love so far—I've chosen her over several terrific, non-imaginary women—and the thought of letting her go frightens me. Which is to say, I suppose, that I have a basic and rather boring fear of commitment.

"There they are," Calliope says, looking down at the street, where Schecter and team are disembarking from a black limousine, a modest one if that's possible; in nineteen-nineties New York it seems like just a big car. Danny, Paul, and the others linger on the sidewalk, waiting for The Man to lead the way.

"You think I could land a nickel on his bald spot?" I say.

Calliope clucks sadly, violence being the one subject she doesn't like to joke about. "Have you been doing the breathing exercise I showed you?"

"I tried during the party. Made me feel worse."

"You need to keeping working at it," she says, rubbing my back, the two of us now shoulder to shoulder. "It's like anything." Her hand, moving in a tight circle, generates a patch of warmth that I want to stretch out and pull around me like a blanket.

"You're good people," I say.

She takes back her hand to pull out another Camel, then licks her upper lip to ensure that the cigarette doesn't stick. Caught in the corner of her mouth is a strand of hair, which she scrapes away with her middle finger. At times like this it seems unhealthy not to be having sex with her, a suppression of animal need. But at other times it seems like a mature departure from my pattern in relationships, which is to fuck early and then fuck up, sometimes within the span of a single night. Becoming friends first is something I've never done before; smart people tell me it makes sense.

And both of us are reluctant to alter the status quo, which has its excitements; nothing ruins sexual tension like sex. Beyond that, I have doubts and she does too and my doubts feed off hers and visa versa. A few months ago we had a series of conversations about us, as in "us." The only thing we concluded is that it's a bad idea to get involved while we're working together. Which is reason enough to leave the campaign. Or to not.

"It was nice what you did with Mona," I say. "Comforting her."

"I don't know how much good I did."

"At least you did *something*."

With a wide-open mouth, she tilts her head back, a halfnod that's more than a nod. It all makes sense to her now. "You wanted to raise a ruckus."

"At least speak out. But I couldn't get it together."

"Ben, Ben, Ben, Ben. Ben. You've got to make a move. Or not make a move and be okay with it, you know?"

3

I live just south of Union Square. The noise aggravates me, but I like the location. Most of the places I want to go are a walk away, and for those that aren't, a bunch of subway lines converge on the square. Growing up, I felt far away, on the edge of things. It's part of my psychology—I still feel that way sometimes—but it was also a matter of simple geography: I lived in Maine. Now on good days, it seems as if I'm in the center of the world.

At the moment my apartment is messy but not out of control. The state of my place was one of the reasons I left DC: moving seemed less daunting than cleaning. I'm doing better now. There's nothing disgusting here, or at least nothing dangerous. I've learned to make piles. There are piles everywhere: clothes, dishes, piles of mail on top of piles of books on top of piles of magazines. In the patch of vinyl that passes for my kitchen, I find a notebook I must have written on last night. *Private Prisons* it says. I stick it in a pile, between a pizza box and a hiking boot.

The insistent blinking of the light on my answering machine suggests that the message is from Mom, and it is, one of her weekly missives from Maine: "So I'm thinking of getting new carpeting in the living room. I was wondering if you had any thoughts about color. I guess you wouldn't, would you? Now it's off to French class. How are you? Okay, I hope. It's freezing here, just *awful. A bientôt, mon fils.*"

I'm exhausted but restless—restless because I'm exhausted—so I go back down to the street, and the energy slaps me in the face. I take a right on University and pick up two plain slices at Stromboli. Coal oven pizza is the rage, but I go for the regular slices, the ones that are so cheesy the grease streams off the tip. I get a 24-ounce can of Bud and sit on a bench in the square, next to a black guy muttering to himself.

When I was in seventh grade, I visited Manhattan with Mom and my brother. My first New York slice was a formative event. In Maine, the sauce on pizza was sickly sweet, and the crust was either too soft or too brittle. The NYC slice was remarkable yet unsurprising. It was what I'd been searching for. *Here it is. Finally.* Since moving here, I must have had two hundred slices. I'm sick of pizza. And tonight's batch is subpar, the crust wilting under the weight of the cheese. The beer's good, though. You can drink in public if you bag your beer, and I feel smart when I do. In bars around the square, people are buying beers for five bucks; I got two beers worth for $1.89. The muttering guy next to me is bag-drinking too.

It seems as if it should be dark by now, but twilight's hanging on. People pass by: professional people, poor people, men walking dogs, women pushing strollers, skateboard boys, crunchy girls. A bald girl across from me, her mouth on her knee, blows out, her cheeks puffing up, and I imagine the warm spot on her black jeans. This is what I do. I walk around and I sit and I watch people walk around and sit. I've been too busy, tired, or lazy to do much else. Sometimes, though, I go deep into the East Village, where the intensity clears my head and then sends me scrambling for home.

I think I could like the city. I like to think I could. New York was what drew me to the job. That, and the energy of a campaign, which is the emergency room of politics.

I'd been aching to leave DC for months and almost did twice. A woman I maybe loved invited me to come to South Africa, where she was going to travel and write. I must have had reasons for not joining her, but I can't remember what they were. Then last summer a friend asked me to run his no-chance campaign for a House seat. I declined, saying I wanted to leave politics altogether. When the idea of my moving to Schecter's campaign came up, I hopped at the chance (hopping being relative: it took me a month to decide). Sick of the Hill, bored with DC, and afraid of my shower, I came up here, choosing not to see that the aspects of politics I don't like are magnified on a campaign. Right now I could be running on white sand beaches with a woman I love, or running the campaign of a politician I believe in. Instead, I'm in the belly of the beast. Or the colon, perhaps.

My post-college life looks fine on paper: half a year traveling around the country, a year as an editorial assistant for a magazine in Los Angeles, three-plus years working for a congressman—a congressman with a genius IQ and perfect ratings from NARAL and the Sierra Club. But I can read between the lines; that's where the story is. It's a story of sideline-standing, of cleverly criticizing, of not making phone calls, of hedging bets, of sleeping in and sleeping off, of laughing at myself, of drinking to numb and talking too much, of flirting with other guys' girlfriends.

That's not to say I was a brave soul *before* graduating from college. Or high school, for that matter. My cowardice dates back to at least fifth grade, when I repeatedly shied away from talking to the lovely and good-at-dodge-ball Kimmy Blake. At the time, I wasn't fully aware of how much I liked her. Or of how much I disliked myself for not acting on my crush. Back then, and for many years after, my most difficult feelings burned beneath the surface of my consciousness. I was content, repressed, and probably depressed. People saw me as carefree, and that's how I saw myself. But I know now that I did care, and that I certainly wasn't free. Only in recent years have I begun to feel the heat of my emotions. I can't say what accounts for the change. The onset of adulthood, perhaps. Or my self-imposed sentence in the American political system. Or the ounce of galactically strong hydroponic weed I smoked in late '96. Whatever the cause, I've become painfully aware of the chasm between the person I am and the person I want to be.

The muttering guy taps my arm and points at my chest. My first thought is that I've sauced up my shirt, but no, he wants a cigarette. Giving him one, I touch his hand, which is hard, like a heel.

"Ain't no need to be parsimonious," he says. I hand him two more. He laughs in apparent resignation and says, "If you want to rub butter on my belly, go right ahead, but you better bring everything you got, 'cause I ain't got the time, nigger."

If this were a movie, he'd be spouting wisdom and exuding soul; instead, he's spouting nonsense and exuding *l'air du* monkey house.

In the deli on the northwest corner of the square I buy another big beer and, back on the sidewalk, shake a cigarette free from the pack. As I suck it into my mouth a man slides up holding a flame, its heat making me think of a beach bonfire. "Here you go, buddy," he says in an Arabic accent, and he's gone before I can thank him.

"Oh my God."

The words are for me, and I turn toward them: Mike Levy, smiling in a group of hipster professionals: bright tight shirts, too-short pants. Mike has shaved his head and put a loop through his eyebrow.

"Ben Bergin," he says. My name is the kind that compels people to say it in its entirety. My given name was Palazzo, but my father left when I was two, and my mother went back to her maiden name, making me alliterative.

"Mike," I say, feeling invaded. I tuck the beer in my armpit and clutch his hand.

He introduces the others; Brita is the name I catch.

"Nice to meet you," I say, making an effort to be animated. If I don't make an effort to be animated, I sound like I just woke up; that's what people tell me, anyway.

"How are you, Mike?"

"Good, good, good. I *love* my job. I'm working for a foundation that supports the arts. I don't miss DC at all, do you?"

"No."

Levy was an intern in Schecter's Washington office when I first started there. I wanted to like him, but he was hard to be around. He had a knack for saying things that made me feel exposed, seen through, and there was something skewed about him; it was a problem of tone. Then, the last time I was with him, we were crammed into a car, smoking a bowl on our way to a party. He was explaining why he broke up with his girlfriend, and I realized in a rush of stoned clarity that he was gay. I didn't share my discovery with him and, judging by his two fake dates this evening, he hasn't made it independently.

"We're going to get a drink," he says. "You want to join us?"

I hold up my bag, proudly. "Got one." Then I see what they're seeing: bag o' beer, crinkled cigarette, dirty trench coat. I start to sweat, completing the picture.

"Doing the down-and-out writer thing, huh?" Mike says.

Someone snickers, Brita maybe.

"I'll join you in a bit," I say.

"Bullshit, but I'm going to give you a call sometime."

He rubs my upper arm, and takes off across Seventeenth. I sit down on the trashcan, my chest tightening like a muscle.

Everyone is expected to work long hours and everyone notices how much time everyone else puts in. Being productive is less important than being here. At first, when I came in late, I'd stash my coat in the equipment closet next to the bathroom and walk in as though I'd already been there. For hours, possibly. I don't bother anymore.

Bernice, the woman at the front desk, gives me a nod when I say good morning, and I'm lucky to get that much. Most people in the office think she's cold, maybe even dull, but I suspect that Bernice simply chooses not to show herself to her coworkers, who are probably too eager to befriend her; it'd be easy, I sense, for her to be the wisecracking secretary everyone loves and laughs for. No thank you, she seems to be saying. She just wants to do her job. I respect people who don't need to be liked. I pretend to be one of those people because people like people like that.

It's peaceful this morning, eerily so. Tod isn't in his office; Danny, the campaign manager, is reading the paper in his. The little smile he gives me says: "You're late."

I appreciate his subtlety, a quality in short supply around here. Danny's a nice guy, too nice to run a senate campaign, especially one that requires him to butt heads with Tod. The word is that after college Danny was working happily as a carpenter until his father, an advisor to three presidents, "urged" him to join the family trade. Danny handles himself with poise, although all of us would be relieved if just once he tossed a chair through a window. The pressure is wearing on him. His physical deterioration is a popular topic of conversation in the backrooms. Amused and concerned, we chat in hushed tones about the growth of his stomach and the red sacks under his eyes, which seem to be hardening into permanent features. I picture his eyes closing up like a boxer's. Campaigns are tests of endurance for staffers as well as candidates, and it seems that Danny, our kind and able sergeant, might not make it.

Shawn's in the kitchen, waiting for the coffeepot to fill. I'm forced to wait with him. "S'up, bro?" he says. "Guess *you* got some nice sleep."

Wanting a high five, he holds up his hand, and I punch it.

"Yo, Bee," he says, shaking out the pain.

I don't dislike Shawn—he's not smart enough to dislike—but I don't like being around him. His personality, if you can call it that, is a patchwork of expressions and mannerisms he's picked up from celebrities. There's something very sad and modern about the guy. I picture him alone in a plush suburban basement, staring wide-mouthed at three square feet of MTV. He's a field organizer— a good first job for someone who got bad grades at a bad school. (There are few secrets on a campaign.) His mother, the head of some foundation, is a big Schecter supporter. Clearly, she made a phone call.

"Coming up on the debate," he says. The last of three debates is next week, and the Primary election is the week after that.

"Yup." One nice thing about talking to Shawn: I don't feel a need to be interesting.

The coffeemaker lets out a Darth Vader breath.

Shawn sighs. His hand goes searching for something to play with and settles on the skin underneath his eye, which he pulls out a good half-inch. He's got a sloppy-preppy thing going: wrinkled khakis, untucked shirt, loose tie, which he loosens further when he sees me looking at it. I make him feel overdressed. Shawn thinks I'm laid-back.

The coffee is bad, even for office brew, but it strikes me as authentic and American, a bitter drug of the common man. I down a cup, refill my mug, and proceed toward my desk, preempting comments about my lateness by bellowing exaggerated greetings: "Great to see you . . . How I've missed you."

"Stop it," Calliope says. "I can't stand you being perky."

She's at the photocopier, which flashes yellow as it snaps a shot of the American history textbook her palm is pressing to the glass. The copies are probably for one of her unorthodox organizing efforts. The other night she went to an Indigo Girls show and handed out little bags that contained gummy fish, a Schecter pin, and her business card. She's wearing a dress over pants—a hippie style I don't care for—but Calliope can pull it off. Her aesthetic isn't pure hippie. At the moment, for instance, she has on lipstick, and the Buddy Holly glasses she sometimes wears strike me as less hippie than hipster.

"Are you stoned?" she asks half-seriously.

"You *are* acting weird," says Shawn, who's followed me down the hall.

"It's a big change, all right," I say, chopping the air with my hand. "'But it's not the kind of change America wants, it's not the kind of change America needs, and it's not the kind of change we can abide in a nation we still call God's country.'"

Shawn points at me. "Falwell?"

"Buchanan," I say, and Shawn cringes, thinking he should have known.

"Freaks," Calliope says.

"But you got to love 'em," Shawn says.

"I'm talking about you two," she says, and takes off, Shawn on her heels.

Shawn likes the performances and personalities—probably a sensible approach to politics, but to truly enjoy it as entertainment, you can't believe in much. There are fans like Shawn, idealists like Mona, players like Tod, wonks like Gerry, and people like Danny: malcontents and/or cynics who should get out—move to the country and eat veggies and never even watch the news. And me? What's my niche? I'm a bit of everything: a somewhat wonkish, idealistic cynic who has a love-hate-hate relationship with politics, with power itself, and who should probably get out. Or something.

I sit down at my desk, my legs shaky from the caffeine, my empty stomach munching on itself, thoughts flying around my head—Pat Buchanan, Mona, Mike Levy, Israel, Pat Buchanan—coating my brain with goo, like moths spinning a cocoon.

I feel Calliope come into the room. Or maybe Gerry's reaction tips me off. He's on the edge of my vision, staring. He shows a keen interest only in Calliope and The Man, who almost never comes back here.

As she falls into the couch, my thoughts slow; her presence grants me a reprieve.

"So I'm making these get-out-the vote flyers," she says, "with pictures of all these famous civil rights leaders, and it's going to say, 'We fought and died for your right to vote. Now use it!'" She rubs her palms together, claps twice. "Pretty good, huh?"

"Yeah," I say, impressed by her excitement. She takes a child-like pleasure in things. I, on the other hand, seem to be losing the ability to enjoy myself. One by one, my pleasures are getting consumed by my distraction.

"I don't know that we want blacks to vote," I say.

"Why? Oh, 'cause they're going to vote for Stein?"

"Most of them, probably. We need forty-five percent."

"We should pay them."

"Happens all the time."

"Vile."

"Voting fraud is rampant," Gerry says, his final word evolving into a guttural groan that goes on for several excruciating seconds.

"I'm going to my parents' for dinner tonight," Calliope says. "Want to come?"

Calliope is a native New Yorker. She moved back here in August, after living out west for seven years, including college.

"No thanks." I've been reluctant to see her outside the office. I'm not sure why. My self-loathing self tells me that I'm simply lazy and afraid. But my self-liking self has a compelling rebuttal: given my uncertainty, parameters are a good idea. I shouldn't have sex with her unless I'm ready for a relationship. ("But how will you know unless you have sex?" shouts Self-Loathing.) Sex without romantic follow-up could ruin our friendship, while a buddy-buddy, phone-chatty friendship—in which we, for example, tell each other about dates with other people—could undermine our chance for romance. Not so compelling, after all. Self-Loathing wins!

"I'm going out with Ethan," I say.

"Can I come meet you guys?"

"If you want to, but we're watching baseball." A lie to cover my lie. Come to think of it, though, I wouldn't mind going to a sports bar tonight, Red Sox-viewing being one of my pleasures that seems to have survived intact.

"Sports," she says with amused disapproval. "Come eat with me first."

"Game's at seven. Sorry."

"Please."

"Why is it important to you?"

"I want you to meet them."

"You don't want to be alone with them."

This comes out of nowhere, but it smells true. She doesn't talk about her parents much, but in what she does say I sense anger. It's probably related to her younger brother's death. He killed himself. When I first met Calliope, I thought she was the healthiest person I'd ever known. Now I'm not so sure. Sometimes she seems more in tune with my problems than with her own.

"I'm alone with them a lot," she says.

"And you have a bad time whenever you are."

"All you had to do was say no." She stands up and steps into her orange clogs, which she had taken off. "I don't really need your schmuckfuck psychoanalysis."

"I *tried* to say no."

"Go . . . watch your football," she says, walking away.

"Baseball."

"Bite me."

"Why don't you two just *do* it?" Jen says.

On the toilet I decide to have some fun. More fun. Calliope is my go-to girl, but after our argument, I don't want to give her the pleasure. Monica Lewinsky is who comes to mind. She could have been an intern in Schecter's office. We could have been best buds, so tight that she sent me letters about her heady times with Clinton, letters that I'm refusing to hand over to Ken Starr. Risking arrest, I've become an anti-impeachment hero, and Monica, aroused by my moral bravery, shows up at my door in the middle of the night, wearing dark glasses. She pushes me back onto the couch, drops to her knees, and gives me the presidential treatment.

Tod, shooting out of Danny's office, snaps and points at my face. Be ready, he seems to be saying. Something happened, something that we'll have to respond to. We'll release a statement and either our spin will win or theirs will and either way we'll release a statement saying our spin won. Part of me wishes I could tuck my head away like a turtle and walk past.

But the game is hard to resist. It's a challenge, a dare. Stein's people are calling us out. They're talking trash. They think they can take us to the hole. They're wrong.

In the volunteer room Calliope is sucking on a Sugar Daddy and chatting with Eileen, an envelope-stuffer suspected to be in the early stages of Alzheimer's.

I take a few steps forward, allowing myself to be seen, and

Danny uses his jelly donut to wave me in. Paul is standing behind the desk, his white shirt smooth as a sail in the wind, striking against his dark skin.

"Someone confessed to the Wayne White murder," Danny says, chewing.

"Wow," I say, thrilled to be surprised.

Wayne White killed a cop, Frank Zito. Probably. Maybe. White has always maintained his innocence, as have a few of the more radical black activists. The murder happened in Schecter's district so all of us followed the case. A crack house at dawn, a dozen people sprawled out in two rooms separated by a long hallway. Zito's partner was in the other room when he heard shots. He found Zito bleeding from his chest and White holding the gun. White claimed he was tossed the gun after the shots were fired. As a longtime dealer and addict, he wasn't exactly a pillar of credibility on the witness stand, but he was no worse, I imagine, than the guys who testified against him.

"Who confessed?" I say, trying to remember the other players.

"Another convicted killer," Paul says. This, like many things he says, strikes me as vaguely combative—a tweak from the resident conservative—but maybe I'm hearing what I want to hear. "He wasn't part of the trial, wasn't even detained by the cops."

"A mystery shooter," Danny says.

"Cool," I say. "What's this mean for us?"

"You tell us," Danny says, his mouth finally donut-free.

"All right," I say. "Easy Ed Stein is stepping oh-so-gently onto the Free Wayne White bandwagon while accusing us of, I don't know . . . hating black people?"

I like saying things like this in front of Paul; it shows him and everyone else that I'm enlightened enough not only to talk about race, but to joke about it. That's right, folks, I might be liberal but I'm *loose*.

"Not even close," Danny says. He licks sugar from his fingers. He looks terrible: shaky hands, fat neck. You can feel his heart straining, like a little car on a big hill.

"Washburn," Paul says. Chet Washburn is the incumbent senator, our opponent if we win the Primary. He's conservative, but unconventional enough to keep winning elections in liberal-leaning New York.

"Chetwood Washburn The Third," I say, trying to figure out what the senator is going to say. It's one of my favorite games, predicting the moves of our opponents.

Since bringing back the death penalty a few years ago, New York hasn't executed anyone. White could be the first. It'd make for good PR, killing a cop-killer to inaugurate the new death penalty—except for this problem of his possible innocence. Schecter used to oppose the death penalty and stayed neutral—waffled—on the referendum that brought it back, saying it was up to the people to decide. But in anticipation of this race, he's strained to seem tough on crime, an issue that Republicans have owned since the seventies. Schecter fights for gun control, exudes buckets of moral outrage, and advocates severe punishment, including and especially the death penalty, which he now supports with a convert's zeal. It's not enough, apparently, for Washburn.

I say, "Washburn's claiming that if Schecter had had his way, White wouldn't even be on death row."

"Something like that," Danny says. "Tod's getting the transcript."

On cue, Tod comes in, his grin suggesting he's happy to have a chance to go at Washburn. As am I. All of a sudden I'm looking forward to the General Election?

"He was having a little press conference to talk about Medicare or some shit," Tod says. He holds the accordian printout in front of his face, and five pages fall. "A reporter asked if he knew about the confession, and Washburn said, quote, 'Yes, I heard, but I don't know the details, so I don't really want to comment on the specifics of the legalities involved.'"

"The specifics of the legalities," I mumble.

"'But I will say this,'" Tod goes on, "'White was convicted in a fair trial by a jury of his peers, and New York State has the finest capital defender office in the country. And I think it's also important to think about what this kind of publicity is like for the family of Officer Zito, who shouldn't be forced to relive this terrible tragedy.'"

Tod looks up, smiling in admiration. Then he goes back to the transcript. "Another reporter asked him if he thought this would have any effect on the Democratic Primary."

"That's a planted question," Danny says.

"He said, 'I don't really know. I'm not a political analyst. It's worth remembering, though, that Congressman Schecter didn't support the death penalty back when I and others were fighting to reinstate it to New York. By the way, it's helped reduce homicides by almost forty percent. Schecter says he supports it now. Maybe he does, I don't know. He certainly didn't when Officer Zito was brutally murdered.'"

"That's a lie," Paul says.

"A nice one," Tod says.

"Washburn wants to face Stein," Danny says, stating the obvious. Stein and Schecter are similar, almost comically so—they're both once-liberal, now-moderate Jewish lawyers in their mid-fifties—but our guy is tougher, nastier, and smarter: a heavyweight.

"He wants us to choose between the blacks and the blues," I say.

"That's a false choice," Paul says.

"Not really," Tod says.

"It's a choice we don't have to make right now," Danny says, and then nods at me. "You know what to do."

"Talk about Monica?" I say.

"I wish," Danny says. The scandal has been bad for Democrats in certain areas of the country, the pickup-truck areas, but in New York, some seventy percent of people are opposed to the effort to take down Clinton. "We go after him for going after us," Danny says. "It shows he's afraid of us. And we get him on gun control. And we talk up Schec's record on crime. You know." He yawns. "The usual."

"What if White's innocent?" I say, because someone should. And because he might be. My little rush has already ebbed.

"Then he should get himself a better lawyer," Tod says.

"I don't know if you even have to mention White," Danny says.

"He's not White anymore," Tod says. "He's Mohammed or something."

"Mustafa?" I say.

"My mama," Danny says.

"Ramada."

"Roof-toppa."

"Kill-coppa."

"Enough," says Paul, the adult among us. I'm surprised we couldn't slip this stupidity by him since we were making fun of Muslims, who in his view, I'd guess, aren't going to make it to the safe senate seat in the sky. God knows what he thinks of the three of us: two Jews and the Devil himself. In fairness, I probably wouldn't even know about his godliness if not for Calliope, who often eats lunch with him. Bless them both.

"Here it is," Tod says, showing a rare desire for exactitude. "Hakim Mohammed. Danny's right. This can't be about him."

"That's what Washburn *wants* it to be about," Paul says.

"Schec's in DC?" Tod says.

"Yeah," Danny says. "I'll run it by him."

Tod hands me the transcript, not bothering to fold it.

I walk out, but before I can escape to the relative integrity of the backrooms, Paul calls to me. He's going to ask to take a look at what I end up writing. It's not in his job description; he doesn't *have* a job description. He joined the campaign late, in February. As political director, he's technically the number two guy, but he was given no mandate, leaving him to cobble together responsibilities, and putting him at the mercy of Tod, who barely deigns to acknowledge him. It's safe to assume that the architects of the campaign—the higher-ups in DC and their consultants—created the job to add color to the campaign. No crime that. The good news is that Paul is bright and principled. The bad news is that as far as I'm concerned he's a bright and principled Republican.

He waits to speak until we're face-to-face. He's an inch taller than I am, three if you count his hair. His short Afro stands in contrast to the rest of him, which is decidedly white-person-friendly. He's even expunged the street from his voice, though it occasionally slips back in, and I have to confess to being excited every time that it does. I don't think it's fair to say that he's acting white or selling out or anything like that. Or maybe it *is* fair, but I don't feel qualified to say it.

"I'd like to take a look at the release," he says.

"All right," I say.

He nods. "All right."

There's a silence, a silence I'm anxious to flee; but Paul, shaking his head, wants to say something.

"What?" I say.

"A black man killed a cop."

My mind, searching too hard for words, goes blank.

"Or another one did," he says.

"But one of them *didn't*."

He turns his lips inward while he considers what to say. Our conversations are like this, tight and halting. It's tough to know where the discomfort begins, with him or with me. He's generally ill at ease around people, and I'm generally ill at ease around people who are ill at ease, but he'd likely intimidate me even if he were socially adept.

And we can't seem to find safe conversational ground. He's not interested in talking to me about sports or music or any of the other topics that sustain most male relationships. He always wants to talk to me about *issues*, sensing correctly that moral questions interest me. The problem, I think, is that he has a way of making the political seem acutely personal, as though his opinions were family members.

"At the time of the trial," he says, "I was an assistant district attorney. In Manhattan, not Brooklyn, but I followed the trial quite closely. I'd be surprised if he's not guilty. To tell you the truth, I *hope* he's guilty. But let's say that he is not. Then he becomes a hero. A crack dealer. We don't need heroes like that."

"I don't think he'd become a hero," I say. "A symbol, maybe."

"Of what?" Paul says.

"Injustice?"

He winces. "We have got plenty of symbols of injustice. What we need are symbols of *achievement*, of overcoming injustice."

He holds up his hands, long fingers spread, indicating that he has more to say. He's gone preachy, as he tends to, but I don't mind. His sermonettes are a relief from the effort of conversation, and they pack a punch despite themselves. His is the kind of eloquence that comes not from smoothness, but from conviction. And he's got a good deep voice. "Every black child should grow up believing they can be something in this world. Instead we've got them learning they *can't* be. The biggest barriers for black people these days are psychological. I see it all the time: self-sabotage. I mean, do you really believe that The Man is what's stopping most black people from getting ahead?"

"Yeah," I say, feeling both deferential and presumptuous for not feeling more so. Paul grew up fatherless in East Brooklyn, then graduated from a public high school, City College, and the Columbia Law School. Like everyone else in the office, except maybe Tod, I admire Paul, but I don't want to admire him too much—at least not before I get to know him. Talk about symbols: it must be exhausting to embody everything everyone pretends to stand for. "The point is," I say, " is that it's all connected. If there are psychological barriers, it's because of actual ones."

"Maybe, but we need to get past this . . . this separation, where blacks are on one side and authority is on the other."

"I agree," I say. "But executing the wrong man isn't going to help."

"That's why I hope he's guilty."

"Maybe Zito shot himself," I say, loosening up a little. "Maybe it's all a plot to keep the black man down."

"Don't you get me started now," he says with a smile. His front teeth are huge, and they're separated by a space you could put a penny through. "There are plenty of brothers out there who believe that."

5

Tod has e-mailed me the story about the confession, which isn't as solid as Danny and Paul suggested. A man named Roger LaBrie, serving fifteen years in Sing Sing for second-degree murder, has bragged to friends and other inmates that he killed Zito, and shortly after the shooting he was seen in a bar nearby, but when he was asked by the reporter about his claim, he didn't quite confirm it. "I done a lot of things I ain't proud of," he said. Of course, he has an incentive not to issue a formal confession: it could get him killed.

In a way, it's a credit to New York that a second-hand confession has become a story. In other states, death row prisoners have wasted away in obscurity for years despite evidence of innocence. But then New York intends to be different when it comes to the death penalty. We give capital defendants good lawyers and fair trials. Alabama we're not. Yes, we're going to execute people now, but with compassion.

I've been skeptical about White's claim of innocence because I assumed they'd make sure not to mess up one of the first death penalty cases. As if they could just choose not to.

Still, I'm not quite ready to don a "Free Hakim" T-shirt. Nor am I ready to write the official release. Instead, I'll write my own version, as I do sometimes. This one will join twelve or thirteen others on my hard drive. They're my therapy, my diary, my fantasy campaign.

★

Schecter Decides Not to Mention Death Row Prisoner

Today it was revealed that another man has confessed to the killing for which Hakim Mohammed was sentenced to death. Senator Chet Washburn, never loath to exploit racial prejudice or fear of violence, charged that if Congressman Schecter had had his way, Mohammed wouldn't be on death row. This may sound like a compliment, but it most certainly is not. After minor deliberation, Schecter decided to avoid the issue altogether.

Washburn wants Schecter to take a position that will hurt him either in his current race against Congressman Ed Stein or in the prospective General Election. But Schecter will remain on the fence for as long as possible. It would be unwise for him to align himself with a convicted cop-killer. But it would also be unwise to dismiss the possibility of Mohammed's innocence, given the prominent role played by blacks in the Primary. So silence it is. "We don't even have to mention Mohammed," said Campaign Manager Danny Cohen, picking at his crusty face.

Ben Bergin, deputy director of communications, was his normally tepid self, although he did ask, somewhat wearily: "What if Mohammed's innocent?" "Then tell him to get a better lawyer," replied Tod Wilcox, communications director and chief prick.

Heartened by my fake release, I walk into Tod's office in the futile hope of changing our non-position. I find him in the middle of a round of air-golf. He alternates clubs as though actually playing: wood, iron, putter.

Taped to the wall behind his desk are articles, mostly profiles of Schecter that we helped craft. There's also a photo of Monica in a spiked leather bikini. Actually, it's Pamela Anderson, with Monica's face superimposed. The creativity has muted but not silenced charges of sexism. Mona had often threatened to tear it down.

"What if Stein rides this issue?" I say, knowing I have to make a political argument, as opposed to a moral one. "What if he goes Jesse Jackson on us? Blacks are our weakness."

He flips his club around and picks at the blade, scraping off imaginary dirt. I can't believe I'm taking orders from this guy. He once told me that he sees himself in me, which is absurd, but I know what he was getting at. The truth is, I like his guyness. Last week, having just been chastised by Mona for failing to use gender-neutral pronouns in a memo, I came in here, shut the door, and let go. Forty minutes of sex talk: best blowjobs ever, the different sorts of vaginas, the strange humor and hygiene of anal sex.

"There's not enough time for him to get traction on this," Tod says. "We can run out the clock. Then in the General, blacks will come home."

I picture a fleet of ships, headed back to Africa. "Some home."

He shrugs. "Remember Judy?"

"Inverted nipples?"

"Right. Lovely lips and inverted nips. You remember. She was depressed, a little psycho. I guess she'd been raped in college. I treated her like garbage, didn't introduce her to a single friend. I actually felt bad about it. She threatened to break up with me, oh, twenty times, but whenever I called, which I did only when I *really* needed some—"

"I get your point."

"She'd be at my door in like ten minutes, looking for love. But all she got was, you know . . . " He holds the head of his driver in front of his crotch, the shaft jutting out, and pumps his hips. Then he tosses the club into the corner, as though he had a caddie to pick it up. "We need a strong release," he says. "One of your bad boys."

FOR IMMEDIATE RELEASE:

Schecter Campaign Responds to Senator Washburn's Comments

Senator Chet Washburn launched an unprovoked and unfounded attack on Congressman Arnie Schecter today. He falsely claimed that Schecter didn't support the death penalty in 1996, "when I and others were fighting to reinstate it to [sic] New York."

The truth is that Schecter was a co-sponsor of the 1994 crime bill, which greatly expanded and strengthened the federal death penalty. He supported capital punishment then. He supports it now.

Schecter is running against Congressman Ed Stein in the Democratic Primary. Washburn's comments were clearly an attempt to influence the outcome of the race. "I guess we know which candidate Washburn is afraid of," said Danny Cohen, Schecter's campaign manager. "It's not going to work. The people of New York know that Arnie Schecter has been one of the country's leading crime fighters."

Schecter has been a national leader in the effort to crack down on violence against women, abuse of children, drug trafficking, and illegal guns. He has sponsored eleven pieces of gun-control legislation—ten of which Washburn opposed. "No one hates violence more," Cohen said, "and no one's done more to stop it."

I'm on the couch, reading Paul's edits when Calliope walks in shoeless, her face showing no carryover from our argument this morning. She's good at letting tension go. She sits down in my chair, and the reversal of positions makes me feel exposed.

"Listen to this," I say. "Paul wants me to say, 'Schecter is tough on crime as well as a fighter for our elderly citizens.' He's the worst *fucking* writer."

"Doesn't sound bad to me. Why does his editing piss you off so much?"

"'Cause it's awful."

"I think it's more than that."

"Oh, please."

"I'm serious."

"Yeah, if he were white, I wouldn't care that his constructions weren't parallel."

"That's not what I mean."

"If anything," I say, lowering my voice, "I'd be more likely to *not* be pissed about his writing."

"That's"—she points at me with a pump, as though pushing a button—"what I'm talking about."

"Hunh?"

"You go out of your way to be evenhanded, to not be too nice to him. But then you overcompensate."

"That's a stretch," I say, unsure if it is. It sounds like something I'd do.

She giggles. "Poor you. It's so *hard* being well-intentioned. You can't get past black people's blackness."

"Me and just about every other white person."

"You're worse, 'cause you grew up in Maine."

She's right, and why wouldn't she be? I've confessed this to her before. It's not the first time she's repeated my words back to me, trying to pass them off as her own.

"And we all know you have intimate knowledge of black people," I say.

"Not this again."

Drew, her last boyfriend, was black. I was happy to learn that he was a lawyer. Then I found out he was a legal aid attorney on an Indian reservation. Then I found out he played sax in a jazz-rock band. He lives in Seattle, which is good and far, but I wouldn't mind if he disappeared. I don't want him to die or anything, just sort of vanish.

"Are you attracted to Paul?" I ask.

"Ben."

"What? I'm not asking in a jealous, annoying way. I'm asking in a friend-wanting-to-know kind of way."

"I'm glad you cleared that up."

"So *are* you?"

"No more than you."

"Cute."

"He is cute, isn't he?" She bites her bottom lip and tilts her head to the side, studying me. "I've never thought about your sexuality."

"Thanks. Thanks a lot."

"I mean, I've never wondered if you were gay. Usually that's one of the first things I do with guys. *Are* you gay?

"No more than most guys."

"No, I guess not. You really don't seem gay. But you *do* seem like a woman."

"I seem like a heterosexual woman?"

She nods and giggles and puts her hand over her mouth. I, too, might be having fun with this conversation if I were in a better mood. I crinkle the release into a ball and toss it at Gerry, missing his head by an inch. He goes on reading, undisturbed.

Calliope reaches out, touches my hand. "You okay?"

"Yeah."

"I saw you come out of the Pod's office. You didn't look okay."

"Par for the course."

She leans back, then pulls her knees into her chest, letting her hair fall over her face. She's angry I'm not letting her in, but I can't whine to her anymore, I just can't. The bluish veins around her ankles strike me as a reason never to go out with her.

"Did you know Tod grew up poor?" she says through her hair.

"No, and I don't want to hear about it."

"Why not?"

"Because I don't want to have to change my image of him."

"Okay."

"Okay."

"Okay."

She rises and glides away on bare feet, seeming unreal, an apparition.

I input the two least horrendous of Paul's edits. All in all, it's one of my worst releases yet—so bad, in fact, that I'm struck by an urge to add an outright lie, one that Tod will have to cut out. Unless he doesn't want to.

At the end of the release, in Danny's quote, I write, "There's a reason the congressman's constituents call him Schecter the Protector."

Then I flush the piece of crap into cyberspace.

6

As soon as I walk into my apartment, the TV summons me. Lately I've had trouble reading, and even movies, once one of my great pleasures, have proved too much for my catlike attention span, so on nights like this, when I want to hide from the city, I end up fondling the remote into the early morning.

I click on the TV, and Arnie Schecter stares at me. His bristly hair is slicked back, giving him too much forehead, and his mustache is newly trimmed but still full, a relic of the early seventies. Gone are the sideburns, the Jew-fro, and the dreams of changing the world, but the 'stache remains, a sliver of tacky machismo, making the nerd from Flatbush, the smartest guy in the room, look like an aging porn star.

The interview is national. You'd think that I, as deputy director of communications, would have known about it.

"I'm not defending the President's behavior," Schecter says. "The question, though, is whether it rises to the level of a high crime. I think the answer *has* to be no."

Watching a Schecter interview has gotten easier for me, but it's still a little like watching a friend do stand-up: I'm so afraid he's going to bomb I have trouble paying attention. There's no rational reason to fear for Schecter: he hasn't uttered an impolitic or incoherent sentence in years. He's a pro. He's never as natural or as eloquent as I want him to be, but he's forceful, quick, persistent, grinding, loud. Okay: Jewish. An unspoken concern among the higher-ups is that he seems too Jewish to play upstate. Which, in the General, would put extra pressure on us to mobilize our base.

Schecter is smiling as the anchor tosses him a softball about the Republicans' position on Medicare. I should change the channel—the interview has sent my brain back to the office—but the possibility of a question about LaBrie's confession keeps me glued.

And there it is. It's about Washburn, not Mohammed, just like we wanted. "Senator Washburn has criticized you for not supporting capital punishment. He says you didn't support it when, quote, 'Officer Zito was brutally murdered.'"

"That's an egregious lie." Then: "A big lie," in case egregious was too fancy. Schecter has to work to speak like a normal person. Of course, he's *not* a normal person: Harvard, Oxford on a Rhodes, Yale Law. But he doesn't come across as a wine-and-brie liberal, either. At his best, politically speaking, he seems like the feisty prosecutor he once was. "I've long supported the death penalty," he says. "I was the co-sponsor of the crime bill back in 1994, which greatly expanded and strengthened the federal death penalty."

"But are you concerned, Congressman, that the senator will be able to paint you as soft on crime?"

"I'm not running against the senator. I have a Primary election in twelve days, and that's what I'm focused on. Should I be fortunate enough to win, I'll be eager to talk to the senator about a lot of things, including his opposition to gun control. The truth is, I've worked tirelessly to make the citizens of New York safer. You know"—a smile blooms on his glossy face—"there's a reason my constituents call me Schecter the Protector."

Pride, embarrassment, and lunch rise in my throat.

My words, his line, national TV.

I pour Jack Daniels over ice and climb out the window, onto the fire escape and up to the roof. I pace around and take quick sips and try to shake it off. But then, as I'm looking down at a ragged woman screaming at a parked car, I decide that it's better to try to hang on to it. It's easy, after all, to let it go. You wake up and go to work. You have a "good" day. You look on the bright side. You focus on "more important" parts of your life. You rationalize and look forward to lunch and decide that it's not that bad. I need to remember that it really *is* that bad.

When I climb back into my apartment, Ethan's talking into my machine, so I pick up the phone. "What are you doing?" I ask, interrupting his ramble.

"Taking a break."

"From what?"

"I can't remember . . . something bad. Can I stop by?"

I should say no—tonight, like every night, was going to be laundry night—but I have trouble saying no to friends, especially Ethan. I met him during the first week of college, in a seminar called "I'm Okay, You're Okay, We're All Okay." The first day, after four people had claimed they treated people of all races the same, Ethan, doing an AA bit, stood up and said, "My name's Ethan and I'm prejudiced."

"Sure," I say, "but I've got to get to bed early."

I consider straightening up until Ethan arrives. Then I lie down. Chores pain me, the mere thought of them, and the more I neglect them, the more they pain me. Cleaning, shopping, planning, packing, paying bills, looking for things, reading instructions. Life's maintenance, which is so much of life, fills me with a combination of boredom and self-disgust, like a superficial conversation.

I've always been sloppy and disorganized. I started making messes as a baby and never stopped. Perhaps I was reacting to my older brother Michael, who is as neat as I am not, or to my mother, who was strict but whose schedule didn't allow her to consistently enforce the rules she set down: she was a dictator without an army. Or perhaps I'm simply hardwired that way: if there's a lose-your-wallet gene, I've got it.

Whatever the reasons for my retardation, the chaos that swirls around me didn't seem like a problem until fairly recently. I used to be almost proud of it. I remember thinking as a college senior that my indifference to life's "small" matters put me ahead of the game; it freed up my mind to focus on "important" matters. While my contemporaries were, say, cleaning kitchens, I'd be pondering the meaning of existence. But now I'm starting to know that on any given day there's nothing more important than washing dishes, and that there won't be freedom in my head until there's order in my life.

I'm munching on a bacon-and-butter sandwich when Ethan walks in. He fills a coffee cup with Jack and joins me on the futon, the only place to sit. He's wearing a royal-blue bowling shirt, which once belonged to a fellow named Bobo.

"How you doing?" he asks.

I shake my head. "My job."

"You said it's been okay lately."

"It gets a little better, it gets a little worse, but the core of it never changes. It's killing me, it's shitting on my soul, it's—"

"Come on. It's that bad?"

"It's bullshit."

"But it's interesting bullshit, right? It's an *experience*." He holds up his hand to make sure I don't cut in. "You'll learn a ton, and you'll use it later."

"Maybe," I say, in a tone that should put an end to the discussion.

There's never been any ugliness between us. The only envy or competitiveness I can detect comes from me, not Ethan. His support is unconditional. And each of us makes an effort to inspire the other because our relationship can have the opposite effect. When we lived together during college, and afterwards, commiseration was too easy to come by. Failing was almost fun. That said, I don't like it when he tries to talk me out of well-earned misery. Sometimes all I want to hear is: "You're right. It sucks."

"Want to smoke pot?" he says.

"Yes I do, Bobo. Yes . . . I . . . do."

He smiles lopsidedly, the unlit joint already between his lips. "Calliope?"

"I told you. We're not doing anything till the campaign's over."

"So responsible," he says, holding in a hit. "And ridiculous."

"It makes sense to me."

"I'm sure." He hands me the joint, his eyes already showing signs of stoned. "So if Schecter loses the Primary, you could have a girlfriend in two weeks."

"How'd it go today?" I ask, body and brain needing a new subject.

Ethan works in a coffee shop but always has "projects" going. He's been filming ordinary people performing weird athletic feats: a postman jumping up to touch an awning, a butcher doing a squat thrust, that sort of thing. As I far as I can tell, it's a commentary on very little.

"You're not going to believe this," he says, getting off the couch, smiling. He has curly red-blond hair that sticks straight up, sideburns than slant down toward his mouth, and an angular face. Pretty good-looking, especially in Israel.

I take another hit and lean back, excited; I love to watch Ethan talk.

"I went into a gym, the one in the Woolworth—" He tilts his head like a dog hearing a strange sound, then heads for the bathroom, hand on stomach.

The phone rings. It could be Mom, or Tod, or the woman I met at a party who smelled like cornflakes and described herself as a proud libertarian. On the other side of that ring is my life, and I want no part of it. But it's my voice I hear: *Please leave a message*. I sound dead. And gay. I sound like a gay dead person. Now a woman is speaking Spanish, songful Spanish. I'll save this message, I'll save all wrong-number messages and create something, something about technology and the longing for—

The bathroom door thumps open, making me jump; my ass actually comes off the couch. "There's no toilet paper," Ethan says, his head sticking out.

"Nope. No napkins or paper towels either."

"Of course not. Why *would* there be?"

I walk to the bathroom door and look down at Ethan, small on my short toilet. Hairy legs. The smell is in the egg family. "How we doing?" I say, in the Maine accent we do sometimes.

"Not bad, and you?"

"Not too bad."

"Ayuh. Suggestions?"

"Oh, like this doesn't happen to you."

"Of course it does, but before I stick one of your smelly socks up my ass, I was hoping you had some insights."

"So you're looking to learn."

"Always."

"Well," I say, rubbing an imaginary beard. "Unfortunately, there haven't been many new developments in this area. What works best is what's always worked best. Your choices are essentially threefold. The aforementioned sock is a strong option. A paper product from the trash can be effective, but often crusty, even sharp. Or, and this might be too radical for a guy like you, you can step into the shower."

"Thank you, doctor."

"Doctor Wiper."

"Doctor Y. Per? No, that's not right."

"Doctor Y. *Pass*."

"Right." Ethan giggles. "Doctor I. Y. Pass."

"Yesss!"

I find myself in the kitchen, slapping my thigh with a spatula and thinking about my conversation with Paul: his wince, his smile. I did okay, all things considered.

"Is this weed strong?" I ask as Ethan sits down on the couch.

"No. I don't know. Maybe. The same." He's staring at the TV, now filled with the prominent noggin of Newt, who's talking about Clinton. His enemy. His brother.

"The same as what?"

He giggles, points at the TV. "Newt looks like Slobidan Milosevic."

"Slobidan Milosevic," I say, loving the sound of it.

"Why'd you ask about the weed?"

"'Cause I'm stoned."

"That's the idea."

"Are you W.C. Fields now?"

"What?"

"W.C. Fields?"

The radiator hisses, then clanks like a guy in a dungeon with chains on his ankles.

"What are you talking about?" he asks.

"The radiator?"

"W.C.?"

"Like a bathroom?"

"Right. Europe."

"I fucking *pissed* away my year in Paris."

"Are you going to want to eat?" he asks.

"That's the idea, my little chickadee." Or is that Mae West?

"I didn't say that."

Ethan bites into an ice cube, the crunch impossibly loud, like from a speaker. I'm not sure he's still with the conversation. Probably not. He has a fertile mind, but a turbulent one; thoughts blow away before they blossom.

"What didn't I just say?" he asks.

"Forget it, because—" I suck on my cigarette, and the smoke feels like a solid thing, an egg noodle, an egg noodle coated with stewy sauce.

"Because what?" he says.

"What?"

"You said because."

"No, I didn't."

"I think you did."

"I might have."

"Let's assume you did."

"Okay. I don't know if I want to say what I want to say *because* I may have already said it."

"Who cares?"

"Not me."

"Me neither."

"Okay, here goes: *because* I'm stoned."

Laughter bursts from Ethan's mouth like a sneeze, and he dives onto the floor. I watch him laugh and roll, and then I feel it coming, a tickle moving up from my stomach. I let it fill me up and it feels good, a massage from the inside.

We stop laughing when Ethan conks his head on the coffee table. Unhurt, he stands up, sniffling, rubbing his eyes with his palms.

"So you went to Woolworths?" I ask.

"The gym in the Woolworth building." He moves out in front of the coffee table as I sit down. "It's an all-male gym so a few Hasidic Jews work out there, which I thought was kind of strange. But I figured weight-lifting Hasidim would be perfect for my film."

"Vain," I say. "And rebellious."

"*Exactly*. A young guy named Dov let me film him doing lat pull-downs."

"That's not good enough."

"No. So I convinced him to come out to the park across Broadway so I could film him sprinting. I told him it had to be an all-out sprint, like a race. That was what I said to him, like a race, so then of course he wanted to race. For like half an hour I tried to find someone for him to race. Finally, I recruited this fat guy selling souvlaki, which worked pretty well, I thought, thematically. *Something*, right?"

"I think souvlaki is *lamb*."

He stares at me, confused. "Anyway, Dov got off to a great start." Ethan bends over, pops up. "He exploded out of the blocks. His arms were pumping, his hair thingies were bouncing up and down. It was *awesome*. But I started to get worried because I could see how tight he was." He pumps his arms stiffly, like a robot. "Sure enough he comes up lame. He pulled a hammy." Ethan starts hopping on one foot. "He went like this for a while, then fell down. I helped him over to a bench. He was almost in tears. It didn't help matters that Fat Souvlaki was doing a victory jig. And get this: Dov asked me when the movie was coming out. He thought I was making a real movie, a feature film or a documentary about, I don't know, speedy Jewish people. I felt . . . dirty. I asked him if he wanted help getting home, but he insisted on going back to the gym. He said he still had to do biceps."

"I bet he enjoyed the sprint till he got hurt," I say, trying to remember the last time I ran as fast as I could.

I'm standing up, but why? Maybe to turn up the stereo, which is playing "Green Grass and High Tides." Calliope's always telling me why I'm not supposed to like Southern Rock. She doesn't get it. Maybe she doesn't get *me*.

"Private prisons," Ethan says.

"No shit."

"Huh?"

"I'm not so into the idea anymore. It's not . . . "

"No need to explain. I've got plenty more where that came from."

The joint is in my hand, lit, so I smoke it. "That was my idea."

"Then don't worry, you'll think of another one."

"I want to put together all these phone messages I've been getting from people I don't know, like a collage of loneliness. The loneliness of the long-distance caller."

He puts his finger in his ear and scratches. "I don't get it."

"I lost it, but it's good. Trust me."

Everything has become fascinating: Dov's sprint, Newt's noggin, Paul's smile. Everything is interconnected and profound and interconnected.

"I want to check the Sox score," Ethan says, clicking on the TV. "Pedro went tonight." Pedro Martinez: the Red Sox's new ace.

Hakim Mohammed is on TV, sharing the screen with Roger LaBrie, the guy who sort of confessed. According to the reporter, Minky Lennon, eight months ago LaBrie told his cousin that he shot Zito. Michel Coyne, the Brooklyn DA, is standing by the conviction. Now there's a shocker.

"I had to write a press release about this today," I say as the news moves on to another story, a new killing.

"What'd you say about it?"

"Nothing. Absolutely nothing. It's going to be quite an event when someone in New York gets executed."

"It could be that guy Hakim."

A good thought goes darting by, and I close my eyes to see it. "The first person executed in New York in decades. It's a whole machine, you know? They're going to have to find people for an execution team and a doctor to pronounce him dead and who knows what else."

"You think they've already put it all together?"

"I don't know. I think that's the story right there: what's been done, what needs to be done." I look at Ethan, and the look he's giving me is the look I was looking for. "It's a good freelance piece, don't you think?"

"It's great. You should *definitely* do it. There's no reason not to."

He pours two shots of Jack, and it dawns on me that this night isn't going to end anytime soon. There will be drinks, discussion, food. Life will be lived.

Ethan holds up his glass. "To your new project."

"To Dov." I throw back my shot and revel in the sweet burn.

7

One of those mornings. I had no shampoo or soap to wash my hair, which is gathered in clumps like baby dreads. My breath has already made a mockery of the Colgate. My clothes I pulled from a pile. As I approach a group chatting by the photocopier, Lana, the field director, gears up to make a comment. She has a crush on me, which, like a boy, she expresses by giving me shit. "Ben Bergin," she says. "You wouldn't be bad-looking if you bathed once in a while."

I get coffee and go to my desk, where when I sit down I realize that my fly is open. Gaping. And I'm not wearing underwear. I just paraded through the office baring bush.

I need to be careful today.

Tod sent me two e-mails, one saying he loved the release and another informing me that "Schec kicked ass on TV." I don't want to think about the release or Hakim Mohammed or my story idea, which has, like so many before it, lost luster while I slept. The article wouldn't be interesting. Or someone's already done it. One of the two.

I hear breathing behind me. When I turn around, Shawn tilts his head back to laugh, giving me a view of the webbed snot in his nostril.

"S'up?" he says.

"What are you doing?"

"You know." He jerks his head toward his shoulder. "Just doing my thing."

"You have a web of snot in your nose."

He tries to sniffle it away, to no avail. "Actually, I want to talk to you about something?" When he lets the fake blackness slip, he speaks with the tentativeness that slackens the speech of most people his age, my age, an implied question mark clinging ashamedly to every statement, sign and symbol of our reluctance to commit. "I was thinking of asking Callie out?" he says.

Callie is his name for Calliope. I like it, and I'm pissed he came up with it. The thought of her going out with Shawn is funny, the greatest mismatch of all time. But can I be sure she wouldn't say yes just to be nice?

"You're a little young for her, don't you think?"

"She's only two years older than me? I got held back." He grins: little teeth. "Reading problems."

My phone rings, and I forget not to pick it up. "Hello Benjamin," Mom says, in operatic good cheer. The good news is that it's eight-fifty, which means it will be a short conversation if Mom has a nine o'clock. She's a therapist. "I'm assuming you don't have any opinions about the carpet. So I've gone ahead and ordered a nice beige."

"Sounds good."

"So tell me, how *are* you?"

"All right." I shoo Shawn away from my desk. "Busy."

"I saw the congressman on TV last night. Very impressive, very poised."

"Yeah, he did well."

"How's the campaign going?"

She's talking about poll numbers, about Schecter's chances, but I hear myself say, "I'm sick of it. I don't know if I can make it to November."

Until this moment I've been careful not to let her know I'm less than content on the campaign. She worries about me, and I feel the weight of her worry.

"I'm sorry, sweetie," she says. "I'm so sorry."

"It's not that big a deal. I'm fine. I'm used to not liking my job."

"Yes, I suppose you are." Deep sigh. "I must say, you seem to have inherited his inability to be satisfied."

I put my tongue against the back of my front teeth and do the deep breathing thing that Calliope taught me. Now, as always, the effect is hard to discern, but I manage not to yell, so I'll call this session a success.

"Benjamin?"

"Please don't compare me to him."

Him: my father, her husband, our ghost. James Palazzo was a history professor at a college in the town where I grew up. He left us when I was four and died in a car accident in Paris two years later. As a kid, I never thought about him much. The fucker took off; that was all I needed to know. But last year, while researching free-trade proposals, I came across an article he'd written, urging workers to unite in opposition to globalization. It was good: pie-in-the-sky maybe, but interesting and alive. It was also ahead of its time. Since then, he's been on my mind—not at the center of it, but there; when I think about him, I realize I've been thinking about him.

"I'm not comparing you to him," Mom says. "You're certainly not cruel like he was. But you do remind me of him. Happiness is a choice, Benjamin."

This is a version of the discussion that's dominated our relationship for the last few years. What angers me is less what she says about me—I can't really disagree—than what she implies about herself: does she really think she's happy?

"What does that mean, anyway?" I say. "'Happiness is a choice.'"

"It means outlook is everything."

Calliope sits down on the edge of my desk, smelling fruity-fresh. Her hair is damp and her nose is sprinkled with light freckles. Her freckles make sporadic appearances; I've yet to determine the when or the why.

"Got to go," I say to Mom.

"Love you, Bemjamin."

"Love you too."

"Mom?" Calliope says when I hang up.

"Schecter."

She snorts a laugh, which makes me laugh.

"So tell me, crusty boy, what'd *you* get up to last night?"

"Drank whisky and listened to Southern Rock."

"Did you chew tobacco?" She pretends to spit in her tea.

"Not in the mood."

"Did you watch sports?"

She thinks my interests are banal. She even uses that word, banal, with a French-sounding emphasis on the second syllable. Her mother is a poet and her father is a painter-sculptor-film-maker. Calliope makes fun of their snobbery, but she's inherited it. I've never heard of most of the stuff she's into: it's avant-garde this and experimental that. I believe she genuinely loves the art she says she loves, but I also believe she denies herself honest reactions to things that don't meet her threshold of hip.

"Can we just *not?*" I say.

"Not what?"

"I don't feel like being criticized right now."

She sticks out her big lips, trying to be cute. "I'm not criticizing you. I'm criticizing what you like."

"For you, there's no difference. That's the problem."

"What, you want me to pretend I like Lynrd Skynrd?"

"You could try to understand why I like them. I don't like—I don't know—Gert Fanning, but I want to know why you like her."

"Are you comparing her to Lynrd Skynrd?"

"There's no comparison."

She gives me her I-can't-believe-I'm-friends-with-you sigh, then leaves.

But a moment later she has her hand on my shoulders and her mouth near my ear.

"By the way, did you know what Schecter's constituents call him?"

"Get out of here," I say, her soft touch and warm breath confusing things, making me less annoyed, or more.

She giggles and leaves, pleased with herself, reveling in her power.

I type a sentence that turns into the op-ed about gun control. The words come easily and I even believe what they say. I bang out five tight paragraphs, my fingers gliding across the keyboard with a purpose. It's not unimportant, what I'm writing. A real issue with real choices. So what if it's not literature? Or even journalism. It's not advertising copy, either. Well, I suppose it is, but at least I'm pushing a decent product. After all, I'm not working for Jesse Helms (who, on the other hand, dares to say what he believes, so let's not think too deeply about this). Maybe I *can* make it to November. I'll just sit here, sipping good bad coffee and stringing words together.

"Benny," Tod says before he even enters the room.

"Toddy," Jenny says with a mocking edge. Nice to hear. I seem to be having an edifying influence on my roommates.

"Jenny, Jenny," Tod says, playing on that eighties song. Virtually everything that comes out of Tod's mouth could be construed as sexual harassment.

Tod taps my shoulder. Enough with the touching. "Conference room at eleven," he says, already backing away. "We're meeting to talk about the debate."

"Schecter going to be there?"

He nods with a smile that says, You're being brought into the loop.

It's rare—unprecedented—for me to be included in a meeting like this, and I can only conclude that it's a reward for yesterday's release, my rhyming lie.

The meeting is in twenty minutes: not enough time to prepare but plenty of time to get nervous—and to regret not washing my hair with dish soap. I'm divided on whether to drink another cup of coffee; I'm already jacked up.

I go into the kitchen and pour myself half a cup. At the fridge, studying other people's food, I hear Paul and Calliope chitchatting in the hallway. He's telling her about his wacky aunt, and she's laughing with more gusto than the story warrants. "I mean, she's *tapped*," Paul says. He's looser with Calliope than with anyone else in the office. She chalks up their rapport to her ease with black people. I chalk it up to her body.

Paul comes into the kitchen, probably to get one of the super-sweet ice teas he drinks all day. His only vice, as far as I can tell. That, and politics.

"Hey," I say, feeling warmth from him. I thought he might be miffed that I took only two of his edits, but apparently not.

"All right," he says as if I'd asked how he was. He pulls a bottle from the door of the fridge and takes a long swig, his Adam's apple bouncing. The "ahh" I'm expecting doesn't come. "I hear you're going to the meeting."

I nod as matter-of-factly as I can. The news is making the rounds: the kid's getting called up to the show.

"You're wearing *that?*" he says.

"I was planning to," I say, looking down at the olive T-shirt Ethan and I have traded back and forth since college. It's wrinkled but not ridiculously so. No stains. It's an Armani suit compared to some of the things I wear. "I don't have a choice."

"Come on," he says.

I follow him to his office, which is tucked into a corner, past the front desk and the field department. It's a good location if you want to be alone, but you don't want to be alone, not if you're a player, which Paul is. His office smells industrially clean, like hand soap in a McDonalds. There are photos of his mother and little sister on his desk, and posters of MLK and Arthur Ashe on the wall.

From the bottom drawer of his desk he pulls out a light blue dress shirt, still in plastic. "Should fit all right," he says, handing it to me.

"Thanks," I say, touched. "Brooks Brothers."

"Got to dress like you *mean* it."

"I always do."

"Yeah, you mean *something*."

I take off my shirt. I take it off too soon, before I've unwrapped the other shirt, and I have to stand there sporting my once-solid, now-soft, handles-heavy, increasingly hairy, shockingly pale upper body. My guess is that Paul has a great body: the roadmap of veins in his forearms suggests low body fat.

"Any advice on the meeting?" I say, sucking in my gut.

He has his answer ready: "Don't expect anybody to do you any favors. Nobody's going to ask for your opinion. You got something to say, say it. Say it quick and say it loud. Congressman's got like a one-second attention span. You got to grab him, know what I'm saying?"

A jolt of nervousness shoots from my stomach to my head, bringing heat, and I do that breathing thing again: lots of air in through the nose. I'm starting to believe, and that's half the battle, Calliope tells me, believing.

The shirt fits well after I roll up the sleeves. Feels nice, too. Silky. I pretend to be a model on a runway, walking, stopping, spinning.

"Uh-oh," Paul says. "Look out."

"*Now* I mean it."

"You sure do. You're going to *own* this campaign." He holds out his hand for a slap-shake, which I give him awkwardly, our fingers staying hooked too long, but it's nice nonetheless, the beginning of something, perhaps.

8

We get to the conference room two minutes late, and wouldn't you know: my first big meeting happens to be the first meeting in the history of politics to start on time. The only person to acknowledge my presence is Wes Robertson, our chief consultant. He gives me a two-fingered military salute, which he can pull off nicely, being an ex-Marine. And he nods at Paul, I'm glad to see.

The group is what I expected: Tod, Danny, Wes, Paul, and The Man, who's at the head of the table, listening with no discernable interest as Danny gives what I take to be a roundup. I'm always surprised to see Schecter's big gut. No matter how much chopped liver he consumes, his face stays thin—TV-ready, in other words. He's rocking quickly in the desk chair that someone wheeled in here precisely because he likes to rock quickly. The Man gets what The Man wants. After the first debate, which was held in Buffalo, I drove around for an hour until I found a deli that could make corn beef on rye with brown mustard. The presence of yellow mustard on a sandwich once helped inspire a classic Schecter tantrum, which involves saliva being sprayed and someone being fired. His temper is no secret. It puts extra pressure on the staff to plant there's-a-side-you-don't-see stories in the press, for which he's photographed with his granddaughter on his knee.

"And, uh . . . oh yeah," Danny says. He gives his puffy face a hard, one-handed rub, forehead to chin. "McGrath from the *News* called wanting to know when and where people called you Schecter the Protector."

"What'd you tell him?" I say, just to get in the game.

"What's the issue?" Schecter says, staring at the ceiling, still rocking.

"The issue?" Danny says.

"I don't see the *problem*," Schecter says.

Danny looks at Tod, who looks at Wes. "Well, Arnie," Wes says,,his South Carolina drawl altering the tone like a slow song at a dance. "Daniel, Tod, and I got to chatting this morning, and we were having a hard time remembering exactly when it was that your constituents were calling you that."

"I hear it everywhere," Schecter says, going delusional on us. I glance at Tod, and he winks.

"We should make pins," Schecter says.

"Pins?" Danny says.

"With my nickname on it," Schecter says. "Protector pins."

"Safety pins," I offer, then wish I didn't.

"I'll look into it," Danny says.

"All right then," Wes says. "The congressman and I are going to shack up together tonight in preparation for the debate, but first we wanted to get some feedback from you all. Now, let me have a little looksee."

He picks up his notebook and squints in an attempt to read his notes. He's a large man, two-twenty easy, with a square, pinkish face, and red-gray hair that's thin on top and thick around his ears. It's a measure of Schecter's respect for Wes that he's sitting somewhat peacefully while the big guy gets his bearings. Wes has orchestrated Schecter's move toward the center, but they're hardly soulmates, politically or otherwise. Wes is a populist at heart; the one night I spent with him, in an Irish pub in DC, he drank five double bourbons and lovingly recited William Jennings Bryan's "Cross of Gold" speech. He's to the left of Schecter on economic issues and to the right on most social ones. Wes is here because of two issues that they agree on, at least for the purposes of this election: welfare and crime. These issues have dogged the Democrats since the sixties for a simple and sad reason: each has a black face. It's well known (but not well known enough) that the GOP uses welfare and crime as proxies for race. Wes has become a legend by neutralizing the Republicans' advantage on these issues with crafty positioning and relentless attacks. This Primary stuff is a little tame for good ol' Wes; he'll earn his paycheck in the General.

"First off: welfare," Wes says. "The issue, of course, is the nineteen ninety-six Welfare Reform Act. Arnie voted yes, Stein voted no. It's just about as simple and as complicated as—"

"We shouldn't give an inch," Paul says, cutting in, making me nervous for him. I've *definitely* had too much coffee. "It's been good for blacks."

"We need to be careful," Tod says. "Blacks are against us on this."

"I don't think they are," Paul says.

"Do you just not believe in polls?" Tod says, his eyes on Schecter. We all look at The Man as we speak, even when addressing someone else. Meanwhile, Schecter looks at no one. "The numbers are clear," Tod says. "Overwhelming."

Come on, Paul. Stay strong, brother. I'm rooting for him even though I'm pretty sure I agree with Tod.

I can't speak if I don't know what I think.

"But we *signed* the law," Paul yells, making Danny's head bob. Woke him up, probably. "We can't run away from it."

"Course not," Tod says with a back-handed wave. "But we shouldn't portray it as God's gift. We don't want the *Times* saying you told blacks what's good for them."

"Maybe we do," Paul says, standing up, his hands above his head. Grayish palms. "What you all have to understand is that blacks need to hear some hard truths. We keep on telling them what they want to hear. But I ask you: are their lives getting any better?"

Tod smiles with half his mouth. Paul committed two sins: he was emotional and he was earnest. He retreats back to his chair, looking small. He knows he's lost, but I doubt he knows why: if he were self-aware he wouldn't have sermonized in the first place. It's surprising he hasn't learned to reign in his righteousness; you'd think someone in the DA's office would have told him to shut up. Then again, no one here has.

"It's a good bill," Paul says.

I'd like to come to his defense, but I'm now sure I disagree with him. Besides, I've lost the power of speech. It's no great crime, sitting here silently. This is my first meeting at this level. And I don't really care about the campaign. Already planning my excuses.

"I don't hear much of a disagreement," says Danny, Mister Mensch. "We shouldn't act like the bill was perfection, but we defend the vote. The numbers are on our side."

"Numbers are fine," Wes says, "but we need human beings in the answer."

"The system wasn't working for people," Paul says.

"It was a vote of hope," Tod says. "A vote to change an unacceptable status quo."

"That it was," Schecter says. "That . . . it . . . was." He points his chin at the tray of baked goods, and shakes his head when Danny picks up a piece of banana bread. Sheepishly, Danny puts a blueberry muffin on a napkin and slides it to Schecter, who picks it up and bites into it like an apple.

"Moving right along," Wes says. "There's a new development regarding Mr. *Ha*-keem *Mo*-hammed. Apparently this LaBrie character confessed to the killing the *day* it happened. That's what a friend of his is saying."

"Didn't he already confess like a dozen times?" Danny says.

"A contemporaneous confession," Paul says. "It's a whole other ball game, legally speaking. But let's not get carried away here. The evidence was *strong*. There were witnesses, motive, opportunity, a weapon—"

"Maybe so," Wes says. "But people are digging in. I saw Officer Zito's ex-partner on the radio, and he was *fuming*. As far as he's concerned, they've got the right man in prison, and he doesn't want to hear another word about it. Meanwhile, we've got black leaders like Billy Record doing what they do. It's hot. I think Stein might use it."

"Really?" Tod says. "If it's dicey for us, it's dicey for him."

"*Come* on, Toddy," Wes says, and taps his temple to say, think. He views Tod as his apprentice, his baby bulldog. "Stein's down a touchdown with ten seconds to play. It's Hail Mary time."

"Well, we *know* it's going to come up," Danny says, stealing my line. "I mean, one of the sponsors of the debate is the Urban League."

Schecter says, "So then I'll say, of course, any possibly exculpatory evidence should be investigated, but it's too early to start talking about a new trial—"

"Hold on," Tod says. "I wouldn't say the words, new trial. We're talking cop-killer here. This is dynamite in the General."

"We've got to play one election at a time," Danny says.

"I agree," Wes says. *Ahh-gree.* "That's Campaign 101, right there. However, another basic rule that I adhere to, is let's don't *lose* the General while winning the Primary."

"Right," Tod says. "We don't want to give Washburn an opening."

"Chet will get no opening from me," Schecter says. "I'll say that this is a matter for the courts, there's a process moving forward, and so on."

"No," I hear myself say. "You'll look evasive and political. You need to make Stein look political while you take the high road."

"There's a high road?" Danny says.

"We need to build one," I say, looking in Schecter's direction.

"Here's what you do. You shake your head sadly. You're disappointed in Stein. You would have expected more from him. You're silent just long enough for people to get a little antsy, even a little nervous. This has to be perfect. You need to sell the silence."

"Sell the silence," Wes says. "I like that."

"You speak softly. You're almost too sad to speak. You say, 'Did you see that? Did you *see* what he just did? He took this volatile, tragic issue and tried to use it for political gain. We've seen it a thousand times before, haven't we? Aren't you sick and tired of it? Politicians shortsightedly and selfishly exploiting racially charged issues. We're talking about human life here, and he's thinking about votes. Listen up, friends, if we're not careful, this could reopen wounds that many of us have worked hard to heal.'"

I stop midspeech, worried that I've spoken too long. Schecter is drilling me with his brown eyes. Which is a good sign. But I can't bring myself to look at him directly. A smile opens up in my chest, and I struggle to contain it before it rises to my mouth. As politicians go, Schecter is pretty low on the charisma scale, but he has a quality that the good ones all have, that ability to make you feel honored by their attention. Maybe it's simply the glow of their power that feels good.

"Don't stop, son," Wes says. "You've got the floor."

"You say, 'Any evidence of innocence *must* be looked into, and the courts are doing just that. There's a review process going on. We need to make sure it works, and if it does, as I'm confident that it will, justice will be done. And that's what we all want: justice. We *all* want the same thing. You see, friends, we can use this opportunity to unite. Together we can make sure that justice is done. I, for one, will not allow Congressmen Stein or anyone else to use this issue to divide us.'"

When I stop, I realize that I'm standing. Only a little embarrassed, I sit down, but not before grabbing an apple muffin. Paul smiles and points at my shirt. Wes is nodding slowly, as is

Danny. Schecter has resumed his rocking. A muted response, but if you're looking for backslaps, politics is the wrong business for you. The silence speaks for itself; I put an end to the discussion.

"Anybody got anything else?" Wes says.

"I'm concerned about your mustache," Tod says.

"What?" Schecter says, blank-faced, his mustache suddenly looking gigantic and fake, like a bad movie bandit's.

"I think it could be a liability in the General," Tod says.

"That's ridiculous," Danny says, showing rare anger. Since college he's had to play good cop to Tod's bad, the stud's "nice" friend, the reliable one.

"I want to hear it," Wes says. "Lot more interesting than welfare."

"It could hurt us with soccer moms," Tod says.

Wes says, "You got polling data?"

"No," Tod says, playing it straight. "I've got firsthand experience. I grew a beautiful 'stache when I was living in New Rochelle, and the women didn't dig it."

"Didn't get any?" Wes says.

Tod coughs out an are-you-crazy laugh. He actually points at his own face. "Let's just say I didn't get it at my normal pace."

"Did you control for other variables?" I ask.

"Like your personality?" Paul says, and Wes laughs: a close-to-literal "heh-heh."

"Laugh all you want," Tod says, "but name one senator who has a mustache."

"Barbara Mikulski?" Wes says, and we all smile, but only Tod laughs. Everyone else is conscious of the turn the conversation has taken. We modern, chastened, halfway sensitive men won't let the meeting descend into a bachelor party. There's an invisible woman in the room, call her Feminism, and she wears a different face for all of us. For me she's my ex-girlfriends, my mother, Calliope.

"How about Wellstone?" I say. "Doesn't he have a mustache?"

"That's Minnesota," Tod says, "and it's a goatee."

"It's a Van Dyke," Danny says, wanting to be right about something.

"The mustache stays," Schecter says, projecting for the first time in the meeting. "And I sincerely wish that someone, preferably you, Mr. Wilcox, could give me back the last minute of my life." This is his public voice, which he has sought to make less shrill in recent months. He'd probably be better off just being his shrill self since the touch of gentleness doesn't seem natural. He sounds like a dad trying not to be angry. *That's okay, Timmy, it was an accident.* "I have a little secret for you," he says. "If and when women, suburban or otherwise, vote for me, it will not be because of my sexual magnetism."

He pauses while we erupt in fake laughter, then looks at Paul. "Good to see you, Mr. Teague," he says, as if Paul had just entered the room. "I'm going to be in Lana's office. Stop by and say hello."

Then he sets his eyes on me, and this time I manage not to look away. "Ben Bergin, I'm glad you joined us here today. Thank you for the fine press releases you've been writing and for the impassioned little speech you gave today. It's exactly the kind of *positive* approach we need to be taking."

And to all of us: "We're getting close, folks. Just days away now." He leans back and pauses for effect. Talk about a little speech. "This is serious business," he says softly, making us lean in. "They call the Senate the country's most exclusive club. I'll tell you one thing, this big-eared boy from Brooklyn didn't dare dream of becoming a member. But now that I'm this close, I'm *not* going to let it slip away. We've all worked hard, but for the next two hundred and sixty-four hours we're going to work even harder. Do your part. I promise I'll do mine."

9

After the meeting, I go looking for Calliope. I want to smoke cigarettes, and I want to be around her when I'm in a good mood.

Ten or so people are in the volunteer room, but Calliope isn't one of them. I spot George Blue, my favorite volunteer. Big and hairy, he looks like the Unabomber version of Elliot Gould. He founded a group called Jewish Bikers for Justice and claims to have volunteered on fifty campaigns. His record, he says proudly, is seventeen and thirty-three. Some liberals like losing: it's validation of sorts, proof that they're on the side of the angels. Which points to a larger issue: can you be in power and still be a liberal?

I have to call to him three times to get his attention. He looks up, takes off his shades, and has to squint to see me. "Do you know where Calliope is?" I ask.

"Nah, bro. To tell you the truth, I barely know even where I am, I'm so deep into my folding and stuffing. It's really pretty Zen if you go with it." He smiles as if finally recognizing me. "How *you* doing, bro?"

"Awesome," I say. "How about you, Blue?"

"I'm good. Couldn't be better. Seeing the Allmans tonight at the Beacon. Good times, bro. Good times."

I speed down the hall, trying to preserve my limited supply of good mood. I wish I'd known Calliope a few years ago, when I was skimming like a water skier along the surface of my life, when an Allman Brothers show would have made my month. But back then I wasn't secure enough to take on a woman like Calliope. As if I am now.

She's not in the kitchen or by the photocopier.

Too early for lunch, I think.

I force myself to slow down, because what's the point of a good mood if you can't relax? I decide not to do the breathing thing again, not wanting to abuse it.

When I see Calliope come out of the research room, it's all I can do not to hug her. Overcompensating, I give her a gravelly "Hey," feigning boredom. I've been doing this since high school—hell, since grade school—playing down my passion for girls I'm into, acting blasé. It's the worst. It's a slow death, a drip-drip-drip suicide by soul poison.

"Nice shirt," she says, meaning the opposite.

"It's Paul's," I say, looking down, and the sight of coffee spots on the belly of the shirt unleashes a rush of guilt-tinged concern—concern that the stains won't come out, that I wasn't appreciative enough, that I overshadowed him in the meeting.

"Need nicotine," she says.

It's a beautiful day, a blend of spring and summer, warm enough so that when we get to our corner, Calliope takes off her smocklike shirt, uncovering a light pink tank top that gives me a clear idea, my clearest yet, of her dimensions. Her tits are not monstrous, I'm glad to see: no back problems or hang-down issues to worry about. But they're large enough to push the little tank away from her belly, pale and cute and certainly not flat above her wraparound skirt.

"How *great* is this?" Calliope says. She takes a long drag with her eyes closed, her head tilted back.

"The sun's hot," I say, fearing for the tender-looking skin on her neck. I should put her in a safe deposit box until I'm ready for her.

"I'm psyched for summer," she says. "It's my second favorite season."

This is one of the reasons I like her: she says things she might have said when she was five. I have no choice but to ask what's number one. Actually, I want to know.

"What's your first?"

She smiles, her eyes still closed. "Fall."

"I like fall, too," I say, imagining us in the Maine woods in October. We're walking and talking. No, not talking. Summer seemed like a dream, blurry and sweaty. We feared that it wasn't real, that it wouldn't last once the sex stopped being new. But it's fall now, the haze is gone, and we're strong, the two of us. We're walking through the woods and not talking and our boots feel comfortable and solid.

"So I met with Schecter and the boys," I say.

"I heard."

"Went pretty well, actually."

"I can tell."

Am I that transparent? Not wanting to come across as goofy gloating boy, I say, "So what's going on with you?"

She looks at me, her eyes narrow, her lips twisted to the side. It's her something-doesn't-add-up face, and my bullshit always melts away in its glare. "Tell me what happened in the meeting," she says, turning her back to the sun.

"We talked about the debate, and I came up with a pretty good suggestion. A little speech popped out of me whole. Sometimes I kind of love politics."

"I know you do." She stubs her cigarette out on the ledge. She always takes her butts inside and I have no choice but to do the same.

"I like coming up with ways to get people to understand things in the way you want them to understand them. It's psychology, I guess. It's crap, is what it is. But maybe it's *necessary* crap. What would happen if all the decent people decided not to play, and left it to the Tods of the world? It's not pure, but . . . "

"But nothing. Politics ain't poetry, boss."

"You make that up?'

"Think so."

"It sounds like something people say."

"*We* say it."

"Politics ain't poetry."

"Boss. You've got to say boss."

"Politics ain't poetry, boss."

"Right on."

She's sunbathing again, head back, eyes closed. In the brightness I can see her soft little mustache. She doesn't seem all that interested in my meeting, or all that excited that I'm excited. Maybe she doesn't want what's best for me. Maybe she fears that I won't need her when I'm doing well, or that my doing well will force us to focus on *her* fucked-upness, which always seems to get short shrift in our discussions.

Or maybe she's just enjoying the sun.

And I should do the same, given my good mood. A breeze hits us head-on but gently, a caress; it seemed to run out of steam just as it reached our faces. The city, strangely quiet, seems as soft as the weather. You get these moments in New York sometimes, lulls in the madness, as though everyone had agreed to be mellow at the same time. In the distance, the buildings of lower Manhattan are shining.

"Is that the Brooklyn Bridge?" I say, possibly noticing it for the first time.

She opens one eye, then closes it. "Probably."

"You grew up here."

"I don't know that kind of stuff."

"What kind of stuff?"

"Facts." She's only half-kidding. Her body of knowledge is narrow and esoteric. Some people amass facts like money and use them like weapons, but Calliope's content to know what she knows. It seems like a good way to be. "I've always wanted to walk across the Brooklyn Bridge," she says, her eyes still shut. "We should do it someday."

"Yeah, let's," I say, excited by the plan even though it's vague. Or *because* it's vague, the "someday" suggesting a distant future, which in turn suggests sex, romance, all that. We won't make it to someday as friends. We'll be lovers or nothing. And at the moment at least, the thought of being nothing gives me a flu-like feeling.

A thumping sound tells me that behind us, on the building across the street, our fellow roof-dwellers have begun their lunchtime game of handball, slapping a tennis ball against a thick brick tower. Not counting the tower, their building is a floor or two lower than ours. Normally they take off just their suit jackets, but today they're stripped down to their T-shirts. "It's Nick and Rufus," I say, using the names we gave them.

We walk to the corner closest to them and wave our arms until Rufus sees us and points. Nick fires an imaginary machine gun, and I have little choice but to pretend to be shot. I put my hand on my heart and stagger and fall against the ledge. Nick's laughter rises above the sound of the traffic. He's my favorite of the two.

Calliope claps her hands above her head as though wanting him to throw the ball. We make this joke every time, but now it seems that Rufus is going to call our bluff. He uncorks a hard, accurate throw, and the ball glances off Calliope's hand, smacking her in the forehead. Giggling and unembarrassed, she puts both hands on her forehead, one on top of the other. I go to her and gently peel her hands away. She assures me that she's okay, and I believe her, the red mark notwithstanding. I retrieve the ball, eager to show off my arm, which was strong—I mean, downright cannon-like—about a decade ago. But Rufus, holding up another ball, signals for me to keep this one.

"Let's have a catch," Calliope says.

"What do you know about having a catch?"

"I like sports. I just don't like to *watch* sports."

"This isn't much of a sport."

"Come on, don't be a poop."

"How's your head?"

"Fine." She claps her hands, then holds them out and squats down. "Come on, pitcher, pitcher, pitcher. Put it right in there, chuck it right in there."

Her approximation of baseball chatter makes me want to squeeze her. Instead, I toss her the ball, underhand, and she reaches up to catch it, giving me a glimpse of a mole near her ribcage. "You can toss it harder than that," she says.

We back up, until most of the roof is between us. Even if Calliope hadn't already been plunked, I couldn't throw it half as hard as I'd like, but it's fun trying to catch her erratic tosses. She has a wild throwing motion, distinctively girl-like yet distinctive. She unfurls her arm as though handling a whip and arches her back—something goes awry around the shoulder—then flings the ball, her hair falling over her face.

"I'm going to throw this one extra hard," she says. She lifts up her skirt to free her long leg and winds up the way she thinks a pitcher would. The ball bounces, picking up speed on the second hop. Darting to my right, bare thigh on my mind, I stretch out to snag the ball, and she yells "Good hustle" like the good mom she'll be.

It's a relief to be doing something other than talking and smoking, an actual *activity*. Over the blurry last seven months, our conversations have sustained me—they stand out like the parts of a dream I can recall—but sometimes they feel like work. It's mostly my fault. I have a need for our conversations to be intense and meaningful, and though they sometimes are, it's too much to ask of mere words, especially when there's much we're choosing not to say. If you want to be intimate, you have to be intimate, sexually and otherwise, you have to surrender, and even then there are limits—limits that I've had trouble accepting in relationships.

More than that, though, Calliope and I challenge each other to be honest. I love this about us, but it tends to shove aside other qualities that a relationship needs, like simple kindness. Sometimes we need to give each other a break.

Sometimes we need to have a catch.

Down on the street, horns are honking, chasing away the calm. But up here on the roof, it's still peaceful.

Rufus and Nick wave; their lunch break is over. I hold up the ball to thank them, then toss a curve to Calliope, who drops it and says, "Stop spinning it, fancy pants."

A good mood for real, and we have a future.

10

The Stein camp's first choice for the final debate site was the Apollo in Harlem, which we rejected because it was too, well, you know. Our first choice was Brooklyn College, which they rejected because it was in Brooklyn. The compromise site is Columbia. In the end, the site doesn't matter much: the crowd is split regardless, and the people you need to reach, excluding reporters, are in their living rooms.

The debate over the debates tapped into an undercurrent of borough rivalry, with Schecter portraying himself as an outer-borough underdog—an effort that required a fair amount of chutzpah given his fundraising advantage. Of course, he has a chutzpah advantage, too. The rivalry turned blatant, and embarrassing, when Schecter showed up at a press conference sporting a straight-brimmed and oddly tall Brooklyn Dodgers cap. It's still not clear whose idea *that* was.

The day of the debate is the first that feels like summer, dark and humid, the sky like a bag about to burst. I allow myself plenty of time to go home and get ready to avoid having to perform the hurrying and sweating routine that has won me both laughs and ridicule at weddings in churches and synagogues up and down the eastern seaboard.

I arrive at the conference hall feeling relatively together. I'm showered and shaved and wearing my suit, which I remembered to bring to the dry cleaners along with Paul's shirt. The good news is that the coffee stains came out. The bad news is that I forgot to bring a shirt of my own to the cleaners, so I'm wearing Paul's again, the long sleeves folded back underneath my jacket. My forearms are cuffless and puffy, like a Popeye Halloween costume. But I'm wearing clean underwear.

I'm surprised by the intimacy of the hall. The sight of TV cameras, which crews are setting up some thirty feet from the stage, unleashes a surge of anxiety that makes me grateful I'm not the one debating tonight. I'm not even going to be in the audience. I'll be backstage, then in the spin room. As part of my undeclared promotion, I can talk to reporters but can't be quoted. I'm a mute spokesman.

I find Tod in the spin room, chatting with a radio reporter, Melanie something. Having worked on campaigns in New York for ten years, including three of Schecter's, Tod knows most of the reporters and has slept with at least two of them. "The ultimate spin," he calls it, but the coverage by reporters he's boned seems no less or more favorable than the norm. I admire their professionalism.

"Ben Bergin," Tod says, introducing me. "A rising star."

"Yeah, yeah," I say, embarrassed and excited; his words seemed shockingly free of irony. I shake her hand, hoping she doesn't notice the Popeye puff.

"Big night," she says. "Are you nervous?"

"Yeah," I say. "Nervous for Stein."

"Good answer, Ben Bergin," she says, with a lilt that makes me suspect she might want to get spun by the rising star.

I excuse myself and head for the food table, where a reporter, an old-timer, his belly testing the strength of his suspenders, is trying to piece together a meal out of cheddar cubes, melon chunks, and sugar cookies. After forcing down a piece of cheese, I realize that I'm too nervous to eat. It's more excited-nervous than anxious-nervous, and it's not unwelcome, but I'll be relieved when the debate's over, assuming that my skit, if Schecter performs it, proves to be at least not terrible.

"Hey, Iceberg," Tod says to Julie Greenberg, his counterpart on the Stein campaign. I had a few dealings with her when she was a lobbyist for an abortion rights group in DC. "Double or nothing on the dinner you owe me?"

Julie barely even manages a smile. She's not one of those women who merely *pretend* to dislike Tod. Her hatred is pure, and I respect her for it.

"Come on, Ice," Tod says. "What do you say?"

She's saved from having to respond when her assistant, my counterpart, comes up to her and nods. The two of them race away, exuding the kind of tension that can mean only one thing: their boss has arrived.

"Big one tonight, Big Daddy," someone says, presumably to the reporter with the suspenders. "Whole ballgame right here."

Stein and his entourage shoot through a corner of the room, and three reporters hustle toward them, holding their microphones like torches.

Commotion erupts in another corner. I'm expecting Schecter, but it's Gabe Widener of Channel Five, the moderator.

There's definitely a sizzle in the air. Debates aren't what they once were now that head-to-head questioning has been virtually eliminated; if I had my way debates would have no rules. But the stakes are huge and, all the scripting notwithstanding, people get a sense of the candidates. Seeking to shut out the unexpected, candidates build a wall of soundbites, but something real invariably squeezes out between the cracks.

"What's with your cuffs?"

It's Paul, smiling but concerned, looking down at my sleeves. There's a little round Band-Aid next to his mouth, probably covering a shaving cut, the rare blemish on his face. The Band-Aid draws more attention than a cut would.

"It's your shirt, actually," I say. "I got stains on it, so I took it to the cleaners and the stains came out, but I forgot to get another shirt cleaned, so I had to wear your shirt again, but the sleeves are too long. I'll get it cleaned again, I—"

"Okay, okay," he says, putting his hand on my shoulder. "Take it easy. Keep the shirt. But I'd take off the jacket and roll up the sleeves. You're going to be shaking a lot of hands tonight, Mr. Spokesman."

"Thanks," I say, feeling for an edge in his words—my post-debate responsibilities have been made equal to his—but generosity is all I can detect. Who knows, though? The guy is hard to read.

Off the spin room is a room equipped with a TV and a mirror—Schecter's locker room—and that's where I am, trying to make my hair look neatly messy, when The Man bursts in with his wife Carol, Wes, and Danny. I exchange upper-arm slaps with Wes and play of-course-I-remember-you with Carol, whom I like. More than like, really. There was a time when she starred in my fantasies.

"Heard you've been writing some great stuff," she says, letting go of Arnie's arm as he huddles with Tod, who's come into the room.

I look at the ground, going all aw-shucks despite my best efforts not to. Carol is never anything but sweet, which might be annoying if she weren't beautiful. Long dark hair, blue eyes, nose that was jobbed but jobbed well. She's the daughter of a Long Island department store mogul. Even if she were younger, she wouldn't be for me, but she's too good, in every sense, for Arnie. Their relationship seems solid, and I've certainly searched for holes. She must find his power alluring.

"Eddie's got a bigger locker room," Wes says. "Should we protest?"

Schecter laughs loudly, which he does when he's trying to seem relaxed. He does seem relaxed. Say what you will about Schecter, he thrives in the spotlight, and people who thrive in the spotlight rule the country (along with their buddies who have the money). It's hard to envision how I'm going to alter the course of history when the mere sight of a turned-off TV camera makes my throat parched and my ass sweaty.

Someone from Channel Five comes in to do Schecter's make-up and everyone else except Carol leaves. I wish someone would put make-up on Danny, whose eye-bags have begun to crack like chapped lips. I ask him if he made sure Calliope had a seat; not everyone who works on the campaign is able to attend.

He nods, then nods again, this time to point. "Speak of the devil woman."

Calliope, the poor girl, is making her way toward us, walking unsteadily on high-heels, her face twisted up in a semi-smile, inspired no doubt by her attempt to look professional. The jacket of her pants suit—pants suit!—is too tight around the shoulders, and her hair is collected in a bun that's already unraveling.

"It's Mary Tyler Moore," Danny says, making me reconsider my choice of words, which were going to be nice.

"Well," I say. "It's you, girl."

"And you should know it," Danny says.

She doesn't get the reference—she's never watched much TV—but she knows we're making fun of her. "Yeah, yeah, yeah," she says with a theatrical huff. She tries to put her hands in the pockets of her jacket, then realizes they're sewn shut.

"With every little something and something, you show it," I say, and she walks away, her ass unfortunately concealed by her ridiculous blazer.

I go to the locker room, where I'll settle in. Back here I can get the all-important perspective of TV. Plus I get to hang with Wes, veteran of hundreds of these things. "Eddie ain't going to know what hit him," Wes says. He puts his legs up and slaps the chair next to him. "Sit down, Ben-Hameen. Sit down and watch a grown man cry."

We should have beer.

The opening statements are a predictable melange of passages from stump speeches. The entire debate will be like a greatest hits album.

Once the questions begin, I have trouble paying attention because I'm trying too hard to pay attention. Words echo in my skull as my brain tries to analyze my response before I have a response, and I end up with no response that I trust. We should really have beer.

Wes is my gauge. "Heh heh" means good and "Hmm" means bad. In the first hour, there are more heh hehs than hmms, so I begin to relax.

Stein is asked about welfare, and his answer is too full. He keeps interrupting himself. Stein's stocky and hairy, a hairy-fingers kind of hairy. A photo-op of him playing basketball in a tank top was one of the worst ideas of the campaign, trumping even Schecter's baseball cap debacle. Stein actually seems like a good guy. My guess is that he's pained by all the bullshit, but can't quite bring himself to rise above it.

Schecter, in rebuttal, gives the numbers, then says, "Given a choice between an uncertain future and an unacceptable status quo, between hope and resignation, I voted for hope, and I'm proud that I did."

"Heh heh."

So far the heh hehs have it over the hmms by ten, but I haven't heard the heh heh I'm longing to hear. Stein hasn't mentioned Hakim Mohammed; he's probably waiting for a direct question. And so are we all.

It's a cleavage-baring black journalist who asks the question. Stein nods as she asks if "given the recent revelations we can be confident in Mr. Mohammed's guilt."

I sink down, going horizontal from my knees to my neck.

"For certain heinous crimes," Stein says, "I support the death penalty." There are boos; the audience, which is about half black, has been sedate until now. "But there's nothing worse a state can do than take the life of an innocent man. This issue is of special significance to African-Americans, who've seen way too much police and prosecutor misconduct. Yet my opponent refuses to take a stand. I believe that every remedy must be on the table: a new trial, clemency, perhaps even a special judicial panel to review death penalty cases." He turns to face Schecter. "Congressman, do you not realize how vitally important this issue is to many New Yorkers, or do you just not care?"

And then it happens: Schecter shakes his head sadly.

As the silence stretches out, even *I* start to worry for him. He's selling shit to the shit salesman.

The room quiets, and quiets further when Schecter begins to speak in a voice just louder than a whisper. "You see that? Do you *see* what he just did? He took this volatile, tragic issue and tried to use it for political gain. We've seen it a thousand times before, haven't we? Aren't you tired of it? Politicians shortsightedly and selfishly exploiting racially charged issues. We're talking about human life here, and he's thinking about votes. Listen up, friends, if we're not careful, this could reopen wounds . . . "

When it's clear he's doing my bit word for word, I shut down. I can't hear a thing. I don't want to hear a thing. Schecter turns to face Stein—a touch of his own—but this is a Bergin original, out there for all the world to see.

He's stopped talking. Part of me, knowing he nailed it, wants to yell, but part of me feels naked and guilty, and that part has me locked in a cringe. I'm holding my breath, dreading laughter, derision, punishment.

The response from the crowd is loud, the loudest of the night. There are boos, but there is also applause, plenty.

"Heh heh. Man has a tape recorder for a mind."

"Good, right?" I say.

"Heh heh heh heh."

I exhale and laugh at the same time. "We've won."

"Long as Arnie don't fall asleep or fart."

You can see the energy seep from Stein. Speaking quickly and softly, he doesn't use even half his allotted time to answer a question about the Lewinsky scandal, unmentioned until now because they basically agree on the issue.

Tone-deaf or maybe just mean, Schecter blasts Stein for calling Clinton an embarrassment—a comment he's retracted about a dozen times. "Congressman Stein wouldn't be able to defend the President when Senator Washburn goes after him," he says, his eyes on fire. "There's only one man on this stage who has the political judgment, the character, and the toughness—"

"Hmm."

". . . to beat Senator Washburn."

"Hmm. Down boy."

"There's only one man on this stage who will be able to look Senator Washburn in the eye and say, 'Stop speaking ill of our Commander in Chief.' There's only one man—"

The moderator cuts in, and Schecter talks over him, his voice consuming everything in its path. "That man, ladies and gentleman, is not Congressman Edward Stein."

Time for closing statements.

"Let's go do our thing," Wes says.

"How bad was that?"

"Not too." He chuckles. "It's a struggle to get most candidates to throw punches. It's hard to get Arn back into his corner. We'll be glad for that just as soon as we get past this intramural, pansy-ass Primary shit."

The spin room is abuzz. Some forty journalists and operatives are making the rounds, stalking each other. Tod's handing out the victory-declaring press release I wrote this afternoon. When a gaggle of reporters flocks around Wes, it occurs to me that the only ones who would be eager to talk to me are those hoping to get info they couldn't get out of an experienced spinner. I might just oblige.

Tod hands me a stack of releases to distribute. "How awesome was that?" he says under his breath. "Fucking bloodbath. Put on a nametag and go talk to reporters."

The thrill of hearing Schecter deliver my lines is long gone. There was the ugliness at the end of the debate, and now the burden of having to talk to strangers, to *sell* to strangers—about my least favorite task in the world.

But damn if I haven't become a good soldier. *Deputy Director of Communications* is too long, so I write *Ben Bergin: Schecter*, stick the nametag on my shirt, and set out in search of an approachable face. Campaign coverage is an abomination. There's all the dirt-digging and finger-sniffing, but that's the least of it. Reporters can't see beyond the conventional wisdom they create. *He's not lying because he's not a liar.* Strange, then, that the political reporters I've met seem sharp, if jaded; we've all seen it all, but they've seen it all a thousand times. My sad silence bit was designed to satisfy their hunger for something even remotely fresh.

Though I expected the bit to work, and though I watched it work on TV, I'm nonetheless surprised to discover that it worked on the first journalist I speak to, a youngish guy with glasses. "That was by far the most dramatic moment," he says.

Where's his cynicism? Has he ever even *heard* of political theater?

"That was the longest silence I've ever heard from the congressman," I say, getting the smile I was looking for.

"That must have come as a shock."

For a flash I'm tempted to tell him about the planning that went into the spontaneous moment: he'd have a story, a real story, and I'd be clean. But I say, "He's worried that this issue could tear us apart. He's always been a uniter."

The guy asks for a business card, but I didn't bring any, so I write my phone number on a press release and manage to look him in the eye when I shake his hand.

I spot Calliope by the door, leaning against the wall, fighting her shoes, her suit, and her hair all at once. She'll be lucky not to fall.

I'm expecting a crack about my nametag, but she says, "I hate these fucking heels. You going to be here a while?"

"I think so."

"I'd really like to get out of here."

I can tell by the way her chest heaves, tits growing huge, that she's doing the breathing thing. She's more than uncomfortable, she's miserable, and a bad outfit is not the only reason.

I look at the growing swarm of people. Tod and Wes are caught up in their spinning. Across the room Paul is chatting with the reporter I just lied to.

"All right," I say, peeling off my nametag. "Let's go."

11

It rained while we were inside, and Broadway has that sheen and summer smell I like: warm wet pavement. It's rare for us to be together outside the office at night, and I feel unsure of myself as we walk south in silence. It seems that I might not know what to say or do, that more will be required of me out here in the big bad city.

Calliope isn't going to help me out. I've felt these moods of hers before, and they always have to do with her brother. My attempts to talk about her brother's death never go well. She's relatively free with the facts—I know that Ari was seventeen and that he had tried once before and that her mother found him in a puddle of blood in her father's studio—but she never tells me how she felt or how she feels. And when I ask, she gives answers that makes me feel naïve and shallow.

"You okay?" I ask.

"It's my feet. They're killing me." On the island in the middle of Broadway she sits down on a damp bench and pulls off her shoe. "I'm going to carry my shoes."

"Really? The sidewalk's kind of gross."

"I didn't think you thought anything was gross."

"I do for other people."

"I'm wearing pantyhose."

"What about glass?"

"Well I can't walk anymore. Maybe I should just get on the subway."

"No," I say, an abrupt end to the night feeling like a tragedy. "Let's hang out."

"Where?" she says, and we both scan the street. A Cuban restaurant, a diner, a dive.

"Let's sit right here," I say. "I'll go to a deli and get us stuff."

"Really? Okay." She takes off her other shoe. "I'd love a big beer."

"Anything to eat?"

"Yeah, whatever."

"What do you mean, whatever? You're a vegetarian."

"Whatever vegetarian. Except portabello. It reminds me of a brain. And candy."

I walk past the first deli because it doesn't seem like the kind of place that would have interesting vegetarian sandwiches. The second deli doesn't look any more promising, but I go in, speed seeming important. I get my sandwich out of the way: chicken cutlet on a hero with melted swiss, peppers, tomato, and mayo. Then I ask the sandwich guy, a squat Latino, if he has avocado, which Calliope loves. Not behind the counter, he tells me, but they sell them whole, and in the produce section I find a ripe one and a thing of sprouts, which I hand to the sandwich guy, who seems amused by my effort. Swiss cheese, avocado, tomato, and sprouts on rye. Not bad, but what about condiment? Calliope hates mayo, mustard's wrong, and basic oil and vinegar won't do, so I find a bottle of balsamic and a jar of dijon, and the guy stirs up a vinaigrette in a paper cup while I fetch a Bass, a Bud, original Lay's, and a Cadbury with roasted almonds. The bill is twenty-eight forty, the most I've spent on a meal in months.

I don't want Calliope to know about the production, so I drop the mustard and the vinegar in a trashcan. Then, feeling wasteful, I dig them out of the trash and stand them up on the sidewalk. In case a homeless guy wants to make a nice dressing for his pizza crusts.

Calliope has the island to herself. I watch her from the sidewalk, where I'm waiting for the light to turn. She's sitting in yoga posture. Her eyes are closed, her hair is down, and her hands are resting, palms up, on her knees. Cars zoom by.

What would I think if she were a stranger? I'd want to talk to her but wouldn't dare. There's a chance I'd come to the conclusion that she was full of shit—if only to relieve myself of the desire to talk to her. More likely, I'd detect a positive energy out there on the island. And I'd wonder what that freaky chick was doing in a pants suit.

Reluctant to disturb her, I sit down on the bench. She opens her eyes, and it takes her a moment, it seems, to see me. "Beer?" she says.

Her beer's in a bottle, and I forgot to open it. I spent all my time on the sandwich, neglecting what was most important. But I can fix it. I can make it right.

"I forgot to open it," I say. "I'll run back."

"No need," she says. She rummages in her bag and pulls out a Swiss Army knife. That's the camper in her.

"Thought you were trying to eat healthy," she says, looking askance at my sandwich, which is like a third forearm.

I like the idea of her looking out for my health, but not when I'm eating. "At least I got it without lettuce."

Her first bite is a nibble. She's chugging her beer, though. I should have bought her two. I can always go back.

"That was really something," she says. "I was expecting a show, but God. Like when Arnie got sad? That was some *seriously* bad acting. I got the bad-theater bumps all over my body."

My face goes hot, and I peek at her from behind my sandwich, trying to gauge whether she knows that she's dining with the playwright. "How's your sandwich?"

"It sounded good, though. Unless you really thought about

it. 'We must unite to see that justice is done.'" She giggles.
"Garbagio."

No, she doesn't know; it's not her style to be indirect. Still, I
feel exposed and ashamed, like a fourth-grader caught cheating
on a test. There was a reason I didn't tell her the substance of
the speech that popped out of me whole. It's not that she
would have had qualms. It's that she would have forced me to
see *my* qualms. Made gay and giddy by Schecter's praise, I did-
n't want to think about what I'd done.

Fuck, the death penalty used to be my issue. I remember the
moment in college when it dawned on me that the death
penalty was wrong. Always wrong. Like a good bad mystery
novel, the issue just fell into place, and the clarity felt almost
sexual. Friends and strangers in bars from Paris to Boston to
Los Angeles have been forced to listen to my diatribes. When
I started working for Schecter, I was glad that he came from a
state without the death penalty and that he wasn't an outspo-
ken proponent. You'd think that his change of heart, his *lack*
of heart, on this issue would be enough to push me out the
door. Instead, I help him avoid the matter of a death row pris-
oner's possible innocence.

I have to stop pretending that I'm better than my job, that my
anger and awareness keep me at all pure. At some point you
become your job. And I hate my job.

"Your sandwich okay?" I say.

"Yes, sweetie," she says, her baby-talk tone splitting the difference between affectionate and mocking. "It's yummy."

The two of us are silent as street-crossers pass: a silver-haired
man and a young Asian woman in a short skirt and knee-high
boots. Nice thighs. It turns out that they're a couple, the woman
speeding up to grab the guy's hand.

I find myself trying to think of something to talk about. I'm
not good at taking people's minds off their problems. If I'm
going to make her feel better, I need to take aim at the problem, and push through.

"You don't seem good," I say. "And that's fine. I don't want you to feel like you have to be *on* around me. But I want you to feel like you can tell me about it."

"It's nothing."

"It has to do with your brother, right?"

She looks at me, a sprout on her lip. "How'd you know?"

"'Cause it usually does when you're down."

"Hunh," she says, surprised. Yeah, she has some dealing to do. We're silent again, Calliope practically sucking on her sandwich, probably trying to finish it for my benefit, pathetic soul that I am. I plowed through the bulk of my sandwich without giving it the attention it deserved. I focus on the last bite, which tastes excellent even through it contains no meat, just grease-stained bread and mayo.

"Want to talk about it?" I say.

"Tomorrow is the fifth anniversary of his death."

"Oh."

"My parents don't even acknowledge it. They barely ever talk about it."

"Must be hard."

"I'm not judging them. That's the way they deal."

"Still, it must be hard for you."

"And it'd be hard for them if I talked about it."

"You don't think talking about something is better than not?"

"Of course," she says, annoyed, seeming more like herself. "But I also think people can do what they can do. I'm not going to judge them or . . . be angry at them."

"It's not something you really have control over."

"Where's my candy?"

"I think you *are* angry at them."

"I'm not talking about this until I have candy in my mouth."

Trying not to smile, I hand her the chocolate bar, which she unwraps carefully, making sure not to rip the foil. "Good choice," she says. "But if you really want to impress me, and I *know* you do, one word: Lindt." She snaps off two rows, bites off a square. "I hate the whole parents-screwed-me-up mentality. It's so upper-middle-class, so East Coast. We're the luckiest, most spoiled generation in the history of the world. We can do whatever we want to do. Except we don't. We don't dare. Or we can't figure out what we want to do. God knows we're not fulfilled. It must be Mommy's and Daddy's fault. They didn't love us enough. Or they loved us too much, the assholes. Bad job? Bad love? Bad weekend? Let's do a little fake introspection and blame the folks."

"Even the best parents make their kids angry. It comes with the job. But it's not about blaming them. It's about forgiving—"

"Oh God."

"It's true," I say, determined to risk being trite. "But you can't forgive them till you admit you're angry."

"Have *you* forgiven your parents?" she asks.

"No. I'm still in the being angry stage."

"Why are you angry at them?"

"Well, my father's easy: he left and he died. And I'm angry at Mom for thinking I'm going to be like my father. I understand why she worries. It makes psychological sense, and it comes from love—maybe it *is* love—but that doesn't make it any easier to take."

"And you can't picture a person in your position not being angry?"

"I don't know. I can only speak for me."

"Exactly," she says, meaning, don't speak for me. "Of course it's hard that they don't talk about Ari, but I'm truly not angry. I mean, they lost a son."

"And you lost a brother."

"Yeah, thanks, I'm aware of that."

This is the kind of statement that usually shuts me up. "Maybe you ought to do something for Ari yourself, a little memorial."

"Like what?"

"I don't know. What'd he like?"

"Nothing. That's why he blew his brains out."

A fire engine, siren blaring, goes hauling uptown. Two cabs try to ride its traffic-free wake, but it closes up in a hurry. "He must have liked something."

"Of course he did."

"What?"

"He liked bagels and let's see . . . skateboarding and . . . Central Park and David Bowie. He loved Bowie. I introduced him to him."

"So bring a bagel to the park and listen to Bowie on your Walkman. I think you can skip the skateboarding."

"It's a nice idea. Except I have to work twelve hours for Schecter the Protector."

"So come do it on my couch."

She smiles. "I'll do something. I'll at least think about him. I want to think about *him*, you know? As opposed to his death."

She squeezes my hand and, to my surprise, grabs hold of it. This is the first time we've held hands, and it seems shockingly intimate, almost too intimate, but I hang on, and when I feel her grip loosen I tighten mine.

"You don't seem so hot, either," she says. "I thought tonight would be a nice night for you."

"Debates are always a letdown."

"Yeah. Schecter got mean."

"It was his only honest moment."

"Was that a big deal, performance-wise?"

"Wes didn't think so."

More pedestrians pass by, the biggest group yet. Middle-aged people, walking slowly. A movie crowd.

"So we're going to win?" she says, looking at me.

"Unless something weird happens."

12

Primary day. I wake to the sounds of the street: a car alarm, a siren, the thud of newspapers hitting the pavement. I doubt I'll be able to fall back asleep. Excitement, I guess. I'm excited not only because Schecter might win, but because he might not. The polls have remained closer than we expected, so this could this be my last day of work. On the other hand, a win means I'd have a pretty good position on one of the biggest senate races in the country.

Unless I quit. Now's the time to do it: there's a lull before the General Election gets going. I wouldn't even have to give a reason. They'd probably throw me a fucking going-away party. Leaving on good terms wasn't what I had in mind. In my daydreams, I quit for a specific, noble reason. My controversial stand splits the office, infuriating some of my coworkers, inspiring others. The right people are on the right side.

But that's vanity. If I'm going to quit, I need to do it soon.

I stay in bed, giving myself a chance to slip back under. Last night we all stayed at the office till one-thirty because it seemed like the thing to do on the eve of the election. I've been working late every night, and my schedule shows in my apartment, which has gone to hell. I don't know the details of the disarray. I've stopped seeing it.

I start to beat off, hoping to fall asleep in the post-ejaculation lull. I scan my mental archives, trying Julia, an old girlfriend, then Schecter's daughter, but it's Calliope, as usual, who gets things flowing. Yeah, I'm not sufficiently attracted to her. Right. Time to kill that lie. She makes me hard—the thought of her, the sight of her, the smell of her—and that's what attraction *is*.

With that excuse gone, there aren't many left. Quitting would do away with another, and that one was never strong. Enough with the talking, the thinking. I'll grab her when we're on the roof. I know what to do. I kiss her soft, then hard. I turn her around and lift up her dress and yank down her panties. She gasps when I enter her.

★　★　★

I take my time getting to work, knowing that most of my colleagues will arrive late because they have to vote—which I'm not permitted to do today. A few years ago, fed up with Schecter and other Democrats, I registered as an Independent. The question is, if I had a vote, which candidate would get it?

In the office everyone is wearing a stern expression and moving quickly, as if we had a lot of work to do, as if the more humorless we are, the more votes Schecter will get. Overconfidence is a no-no, but anything less than confidence is also frowned upon. Don't worry and don't relax.

The kitchen is full of donuts, five dozen Krispy Kremes. Still warm! Last month, I gave up hot dogs and donuts, which strike me as the two most blatant offenses against good health. It's not a rigorous diet plan but it's at least a limitation.

And it's over. I catch sight of myself in the glass of the microwave, munching with a custard-rimmed grin, looking fat and perverse. It could be worse: Calliope predicted I'd fall off the wagon by eating a donut looped around a wiener.

People cruise by in the hall, oblivious to both the donuts and this donut-eater. Caitlin Shays, my old boss—one of a group up from DC—passes by three times, head down. It's a big day for Schecterites, the biggest ever.

I'm relieved to get to the research room, where Gerry, Jen, and Jenny are their steady selves, consuming info. "What could you guys possibly be doing?" I ask.

"Getting ready for Senator Washburn," Gerry says, lining up a ruler under numbers in different columns. "He is going to be in a world of pain."

"Did you know his rating with the NRDC isn't that bad?" Jen says.

"Misleading," Gerry says.

"Totally," Jenny says.

There's an e-mail from Tod telling me when and where Schecter's going to vote—information that I combine with four clichés, two half-truths, and a boldfaced lie to produce a short release. Done for the day, maybe forever.

Calliope time. The thought of grabbing her as I imagined this morning makes me trembly—too much sugar—and I'm relieved to discover that she's busy overseeing the get-out-the-votes phone calls. There are volunteers filling up the room and over-flowing into the hall. Calliope tells me to sit down, and what can I do but obey?

I make a point of sitting next to George Blue, who's wearing black bandanas all over his body. Calliope hands me a list of numbers and a script, which Blue seems to be ignoring. He's urging someone to "Get out there, man, and do your democracy."

"Make sure you mark the result of the call," Calliope says to the crowd, her glasses adding to her air of authority. She's become a den mother to the motley crew of regulars, and the discipline and *esprit de corps* she's instilled in them is impressive.

I get answering machines on my first three calls, and I leave messages.

"You guys are doing great," Calliope says, making the rounds.

"*You're* doing great," Eileen says, and everyone claps.

"Calliope!" someone shouts.

Blue lights his Zippo and holds it over his head.

An old guy reaches for Calliope's ass.

She grabs his hand and shakes it. "And hello to you, William," she says. "How about using that hand to dial."

On my fourth call, a woman picks up, and she cuts me off as soon as I identify myself. "I know, I know," she says. "I'm for Schecter, I vote for him every time, but my ankle, it's broken. I can't even make it to the store."

"There's nobody who can take you?"

"Lonnie comes to clean and cook. She said she was getting me a wheelchair, but she says a lot of things. She's a real big talker. I don't trust her for a second."

"Maybe we can help you. I'll call you back."

I'm thinking that someone out in the field can take care of it, but the woman, Rosa Marchetti, lives in Red Hook, Brooklyn— not an area, it turns out, where we're doing door-to-door work. "We have any wheelchairs?" I ask Calliope.

"You joking?" she says, pulling up.

"A woman broke her ankle. I'm going to help her get to the polls."

"Lot of work for one vote," Calliope says.

"But it's guaranteed. She says it breaks her heart she can't vote."

"You're breaking *my* heart," she says with a stifled smile. She picks up my list and hands it to Blue, who gives her a double thumbs-up. "Go," she says. "Get out of here."

I call up Rosa and tell her that the cavalry is on its way.

How to get to her is the question: no subway goes to Red Hook, I doubt I'd get reimbursed for a cab, and I don't want to take a bus, my desire to be free from the office having its limits. Tod's car is the answer. On the way to his office I run into Paul, who looks different: it's his hair, which he's just about shaved off. The change is striking, but I'm reluctant to comment on it. Then I decide I should.

"Good haircut," I say.

"Thanks," he says, rubbing his head in a way that, I confess, reminds me of a monkey. "It's my summertime look."

It occurs to me that I might need help lifting Rosa. "You doing anything?"

He looks left, then right, as if to say, what's there to do?

"Want to go for a ride?"

"Definitely."

Tod's office is crowded, mostly with people from DC. Paul and I bring the total to eight. Caitlin, finally noticing me, gives me a hug. She was a good boss, a kind one, anyway. She's a lesbian, and I was like the son she never had. I took advantage of her matronly inclinations, allowing her to straighten up my desk, bring me lunch, and buy me clothes. The rumors about us having an affair flattered us both.

"I miss you," she says, rubbing my arm. "How's Wilcox treating you?"

"Wilcox is an ass," I say. That's the only way you can tell the truth around here: pretend you're kidding.

"A nice ass," Tod says.

"Schecter the Protector, hunh?" says Lisa Karsch, the legislative director and my old nemesis in DC.

"He hears it everywhere he goes," I say, deadpan, sickened to realize that even the DC people know about the imaginary nickname. And they also know it was what propelled me to semi-stardom. Worse, they might suspect that I came up with the lie precisely to promote myself. I should quit right here, right now: that'd show them how much I care about self-promotion.

Tod stands up and steps in front of the Monica photo to prevent Caitlin from tearing it down. "It's a tribute," he says. "She's our spiritual leader."

"Mr. Communications Director," I say, not wanting to get pulled into this disagreement. "Paul and I need to use your car. We're going to help a woman who broke her leg get to the polls."

"Haven't you gotten in like five car accidents?" Tod says.

"None of them were my fault," I say, getting nary a smile. "Paul will drive."

"Don't you guys have something better to do?" Lisa says.

"No," Paul says, willing to tell it like it is.

Scratching my chest between buttons, I find a clump of hair, crusty with what I realize is dried come. I scrape it off and roll it into a ball. "What could be better than this?" I say. "She's an old, sweet Italian woman. She told me it breaks her heart she can't vote for Schec."

"Maybe we should get the press there," Tod says, not completely kidding.

"How about this," I say. "Arnie goes there, scoops her up, and carries her to the polls. She looks up at him lovingly as the cameras roll."

"Don't give him any ideas," Caitlin says.

"Can't you take a cab?" Tod says.

"Can't you feel the karma," Paul says, sounding un-Christian to me.

Tod reaches into his pocket and tosses his keys to Paul, who reaches up with both hands and catches them in a surprisingly awkward clap.

★ ★ ★

The day is sunny, and like school kids cutting class, Paul and I are giddy as we walk to the parking garage across the street.

"I can't wait to call up Tod and say we got in an accident."

"Definitely," Paul says.

When the BMW goes on, a familiar song blares. Familiar and bad: Billy Ocean's *Caribbean Queen*. To my shock and amusement, it's not the radio, but a CD.

"I guess we know why he didn't want us to use his car," I say.

"I remember this one," Paul says as Billy belts out the chorus. He cracks up, covering his hand with his mouth, a habit he must have developed as a kid embarrassed by his big front teeth. "What do you suppose this says about Tod?" he asks, his voice booming over the music.

"Well," I say, thinking hard, glad to be having a conversation like this. "Most likely, it reminds him of high school, where I'm sure he was the king." Paul nods in pensive agreement. "Or it could just mean he's gay."

"Ha!" Paul barks, then gets serious. "Wouldn't surprise me, to tell you the truth."

The directions Rosa gave me start in Red Hook, and neither of us knows how to get there. We drive around for about ten minutes, thinking we might get lucky and happen upon it. Paul wants to buy a map, but I manage to convince him to ask a traffic cop for directions. The cop, surly at first, warms up once he hears Paul's politeness. I'm pretty sure Paul gets a kick out of talking to him from behind the wheel of a BMW. By the time we pull up in front of Rosa's little red house, we've listened to most of the Billy Ocean catalog, including "Suddenly" and "Get Outta My Dreams, Get Into My Car." For all our making fun of Tod, we left the CD spinning.

The black woman who answers the door has an Island accent: Jamaican, I think.

"Are you the boys from the political office?" she says.

"Let them in, Lonnie!" Rosa squawks from behind her. "I've got to go vote."

She's sitting on a chair in a tiny living room that smells like sauerkraut. Her face has collapsed in behind her nose. With her pale skin, dyed black hair, and heavily made-up eyes, she looks Goth, like Marilyn Manson's grandma.

"Where's your wheelchair?" she says.

"We're going to carry you," I say. "We've got a car out front."

"I don't know about that," she says, patting her belly, a lump under her blanket.

"With my broken ankle I've put on weight."

"And you were thin like a stick before," Lonnie says.

"What'd you say, Lonnie?" Rosa says.

"I said these strong young men can lift you easy."

"Oh all right." Rosa peels off her blanket, revealing a knee-high cast, and puts her hands over her head. "Take me away, boys."

I hold her from behind, her armpits hooked on my forearms while Paul, walking backwards, has her legs. Her scalp looks white under her wisps of hair.

"The cast weighs twenty pounds," she says as we navigate the narrow front hall. "I'm not this heavy."

"You're not heavy at all," I lie, my biceps burning.

"I used to have a body like a movie star, curves everywhere. Now my titties are in my belly. Getting old is the worst. I don't care what anyone says."

"Hey, Lonnie!" she yells as we edge down the steps. "I don't keep any money in the house." Then, to us: "She's Jamaican." Then, to Paul: "No offense."

"Stop!" she yells, and we do. "Careful, now. This is where I tripped. Kids left a ball in the middle of the sidewalk. You should see these kids. They're beasts."

Red Hook is peaceful and industrial: cobblestone streets, warehouses, trash-strewn lots. I can tell by the feel and the smell that the water is nearby. We see a lot of the neighborhood as we search for the community center. I could call the office and get directions, but we're in no hurry.

"Vote early and often," Rosa says from the backseat. "That's what Mike used to say. He was big in the union. A longshoreman. That's how I met Mr. Schecter. I thought he was Italian, but he's Jewish. But he's a good congressman. Now he's going for senator. My daughter, she married a Jew. What are you going to do?"

Paul and I smile at each other, our new friend's bigotry uniting us. We pass a pocket of gentrification: a café, condos for sale, an art gallery.

"This is the block," she says, and Paul makes a sharp turn, the tires screeching.

"Christ on the cross! You trying to kill me back here!"

There's no line in the voting hall, and we get Rosa signed in without having to set her down, all the volunteers enjoying the spectacle. "Now that's dedication," says the woman in charge of the A-through-G list. Another volunteer, a white-bearded guy, walks ahead with a chair as we proceed toward the booth, my lower back aching.

"It's too low," Rosa says when we set her down. It's one of those old crank-turning machines, and she can't see the board. "Hold me up, boys." But we're not allowed to be in the booth with her, so white-beard brings her a paper ballot.

Paul and I wait in the vestibule, luxuriating in the peace of a Rosa-free moment. The community center, dimly lighted and drab, is like municipal buildings everywhere, which I guess is why I like it.

"What are you going to do?" Paul says, doing Rosa.

"We'll take any vote we can get."

"That's right. I would have helped her into a white hood as long as she was going to vote for the right guy."

"We did a good thing," I say, and I mean it. Not because we scored a vote for Schecter, but because we helped a woman, as Blue would put it, do her democracy.

Check me out, feeling good about myself even though I came here just to get out of the office. But hell, the concept of voting still gets to me. You have to be more cynical than I am to deny its power. Its promise.

"All right, boys," Rosa yells. "Come and get me."

Paul suggests we change positions, and I agree on the assumption that Rosa's leg-end is lighter. Not by much, it turns out, plus the cast gives off a scallion-poop odor. All the volunteers wave goodbye, and Rosa waves back, the electoral hero of the precinct.

"That's that," she says as we prop her up in the backseat. "Did my duty. If you don't vote, don't complain. That's what Mike used to say. He always voted, and he always complained. Not a minute goes by I don't miss him. He was my life."

Paul somehow gets us back to the house without Rosa's help. She's gone quiet, lost perhaps in memories of her husband. She stays silent as we lift her out of the car.

Lonnie, it seems, has left. We put Rosa back in her chair, and she points at the blanket folded up on the coffee table. Paul drapes it over her, and she pulls it up to her chin. Her mascara is running, making her look even more vampirical.

"You boys want to stay a while? There's probably something in the fridge Lonnie made. It might not kill you. If I could stand, I'd make you a nice lunch."

"We should get back," I say. "But thank you."

"Thank you, boys. You're very kind, helping an old lady. I'm glad I could vote for Congressman Stein. Or should I say *Senator* Stein?"

I glance at Paul, who looks terrified, then down at Rosa, who smiles. "Just joking with you," she says. "Didn't know I was a jokester, did you? I used to be life of the party. How we laughed, Mike and me."

She holds up both her hands, palms down, her fingers bending back toward her arms. She seems to want us to kiss her hand, and that's what I do. Paul, after a moment's indecision, does the same. "Oh," she says, literally batting her eyes. "Such gentlemen."

I have to stifle a laugh as I walk away. "Lock the door!" she yells. "There are criminals out there. Animals!"

As soon as the car starts to move, we crack up. Five minutes and ten blocks later, we're still chuckling. "Did I really kiss her hand?" Paul says.

"I won't soon forget Mrs. Rosa Marchetti."

"Mrs. *Michael* Marchetti."

"Yeah, he was there the whole time. Sad."

"And sweet," Paul says, making a decisive right turn; at least *he* has an idea how to get back. I suppose he's never had the luxury of being irresponsible.

"To tell you the truth," he says, "the Democratic Party needs people like Rosa. I bet you her children are Republicans."

"Even the one who married a Jew?"

"Maybe. We're losing the Jews too." He rubs his head, slowly circling down to the back of his neck.

"Can I ask you a question?" I say, doing some head-rubbing of my own.

"All right."

"Why are you a Democrat?"

"What do you mean?"

"Well, you seem pretty conservative."

"Conservative? No, not at all."

When I look at him, tucking his lips inward and running the tips of his fingers along his hairline, I can tell there's a statement coming. He's driving fast, Brooklyn hurtling by outside my tinted window, brownstones giving way to office buildings.

"I consider myself a Clinton Democrat," he says. "The way I see it, President Clinton is saving liberalism from liberals. I believe in government, a good strong activist government. But a lot of liberals put too much faith in government. It can only do so much. It can't speak to people's souls. At its best it can help people help themselves. At its worst it undermines their ability to do so. That make sense?"

"Yeah," I say, impressed with his conviction if not the substance of his views, which are straight out of the New Democrat playbook.

"I take it you're more liberal than I am," he says.

"I'd say so, if those labels mean anything anymore. A few years ago I sat in on the Waco hearings. A couple of right-wingers were the only ones who questioned the government."

"Because the government was being run by Democrats," Paul says.

"Maybe, but that doesn't make them wrong. They stood up for the powerless. Our boss certainly didn't. And he was awful to the witnesses, who'd lost people they loved."

"Talking smack on Election Day!" he says in his black voice, probably for my benefit. "You don't have much respect for Schecter, do you?"

I wait to answer, thinking I should come up with a tactful response, but any qualification, it occurs to me, would be a lie. "No."

"So let me ask *you* a question: when he's up there tonight, giving his victory speech, you going to be happy even a little?"

"Yeah," I say, holding out hope that this much is true.

We turn into the parking garage and speed up the ramp. I'm already nostalgic for our visit to Red Hook, for that time Paul and I carried a woman to the polls. That was the day we became friends.

"By the way," I say. "When Schecter's up there giving that speech, I'm going be wearing your shirt again."

"I told you, it's yours. Just don't wear a jacket with it."

"I couldn't even if I wanted to. I lost it at the debate."

Paul smiles slightly and shakes his head.

"I'm an idiot," I say, sounding more serious than I intended.

"You're searching, aren't you?"

"For what?"

"You know, truth, peace, love."

"Isn't everyone?"

"No. Some people have found it, and some people have stopped looking."

"Are you talking about God?"

"No, not necessarily." He pulls into a spot, the spot where the car was originally parked, and kills the engine, its loud power striking in retrospect. "I'm talking about finding someone or something you love with all your heart. For me, it's Jesus. But I think for other people, it could be a person or a passion. I'm talking about commitment. I'm talking about something that anchors you. My pastor told me that only through loving someone more than you love yourself can you come to love yourself. I know it sounds touchy-feely and all, but it's the straight-up truth. I was on the path to destruction, Ben. I was thirteen years old and headed to the morgue. There was a gravestone with my name on it. But I was fortunate enough to have a mother and a pastor who helped me see the light. I *know* you want more out of this life. All I would ask is that you don't just dismiss God out of prejudice or fear or laziness. Be open, man."

"All right," I say, mad at Paul, mad at myself, mad at Jesus.

13

The news is good—good for Schecter, that is. Wes, bopping down the hall with our pollster, stops to tell me that according to exit polls we're doing well in bellwether precincts, a black one in Queens, a Latino one in Buffalo, an Italian one in the Bronx.

"And we're holding our own in Manhattan," says Peter Meltzer, the pollster.

The three of us go into the conference room, where a TV has been set up. The room is full, people finally giving in to the absence of work.

"Turnout's high," Caitlin says with concern: high turnout means more blacks; more blacks means more votes for Stein.

Wes shakes his head. "I swear, you city folk *search* for reasons to worry."

Tod comes in, using his putter as a walking stick. "What's the word?" he says.

"Turnout's high," Caitlin says.

"Hey, Tod," I say. "If it's not too much trouble, do you think you could maybe get out of my dreams and into my car?"

"Yeah, yeah," he says. "All I can tell you is, ladies dig it."

Heads turn: Caitlin, Leanne, Lisa. At least he didn't say "chicks." It's funny, the thought of Tod using Billy Ocean to woo women, or wooing women at all. Funnier still is his belief that anything is justified if it gets you laid. Not that he needs to justify his taste in music. He likes Billy Ocean, so what?

I go to the volunteer room, which is even more packed than before. There aren't enough phones, so Calliope has a few people working on a mailing. When she sees me from across the room, I point to the roof.

"I can't," she mouths, but holds up a finger, telling me to wait. She bends over to talk to Blue, shakes her head, laughs, taps Blue's script, then bounds toward me. "Hey, Benny, Benny. Welcome to the call center. We've made thirty-thousand calls, and we're just getting going." She claps twice, then pumps her fists.

"You look good," I say, because she does, greasy but good.

"Yeah, right."

"You *do*. False flattery's not really my thing, you know."

"Good point. Okay, I admit it." She spreads her arms, the sleeves of her dress falling almost to her waist. "I'm gorgeous." Chuckling, she pretends to punch me in the stomach. "Big guy. Hey, big guy. What's up, big guy?"

"You're cranked up," I say, trying not to sound critical, because I'm not. I like seeing her like this. I'd like it more if I could join her.

"I've got to get back. Tonight, Benjamin, you will buy me many drinks."

"Wait," I say, wanting to tell her that I'm thinking about quitting, but I can't, not now. "We're going to win," I say.

"Shhh. Don't say that."

"Don't tell me you buy into that."

"We can't get cocky, especially here in the call center."

"Right."

"I've got to go." She dance-walks around the main table, her shoulders see-sawing. Blue, feeling her groove, mouth-farts a beat, and others clap along.

"What do I do if the number's busy?" someone says.

"What's he do if the number's busy?" Calliope says, talking to the beat.

"Mark it down and call back later," says a chorus of voices.

"Right *on*," she says. "You're the best team ever. I *love* you."

★ ★ ★

When the polls close, the TV tells us that Schecter is ahead by five points with most of Brooklyn, his stronghold, yet to report.

"It's over," I say, standing with Wes by the door.

The response is more reserved than I expected, although Lisa doesn't disappoint. "Shut up, asshole," she says, making me recall fondly our tussles in DC. Mistaking sloppy for lazy, she badmouthed me to everyone in the office, and I, in turn, crank-called her almost weekly. She was the legislative assistant for economic issues, and I'd pretend to be the lisping, hack-coughing CEO of a Porta-Potty company or the assistant to the Undersecretary of the Treasury, who needed to know, pronto, the most cost-effective method of treating the crusty pimple on Lisa's nose.

Schecter moves ahead by seven, with half the precincts reporting—a "commanding lead" says Sandra Cho, the anchor. Even Caitlin ventures a few claps, and several people rise to make their way to the Marriot in midtown, the site of the "event."

Danny comes in, having spent the afternoon in the field; Schecter, being Schecter, made a half dozen public appearances today. Questions are thrown Danny's way, all inquiring about The Man's state of mind and whereabouts.

"He's fine," Danny says. "He's here."

"He's queer," I say. "Get used to it."

I'm disappointed that people aren't offended; they seem hardly to have heard me. Then I'm worried that Caitlin *is* offended; but no, her face shows concern, not anger. My old mother-boss is worried about me. I smile at her to say, I'm fine, and I am, aren't I? Schecter won, but I was sure he would. I already knew that if I wanted to rid myself of this campaign, I'd have to quit. So nothing's changed.

"What's the latest?" Danny says.

"Schec by seven," Lisa says.

"Nice," Danny says with a reserve that seems unforced. He wants Schecter to lose. Yes, down deep—beneath his sense of duty and his need to please his father—he longs to escape. But even if Schecter wins, he and I could take off. Come on, Danny boy. We'll leave tonight, the two of us and Calliope. You'll build us a cabin in the woods with those carpenter's hands of yours. We'll get healthy. Purify. We'll live off the land until this campaign has become a bittersweet memory.

"What are we watching?" Schecter says, Carol on his arm, his voice waking up the room. "The Yankees game?"

Everyone laughs, including me, although I want to knock him down and steal his wife. He knows nothing about baseball but insists on pretending he does. I've conveyed to him through Tod that if he's going to use baseball to shore up his populist credentials, he should pick the Mets as his fake favorite team, since they're the descendants of the Brooklyn Dodgers, a working class squad if there ever was one. But Schecter keeps invoking the Yankees, baseball's royal family. Even when he's pretending to be down with People, he aligns himself with Power.

Schecter says, "Is it true that a few of you literally carried someone to the polls?"

Paul's not in the room, so it's up to me to answer, but I stay silent, not comfortable kissing ass in front of a crowd, if at all.

"It was Ben and Paul," Caitlin says.

Schecter and Carol look at me, their eyes wanting to know every little thing. "We helped out a woman in Red Hook. She broke her leg. She met you once because her husband was in the longshoreman's union. She's a big fan."

And I'm a big fan too, Arnie, even though I pretend not to be. The truth is, I love you, and I want you to love me back.

"That's wonderful," Carol says.

"Make sure she gets a note," Arnie says.

He hands a short stack of papers to Wes, who taps my shoulder and heads for the door. In the hallway, he hands me the papers.

"Let me know what you think," Wes says. "It's the speech."

"The speech?"

"The victory speech."

"The victory speech he's giving tonight?"

"God willing. Ending needs a little oomph, I think."

I walk to my desk, dazed by this turn of events. Here in my hands is the speech that will set the tone for the General. To help craft it is to commit myself to staying. I might as well be signing on the dotted line. But then the notion that I was going to do otherwise was nonsense, wasn't it? Did I actually believe that I was going to pull Danny aside tonight and quit? That was self-delusion. It seems wise to see it as such.

14

I arrive at the Marriot as late as I gracefully can, tired of the artificial air of uncertainty, which won't blow away entirely until Stein concedes. But the crowd isn't waiting to celebrate. Hundreds of people are waving at the TV cameras, half-dancing to an Alanis Morrisette song, and giving ovations to the Schecterites they recognize: Danny, Tod, Caitlin, Chief of Staff Dov Eder, and Wes, who buys me a shot of Jack at the bar. Tonight, if nothing else, is going to be a party.

"Liked your edits," Wes says. "Took most of 'em."

I'm aching to ask him to elaborate, since a couple of my suggestions weren't minor, but all I say is, "Cool," trying not to be one of those neurotic city folk he likes to skewer. If Wes has taken to me, and I think he has, it's partly because he thinks I'm down-to-earth, which I suppose I am. I'm neurotic *and* down-to-earth.

Walking around in search of Calliope, I go to great, circuitous lengths to avoid Dov Eder, who makes Schecter seems cuddly. Last summer, when I went into his office to discuss the possibility of leaving DC to work on the campaign, he said,

"Let's pretend that I care and that I give you advice and that you take it."

Calliope, Blue tells me, is going to be late: William, the ass-grabber, collapsed, and she took him to the emergency room. "He's going to be all right, bro," Blue says. "Just made a few too many phone calls, that's all."

A murmur goes through the crowd, and it rises into a cheer. For an irrational moment, I think Calliope has arrived. But of course it has to do with the race: Channel Five has called it. Wrapping his arms around my waist, Blue picks me up, and I fall against his leather jacket. I push myself up and put my arms in the air as he spins around and bounces up and down and emits a twangy sound that by the fifteenth twirl or so has taken on the tune of The Grateful Dead's *Shakedown Street*.

When he puts me down, I'm too dizzy to stand, my head pulling me to the right, toward Shawn, who tries to catch me, but I take him down, my chest ending up on his face, and there's cold wetness on my back. "The fuck?" he says.

"Sorry," I say, rolling off, my body hurting more than it should after such a cushy fall. Soreness from carrying Rosa, perhaps.

People around us, having realized that our tumble was buffoonery rather than violence, clap mockingly, and the attention mollifies Shawn, who sees this as a chance at notoriety. "Think we were on TV?" he asks, his head swiveling in search of cameras. "You owe me a rum and coke."

"Coming right up." I spring to my feet, not wanting his company.

Wes is still at the bar, drinking now with Dov Eder, whose fascist face makes me want to turn around. But Wes waves me over, and hands me a shot when I get there. I keep my distance, trying to conceal the wet spot on my back.

"Here's to Mr. Chet Washburn," Wes says.

"Indeed," Dov says, holding up his wine.

Dov has Aryan good looks—thin lips and all—but he's a Jew, an Orthodox Jew, the leader of a faction of Schecterites who are especially hawkish on Israel. Danny, whom I initially mistook as a member, calls them the Natan-Yahoos. The Washington office has a strong Jewish presence, which is why I downplayed my Jewishness when I worked there. (I once annoyed Dov by telling him I was sort of Jewish.) Of course, I managed to find religion when Jewish holidays fell on workdays.

"Washburn's been talking like a moderate," Dov says.

"Ain't gonna work," Wes says. He looks over his shoulder, then leans in. "By the time we get done with him, he's going to look like the lovechild of Jesse Helms and Anita Bryant." He cups his ear, pushes it forward. "You hear that? It's Washburn, hanging out with the boys at his country club. Why, I do believe he just used the n-word."

"Jesus," I say, sounding unfortunately naïve.

Wes, covering for me, puts his hand on my shoulder and says, "This here is the sergeant who fortified our left flank on that prickly death row issue."

"I always knew he had talent," Dov says, implying I lack something else: balls, toughness, the killer instinct.

"But he threw it all away on wine and women," I say after a pause that makes my words sound like nonsense. Dov looks at me so that he can then look away.

The conversation turns to the telecommunications bill working its way through committee. We're siding with the industry—the least we could do after all it's done for us. Although Washburn will vote the same way, it'd be nice, Wes and Dov agree, if the bill didn't reach the floor before November, the unspoken reason being that Schecter will spend the next few months portraying Washburn as a shill for corporations. I know not to suggest that we vote the other way and they know not to explain why we can't. Like a Waspy family, we don't talk about money. The inner, inner circle—the bull's-eye—manages the intricacies of the bribery. For the rest of us, campaign contributions are like gravity, the invisible force dictating what we can and cannot do.

From the ballroom comes another cheer, this one louder than the one before.

"That'll do it, boys," Wes says, tossing bills onto the bar, dealing them like cards. "Stein's throwing in the towel."

The three of us walk into the ballroom, pulling eyes toward us, drawing applause.

"Are you someone?" a woman asks me.

"Yes," I say, and wink almost seriously, which I've never done before.

A shush goes through the room as Stein appears on the TV monitors. "We put up a good fight, didn't we?" he says. His partisans cheer wildly while we, in this room, give him a round of applause that is obligatory and patronizing.

I see Calliope across the room, and I go to her, slowly, having to weave among people who are frozen while Stein speaks. Calliope sees me coming and wiggles two fingers in a wave. The last bit of my path is blocked by a cluster of Latino transit workers—a very specific special interest group—and I pick my way through them. Calliope grabs my hand and helps me with the last couple of steps.

"How's William?" I ask.

"Fine."

"And you?"

"Okay, I think. Good, maybe? *Crazy* day." She shrugs. "We won."

"We sure did. Congratulations." I give her a hug, burying my face in her hair, which smells not dirty but not clean, like a wool sweater.

She pulls away. "Your back's wet."

"You should see the other guy."

"It's water?"

"Rum and coke."

"That's strange." She pauses for effect. "You don't like rum."

I laugh not at the joke but at her smiley pleasure in telling it. She gets a big kick out of herself. And that's it, I guess, the simple reason she glows. She likes herself.

"It's weird to me, the whole idea of winning," she says. "I can't remember the last time I thought in those terms."

"Not since your days playing college hockey?"

"I don't even play cards. This is the first thing I've won in like fifteen years."

"How's it feel?"

"I don't know. Better than losing, I bet. I feel bad for Stein."

Her eyes go to the TV, where Stein is talking through tears. When did it become cool to cry in public? "Thank you all so much for your support," he says. "I want now to lend my support to the next senator from New York, Arnie Schecter."

I'm interested to hear how Stein's crowd reacts—the clap-to-boo ratio—but it's impossible to tell over the cheers of our crowd, which returns to party mode, the music coming back: "Celebration" by Kool and the Gang. A trio of dancing lesbians has gotten in between me and Calliope, who's turned to talk to Shawn. I know from his body language that he's telling the story of our tumble, trying to make it part of campaign lore.

I smile at one of the three dancers, a pleasant-faced aunt-type with a skunk-streak in her hair. We're smiling at each other and bobbing our heads. I instruct myself to let my body go, and soon. I'm dancing, or doing an impression of a person dancing, and the parody deepens when I see Calliope and Shawn watching me. I bump hips with skunk hair. I grind against one of her friends. I keep my smile so that everyone knows I get the joke. I'd love to shake off the weight of irony, but you've got to be brave or drunk to dance earnestly to a song like this. I can't get brave but I *can* get drunk, so after cheek-kissing my dancing friends, I go to the bar, where Tod takes a break from chatting up a black woman with shellacked hair to buy me a shot. Back in the ballroom, "Celebration" has given way to a song that my mind at first misidentifies as Clinton's theme song: it's a less-bad Fleetwood Mac song, the lay-me-down-in-tall-grass one. Calliope and Shawn are dancing, Shawn crossing and uncrossing his arms with faux hip-hop fervor, Calliope spinning around like a girl in the rain, her hair and dress catching wind. By the time I get to them, the song is over, and Burt Sellers, the campaign chairman, is calling the staff up to the stage, stirring up applause that's still going strong when we get there. I make sure to stand next to Calliope, who says, "Now *this* is kind of nice," and it is.

"Smile for the cameras," I say.

"Great," she says, running her hand through her hair, which she's danced into a tangle. "I look like Jane of the Jungle."

"You look good," I say, comforted by her rare display of vanity.

Schecter comes out with Carol, their eighteen-year-old daughter Lara, their twenty-nine-year-old son Teddy, and Teddy's wife Mia. One of the women, probably Lara, inspires a moan from Tod.

We clap for Schecter, and he claps for us. Then he works his way across the stage, shaking hands and kissing cheeks. As he approaches me, I'm preparing to give his hand a firm shake and say, "You earned it," but he puts his hands on my shoulders and his mouth by my ear. "You've got talent to burn," he says.

"Thank you," I say to his cheek, and squeeze Calliope's hand.

He eases into the speech, which would ring familiar even if I hadn't read it fourteen times: it's standard stuff, and the changes I suggested are no exception. But it seems to be doing its job. The faces of my dancing friends are beaming. An Asian woman in front has tears in her eyes. I think of Rosa, watching the scene from her chair. These people aren't dupes. They know what Schecter is and what he is not.

"Make no mistake, ladies and gentlemen," Schecter says. "The choice that faces the people of this great state is dramatic."

He's right. There's a reason the room is filled with all different kinds of people, people who've traditionally been shut out. There's a reason Schecter can honestly say, "Tonight is a bad night for the enemies of justice." There's a reason women like Calliope and Caitlin are standing up here, clapping.

I put my arm around Calliope, Tod puts his arm around me,

and then all of us, across the stage, put our arms around each other.

"Women need to have control of their bodies," Schecter says, and Calliope kisses my cheek. Yes, it's a relief to know I'm staying.

Giving myself over to the words, I'm fired up when Schecter challenges Washburn to "Bring it on," and I'm moved when he says, "Tonight marks the beginning of something more than a campaign. It is a movement. A movement that will dignify everyone who takes part in it. Not only are the goals of this movement compassionate and just, the movement will be compassionate and just in pursuing its goals."

But then it's no surprise that I'm moved. The words are mine.

15

There are things Tod is good for, and picking a bar is one of them. We're all standing around the ballroom, trying to make a decision, when Tod, having wrapped up his final interview, instructs us to go to a place a few blocks away. The bar turns out to be fine for our purposes: not too fancy, not too seedy, and empty enough to accommodate our group of fifteen, which includes Danny's wife Jo and Ethan. We sit at three pushed-together tables, Wes at one end and Paul at the other. Paul's presence is a surprise, and I can't say I'm happy about it. His God-talk has left me feeling uneasy.

"I guess you ain't the worst group of party people I've worked with," Wes says, receiving a cigar from Tod, who's already circled the bar twice in search of women.

I hate my seat. I'm between Shawn and Tod's empty chair, and across from Danny and Jo, who are talking quietly. He has his eyes closed and she's rubbing his neck. As I steal their pitcher of beer, which I'll drink along with my Maker's Mark, I decide not to feel sympathy for Danny ever again, not when he has someone to rub his neck. On the other hand, if the rumors are true, Jo wanted Danny to take this job because she didn't like being a carpenter's wife. The rubbing comes with a price.

Calliope and Ethan have been chatting nonstop since we left the hotel. It's the first time they've met. I'm glad they're getting along, but enough already with the giggling.

Paul is taking in the scene and sipping an orange soda. He looks serene. He doesn't need attention, doesn't need to fill himself up with other people.

"Hey, Wes," I say, trying to get a group conversation going. "I heard you got a guy elected who beat the crap out of someone *during* a campaign?"

"I heard that, too," Wes says. "But according to the story I heard, the man was never charged, and the morning after the fight he held a press conference to explain that he was defending the honor of a young lady. His poll numbers shot through the roof."

"Made him seem like a real guy," Danny says.

"Yup," Wes says. "Personality is the best politics." He smiles around his cigar. "One time a candidate I was working for let out a belch like a foghorn during a debate. There was dead silence. Then my man, God bless his heartburn, smiled and said, 'My mama's ribs, I can't get enough of 'em.' Crowd went wild."

"So who wins the personality contest, Schecter or Washburn?" Danny says.

"Well, nobody wants to have a beer with *either* one of them," Wes says. "Good God Almighty, this race just might come down to the issues." He takes a swig of beer from the pitcher, the cigar still in his mouth. "But I doubt it."

Tod, returning from one of his reconnaissance missions, taps me on the shoulder. "I need a wingman," he says. "Two hotties shooting tequila."

"Let me guess: the hotter one is yours."

"Come take a look. If you don't like what you see, you can come back here for naptime with Danny and Mrs. Boring."

The women are what I expected: synthetic lovelies, made to be looked at, especially from this far away. They're smoking long dark cigarettes, their dinner.

"You get the blonde," Tod says.

The blonde is thinner of the two, a slice of a person. There's no way I could walk up to her with a straight face. In my less self-conscious years, picking up women came pretty easily to me. Now I find the whole process tiring and embarrassing and a little icky, from the first smile to the naked morning.

"I don't know," I say, undecided only because I need sex. I walk around in a circle, pretending to deliberate while I sneak a look at Calliope. The contrast between her and Blond Slice gives me my decision. "No thanks," I say.

"What's wrong with you? When was the last time you got laid?"

Susceptible to attacks on my manhood, I have to summon my strength. "I just want to hang out," I say.

"You just want to get on Calliope; that nice big body." He does a pantomime of someone, presumably me, wrestling a woman, presumably Calliope, to the ground. He sucks on his middle finger, pulling it from his mouth with a pop, and wiggles it in some imaginary orifice. "Can you *imagine* her bush?"

I decide not to say that I've spent hours imagining her bush, or that his suggestion that it's huge might not be correct, head hair in my experience being a poor predictor of pubes. Instead, I try to look disgusted, as though I were defending Calliope's dignity, which I *should* be doing.

I start to back away, but he grabs my shirt with both hands. "One-on-two almost never works," he says. "I need you, man." He shakes me. *"Please."* This is the most emotion I've ever felt from Tod, and it makes me sad for him. Sad because he seems sad. I knew his life was shallow, of course, but he seemed to revel in the shallowness.

Maybe realizing what he's revealed, he lets go of my shirt, and I hustle back to the table, where Calliope and Ethan are standing up, going home to giggle and fuck.

"Where you off to, Callyopie?" Wes says, his name-mangling unintentional.

"Actually, Wesleyopie," she says, bending over to talk quietly. "We're going outside to smoke drugs."

"If it's crack, I'm coming," Wes says.

"Sorry," she says.

"I'm coming anyway," Wes says, and the four of us go outside.

We huddle in front of a closed stationery store a few doors down from the bar. Ethan hands the pipe to Wes, who holds it out for Calliope. "Ladies first," he says.

She shakes her head. "Old people first."

"Heh heh. I forgot chivalry don't fly up north." He takes a long hit, his pink face turning pinker as he holds it in. He exhales with a wide-open mouth, smoke coming out in a billow. "What are the chances Guiliani's boys bust us?" he says.

"How would we spin it?" I ask.

"Damned if I know," Wes says. He makes a strange sound, something like he-u-ee, and knocks on the side on his head. "I like the wacky weed. And I like you, Callyopie. And I like you, Ben Bergin. And I like you, whoever you are."

Ethan introduces himself. They shake hands; then Wes puts his hand on top of Ethan's head. He pushes down on his hair and watches it bounce back into place.

"Nice, huh?" Ethan says.

"Sure is," Wes says, now using both hands to push. "They don't make it like this where I'm from."

They've coupled off, so I turn toward Calliope. "Ethan's great," she says.

"I knew you'd like him."

"He's great."

She hands me the pipe, and I hesitate before bringing it to my lips. Pot for me is the great intensifier, and I'm afraid of what it might intensify. Wes chuckles as Ethan tells him about one of the subjects of his film, the nun who shotputted a Cantaloupe.

I take a hit, deciding it's a chance worth taking. "Much to discuss," I say.

"So discuss," she says.

All that I wanted to tell her about seems suddenly distant. There are more important things to talk about, though what they are I don't know.

I take another hit, then another. The one time Calliope and I smoked pot together, late one night on the roof, I felt far away from her. She also looked like a gorilla. Not now, though. Now she looks great, positively bitable.

Wes has dropped to his knees in the middle of the sidewalk. He spits on each hand, rubs them together. "I'll have you know that you just challenged a former officer in the United States Marine Corps." He falls forward, onto his hands, and starts doing pushups.

"Boys," Calliope says with affection.

"That's not a full one," Ethan says.

"I'll give you a full one," Wes says, resting at the top of number ten.

Ethan looks at me as if to say, this is hilarious. Having a good time, as he often does. "I want to meet your Mom," Calliope says, drawing a connection between Ethan and my family, making my jealously absurd. Ethan, for her, is part of me. She wants to know me.

Calliope gasps and beats her chest. "Let's have a cigarette," she screams in a whisper, as if it's a brilliant idea, which it is. My first drag tastes like excitement, and it makes me want everything.

"Thirty," Wes says with a grunt. Two women walk around Wes, ignoring him with New York nonchalance.

"I'm sorry I've been so reluctant to get together outside the office," I say.

"I have been, too," Calliope says.

"But I want to. I want to hang out more. I want to stop being careful."

She looks me in the eyes, giving me access, and my stomach

goes achy-tingly. It's almost too much, the reality of her. Or the *un*reality of her. Who is this woman?

"What do you mean?" she says.

"I don't know, I just . . . " I pause, afraid of not saying the right thing. "I'm staying on the campaign."

She looks at me with an open mouth that closes into a tight smile. "I'm glad," she says in a voice not hers.

"Why doesn't it seem like you are?"

"Oh come on, Ben. *Of course* I'm glad. I can't imagine working there without you."

"You seem kind of blah about it, and you're someone who almost never seems blah."

"Blahhh!" she yells.

"That's not funny."

Her body goes rag doll, chin on chest. She looks up at me from under her forehead. "Aren't we supposed to be celebrating?"

"Fifty," Wes says, and collapses. He rolls onto his back and lies, spread-eagle, on the pavement, his stomach rising with each gasping breath.

"I owe you a drink," Ethan says, lying down next to him.

Calliope grabs my arm, and we take a few steps back toward the bar—away from Wes. "I'd be reluctant to show a strong reaction either way. It's like you need me to tell you what to do. You have to make the choice for you."

"And I did. I'm staying."

"Okay."

"You see? You don't trust me."

She puts her hands over her eyes, squeezing her nose between her pinkies. This is a romantic relationship, a romantic, codependent, neurotic relationship without orgasms. The worst of both worlds.

"Tell me what you think," I say. "You're holding back."

"All right. It doesn't seem like you've given it much thought. Or maybe you've given it *too* much thought. Now is the time to quit. You can't in two weeks. You can't even in a week."

"Who says I can't? I can quit whenever I want."

"No, you can't, Ben. It wouldn't be fair."

"Oh, please."

"It's true. I'd be pissed if you baled in the middle of the campaign. You have a responsibility to the campaign, a commitment."

"Please don't give me your speech about the importance of community."

"Fuck you."

Both of us cross our arms and turn away, parodies of pissed-off people. Ethan is walking on his hands, not well at all, and trying to get Wes to watch. Wes, still spread-eagle, is smoking, his cigar sticking straight up, like a little chimney.

"Sorry," I say, my mood mellowed by the sight of my two inebriated friends. "That was mean. I actually like that speech quite a bit."

She moves in close, her warmth on my face. "I want you to do what you want to do, and I'm not convinced you want to stay. I'm worried you're doing it because it's easier. It's easier for a lot of reasons."

"What's that supposed to mean?"

"You know what it means."

"Yeah, I do, and I think it's my turn to say fuck you."

I look at her face, which I usually take in as a whole, a satisfying sum of its parts. But now I'm seeing it as I did the first time I saw her, zeroing in on her features, each one oversized, grotesque, especially those lips, those wide wiggling worms that are saying something I can't hear. I could slap her.

"Right?" she says. "Right?"

"Yeah. Sure."

"You wanted to know what I thought."

"I didn't promise to like it."

"Back from the dead," Wes says, ambling toward us. He puts his arm around Calliope and pulls her away. "You see, Ms. Callie, Bob Marley didn't like how the white mon turned herb into a lazy drug. You're supposed to move, enjoy your body."

"Is that what you were doing?" she says.

Ethan pulls the cigarettes from my chest pocket. "What's the matter?"

"Oh, you know," I say, watching Wes hold the door open for Calliope. He steps in front of her to make a point about chivalry, about hypocrisy, and the two of them laugh as they hip-check their way into the bar.

"You'll figure it out," Ethan says.

"When?"

"After you have sex with her."

"You think I need to have sex with her to figure it out?"

"No, but I think you should have sex with her. She's great."

"You think she's good-looking?" I ask, child that I am.

"Definitely," he says after a pause. "She's cool-looking. You should go for it. Just do it, you know? Try not to think about the next day. Try not to think, period."

Good advice, though at the moment not thinking seems about as feasible as jumping to the top of one of these buildings.

"Wes is awesome," Ethan says. "I need to buy him a drink. You coming?"

"In a minute."

When Ethan goes in, I walk to the front of the bar and look in the picture window. Calliope is sitting next to Shawn, giving him her smile for free. She sees Ethan sit down, sees I'm not with him, yet doesn't come looking for me.

I bark. It was meant to be a yell, but it came out a bark. No one inside heard me, so I bark, and bark again. Paul looks up, and I sprint away, to the stationery store, where I pace in a circle around Wes's sweat stain on the sidewalk. The yelling and the sprint took an edge off my anger, which, I now see, is shallow, a cover for other emotions. I light a cigarette, my brain digging into itself.

Calliope's right, but not as right as she thinks she is. Wanting to explain this to her, I jog back into the bar, but by the time I'm sitting down next to Shawn, my line of thinking has unraveled, and I'm still angry at Calliope, who's telling a story I've never heard about her stint working at a nudist yoga institute, everyone listening and laughing, even Paul. Without pausing, she reaches around Shawn and pokes my arm, the smallness of the gesture making me want to tip the table over.

"Ah, man," Shawn says when the story's over. "That is *off* the hook."

"Doesn't that bother you?" I say to Paul. "Shawn's black act."

"Hey," Shawn says.

"It bothers me," I say.

"Ben," Calliope says.

"It's fucking excruciating," I say. "I can't stand it."

"To tell you the truth," Paul says, "most whites talk a little black, the same way most blacks talk a little white. That's a good thing, cultures influencing each other. Eventually there's going be no such thing as white or black."

A nice little theory to justify his own whiteness. But maybe he's right: why shouldn't Shawn act black? Because it's an *act*, that's why, and I'm about to make this point when I see Calliope glaring at me. With her eyes she points to Shawn, who's looking down, all droopy-dog. She wants me to apologize, and the maddening thing is that I'm going to, not because I know I should, though I know I should, but because I don't want Calliope to think I'm not nice. You'd think she'd be clear about that by now, one way or the other.

I put my hand on Shawn's shoulder. "Sorry, that was mean," I say for the second time tonight. "You should be able to say whatever you want however you want to say it." I'm tempted to look at Calliope to see if my apology sufficed, but I manage not to.

"You still owe me a rum and coke," Shawn says.

I stand up, feeling hot and guilty, my behavior seeming worse than it could possibly be, like an abuse of power, a moral failing, a stain on my life.

Tod's at the bar, chatting up the blonde who was going to be mine. Her friend has left. Another mistake: not joining Tod. Sex seems like one of the few activities that could mellow me out. Violent sex, with knives and punches.

When the bartender sets down my drink, I realize that I'm biting my hand. Back at the table Paul's putting on his jacket. Talking to him seems crucial, more crucial than trying to make things right with Shawn, so I walk out with him, the night air on my face warmer than before.

He needs the 1-9 train, and I offer to walk him there. If he thinks it's odd, my going with him, he doesn't let on.

At a busy intersection we stop to let the last row of cars go by. Behind us on the sidewalk, teenagers, just out of school for the summer, are hanging out like kids anywhere, the boys hamming it up for the girls, scoring laughs.

"Can you believe we were in Red Hook today?" Paul says.

"Our conversation fucked me up a little bit."

"I could tell."

We're walking again, the subway station in sight. "It felt a little bit like a conversion attempt, like you were giving me the soft sell."

"Nah, man. It wasn't like that." We pull up in front of the subway entrance, one of those rare ones in a building. "I have an idea on how to live life, and I wanted to share it with you. I was just asking you to consider it, that's all."

"I have. Enough to know it's not for me. In many ways it's the *opposite* of how I want to live my life."

"And are you fulfilled?"

"God, no."

"What you went outside to do isn't going to do the trick."

"You'd be surprised."

He smiles. "What are you're going do?" he says, imitating Rosa.

We shake hands, and he pulls me in for a one-armed hug. It's rare for me to relax enough to enjoy a hug from a man, but this one calms me, makes me feel my fatigue.

On my way back, I linger by the teens, longing to be included. I want to joke around with the boys and gets laughs from the girls. One of the girls is a Latino beauty, her butterscotch smoothness visible in the light of the Papaya King. The boys are wearing football jerseys that seem too hot. Their movements are aggressive and jerky, like spasms, as though their hormones were exploding.

"Yo mister," one of the boys says. "Buy me a dog?"

"Sure," I say.

"What about me?" says another.

"Who wants one?" I wave the boys toward Papaya King, praying the girls come too. "Hot dogs for everyone."

16

Everyone looks ugly. It's my mood. It's the light.

I came into the conference room late, thinking I'd stand by the door, but staffers from the main upstate office arrived after I did, and I was stuffed into a corner. "If you know what I'm sh-zayin," Shawn says, Snoop Dog style. He's a bunch of bodies away from me, but the blackheads on his forehead are alarmingly visible in the newly installed florescent lights. Several of the old bulbs were flickering all August, inspiring dozens of how-many-Schecterites-does-it-take jokes. (Ten was my answer: one to screw and nine to spin.) In anticipation of this morning's meeting, someone finally had new bulbs put in, and they cast a merciless white-blue glow. Like TV stars making big-screen debuts, we've been transformed for the worse, our facial blemishes now as prominent as our noses. I have a fingernail-shaped scar on my cheek that people are probably noticing for the first time. Not that anyone's looking at me; all eyes are on The Man, who's rocking quickly. There's nothing on his face I haven't seen before, but the vein snaking from the outer edge of his eye socket up to his hairline seems to be bulging perilously.

I'd like to examine Calliope's face, but my view gives me only the back of her head. Her hair is split down the middle, pulled into braids I can't see.

"Hope you all had a nice Labor Day," Danny says, the razor burn on his neck almost a welcome distraction from the wounds under his eyes. "It's your last day off."

With a groan I mourn my yesterday, which I pissed away watching golf and trying to write my political manifesto. I didn't get past the title: "On Populism." The blank page was a mental mirror, and I found myself regretting all my big decisions in recent years: getting a job on the Hill, moving to New York, not leaving the campaign after the Primary. In an unsuccessful attempt to feel sad rather than depressed, I drank beer on the roof as the sun went down.

"Ladies and gentlemen," Danny says. "The next senator from the State of New York, Arnie Schecter."

With one final rock of his chair Schecter rises to his feet. We all clap, except for Shawn, who finger-whistles. Schecter nods and smiles and raises his hand as if we were a normal audience. Today's the beginning of the "real" campaign. Until now only activists and political junkies have been paying attention.

During a normal August we might have been able to generate a few headlines, but this was the August of Monica; the hullabaloo over Clinton's videotaped deposition drowned out all other political noise. Surreal seems too mild a word for this summer of semen stains and penile cigars. Everyone here thinks the attempt to impeach Clinton is a travesty, but beyond that central consensus, which has unified the campaign, opinions vary. Some are furious at Clinton, others are sympathetic. I'm neither; that's because I didn't think much of him before the scandal.

Clinton, I admit, is a tough case. Some of my favorite people in the world like him, and I've had to work not to, as if he were a beautiful woman I didn't trust. He's smart, possibly brilliant, and there's something appealing about his pussy-lovin' humanness, which seems like a rebuke to the politicians and parents and preachers who keep lying to us about sex. But the dude's a big part of the big problem. Thanks to Clinton, the Democratic Party is now almost as plutocratic as the GOP. More to the point, he's long fed the beast now trying to devour him. He himself is a scold, always quick to lecture the poor and the young on "responsibility." And he's expanded government at the expense of freedom. And he trashes people who get in his way. If you choose to play the game, don't cry foul when you lose.

Schecter looks up at the lights, theatrically shielding his eyes with both hands. "This isn't good. I don't like sharing the spotlight."

I check to see who laughs the loudest: Mara Cohn from upstate. Her obsequious cackle makes me long to see Calliope's face, and I'm hurt when she doesn't turn around.

"I know that all of you have been working hard to get our message out," Schecter says. "I want to thank you and to tell you that nobody's been listening."

Cohn again: cackle with snort.

"But seriously, folks. Everything matters more now, our successes as well as our failures. But view this, please, not as a chance to slip up—I know none of you will—but as a chance to shine. This is a time for heroes."

A sucker for such talk, I find myself clapping, and as the meeting breaks up, I fight my way out the door, wanting to be the first one back into the fray. But my adrenaline evaporates when I remember that there's no chance for heroism on the seventh floor. Of course there isn't. There *is* coffee, however, and I go into the kitchen to get some.

Calliope walks in, her face full of conspiracy. "Terrible," she says, the word bringing out her New York accent. She's talking about the too-bright light, not the pep talk. Her braids are like thick rope, the kind of rope used to pull pianos up to windows. She opens the cabinet that holds her herbal tea. "It was like waking up next to everyone," she says.

She's inviting me to catalog all the moles, bumps, and wrinkles. I decide not to. I've been trying to curb our junior high tendencies. "Can you imagine?" I say.

"What?"

"Waking up next to everyone."

She gives me a blank stare. My jokes have been missing the mark. But was that even a joke? She drapes the string of her tea bag over the side of her mug, which a kid at her camp gave her. "Best Counselor in the World," it says, next to a magic-marker drawing of Calliope that makes her look like a retarded lion. I know enough not to make fun of it, but I wouldn't object if someone else did.

"We can be heroes," she says, doing Schecter, quoting Bowie. She bends over to get hot water out of the water cooler, and I look at her ass, which is lost beneath her maternity-like dress. Last week she wore a pair of jeans for the first time since I'd been noticing. Calliope Faye Berkowitz, I was pained to discover, has a nice ass, a nice big ass that bulges out, beautifully —its own thing. Her ass is the new locus of my fantasies.

She blows on her tea, its minty smell blending with the coffee in my mouth. "I'm having dinner at my parents' tonight," she says. "Care to come?"

"Sure," I say, wanting to be a hero.

"Really?"

We need movement, she and I. New people, new situations. The retarded lion is looking at me, awaiting my response. "Yeah," I say. "I'd like to meet them."

"Good," she says with something less than excitement. "I should warn you, they're a little—they don't really listen."

From the doorway of the kitchen Tod summons me with a tilt of his head, and I follow him into Danny's office.

"What?" Danny says wearily, disappointed to be distracted from his brunch of cold meatball pizza. He tugs a slice from the box, the cheese droppings clinging to the cardboard like tentacles. Paul walks in, sensing action.

"Guess who's back," Tod says. "Hakim Mohammed. The other guy, Roger LaBrie, has gone public. He confessed to a reporter."

"That's not an official confession," Paul says, resting his hands on his head. He's gone back to his big cool-weather do.

"No," Tod says. "And apparently he got facts wrong, the street where it happened, the time of day."

"I can't remember the street I lived on in DC," I say.

"He says Zito shot first," Tod says.

"Of course he does," Paul says.

"Then he says he shot him, tossed the gun, and took off," Tod says.

I say, "Why would he confess if he didn't do it?"

"Rep-*u*-tation," Paul says. "Now that's some bad-ass shit, offin' a cop. Meanwhile, I take care of a brother. That Islam dog set me up with smokes rest of my stint. And hell, I is already in the can."

"But not on death row," I say, pointing at Paul. As we grow more comfortable with each other, we're arguing more aggressively—which, in turn, makes us less comfortable with each other. My relationship with Paul, like my relationship with Calliope, is in standstill. And there's the same amount of humping in each.

"That's why he hasn't made it official," Paul says. "LaBrie's angling for a plea."

"Hakim might really be innocent," I say. "Can we at least *consider* that possibility?"

"There's still all those witnesses," Paul says.

"Crackheads," I say. "Conservatives don't like crackheads unless they're testifying against other crackheads."

"Who you calling conservative?" Paul says.

"Excuse me, counselors," Tod says, "but we're running a campaign here."

Paul says, "We're not going to kick off the homestretch talking about a cop-killer." He says this casually, more statement than plea. In recent weeks he's traded in his loud sanctimony for a quiet confidence. The change is sharp enough for me to suspect that Wes had a sit-down with him. Also, Paul can afford to relax as we move rightward: the politics of the campaign and his own politics are converging.

"It's going to be an issue," I say, "whether we like it or not."

"Doesn't need a push from us," Paul says.

"I agree," Tod says.

"So we say nothing?" I say.

"Or something that says nothing," Tod says.

"Fun, fun," I say.

"What do you suggest we do?" Paul asks with a little smirk. "Call for a new trial?"

"No," I say. "We don't have to go that far. But we should, I don't know, talk about the importance of making sure he's guilty."

"That's an issue for the courts," Paul says.

"And they're not going to let an innocent guy die," Danny says.

"Why not?" I say. "And the appeals could take years. We're going to let an innocent guy rot in prison till then?"

"Who's 'we?'" Paul says. "And who's innocent?"

"No shit," Tod says. "Bergin, you're starting to sound like Mona."

"You're starting to look like her, too," Danny says.

I lift up my shirt and grab my gut with both hands, squeezing my belly button into an ass-like puppet. "I got into this business to make the world a better place," I say in Mona's voice, moving my ass-belly-puppet accordingly, "and I still believe we can help those who most need to be helped."

No one laughs. Serious discomfort in the room. "So we're saying nothing?" I say casually, as if Mona had never made an appearance. "Or something that says nothing?"

"Nothing," Tod says.

That should be the end of the discussion, but for some reason Danny doesn't make it official. He calls up Wes, who's in the office today, and a moment later the big guy walks in, smiling but serious. He's wearing suit pants and a tight T-shirt that says "Clemson" in orange. It seems we caught him in the middle of changing.

Tod says, "Hakim—"

"I heard," Wes says. "I don't think we say a word till we see what Washburn does."

"That's what *I* think," Paul says.

"Who thinks different?" Wes says, and when all eyes go to me, he adds, "Ben Bergin, you goddamn hemorrhaging heart, let's hear it."

"Well, aside from the fact that I don't think we should support the execution of innocent black men—"

Blank faces. My humor bone is broken.

"This isn't going to go away," I say. "Mohammed's going to become an issue. A cause. Black leaders are going to beat us up."

"Let them," Paul says.

"It's a lot better than Washburn holding a press conference with Zito's widow," Tod says. "It'd kill us with the cops."

"And the you-know-whos," Wes says, meaning white working-class and lower middle-class voters, known as white ethnics or Reagan Democrats. Their economic self-interest pulls them left; their cultural sensibilities—and their fear—pull them right.

"And what about blacks?" I say.

"They've got no place else to go," Tod says.

"No, no, no," Wes says. He points a scolding finger at Tod, delighting the rest of us. "I don't want to hear that kind of talk. You know how many elections have been blown 'cause campaigns didn't get their people to the polls? That said, we don't need this issue to get the job done. We've got something a whole lot better."

Wes looks over his shoulder, into the hallway. Then he shuts the door and leans against it, his hands tucked behind his tailbone, his stubby legs slanting down. "I, uh, got wind of a story that's going to break tomorrow, if not sooner."

"Yeah, right," I say. "You created the wind."

"Hush, child," Wes says. The *Clemson* on his shirt is warped by the curve of his belly. "It seems that Washburn's daughter, Mindy, was dating an African-American gentleman at college, and Mommy and Daddy were none too pleased."

"And you know this how?" Danny says.

"The *reporters* know this because they talked to people who knew Mindy at the University of Pennsylvania."

"Delicious," Tod says.

"Like a dog-shit brownie," I say.

"It's legit," Danny says.

Paul nods. "Definitely."

"I have trouble believing it'll be cut and dried," I say. "My guess is, Washburn will be able to plausibly deny it."

"Plausible schmausible," Wes says, opening the door. "Once you have to start denying you're a racist, you're fried."

He walks out, and I follow, wanting to talk to him about Hakim Mohammed, who seems to be emerging as *my* cause.

"End of discussion," Wes says without turning around.

I jog to get in front of him, stopping him by the front desk. Bernice, focusing on her crossword, doesn't look up. "You marched with Martin Luther King, right?" I say. This gets Bernice's attention.

"Not really," Wes says. "But I did meet the man, in sixty-one. I was helping to register blacks in Georgia. I thank the Lord I was on the right side of the big issue."

"My point is, doesn't the idea of an innocent—"

"Of course it does." He looks at Bernice, who's gone back to her crossword. "But the courts will take care of it. Or they won't. His fate is not in our hands."

"Oh, come on. That's not why we're not taking a position."

"No."

"There's got to be a way of talking to everybody at the same time, all the ordinary people we're always waxing about: the waitress in Westchester, the Italian grocer in Buffalo, the black cop in Crown Heights. If you're honest and straight with people, they'll get it, they'll understand. We should be able to bring them all together."

He puts his hand on my shoulder, and I brace for condescension, for a you-remind-me-of-myself-at-your-age speech. "That's a beautiful goal. Hell, that's the *revolution*. But whenever we try, the Republicans break out the wedges: race, gays, the flag, whatever."

"And then we break out our wedges."

"Yessir."

"Are you telling me we couldn't sit down with the guy in Buffalo and explain to him that a poor man might have gotten screwed."

"Not if we only had thirty seconds, and not if Washburn's boys were in there too, yelling, showing him pictures of Hakim's black face and Zito's bloody body."

"But we don't even try. We play their game."

"It's the only game in town." He moves his hand from my shoulder to my cheek. "And guess what, Ben Hameen,"—he slaps me softly—"we're going to win."

I wander back to my desk, deflated. But I'm pleased that I don't have to write anything. I recently realized that I don't work very hard. It came as shock, since I like to complain about how hard I work.

But the truth is, I wouldn't mind having more work; it would give me less time to consider how much I dislike the work that I do do. Doo-doo.

I open up a file on my computer, wondering if I should write down a few jokes for this evening. Making it through dinner with a broken humor bone could be painful. I certainly won't be trying the belly-button bit on Calliope's parents.

★
Schecter Stays Mum on Mohammed

Roger LaBrie, an inmate in Sing Sing, today told a reporter that he committed the murder for which Hakim Mohammed was sentenced to death. Congressman Arnie Schecter has decided to say nothing for fear of opening himself up to charges that he is soft on crime. "It'll kill us with the cops," said Tod Wilcox, chief propagandist and all-around moral cretin.

The only dissenting voice came from Ben Bergin, deputy director of communications, who was vague and meek in arguing for a different course of action. "What do you suggest we do?" Paul Teague asked with a jerk smirk. "Come out for a new trial?"

"No," Bergin should have replied. "We call for an investigation into LaBrie's claim. We stress the urgency of removing the cloud of doubt and the importance of making sure they've got the right man. We talk in simple, moral terms. If we did this, we'd attract more voters than we'd turn off."

He thinks. He hopes.

17

Jeremiah Berkowitz and Lila Miller own two lofts, one on top of the other. "That's my dad's studio," Calliope says as we pass by on the elevator, which a moment later opens into their home. We're greeted by an enormous sculpture, a tangle of black metal that looks like an evil Christmas tree. Four paintings—all black and gold splatterings—just about cover the walls.

Beyond this gallery space is the living room, where Calliope's mother is standing with her back to us in front of a wall of windows. She turns and smiles, a phone on her ear. "Got to go, Sue," she says.

"Hey, Mom, this is Ben."

"Nice to meet you," I say, extending my hand.

She wraps her tiny hand around my fingers and gives them a squeeze. She's about half Calliope's size. Their only physical similarity is the color of their hair, but Lila's is short and thin. She's wearing shorts and funky green sneakers.

"Ben Bergin," she says, not quite looking at me. "Nice to

finally have a face to go with the name. How was work? Can I get you a drink, either of you?"

"I'll do it," Calliope says, heading for the kitchen, which is set off by a counter. If you pushed aside the furniture and put up some rims, you could get a decent basketball game going in here. It'd be a perfect rectangle but for the rooms built in two corners. The shiny wood floors, as beautiful as they are, could use a cushy rug or two. There's a woven mat under the coffee table, but that's it.

Both of us watch Calliope walk away. "Great place," I say.

"We got it at a time when you could actually get them, you know? Today we couldn't afford one of these places, much less two." She puts her hand on my forearm. "You're from Maine! Jeremiah and I used to go to Monhegan Island."

"It's beautiful there," I say, never having been.

"It used to be a refuge for artists. Now it's probably just another tourist hell. But what isn't? There must be a new coastal frontier. New Brunswick, I suppose. We should all quit the city and move to New Brunswick."

"Sounds good," I say in a Maine accent that's not quite a joke.

She smiles—perhaps at what I said, perhaps not. She has a relaxed manner, not unlike Calliope's, but Lila seems to lack her daughter's capacity for engagement. From the moment I met Calliope she was processing every word I said, making every moment matter, matter too much perhaps. With Lila I feel barely noticed.

"Who wants red wine?" Calliope says from the kitchen.

"Sounds good," I say for absolutely the last time tonight.

"Oh," Lila says, looking at Calliope. "Not that bottle."

Lila goes into the kitchen, leaving me to wonder if the bottle Calliope selected was too good or too bad for Ben Bergin.

In the corner facing the window is a writer's table that must belong to Lila. She stopped writing a year before Ari died. She spent her time that year trying to talk to Ari and worrying and schlepping him from shrink to shrink. Meanwhile, Jeremiah plunged ever deeper into his work. That's their pattern, Calliope told me: Lila deals with life while Jeremiah retreats from it. When Calliope talks about her parents, it's usually to express sympathy for Mom, whom she sees as a victim of Dad's self-absorption. "Don't let the bohemian exterior fool you," she said. "It's a traditional marriage."

From the kitchen come girlish giggles, which I'm glad to hear after their subdued, touchless greeting.

There's a small sculpture hanging on the wall, a spirally aluminum piece that I pretend to study while I use it as a mirror. Luckily I wore a decent outfit today: short-sleeved navy button-down and gray pants that deny their dirtiness. Still, I look like a mess. Threads drip from my sleeves. Slovenliness as a substitute for style. It *could* be a style, I suppose, if I wore it with confidence. Or if I were, say, a painter. Artists must become artists so that they can get away with acting like teenagers. If you're a writer or a rocker, drug abuse looks like freedom and fistfights look like passion. Greasy hair and wrinkled clothes are your crown and robe.

It seems that Calliope's parents removed reminders of Ari from their home and in so doing removed signs of themselves. Even the artwork seems impersonal. The only photo in the place sits on the low bookshelf that stretches from the gallery to the living room. It's of Lou Reed, sitting next to a man who must be Jeremiah, his gray hair pulled back into a ponytail. He has his hand on Lou's shoulder.

I confess: I'm envious. Yes, I'm afflicted with that great American sickness, a hunger for fame. Not that I want to put my hand on Lou Reed's shoulder. On the contrary, I want to be famous so that I can refuse to put my hand on Lou Reed's shoulder. I'd be the rare celebrity who doesn't sell out or suck up. Gore Vidal, for Chrissakes, is doing vodka ads. Where are the incorruptible famous people, the ones who turn down awards and tell presidents to fuck off and never, ever sell anything? The world needs celebrities like that. As if I care about the world: I want to reject the trappings of fame for the same reason I want to be famous, so that people will love and admire me, so that strangers will say, "Not only is he brilliant, he has integrity."

I circle back to the living room and sit in a low chair that I guess is sixties kitsch, vinyl on wood. The women are still in the kitchen, having a discussion I can't hear. Lila might not weigh a hundred pounds. It's amazing to think that Calliope came out of her body.

The elevator slides open, and from behind the evil Christmas tree emerges the largest human being I've seen in a while. Jeremiah's hair, now white, is balled up in buns like Mickey Mouse ears, and his scruff starts just below his eye sockets, creating the impression that he's peeking out from behind something. His arms ooze from a white New York Knicks jersey. The rest of his outfit consists of cutoff cords, gray socks pulled up to his knees, and sandals. He looks like a joke Moses.

I stand up, but he doesn't see me.

"You remembered," Lila says, referring to the bag he's cradling, which must be the source of the garlicky smell he brought in with him.

He drops the bag on the dining room table and holds up his arms, spread-eagle. His armpit hair curls around his shoulder, joining forces with the wisps crawling up his back.

"Hey, Daddy," Calliope says, beaming.

Daddy? She goes to him, and he swallows her up. He kisses her head about a dozen times. I'm relieved when she squirms free.

"Turn around, Dad," she commands, her little-girl demeanor having been squeezed out of her. "This is Ben."

He turns one way, then the other, almost doing a three-sixty. I shake his hand, which is both hard and soft, hard with softness behind it, like a crusty loaf of bread. "I'm Jeremiah," he says, his voice gentle. "Welcome to New York."

"He's been here almost a year, Dad," Calliope says.

"That's nothing." He scratches his belly. "It took me at least five to find my footing when I moved here."

"You found your footing?" Lila says, putting plates on the table. "We better eat before it gets cold."

"We got take-out," Calliope says to me, an apology.

"I didn't know we were going to have company," Lila says.

"Your daughter's not company?" Calliope says.

"You like the Knicks?" I say.

"Oh, Jesus," Calliope says.

Jeremiah says, "Cal thinks sports are—what's the word I'm looking for?"

"No, I don't," Calliope says.

"What's that word?" Jeremiah says.

"Ben watches tons of sports on TV," Calliope says.

I smile to mask my annoyance at Calliope: she should find a more flattering way to bring me into the conversation, if conversation is the right word. We're sitting down now, passing around tin-foil containers of Middle Eastern grub: felafel, hummus, etc.

"Antediluvial," Jeremiah says.

"That's not a word," Lila says. "Diluvial is a word, but not with the ante. Antediluvian is what you mean. In any case, it's not *le mot juste*."

"I think it's *juiced* about the most *juiced* word I ever heard," Jeremiah says in a Southern accent. He leans toward Calliope. "Juiced!" he says, poking her in the side. She giggles. "Did you notice, Cal?" He points his fork at the food. "All vegetarian."

"Great," Calliope says. "You've got it down after ten years."

"So I was in the place," Jeremiah says, "and a woman comes up to me and grabs my hand: 'How are you, Jeremiah? It's so good to see you.' She was attractive. Nice green eyes." He pulls open a piece a pita and looks inside. "I had no idea who she was."

"*Come* on," Calliope says with mock astonishment.

"I didn't know what to do, so I just played along," Jeremiah says. "Then she mentioned someone named Abner."

"It was Bette Slocum," Calliope says.

"Who's that?" I ask, understanding that I have to pipe up to participate: no questions are going to come my way.

Calliope's lips pulsate, a nervous twitch. But a sexy one. "Abner was a friend of mine in high school," she says, looking at her father.

"A boyfriend," Lila says. "He was an absolute sweetheart." Either she's tactless or Calliope has portrayed our relationship as platonic. Which it is.

"And this was his mother, Beth," Jeremiah says.

"Bette," Calliope says.

"She told me Abner's an artist in Berlin," Jeremiah says. He takes a bite of his overstuffed pita, and it falls apart. "Or Vienna. She showed me a picture of his work. It was an installation with what she told me were real people, a black man and woman, naked, with words written on them in white paint."

"Is it good?" Calliope asks.

"I'm sure," Lila says. "Abner was always bursting with passion."

"You can't tell from a photo," Jeremiah says, wiping his hands on his placemat. His buns of hair are secured with blue rubber bands. "But—"

"But that's not going to stop you from saying it sucks," Calliope says.

"Words written on black people?" Jeremiah says with derision. I'm starting to like the man. "That's not art. That's an op-ed."

"Critics used to call your work pedantic," Lila says.

"They still do," Jeremiah says. "That's what they say about challenging work they don't understand. Meanwhile, they'll fawn over easily digestible work. Ambitious movies are considered pretentious, while slight little films are lauded for, quote, 'working,' as if art were an appliance."

He takes a violent bite of his newly stuffed pita; his voice has remained soft, but his bitterness is clear, and his wife and daughter, who've been sniping at him since he came in, have gone quiet with what might be sympathy. "If you want to be celebrated," he says, tahini sauce frothing in the corners of his mouth, "set a low bar."

"You've been celebrated plenty, Dad," Calliope says.

"Come on, Jer-Bear," Lila says. "You're acting like the embittered artists you used to mock."

"Well, if the Jew fits," Jeremiah says with a smile. He seems to enjoy his angst, which I guess makes it something else. "Anyway, Beth told me that Abner's going to be in New York next week, and I ended up inviting them over for dinner."

"What the fuck!" Calliope says. "I haven't seen Abner in seven years."

"Chill down, Cal," Jeremiah says, continuing to chew. "You don't have to be here."

"Of course I do," Calliope says.

There's a silence, the dinner's first. It's not my place to break it, but I'm aching to hear my voice: I've said next to nothing. My performance is only mildly embarrassing because both Lila and Jeremiah seem to exist in a fog. I doubt I'd be breaking through even if I were coming across as smart and substantial. Still, the thought of Abner sitting in my seat, bursting with passion, makes me nauseous.

"I'm sorry," Lila says, mostly to me. "The grape leaves are too soggy."

Calliope looks at me, her eyes asking for a smile of sympathy, which I give her. Then I realize that she deserves it: what her father did was wrong.

Jeremiah pinches Calliope's upper arm and says, "Guess what, m'gal Cal. We've got ice cream. Want some?"

Calliope—or some inflated child who looks just like Calliope—nods with her lips puckered in a pout.

Lila stands up to clear the dishes, and I stand up to help. In the kitchen she hands me five containers of ice cream, which I take to the table. Following the example of Calliope and Jeremiah, I serve myself a scoop of each kind. Lila puts some mint chocolate chip shavings in her bowl.

"So you're an ice cream family," I say.

"We've tried to instill Cal with an appreciation for the finer things," Jeremiah says. "Mozart, Shakespeare . . . coffee Haagen-Dazs."

This could be the start of a conversation, but no one builds on it. Calliope and her father eat ice cream the same way, leaving lumps on their spoons.

"I heard a story on NPR about this Hakim Mohammed," Lila says. "It's so awful."

"Who?" Calliope says.

"He's on death row for killing a cop," Lila says. "But someone else confessed."

"Then why is he still on death row?" Calliope says.

"Because he's black," Lila says.

"No," I say, bothered by Lila's claptrap. "The other guy hasn't formally confessed. And he's also black, by the way."

Lila is looking at me, seemingly for the first time. "You don't actually believe he should be executed, do you?"

Her tone makes me want to say yes. Lila Miller, I fear, is a too-familiar type. *The New Yorker* and the *New York Times* tell her what to think. She was politically active in the sixties; now all she does is send a check to the Southern Poverty Law Center. She claims to believe that people in her income bracket should pay high taxes but hires an accountant who makes sure she doesn't. To Lila Miller, religious people are weak-minded and right-wingers are racists (unless they're in the Israeli government). The Lila Millers of the world have ruined liberalism. They've allowed it to atrophy. It's grown fat on their elitism and self-righteousness.

Or maybe she just doesn't think innocent people should be executed.

"No," I say. "I don't think *anyone* should be executed. But I don't think it's as black and white as you were making it out to be." Liking my pun, I suck on a spoonful of butter pecan, the first bite of food I've enjoyed tonight.

"Well," Lila says, stretching out the word, as though it were being pulled from her mouth. "It seems pretty black and white to me, and I assume your boss agrees."

"Yeah," Calliope says. "What *is* his position?"

"He's trying not to have one," I say.

"Because he's afraid of looking soft," Calliope says.

"Right," I say, both pleased and sad that Calliope is starting to get it.

"Oh Good God," Lila says, as though it were a crime to worry about the politics of the issue. Sometimes people you agree with are the most aggravating of all.

"So we're not saying anything?" Calliope says.

"No," I say. "Maybe we should write words on him in white paint."

★ ★ ★

"That was nice," I say as we emerge onto Prince Street.

"Really? You had an okay time?"

"Yeah. Yeah. I liked your parents."

"They're crazy."

We're walking east on Prince toward the Second Avenue stop of the F train, which will take Calliope to her apartment in Brooklyn. I'm going to meet Ethan for drinks on the Lower East Side, where he's watching his friend's one-man show. It's humid tonight, the air something to push through.

"I wasn't sure how you were doing," she says. "You were so quiet."

"Your parents aren't easy to talk to."

"Yes, they are."

"You yourself said they don't listen."

"They don't listen, but they let you talk."

I smile, and she gives me a sharp look; apparently her irony-gauge falters in the face of her parents. We've pulled up in front of a guy selling handbags, the smell of leather sticking to the air. "What?" she says.

"Nothing." A response I always hate giving, because it's always a lie. We start moving again.

"I don't really appreciate you criticizing my parents."

"I don't really appreciate you criticizing me."

"I wasn't criticizing you. I wouldn't have cared if you sat there and drooled. I was worried you were having a bad time."

Normally this would piss me off—Calliope barely ever takes responsibility for hurting my feelings—but I'm relieved that she seems like herself. At dinner I feared that I was getting a glimpse of her true self: Daddy's little girl, a sad spoiled Manhattanite Jewess with Oedipal issues. But that's just part of her, one half of one of the contradictions that make her interesting. Right?

"So I'm not allowed to say anything less than kind about your parents?"

"Not until you've said twelve kind things."

"I said they were cool."

"No, you didn't."

"I don't think anything should be sacred. Nothing *is* sacred."

"We all have sensitive spots, you more than most."

I stop myself from reacting so as not to prove her point.

"We can talk about my family," she says, "but not right now."

In Little Italy, the sidewalks are narrow, the buildings bunched together. Above us people lean out of windows. Calliope walks in front of me as we pass an outdoor café, where tourists are pinching cups of espresso, their camera cases and wide eyes giving them away. Without stopping, Calliope somehow wraps her braids into a mound. Her upper back, the strip of skin above her dress, is pinkish and moist.

Houston Street, which runs like a river through lower Manhattan, brings relief, and I take a deep breath. But the air between Calliope and me stays thick.

Maybe we missed our chance. Maybe we needed to act during those giddy first weeks when we were excited just to be in each other's presence, when we were unaware of the challenges. It's better to race into a relationship blind. That way, you experience the bliss that then allows you to bear the imperfection, the impossibility. We've waited too long, thought too much, and now we see the hurdles too clearly.

On the other hand, maybe there's a reason nothing's happened. A good reason, I mean. "It shouldn't be this difficult," said my friend Barb on the phone from DC when I told her about Calliope. It seems even more difficult now, after tonight's dinner. What I witnessed up in the loft was connected to our relationship in a way I can't quite name. It's as if I saw the gnarled roots of our difficulties.

When we stop next to the subway stairs, Calliope says, "You like my father more than my mother."

I manage not to say, You do, too, and suddenly I feel better about the evening.

An old guy rolls by on skis. "Let's go out some night," I say. "Let's run around and drink too much and eat greasy food with our hands."

"Don't you do that all the time?" she says.

"Not with you."

Her lips are right there. I say goodnight and give her a hug and not until she's underground do I remember about her lost love Abner, who in my mind is short and cute, a brooding little bundle of earnestness whose greasy hair hangs in his eyes. Calliope will probably have sex with him: she needs it, unless she's been keeping secrets, and who better to do it with than an ex who lives in Europe? Talk about safe sex.

I'm walking east on Houston, slowly. I don't want to get to the performance space before the show ends. I'm not in the mood: if the show's bad it'd make me anxious; if it's good it'd make me envious. In a deli stunk up by the low-tide body odor of the man behind the counter, I buy a can of Bud, which I bag-drink as I walk. I unbutton my shirt and light a cigarette. It's funny to think that I used to fantasize about having a life like this. It was my most attainable dream, the only one that didn't involve glory or a beautiful woman: I wanted to carve out a somewhat scummy, drinking-and-smoking, just-getting-by existence in a big city. The slumming fantasies of a middle-class boy. Well, here it is. It's better from afar. It's not bad, though. I'm pissed-off and horny, but that's part of it. I feel real. I'm walking down the street in New York City.

18

A headache wakes me up at seven, but I feel as though I've been awake for hours, the alcohol in my system having denied my brain access to sleep's deepest chamber, its plush interior. The hangover surprises me: I showed restraint with Ethan, going so far as to reject his suggestion that we have one more. But I had wine with dinner and not enough water for the weather and half a pack of cigarettes, so I guess it makes sense.

Some hangovers offer a certain kind of clarity, a heightened consciousness that allows for sharp, if fleeting, thoughts. This is the other kind, the boring kind. I don't have the patience to wait until midafternoon, which is when my brainsmog usually drifts away, so I walk naked into the kitchen and pour a four-drink drink of gin, the only alcohol I can find. I use a finger to stir in my one ice cube, and I drink leaning out the window, my morning dick hanging heavy.

I'm crossing a line I've never crossed, boozing before work. I like it so far. The gin tastes good, like pine.

Last night comes back in a flash of anger. Ethan, I guess. His friend who'd just performed joined us. He was a friendly guy, full of himself but interested in others, and theatrical; he used the word "exhilarating" three times. Sensing little depth beneath his exuberance, I suspected that his show wasn't good. In fact it was awful, according to Ethan. "But he's doing it," Ethan said after his friend had left. Between Ethan and me, there's no higher compliment, "doing it" being shorthand for chasing a dream, having balls. When we got around to discussing our own dreams, Ethan urged me to start my own political website. I liked the idea but not his tone, which suggested that mine was the only life that needed fixing. Granted, he's on the right track, being creative, but the guy never finishes anything. There are different ways of not doing it.

The temperature has plummeted since last night, and down on the sidewalk people are wearing their suit jackets rather than carrying them in the crooks of their arms. But most aren't dressed up. T-shirts and jeans and sneakers: dot-com people, headed to the start-ups clustered around Union Square. An SUV limousine floats by. I keep forgetting that this is a Golden Age.

Drinking in the morning makes you acutely aware of alcohol's essential nature. It is, you remember, a drug. The apartment, which I've scarcely even seen in months, has become vivid. My life in full color: the profound revealed in the mundane. The three empty bottles of baby oil by my bed, my bed that hasn't been in the form of a couch since July 4, the last time I had a guest. Envelopes on my coffee table—bills, I realize now—trying to warn me with red stripes. A bag of bread on my kitchen floor, the plastic chewed through by what could only be a mouse. The strangely unwrinkled tan linen shirt that I put on, a gift from my friend Barb, who, I must finally acknowledge, has romantic feelings for me—feelings that I've cruelly cultivated and that makes her advice about Calliope suspect.

I've never been in love.

Unless I am right now.

My absurdity is so clear to me that I feel healthy. This is the good kind of hangover, after all. No, I'm drunk.

The world outside my apartment has a poignancy all its own. In front of the deli a Mexican man clips flowers. (Mexicans, I've read, dominate the cheap flower business.) A blind man taps his way across Fifteenth, narrowly missing a massive pile of shit—too massive to be the product of dog or human. Probably a police horse, a cop exempting himself from the pooper-scooper ordinance. But there's a chance the poop is elephantine: when the circus comes to town, elephants are marched through the streets in the middle of the night. Could elephants have passed by my building while I slept?

In Union Square people are setting up the Wednesday farmer's market, a smaller version of the weekend one. The woman at a fruit stand is a muscular lovely in a baseball cap and muddy hiking boots. I ask her if it's too soon to buy a peach. She picks one out and gives it to me for free. As my teeth break through the velvet, there's an explosion of sweet juice, which drips off my chin and onto my shirt, the shirt I got from Barb, whom I need to call, or not call. The peach is perfect, and it dawns on me, for the millionth time, that I need to exert control over what goes into my mouth.

This morning I feel sad solidarity with my fellow New Yorkers, *all* of them: the drunks in the square, the overtanned, outer-borough chick walking up from the subway, phone clinging to her face like a leech, the surly Jewish man behind glass who adds twenty dollars to my Metrocard. Yes, friends, we're all going to die.

I get a seat on the subway, across from a man in a light tweed jacket, holding a battered suitcase on his lap. A professor-type, probably an actual professor, going to Brooklyn College, where he'll try to hold the attention of video-game addicts.

My father was a teacher: I forget that. I think of him as a writer and an activist. "A *true* radical," my mother said to distinguish him from all the fake radicals making the rounds back then. (It's perhaps the only not unkind thing I've heard her say about him. It gave me a clue as to why she fell for him.) I think of him marching and organizing and firing off angry letters to the editor. In one of my few clear memories of him, he's standing in the kitchen with his shirt off, loudly rehearsing what must have been a speech. I seldom imagine him actually teaching, telling a roomful of students about the nineteen-thirties, which was his specialty. I don't know if he liked teaching, or if he was good at it. I know very little about him. It's not that I'm not curious; I am, never more so than right now. But I'm reluctant to delve into the mystery of Jim Palazzo. I don't need therapy to know there's pain there. I can feel its prickly edges. My relationship with my father, or lack thereof, is like my apartment, a mess I don't have the strength to sort through.

A guy in a Yankees cap flips his tabloid around, giving me a look at the front page, and it makes me stand up. I take a step closer to make sure it says what I think it says.

It does.

It says, LOOK WHO'S **NOT** COMING TO DINNER. And underneath: "Washburn Didn't Dig Daughter's Date."

In the office there's an air of celebration, as though we'd won a victory. I need to replace my fading gin buzz with a caffeine buzz, so I go into the kitchen, where Shawn and the rest of the field department are whooping it up. "Why'd Washburn brush his back teeth?" Lana says. "'Cause he likes his little ones white."

"Yo, Bee," Shawn says when he sees me. "You pumped?"

"Yeah, it's a great day for New York," I say. "Our senator's a bigot."

"Why'd Washburn have a sugar cookie?" Shawn says. "'Cause he doesn't like Oreos."

I conjure a smile. Since laying into him in that bar three months ago, I've decided to be nice. It's required a discipline that I should be employing in other areas of my life. As I drink coffee to make room in my cup for more, I scan my brain to see if I have a better joke. I have several, in fact, but none that doesn't play on the notion that Mindy Washburn enjoys a big dick, so I stay pointedly silent, pretending to be above the joking.

"Jesus, Ben Bergin," Lana says. "Did you sleep in the street?"

"There's a pile of elephant shit outside my building," I say. In the silence that ensues, I walk out, and Shawn follows.

"You going to write a release on this?" he asks.

Not wanting to bring him to my desk, I stop by the photocopier. "Of course."

"Word," he says with a nod. "I've got this dope hypothesis I want to peruse with you." He waits to speak, expecting me to compliment him on his use of *peruse*. This is his new thing, trying out fancy words he doesn't understand. Meanwhile, he's retained his black inflection, so that he sounds like Cornel West if West lost the first digit of his IQ. "I read where Alabama just got rid of its anti-miscegnation—"

"Miscegenation."

"Word."

"*Big* word."

He looks at me, blinking dumbly. "I say we inject that into this, know what I'm saying? That way we can, like, bring out the *public* implications, ramifications, and manifestations of his *private* behavior."

"I think people will make that leap without our help. But thanks." I start down the hall, and when I feel him walking with me, I turn and hold up my hand, as if he were a dog about to follow me outside. "Thanks, Shawn. It's a great idea."

My roommates are huddled around a copy of the *News*, Jenny holding it up while Gerry and Jen read over her shoulders.

"We should have come up with this," Gerry says.

"It's not your job to look into his daughter's love life," I say.

"Yuck," Jenny says in response to something in the article. "What a fucking Neanderthal." The display of emotion from Jenny is unusual, and it makes me feel better about the story, more confident that it's getting at something real. Racism, they say, is like pornography, you know it when you see it, and Jenny, a Korean-American, probably sees it more clearly than me.

And she looks cute today. Could be time for an open-faced sandwich.

As always, a stack of newspapers is sitting on my desk, a benefit of working in the communications department. A quick look at all five—the *Times*, the three tabs, and the *Journal*—tells me that Wes gave the *News* an exclusive. The story is only semi-solid. Five sources, three of them named, say Washburn and his wife Linda, especially Linda, objected to Mindy's going out with Devin Pierce, a member of Penn's football team. None of the sources, however, heard the Washburns express their misgivings directly. One of Mindy's friends claims her mother said, "I don't have any problem with blacks. I just don't want one in my family." When Mindy told her father that her beau had cheated on her, he allegedly said, "What'd you expect? They can't help themselves." Adding to the intrigue, Devin Pierce died last year surfing in South Africa.

The Washburn camp's initial round of damage control is woeful. First the story says all the Washburns declined to comment, pleading privacy—which won't work. Then it quotes a spokeswoman who apparently tried to make light of it: "The senator didn't want his daughter to be involved with Mr. Pierce because he was a liberal Democrat."

"Hello, white people," Tod says, his voice as loud and cheerful as a radio jingle.

"I'm yellow," Jenny says.

"You're Korean," he says. "Which means you're whiter than I am, and that ain't easy. What a beautiful, beautiful day." He sits on the couch and crosses his legs, settling in for a change. "You think the senator had the boyfriend rubbed out in South Africa? He must have had connections in the old regime."

"Should I put that in the release?"

"No release. The story speaks for itself. Washburn's holding a presser this afternoon. Maybe we'll do one after that, maybe not. Could be that I like the high road."

"Certainly different."

"So the morning is yours to work on the gay speech. Then this afternoon I need you to meet with Gale Hawkins."

"*The* Gale Hawkins."

"He wants to talk about Hakim Mohammed."

Hakim Mohammed: I'd almost forgotten about him. If there are stories in the papers about the latest development, I didn't see them. The thought of talking to Reverend Hawkins makes me both nervous and sleepy. Usually those feelings preclude each other, but now it's as if my heart is racing while my pulse slows.

"Shouldn't someone higher up meet with him?" I say.

"No. The Hawk is pretty washed up." He smoothes his tie against his shirt. "And Paul will be there."

"Can't Paul do it alone?"

"No, I don't want the Hawk thinking we just gave him the black guy, you know? He's washed up but he can still make noise."

Tod stands up at the same time that Calliope arrives. Her presence surprises me; it's as though after last night I thought I wouldn't get to see her for a while.

"Please, Wilcox," she says. "Don't get up."

He smiles at her, not as confidently as he'd like. Calliope rattles him with her toughness, with her lack of sexual interest in him. She told me that she finds him repulsive, and I believe her; some women have the capacity to look beyond the superficial. Men are different: if Tod were a woman, he'd be a bimbo I'd want to fuck.

"I was just leaving," he says, heading for the door. "I have to go refuse to comment on whether Chet Washburn is an evil bastard."

"Roof?" Calliope asks, and I grab my coat.

The breeze snuffs out the first three matches I light, mocking my cupped hand, so I give the matches to Calliope, who gets her cigarette going on her first try. "You're the worst in the world at that," she says, holding out her cigarette, which I use to light mine.

"Yeah. Among adults, anyway. Among non-retarded adults."

"Among adults with hands."

Our old ease with each other seems to have returned. Or perhaps it's a new ease. We were nervous about my meeting her parents, more so than we'd realized, and now we're relieved to see that it didn't throw us. We're still here, same as ever. Better than ever. Something changed because nothing did.

"So what do you make of this Washburn stuff?" she asks.

"As a story, it seems pretty thin, a lot of third-hand stuff. Mindy might have done some inferring, and her friends might have done some inferring on top of that. It's hard to believe they were so blatant about it, or that Mindy would tell her friends. I mean, they're a public family. She's been a senator's daughter since she was a little kid."

"Maybe she wanted to get back at them."

"Maybe. Anyway, let's assume that the story is true, or mostly true, then yeah, Washburn should pay the price."

"But?"

"When something like this happens, we act like there's a line separating all of us enlightened, completely not-racist people from people like the Washburns." Ahhh. Making that point was like giving myself a satisfying scratch. This cigarette is scrumptious.

"I know what you mean. I always got the sense that my Mom wasn't exactly jumping with joy when I was dating Drew."

It's unusual for Calliope to make a casual allusion to her mother, especially an unflattering one. "And I'm not sure Arnie and Carol would be too psyched if little Lara brought home a black man."

"Unless Schecter was looking for black votes."

"Right," I say, hearing me in her voice.

"But not being psyched is one thing. Telling your daughter she can't date a black guy is another."

"Yeah, Carol Schecter would *never* say that to Lara. She'd say, 'Jamal is wonderful, but your father and I would like you to marry someone of your own faith.'"

"That's still better."

"I guess."

"And Washburn's comment is beyond the beyond."

"Yeah, they're racist pigs."

She giggles as she exhales, the smoke coming out in little bursts. "You think?"

"I don't know, but that's why this story's so strong. The Washburns look the part."

"It's tragic, maybe. Maybe Mindy Washburn was in love with Devin Pierce, but she broke up with him 'cause her parents wanted her to, and then he died."

"Are you going to have dinner with Abner?"

She smiles, and looks at me: some serious eye contact. "I don't think so."

"So sex is out of the question?" Maybe I should be embarrassed, but I'm not: I've earned the right to be jealous, and Calliope seems to agree.

"I would say so, yes. *Definitely* out of the question. We didn't even have sex way back when. We tried a few times, but Abner . . ."

"Couldn't get it up?" He said hopefully.

"No, not that, he just . . . let's just say it all moved a bit too quickly for him."

A tremble vibrates through my undersexed body. "It happens," I say with phony compassion. "Especially in high school."

It occurs to me that Abner might want redemption. Perhaps his failure has haunted him all these years, fueling his bullshit art—are the black people in his work symbols of sexual potency?—and now he wants to exorcise his demons by finally consummating the act. My penis is hard and itchy.

"So then, who was your first?" I ask.

"You really want to know?"

"*Now* I do."

"This guy Mason."

She taps her cigarette over the Chunky Soup can, which Calliope washed out for this purpose. She's decided that it's wrong to ash onto the ground. Pretty soon she's going to forbid us from exhaling.

"And?" I say.

"What?"

"How? Why? Where?"

"His penis in my vagina."

"Jesus . . . Seriously."

"You want to know the whole story?"

"Every detail."

"My father used to have assistants. Starving-artist types. Mason was one of them. I convinced myself that he seduced me, but looking back, it might have been the other way around. It was the summer before I went to college. Mason was from Oklahoma, which seemed kind of exotic. And he was twenty-four, which I liked; after Abner I wanted someone who knew what he was doing. He was staying in my father's studio, sleeping on this ratty mattress. I went down there one night to see if he was thirsty."

"I bet you did."

"Quiet. That's where it happened, among all my dad's half-built sculptures. It's like a weird, fairy-tale forest down there. Anyway, the first time was fine, nothing special. I liked how much he liked it. It was a while before I really got to enjoy it. All summer I crept down there late at night. My parents never knew. It was pretty great, actually. At the time I thought *all* sex was that good. I didn't understand how . . . adept Mason was."

"Hunh," I say, as if she'd just told me her opinion on eggplant, as if I didn't want to cry. I miss Abner, that cute little guy.

Calliope's past hurts me, crushes me beneath its massive,

unchangeable weight. My rational mind knows I'm not com-
peting with Mason or Abner or Drew or Daddy. But my emotional mind—which tends to steer the ship, especially when
Calliope's on board—needs to be smarter, cooler, more *adept*
than anyone who came before.

"Why do your lovers all have names like Abner and Mason?"
I say. "What's wrong with Bill or Bob?"

"Actually, I've had a Bill and a Bob."

"Oh," I say, quarter-considering a dive off the ledge. "So
what happened with you and Mason?"

"I thought I was in love with him. I considered putting off
school for a year, seeing what happened. But ultimately I could-
n't imagine *being* with him. Or I guess I *could* imagine; that was
the problem. He was totally obsessed with his work, totally self-
involved. And he had trouble functioning in the world. He had
no money. He was pretty hapless, actually. I washed his
clothes. I made decisions for him, like whether to apply to grad
school. And he needed me to stroke his ego. I told him I
thought he was a genius because that's what he wanted to hear.
I was seventeen, but I felt like the adult. I had too much power.
But not enough. Course that's pretty much the way I feel in all
my relationships, so obviously I'm, you know, putting my own
poison in the punch."

I look at her: is this a commentary on our relationship? It
seemed too pointed not to be. Does she see Mason in me? Is
she trying too hard to not make the same old mistakes?

"What about you?" she asks.

"Me?"

"Who was your first?"

"Tammy Poulin. She was a senior and I was a sophomore.
We were at a party, on the bathroom floor."

"Fun?"

"Not really. I was drunk. She was on top. I put my hands on
her boobs because that seemed like the thing to do. I remember trying to spread my legs, but I couldn't because my pants

were around my ankles. Afterwards there was a classic awkward silence. I couldn't wait to get back to the party. I said, 'Thanks a lot,' and she said, 'No problem.'"

"And that was it for you and Tammy Poulin?"

"Yeah. I'm not sure I ever talked to her again."

"It's so mysterious to me, your life in Maine." She's squinting, as if by concentrating she could conjure up an image of me at fifteen, balls deep on the bathroom floor. I'd bet that Tammy Poulin is no Mason Sculptor, but Calliope doesn't know that: she finds my past as imposing as I find hers. I hope.

"What do you want to know?" I pull out my cigarettes, this turning into a double session. "I'll tell you anything."

19

Around one I escape from the office—alone, as I like to be at lunchtime. Having eaten only a peach today, I'm angry-hungry, and my mouth fills with spit as I ponder the possibilities. What I want are Chinese dumplings, but knowing I need to start denying myself things—particularly things that are fried dough and meat—I go to my deli and get fresh turkey on a roll with Russian, which I take to the tables in back.

At lunch I usually read the sports pages or the free weeklies: the *Village Voice*, which runs a column by one of my old favorites, and the *New York Press*, which runs a column by one of my new favorites. Today, though, I want to prepare for my meeting with Gale Hawkins, so it's all about Hakim Mohammed. They don't tell me anything about the confession that I don't already know, but tucked into the last paragraph of the *Times* story, mentioned almost in passing, is a startling nugget. A state court has rejected Mohammed's appeal, finding that his trial was fair.

I eat quickly, and the food energizes me—for a few seconds. Then I crash. I put my head down on the table, pretending to be someone who can nap. I'm ready to blame the turkey, that mysterious enzyme everyone likes to talk about at Thanksgiving; then I remember my morning gin.

With my meeting approaching and energy draining from me as if I were bleeding, I walk past the office and into a bar. This must be how it happens: first breakfast, now lunch. But I'm not sliding. I'd never slope down that slip. Just making it through the day. That's what I tell myself as I order a martini, straight-up with olives.

The bar is filled with professionals, all suits and briefcases, and many of them know each other. Lawyers, taking a break from the action at the courthouse down the street. It's the kind of bar you see on *Law and Order*, a place where people you thought were adversaries get chummy and decide people's fates like gods.

★ ★ ★

When I walk into the office, my throat on fire from breath mints, Gale Hawkins and a large bald black man are standing by the front desk, their impatience as evident as the reverend's collar. Hawkins is tall but hunched with age.

"Reverend Hawkins, it's an honor," I say, the words riding a two-martini freedom.

I hold out my hand, which I steer toward the other man when Hawkins points at him.

"That's Car Williams, my assistant." Car squeezes my hand hard enough to make it clear he could kill me in a second.

Hawkins takes off his sunglasses, apparently to see me better. "You're not the campaign manager."

"No, I'm—"

"I was promised a meeting with the campaign manager."

"Danny's tied up," Paul says, surging out of Tod's office. "He sends his regrets. I'm Paul Teague, the political director. We've met once before."

"I was promised the campaign manager."

"I know, I know," Paul says, "and I'm truly sorry. Something's come up. You know how campaigns are." Shaking Hawkins' hand, Paul leans forward, almost in a bow. "I can't tell you how much I admire you. Growing up you were one of my heroes."

I'm surprised by the display—I was worried Paul would be combative—although the inference, if you know Paul, is that the reverend is no longer one of his heroes. Hawkins is a mainstream civil rights leader, an old MLK acolyte with ties to Jesse Jackson. In the sixties black radicals saw Hawkins as too conservative; today black pragmatists see him as too liberal. Which probably means he's been right all along.

Hawkins scowls as if he finds the adulation distasteful, but he softens. "All right then," he says. "Let's get to it."

Paul holds out his arm, directing us down the hall toward his office. We fall in behind Hawkins, who walks with a cane, propping it against his hip for leverage. It takes us a long minute to get to the office, and when we get there we're one chair short.

"I'll stand," Car says, and he does, by the door with his arms folded.

"You know why I'm here," Hawkins says, the cane resting on his lap. In apparent perpetual discomfort, he holds his face in a wince, which makes his lined face look like a walnut shell. "They said it couldn't happen in New York, an innocent man on death row."

"It's a little too soon to make that assumption," Paul says. I'm sitting between them, in a too-low chair that faces the side of Paul's desk. Trying to justify my presence, I pick up a notebook and start taking notes. "With all due respect," Paul adds.

"The point is," Hawkins says, "there's too much doubt for the execution to happen, and I hope the congressman agrees."

Paul says, "His position is that there's a legal process—"

"Don't give me that," Hawkins says, "It's a *po*-litical issue. It might well become *the po*-litical issue. It could cost you thousands of votes."

"I doubt that," Paul says. "We're going to have widespread support from blacks, especially after what we've learned today."

"I'm here to tell you otherwise," Hawkins says. "We will not go to the polls in large numbers unless Schecter takes a stand. He needs to call for a new trial."

Paul bites into his bottom lip, which whitens as his big front teeth dig in. What he wants to say, I'm sure, is something like, Get your idle threats and your rainbow coalition, race-card-playing butt out of my office. But then he doesn't have to; his glare says it all. I've seen Paul's self-righteousness, but this looks more like fury. Paul, it occurs to me, is capable of being one mean bastard.

"I'll pass along your concerns to the congressman," he says.

"I'd hope so," Hawkins says.

Paul says, "Let's not forget that Schecter has said, on more than one occasion, that any evidence of innocence needs to be looked into."

"He's avoiding the matter," Hawkins says.

"And we all know why," I say, just as I was resigning myself to not saying anything. "I mean, let's get real."

"Damn," Car says, pulling my gaze his way. Pressed against his tucked-in hands, his arms are as big as my thighs. It was a compliment, I decide, a comment on my chutzpah, though my man Car wouldn't use that term.

"*Someone* killed a cop," I say. "It's an issue Washburn could ride to victory."

"There comes a point when you've got to stop running scared," Hawkins says, his preacher's cadence making his words bob and weave. "There comes a point when you've got to stand up for what is right and what is just. If Schecter can't make sure we don't kill an innocent man, what good is he?"

"Fair point," I say.

"You have no idea how big an issue this is in the community," Hawkins says.

"And what community is that?" Paul says.

"The black one," Hawkins says. "You familiar with it?"

"First of all," Paul says, "There's not *one* black community. There are hundreds. And I don't think this is a big issue in any one of them."

Hawkins gives Paul a look that says something along the lines of, you housenigger motherfucker. He stabs the carpet with his cane and stands up. His shaky steps don't allow the dramatic exit he must have had in mind. When he finally reaches the door, he starts heading the wrong way until Car grabs him by the arm and gives him a gentle tug.

"Not a single point he made was fair," Paul says. "Hawkins is playing a game."

"And what are we doing? Tell me, Paul, what the *fuck* are we doing?"

I look down at my curlicued doodling. Our relationship hasn't flourished as I'd hoped it would. I don't think it's an exaggeration to say that a few months ago we saw each other as kindred spirits, peons with principles. We respected each other despite our differences. But now those differences are getting in the way.

I peek at him. He's looking down at his bible, which he opens to a page book-marked with a Schecter pamphlet. I suppose it's a victory of sorts that he's becoming just another guy to me, a guy I don't like all that much.

★ ★ ★

At four o'clock everyone who doesn't have something more important to do—and that's almost everyone—is in the conference room, waiting to watch Washburn's press conference. Notably absent is Wes, who's in DC, having fled the scene of the crime.

On a campaign there's nothing more fun than watching your opponent face tough questions. Winning the whole thing is more rewarding, watching a debate more exciting, but for pure pleasure, this is as good as it gets. Two big bowls of popcorn are making the rounds, and someone had the inspired idea of buying black-and-white cookies.

"Oh Jeez," Danny says when he walks in. "Not a word about this to the press."

The press conference is being held at the Albany Area Boys Club/Girls Club. "An already scheduled stop," the anchor-woman tells us. Maybe so, but there's a reason he's taking questions there instead of, say, at an Elks Club. Not that they're being subtle about it: a black man is at the podium, pulling up the mike to accommodate his impressive height. Washburn is standing behind him, along with his wife Linda and Mindy.

"Oh God," Lana says. "Mindy's there."

"And looking fine," Shawn says, stealing Tod's line.

"She'll be performing fellatio on that black guy," I say, my buzz still buzzing. "To show how tolerant her father is."

"Why doesn't Daddy just do it himself?" Calliope says, sig-naling that she's up for being a peanut in the gallery.

"'Cause he doesn't have any lips," I say, and people groan. It's funny sometimes where the line is.

"I'm State Senator Leonard Washington," the black guy says in a voice almost comically serious. "I'm also a vice chairman of the Washburn for Senate Campaign. This morning I called Chet and volunteered to rebut the outrageous charges that have been made. They do not dignify a response, but unfortunately in this media climate it is important that people of goodwill come for-ward to speak the truth. I've known Chet Washburn for almost twenty years. He's not only a friend, he's my senator, and I can tell you that he doesn't have a racist bone in his body . . . "

"Hey, Ben," Calliope says as Washington begins to enumer-ate Washburn's myriad acts of racial tolerance. "How many racist bones do you have in your body?"

"Just one," I say. "My clavicle. It hates Latinos."

"So it's not true what they say about your coccyx?" Calliope says.

"That charge is completely asinine!"

The Ben and Calliope Show. We haven't performed like this in a while; our rapport wasn't there, and it seemed too back-of-the-bus. But now it seems perfect.

So maybe this job isn't the Answer. Maybe it's not nourishing my soul. But it's not sheer misery either. People have to clean toilets, after all. They have to scrape carcasses off highways. I'm getting paid to watch TV and make jokes with the woman I might love. One day I'll look back on the job fondly. "It was an interesting experience," I'll tell my interesting friends as we experience a delicious dinner. At worst, my year on the campaign will look like a necessary mistake. At best, it will look like a step in the right direction, a rung on the ladder leading up to Fulfillment. Sometimes at night, after having awesome sex with the woman I definitely love, I'll think about the campaign, and the memories will ease, not hinder, my descent into sleep.

When Washington is done speaking, he gives Washburn a hug. He squeezes him as cameras click. In political theater it's not easy to come across as too heavy-handed, but I think they've managed it. Judging by Tod's smile, he agrees.

"Kiss him!" Shawn says. His best joke ever.

Once Washington has released him Washburn positions himself at the podium. He waits to speak, as though figuring out what to say. His face is thin but fleshy, unformed, like a child's. His crisp brown hair wouldn't move in a hurricane and his far-to-the-side part is as straight as a seam. He could be a small market newscaster or a loan officer or the doctor you don't like, the one with cold hands.

"When I first learned," he says, "that so-called journalists were not only prying into my daughter's personal life, but accusing me and my wife of racism—" A twitch reshuffles his face, and his mouth tightens into a little line, as if he were trying to hold back tears. And perhaps he is. Racist or not, he's stung by the charges, and he sees their significance. People with power probably know when it's slipping away. On the other hand, he's cheated political death before. A conservative in the Northeast, a bland guy in a state where people like their personalities large, he's survived by being, in a strict sense, an effective senator. He's worked hard, brought home the pork, got his name on bills. He defies the GOP leadership just often enough to look independent, and he makes sure not to alienate major constituencies. He knows, as the saying goes, where the votes are.

"First I was astonished," he says. "Then I was outraged. So absurd were the charges that it didn't occur to me that I would have to rebut them publicly."

"One minute, one lie," Danny says.

"I'm going to read a statement," Washburn says.

"Beautiful," Tod says. "I'm so angry that I'm going to read a statement one of my hacks wrote for me. No offense, Bergin."

"Eat me."

"The charges leveled against me involve my daughter's private life." He looks up, then down again. He didn't even memorize it well enough to keep the flow going. I'm starting to think Wes is up there somewhere, pulling the strings. "And I deeply regret having to talk about it. Two years ago my daughter had a relationship with a man named Devin Pierce, who has since died in a tragic accident. My wife Linda and I welcomed Mr. Pierce into our home and found him to be an intelligent, decent young man. Both Linda and I are very close with our daughter, and based on things she told us, we developed concerns about the relationship. Those concerns had absolutely nothing to do with Mr. Pierce's African-American heritage."

"We just hated his skin," I say, since I hadn't said anything for a full minute.

"I will not discuss the nature of those concerns out of respect for my daughter and for Mr. Pierce's family. As for the implication that I'm intolerant on racial matters, I believe my dear friend Leonard Washington put the lie to that scurrilous charge. Let me add that I supported President Clinton's effort to protect affirmative action—"

"Oh no," Paul says from the back of the room. "He's doing the dance."

"And I, along with some of my Democratic friends, have launched an effort to have a bust of Dr. Martin Luther King placed in the lobby of the Capitol Building."

"And I loves the fried chicken," Paul says.

"If I'm guilty of anything," Washburn says, looking up, trying to do this bit from memory. "I'm guilty of being a concerned father. Maybe I'm even a little nosy; that's probably what my daughter would say." He looks back at Mindy, and she smiles. "But that's only because I love her so much. She's still my little girl, even though she's grown into a beautiful, accomplished woman. I didn't want her to come here today, but she insisted. She's going to say a few words."

With Mom at her side Mindy moves up to the podium. Washburn puts his hand on his daughter's shoulder, and Linda does the same. The tableau works, making the Washburns look united, but it draws unfortunate attention to Mindy's roundness. Linda is a blond-haired skeleton; you could hurt yourself kissing her cheek. Mindy's half a foot shorter and two feet wider. Most striking, though, is Mindy's face: full lips, olive skin, wide nose. Maybe the real scoop is that Mindy was fathered by a black man. Wes is probably looking into it right now.

Mindy unfolds a piece of paper, the crackle loud in the mike. "My parents brought me up to respect people of all races, which is why when I met Devin Pierce I didn't see him as a black man, but as a man. He was smart, articulate, kind. And attractive."

On "attractive," she looks up and pauses. It's a striking move—if move isn't too cynical a word—more subtle and daring and effective than anything Washburn's handlers would have scripted. It makes clear the intrusiveness of the charge.

"When I was involved with Devin, my parents were supportive. The issue of Devin's race never even came up—"

"Ha!" yells Shawn, perhaps the only one of us not chastened—or, in Tod's case, concerned—by Mindy's presentation, which is more powerful than a thousand paeans to Washburn's tolerance.

"When I told my parents about the difficulties Devin and I were having, they urged me to try to work through them. Our eventual break-up had nothing to do with the color of his skin." She looks up again. "Or mine." Chet smiles, squeezes her shoulder. "To suggest otherwise is sickening. Devin and I parted amicably and remained friends. I spoke to him on the phone the night before he left for South Africa, where—"

Her tears come so quickly and forcefully that for a moment, before Mindy buries her face in her father's chest, you can hear them hitting the podium. Chet hugs his daughter while Linda rubs her back. It's impossible to know what's getting to Mindy. Maybe simple grief. Or the pain of feeling betrayed by old friends. Or the psychic torture of having to publicly defend a man whose racism you abhor.

When I look at Calliope, she's cringing in sympathy. I guess I feel bad too, but I'm also angry: Mindy's ruined our party.

Washburn looks too pleased—gleeful at the opportunity to be Caring Father. Still clutching Mindy, he leans toward the mike. "I think she's said enough," he says.

"No!" Mindy says. She grabs hold of the mike with both hands, her face a streaky mess. "My daddy is the best, best, best, most . . . most colorblind person I know. He *loves* black people. You should all be ashamed of yourselves."

20

As I walk up from the subway, Brooklyn's white sky coming into view, it occurs to me that I'm going to make this trek only fifty more times or so. When I try to figure out how many more exactly, I realize that I don't know today's date. I don't even know the day of the week. I have no clue. It could be the drinking (every night now, though not to excess), but disorientation is the natural state of a campaign worker. Calliope and I like to ask each other what happened in the office two or three days earlier, and the answer, to our amusement, is always "I don't remember." But never, until now (I don't think) have I lost my place in the week.

Whether Election Day is forty-five or fifty-five days away, it seems within reach. For the first time, I can imagine sticking it out. I never really believed I would quit, but I never really believed I wouldn't. Now I do. Forty-five or fifty-five more mornings I'll make this trek and sit down at my desk and craft lies in the name of a lesser evil. It's not that bad. I've been doing it for months and I can do it some more.

★ ★ ★

Tod's door is closed. He's either hosting a meeting or performing some cosmetic act, like plucking the hairs from his nipples with the extra large tweezers he keeps in his top drawer. I hear voices behind the door: Danny, Paul.

I continue down the hall, content to be outside the loop, wanting to be left alone.

The place is tight with the anxiety that's dogged the campaign for a week, ever since it became clear that we weren't going to get a big bounce off the Devin Pierce story. It hurt Washburn for a few days, knocking him off message and easing our efforts to make him look like an extremist. What it didn't do, apparently, was convince many New Yorkers that he's unfit for office. The latest poll has us leading by four points (up from three a month ago), an uncomfortable margin against a politician known for late surges.

No doubt his daughter's teary defense helped, as did the statements of her "two closest friends" from school, who questioned the reliability and motivations of the friends quoted in the original story. There's a sense on the seventh floor that we didn't knock Washburn out when we had the chance. He made it back to his corner, cut but okay, and now he's going to come out swinging.

When I say seventh floor, I mean Tod, who more than anyone else controls the temperature of the campaign. (The "heartless and soulless" of the campaign, Calliope calls him.) A few nights ago Tod and I were mulling over the mystery of the campaign: we're on the popular side of the big issues—impeachment, the environment, Medicare, gun control, abortion—yet the race is a dead heat. "I don't get it," Tod said, almost plaintively. It's a mistake to think Tod doesn't care about the campaign: he really really wants to win. His concern has broken through his confidence, and it's leaking into other people's psyches. If anyone can reverse the flow, it's Wes. He'll be here today, with Schecter, and not a moment too soon.

I pour coffee and peel the plastic off a Drake's crumb cake, the least pernicious of the synthetic pastries that have become the lifeblood of the campaign. One morning Danny showed up cradling a box of Yodles. The next day I answered with Ring Dings, which inspired Tod's Devil Dogs, and so on, until our shelves were teeming with the lunchbox treats of our collective youth. The men more than the women have contributed to the supply, and you don't have to be a Freudian to suspect that we feel our mommies in the spongy dough of the pastries. They've proven vastly more popular than the snacks Calliope advocates. It's a little sad watching her try to get people to put down Twinkies in favor of dried fruit. And she thinks *I* have unrealistic expectations.

"Where the *hell* have you been?" Tod says, standing in the doorway.

"Home," I say, as if he wanted an answer.

"You didn't watch the news last night, did you?"

Last night? TV is all I recall, football. Which means today's Tuesday.

He tells me to follow him with a tilt of the head, and the gesture is so familiar, so weighted with déjà vu, that I'm not convinced that whatever's happening hasn't already happened. How does it turn out?

Paul's in Tod's chair, and Danny's sitting on the floor in the corner, his legs arched over a golf bag. Danny looks better than he has in months: not rested, but not dead.

"Channel Seven did a story on the guys who testified against Mohammed," Tod says, handing me papers. "That's the transcript. The case is collapsing like an old lady's rack."

That familiar, want-to-punch-myself-in-the-skull feeling comes rushing back. But of course it's been here all along. I've been hiding from it, numbing myself with beer and TV and routine. It's easy to do.

"We've got to get out of the waffle house," I say, trying to coin a phrase on the spot.

"What?" Tod says.

Danny giggles. "The House of Waffle."

"We've stayed neutral as long as we can," I say. "No more waffles!"

"What are you suggesting?" Paul says. "That we come out for a new trial?"

"Maybe," I say. "This is a big issue now."

"That's *exactly* why we need to be careful," Paul says. "This could consume the campaign. Schecter will become the Free Mohammed candidate."

"So?" I say, freeing myself from politics for a moment, seeing how it feels. "This guy could be innocent."

"That's heartbreaking," Tod says.

"If we don't take a stand, we look scared," I say.

"If we *do*, we look scared." Paul says. "We look beholden." He stands up, waiting for my next volley. Why don't we just whip out our cocks? Actually, let's not.

The sense of déjà vu is long gone. Never-before vu is more like it: Tod seems more stressed out than Danny, and Paul and I are driving the discussion.

"You guys can make your case to Schec and Wes," Tod says. "Meeting at three-thirty. Meanwhile, Billy Record's holding a rally as we speak."

"God help us," Paul says.

"Ben, I want you to check it out," Tod says. "Get a gauge on this."

On my way out I decide that I should pop in on Calliope, though I don't want to. When I'm actively unhappy on the job, as I've just become, I like her less. No, I like myself less around her. Calliope: my mirror.

We've been having pleasant, superficial chats, my trance-like state lending itself to lightness. She must know I've been mailing it in, not dealing. Or maybe not: she has more interesting things to do than track the emotional state of her fake lover, that pussy at work who should have made a move on her months ago.

I lean into the volunteer room, my feet in the hall. Sitting and writing, she looks at me over her glasses. She twirls her hair when she writes, and it's a tangled mess. Sexy: librarian gone bad.

"I'm going to a Billy Record rally. Quite a show probably. Want to come?"

"I'd love to, but I can't."

I wait for a more specific explanation, but she goes back to her writing. "All right," I say in an oddly high-pitched voice. "That's cool."

★ ★ ★

New York subways are efficient except when you need them to be. Stalled between Brooklyn and Manhattan, I start to fear that I'm going to miss the rally, which is being held in front of City Hall. But I don't need to attend the rally to describe it, and whether I'm there or not, I'll end up tailoring my description to support my contention that Schecter needs to embrace Mohammed's cause.

Channel Seven's story was persuasive. Five guys had testified against Mohammed, and the reporter interviewed four of them. Three of these four now say they don't know if Mohammed did it, and the fourth says he's sure Mohammed didn't. All four remember an unidentified man fleeing as Zito's partner rushed in from the other room, and all four say it's possible that this mystery man pulled the trigger. One of the witnesses gave a detailed description of the mystery man that fits Roger LaBrie. According to the reporter's generous speculation, there wasn't outright misconduct by police or prosecutors; it was likely more of a wink-wink kind of thing: say the right thing, boys, and we'll see what we can do for you. All of them had been charged with drug possession.

Responding today in the newspaper, a spokesperson for the Zitos said, "Should we trust the memories of witnesses years after the murder, or days?" He maintained that the fifth witness, not interviewed by Channel Seven, is sticking by his story.

Still, nothing much of the case against Mohammed remains, and you need not be Hercule Poirot or William Kunstler to believe that he should get a new trial. But believing this is one thing; saying so in the middle of a political campaign is another. I need to somehow convince Team Schecter that getting out in front of the Free-Hakim parade is good politics. And perhaps it is.

The meeting today seems to be shaping into a showdown between Paul and me, and the thought of it turns my chest into a large piece of charcoal, hard and hot, glowing orange. I breathe deeply, trying not to think about the East River, all that water above me.

★ ★ ★

The voice I hear as I approach the rally belongs to Gale Hawkins: "Ladies and gentlemen, please welcome the indomitable, the indefatigable, the inspiring, the irreplaceable, the energizing, the ever-ready . . ."

My timing couldn't have been better; the speeches I missed were mere prelude to this, the appearance of Billy Record, who's taking his time getting to the microphone. He walks to a corner of the platform and cups his ear to turn up the volume on the applause. It's a smallish crowd, maybe a hundred and fifty people. Not bad, though, for a Tuesday morning, and if you count the people on the outskirts of the rally, there are two hundred people here. Hundreds, I'll report.

Record, mocking his reputation as an attention whore, is cupping the air and bringing his hands to his mouth. He winks at a reporter for the *Times* and gives someone else his patented smile, bright against his close-cropped beard, which looks painted on. Despite the humidity, despite the two-hundred-plus pounds he carries on his short frame, despite his double-breasted suit, Record's face is dry. A cool customer, through and through.

In fifteen years Record has transformed himself from a bookie into a political force. Using a community center in Harlem as his base, he's become someone the elite can no longer ignore, as much as they'd like to. To his detractors, he's a gadfly, a hustler, an exploiter of racial tensions fortunate to fill a vacuum in black leadership. To his supporters, he's a civil rights leader for a new generation, a media-savvy visionary, a champion of the underdog brave enough to speak truth to power. Whatever your view, there's no denying he has a knack for injecting himself into the middle of the big stories. In fact, his influence is now such that he can *make* a story big.

"I'm not going to talk long," Record says, "because I don't just talk the talk, I walk the walk, and after I do a little talking, we're all going to do some walking."

"Umm hmm," goes the woman next to me.

"You know, friends, a few years ago some of us tried to stop the powers-that-be from bringing back the death penalty. Human sacrifice is what I call it." He pulls the mike from the stands and starts to walk, a man in command. "I call it human sacrifice because people—mostly people whose ancestors were brought to this nation in chains—are sacrificed on the altar of our fear and failure."

"O-kay," goes the woman.

"We told the powers-that-be that human sacrifice was immoral. We said only God should decide who lived and who died. They had no answer. We told them that human sacrifice preyed on the poor and the black and the brown. They had no answer. We told them that the monster of human sacrifice would gobble up the lives of the innocent. They had an answer for that one. They were going to put together the best system of human sacrifice defense in the nation. Foolproof, they said. That was their answer. Fool. Proof." Pausing, he puts the mike back in the stand. "Well, ladies and gentleman, what we've got this morning is proof of fools, and I'm here to tell you that they are out of answers."

There's an eruption of applause, as heartfelt and spontaneous a cheer as I've heard in a long time, and I'm part of it, my cautious claps adding to the noise, loud enough to make a few suits on the steps of City Hall stop and turn.

"Now it's my honor to introduce a woman I've gotten to know quite well these past two, three years. Ladies and gentlemen, Ms. Wanda Carter, better known to you all as Hakim Mohammed's mama."

Wanda Carter is light-skinned and fat, with squinty eyes and bangs pasted to her forehead. She extends her stubby neck to reach the mike. "Hakim ain't no saint and he ain't no angel. But he's my boy and he didn't kill no one. Thank you."

Wanda waddles away, and I watch her through a blur of tears. I stop crying when I realize that I am, but for a moment at least, I felt it: the weight of the real.

"They said the case was strong," Record says. "They said they had a smoking gun, literally. Maybe they did, except Brother Hakim didn't pull the trigger. And it seems, ladies and gentlemen, that there was not just one smoking gun, but two. You see, there's another brother we need to talk about, Roger LaBrie. Brother LaBrie has confessed to killing Officer Zee-to, but he says Officer Zee-to shot first. We need a full investigation. Because if and when our energy and righteousness force them to free Brother Hakim, we're not going to let them turn around and sacrifice Brother LaBrie, whose only crime was being the wrong color in the wrong city at the wrong time. We're not going to rest, ladies and gentlemen, until both Brother Mohammed and Brother LaBrie are free."

He hops down into the crowd, and he's swarmed. Two black men wearing sunglasses clear space for him. "We're going to take the fight to their home turf," he says, his voice barely softer without a mike. "The powers-that-be are going to feel our heat. Powers-that-be. I like that phrase. It's short for the powers that *be* oppressing, repressing, and depressing black folk."

"Say it, say it."

"Come with me, friends. We're going"—he winds up like a pitcher and points at the end of his imaginary fastball—"That way." He scoots away, pulling most of the crowd with him. They're walking toward Brooklyn, so I follow.

The marchers are mostly in their late forties or early fifties—people who came of age in the sixties. Sandals, boots, beards, Afros, tie-dyes, dashikis, an army jacket with its sleeves cut off. You've got to hand it to these people, still doing it after all these years; but they can't help seeming worn out. They're victims of their successes as well as their failures. They're trapped inside a cliché. It's time for them to be relieved. Thanks very much, folks. You've done your part. Now excuse us while we do ours.

As we march through the southern end of Chinatown toward the Brooklyn Bridge, it occurs to me that we might all be headed for the same place.

Up ahead there's a group of college students. The naked back of one of them, a tan smoothie with a butterfly tattoo flying out from her low-cut pants, makes me reluctant to draw too close—my horniness is starting to hurt—but I want to drink in their enthusiasm, so I speed up. The guys in the group, their thin bodies lost inside their clothing, seem meek but comfortable with their meekness. The women in the group hold sway. "This is, like, so the truth," says my naked-backed girl, who's part Asian. She has her arm around a red-haired black girl with freckles on her cheeks and combat boots up to her knees.

Didn't they get the news? There's no need to organize. Everything's rosy at the end of the American Century. We've got peace and prosperity, good coffee on every corner and people playing the stock market in every town. If only the President could keep it in his pants.

They're way ahead of where I was in college. I was too much like too many of my classmates: ironic and inhibited and afraid to seem as if I cared about anything. Back then the PC debates were raging; the only students who made any noise were conservatives and sensitivity-police liberals, who managed to turn conservatives into freedom fighters. The rest of us, the silent majority, watched from a distance, envious and scornful. Even during the Gulf War we were quiet. Almost no one actively opposed or supported the war, although not opposing it seemed the same as supporting it, and we didn't want to do that, but that's what we did. We'd always wanted a cause—a chance to release the passion that we hoped lay dormant within us—and now we had one. Or did we? Sure, the war was partly about oil and the press was rooting for the home team, but it wasn't clear-cut like Vietnam—why couldn't our war be *easy* to oppose?—and there were tests to take and parties to go to . . . so we drank our drinks and watched the war on TV.

I'm not sure I've changed much. Even if I weren't getting a paycheck from one of the powers-that-be, I wouldn't be able to give myself over to this march. I get bogged down in the imperfections. Like Billy Record, who can't resist the lure of demagogy. And the chants. ("Hey, hey, ho, ho, racist cops have got to go.") And the linking by Record of LaBrie with Mohammed, which is bad politics, if not bad, period.

I feel a heavy hand on my shoulder: Car Williams. Hawkins is next to him, motoring along in wheelchair. "Doing some spying?" Car says, not seriously.

"We going where I think we're going?"

"Yeah, we're accompanying you back to your place of employment."

By the South Street Seaport two cops, a white guy and a black woman, are leaning against a cruiser, one of three lined up end to end. At the sight of the cops, staring with their arms folded, most of the marchers tighten, and the chanting takes on a self-conscious air. The red-haired black girl gives the cops the peace sign.

"Get a job," the white cop says. So predictable, his words, yet I want to run to him, tell him that I respect cops and that I have mixed feelings about the march. Could be I just don't have what it takes to be an activist.

"*We're* working," Car yells, walking backwards. "The fuck *you* doing?"

"You bring this bullshit by the Zitos' house," the cop yells, "you and me are going to have a problem." I start to worry about Carla Zito seeing us; then I remember that she lives in Staten Island. More crap from the cop.

"You and *I*," Car yells, correcting his grammar, "already *have* a problem."

As we approach the bridge, I feel unfaithful to Calliope. That day on the roof, the day we played catch, we made plans to walk across it together. I'm relieved, then, to discover that it's not as exciting as I expected. The walkway runs up the middle, between traffic, and thick cables slice up the view.

But it's on the bridge that I relax into the march. Maybe it's the smile the part-Asian girl gives me. Maybe it's being suspended together above water. Maybe it's the better chant. ("Hey, hey, my, my, if there's doubt, then he can't die.") Whatever the reason, the crowd gives me comfort.

With the comfort, however, comes something else, something like its opposite. Responsibility, I suppose. I should probably have quit my job, but as long as I haven't, I've got a job to do. And this is the issue, the only issue. It's life and death, black and white.

21

Near the office I step out of the march. As much as I'd like to see what transpires, I don't want Schecter to know I marched, or the marchers to know I work for Schecter, so I duck into the lawyer bar. What the hell. I haven't had a drink during the day since the day I did, and I want to lube myself up for the meeting, which is the most important thing right now. Brain now; body later.

The lawyers are all here, eating and drinking, the varying quality of their suits revealing them as, from worst-dressed to best, public defenders, prosecutors, or private defense attorneys. There are also a few journalists, including Chuck Nagorski, the *News*'s grizzled crime reporter. I talked to him a few months back about Schecter's position on drug sentencing. He's sipping whisky like the old-school journalist that he is. If he can drink and work, so can I.

★ ★ ★

The marchers are gone when I walk into the office. "You missed quite a scene," Bernice says without looking up.

These are the first unprompted words she's ever spoken to me. "What happened?"

"Billy Record and about a hundred people crowded on in here. They were chanting and hollering about Hakim Mohammed, and Billy Record, that *pimp*, he started yelling at me, demanding to see the congressman."

"Did Schecter meet with him?"

"No, I pretended he wasn't here, but Danny spoke with him for a good fifteen minutes. Meanwhile, the crowd kept right on chanting."

With ten long minutes to kill before the meeting, I go to the volunteer room, where Calliope and four volunteers, including George Blue, are sticking labels on envelopes. George has been away on a bike trip since July. He stands up, a label sticking to his hair, and spreads his arms. I give him a hug, hoping his calm rubs off on me.

"Good trip?" I say.

"*Great* trip, bro. I want to show you pictures."

"You got them with you?"

"Course I do." He points to his head, his dark, bottomless eyes shining like puddles at night. "They're all up here."

He's not calm; he's crazy. I back away, my eyes begging Calliope to join me in the hall. She comes out skipping, literally, and jumps to a stop, landing hard on two feet. Tits quivering to a stop. "Smoke?" she says through the hair that's fallen over her face.

"No, I've got a thing."

She's waiting for me to say more, and I want to. I want to tell her that I'm seasick with nervousness, that I'm drunk but not drunk enough, that it's insane what we're doing, she and I, not rubbing each other every chance we get.

"What's up with Danny?" she says. "He seems different."

"Better, right?"

"I'm not sure."

"Are people . . ." I was going to ask if people are talking about him, but I don't care. I've never cared less about anything.

"You all right?" she says.

"Yeah."

"I don't think you are."

"I've got to go." I shake her hand and gather from her giggle that it's a strange thing to do. "I'll tell you later," I say, starting down the hall. "I'll tell you everything."

The conference room is empty. I sit down and try to shake the feeling that people are looking at me through the one-way mirror. Which is really a window. It's a window and no one's there. I'm sitting where I was during my first big meeting with Schecter. It seems amazing that I came in here and just about took over the conversation.

It's a window and no one's there.

Danny, riding his desk chair, backs into the room, pushing himself along with his feet. He wheels to the head of the table and stands up.

"The king's throne," he says, his voice implying a shrug. He sits down in the chair next to the throne and leans back, using his clasped hands as a headrest.

"How was Billy Record?" I ask, realizing that it might ease my nerves to have a conversation.

"He was like, *so* Billy Record."

Danny's medicating—medicating with something more effective than gin. Whatever he's popping I want three of them.

Everyone else comes in together, all buddy-buddy, The Man's hand on Paul's shoulder. The only greeting I get is from Wes, a light slap to the back of my head.

"No time for chitchat, folks," Wes says. "Arn, Paul, and me got to be on a plane for Syracuse in an hour. First thing, there was a school shooting today in Georgia."

"Jesus," Schecter says as if he hadn't already heard about the shooting. In fairness, a hint of the genuine creeps into his reactions when the subject is children and guns. "It's the sixth one this year," he says, rocking.

"That's right," Wes says. "There's an epidemic of school

shootings going round. If we can't make hay—"

"I'm on it," Tod says. It's comforting to see that he's back to being his cocky self. Across from me, Paul's hands are flat on the table, touching it lightly as if it were hot. He's going upstate with The Man.

"Next up is Mr. *Ha*-Keem *Mo*-hammed, who just doesn't want to leave us be. Let's hear what Billy Record had to say."

That's my cue.

"He drew a line in the sand," Danny says. In the bar I prepared lines, moral arguments disguised as political ones, but now they're a mess in my mind. "If we make an issue of Mohammed, we get Record's endorsement. If not, not."

"That piece of shit doesn't scare me," Schecter says.

"He *is* a piece of shit," Tod says. "But he's worth votes."

"And he costs votes," Paul says.

"He's a net plus, probably," Wes says. "We could be quiet about the endorsement, arrange a get-together in a hole somewhere. The question is, should we do what it takes to get his support. I mean, what does the piece of shit *want* us to do?"

"Wasn't clear," Danny says with a chuckle. He seems to be staring at the air in front of his face. Maybe he has a morphine drip under his shirt.

"That's one of the problems," Paul says. "We certainly can't say he should go free. It's *way* too early for that. What, then, can we say?"

"A lot," I say. "We can, you know, send signals. We can . . . "

"Do what we do," Danny says.

"Yeah," I say, shaking. I'm not sure if the tremble worked its way into my voice. I don't think so: no one's looking at me funny. No one's looking at me at all. "The case against Mohammed is collapsing," I say, a few of my lines coming back. "More and more stuff is going to come out. It'd be smart to get out in front on this."

There's a silence, the bad kind.

"Washburn's going to use it no matter what," Danny says.

"We can deal with that," Tod says, "What we can't deal with is him getting up on stage with a bunch of Zitos."

"He could do that now," I say.

"The Zitos have to agree to it," Tod says.

"Oh yeah," I say, heat rising and bubbling in me, my body a foaming-over test tube.

"And they just might," Wes says. "Unless we're careful."

"Let's give Mrs. Zito a call," Schecter says. "Ask her how far we can go."

By the time we realize this is a joke—at his own expense, no less—it's too late for our laughter to take hold.

"I went to the march," I say.

"And?" Wes says.

"And . . . " There's sweat under my nose, and it smells like martini. "There's real intensity there."

"But it doesn't go very wide," Paul says. "Here's how I see it. Billy-broken-Record is going to do what he always does: try to divide people along racial lines. We—you—can be a unifier on this. You can say that this issue should play out in the courts, but no one should be running around portraying Mohammed as a victim of racism. That's not fair to the family of the victim and it's not fair to this city, which has wounds that a lot of us have worked hard to heal. You see, I have more than a passive interest in this issue."

He stands up, making me want to run away. I'm afraid he's embarrassing himself—passive interest?—and I'm afraid he's not. "As a black man, I'm sick and tired of self-appointed black leaders stirring up the pot of racial resentment. Because when that happens, it's blacks who suffer, not whites. Hakim Mohammed is not on death row because he's black and he's not being kept there because he's black. Now don't get me wrong: as a black man I think we need to talk about injustice. Let's talk about the law-abiding blacks whose children have to walk by drug dealers on their way to decrepit schools. Let's talk about poverty. Let's not talk about one single case of *possible* injustice. Billy Record, all he does is talk about how whites are racists and blacks are victims. That's not leadership. And that's not right. We need to stand up to Record and all the people like him. Their time has passed, man. It's over."

Without realizing it I've placed my hand over my eyes. I spread my fingers to get a peek at Paul, who's beaming; when I see Schecter I know why. He's wearing the moist-eyed, trembly-lipped face he usually saves for tributes to military heroes, memorials for Holocaust victims, and especially mawkish renditions of *God Bless America*. "Well," he says. "I think that about says it all."

"It's got to," Wes says. "Time to go."

They all leave: Wes, Schecter, and Paul, then Tod, who says something to me I can't make out, then Danny, who gives me a Roadrunner beep-beep as he wheels by. I stay seated, my overmatched brain churning away like a coffee grinder, trying to remember everything Paul said, searching for the flaws, and there are plenty. I should know. The bastard stole from the little speech I wrote four months ago.

I stand up, in disbelief that the meeting has already come and gone. I'm not sure if I could have prevailed—only Danny seemed open to my point of view, and he was stoned—but there's no question that my performance was awful.

I find myself walking around the bathroom, my mind replaying the meeting, highlighting all the lowlights. *We can, you know, send signals.* I punch the side of the stall, but it's a half-hearted punch, risking nothing. I want to throw another punch but I'm afraid of holding back again, so I hold back entirely.

★ ★ ★

"Paul kicked the shit out of you," Tod says.

"Yeah."

"It was a bloodbath."

We're both sitting behind his desk, waiting to see what the eleven o'clock news has to say about the race, especially in regard to Hakim Mohammed. It's not among the lead stories:

there was a double murder, an investment scam, and a beating. The beating is a big story because it arose out of a dispute over the quantity of ham on a sandwich—amazingly, the patron thought there was too much—and because the deli-worker victim's eggplant face provided good video.

"Looks like you after the meeting," Tod says.

"Fuck off," I say, thinking he might stop once he gets a rise out of me.

"It was a TKO." He points at the bottle, wanting more. We're drinking Glenlivet and smoking—a cigar for him, a cigarette for me—Tod having used his three-iron to disable the smoke alarm. "I was going to ask Wes to stop the meeting."

I manage a laugh, and it feels healthy, like wisdom, so I laugh some more. It's something I used to be good at, laughing at myself. "I couldn't get off the ropes."

"You pussed out."

"He took over the meeting from you, too."

"I agreed with the upshot of what he was saying."

"But what he *said* was crap," I say. "Mostly."

"As a black man I'm a black man who happens to be a black man."

"Who hates it when blacks play the race card."

"Shec ate it up."

"Unbelievable."

"Not really."

"Yeah."

"It's the right decision."

"We'll see," I say, going for a casual tone, just about pulling it off. The scotch is putting some distance between me and myself.

I spent most of the afternoon rewriting the meeting. In my imaginings I had the opportunity and ability to deliver a rebuttal. For the fantasy to work, I needed an actual speech, and I tried to draft one in my head as I went about my day: talking to Calliope, writing a release about the school shooting, eating fish and chips. I started to type the speech, but after slaving away on one passage, the endeavor—and my entire day—seemed self-destructive and symbolic: fearing failure, failing, regretting having failed. The quintessential cycle of a miserable person.

"You think Paul's a virgin?" Tod says.

"He has a girlfriend," I lie, feeling a silly need to protect Paul.

"Doesn't mean he's not a virgin. The guy needs to get laid, not just laid, but you know, *laid*. He needs to bang some fucking box."

"He's not the only one."

"When was the last time?"

I don't have an answer ready; it's a question I've avoided asking myself. The last woman I had sex with was a childhood friend of my friend Andy, who lives in DC. He came up one weekend, and the three of us went out. Her name was Theresa Carroll. She was what I used to think I wanted in a woman—namely, a man. She burped, knew baseball, used the word *cunt* in conversation. I hadn't yet realized that I was attracted to Calliope, and for about two days, beginning with the moment Theresa put her finger in my ass, I thought she might be my girlfriend. There was snow on the ground: December.

"April," I say.

"*What?* Are you trying to kill yourself? No wonder you got the shit knocked out of you today. You're tight. You're—"

I'm saved by Hakim Mohammed, who's fingering his thin mustache as he speaks, his big-knuckled hand muffling his voice. It's an old interview from prison. He's still Wayne White here, I think. This round-faced guy strikes me as a compelling part of the story; then it dawns on me that he *is* the story. His life will end or it won't.

"I didn't do nothing wrong," he says without the emotion you want, his small eyes darting from side to side. He looks like his mother.

"If you did nothing wrong," asks the reporter, a woman off-screen, "why were you in a crack house?"

He takes his hand away from his mouth and puts it on his head, his eyes finally calming down. He looks almost amused. You're afraid he's going to laugh. It's ridiculous, really: if you want him to be innocent, then you want him to behave the way you think an innocent man would behave. And how do you know how an innocent man would behave? TV probably. NYPD Blue. You want Mohammed to exude righteous indignation, outrage that falls just short of hostility. As if after being sentenced to die and living on death row, an innocent man might not lose the capacity to exude much of anything. As if a man, innocent or otherwise, might not be unable or unwilling to convey his emotions in front of a TV camera to a stranger he has no reason to trust. As if laughter might not be the best, most human response to such a manipulative, irrelevant question. If someone has to die, let it be the reporter.

"I didn't kill nobody," he says, those eyes moving again. It's unfortunate, maybe tragic, that he doesn't make a more camera-friendly hero. Absent rock-solid exonerating evidence, his aura could make all the difference. He's not attractive or articulate or stupid—not easy to like or to pity. But maybe his conversion to Islam softened him. Maybe he's learned to speak in the cornball clichés—"My fate is in God's hands"—that people love. Maybe Allah turned him into a good politician.

"That guy's innocent," I say, just throwing it out there.

"Probably."

"What do you mean, probably?"

Tod takes the cigar out of his mouth, looks at it. "I remember talking to Shec before the trial. He was worried the case wasn't strong enough."

"And he knew this, I assume, because he spoke to the DA?"

"I don't know." He looks at me. "Honestly."

I take a drink from the bottle, my eyes aching as it dawns on me how much I don't know about this case, how much I'll never know. Schecter, by contrast, probably knows a lot, and did from the beginning.

The story, as it turns out, isn't about the possibility of Mohammed's innocence. It's about the issue he's become. There's a clip from Billy Record's speech that includes a shot of the crowd. I see myself, just for a flash. No one else would have picked me out—Tod didn't see me—but there I was, and it seemed to me that I looked enthralled, impassioned, alive—not how I imagine myself appearing to the world.

Now Washburn's talking, his hair holding fast in the wind, a wall of blue uniforms behind him. "Congressman Schecter has never been a strong supporter of the death penalty," he says. "But one would hope that he'd support it in this case, since a police officer was brutally murdered in the line of duty."

"Schecter, for his part, released a statement this evening," says the reporter, the same woman, who interviewed Mohammed. It rises in me, the urge to run and punch, stab and be stabbed. Break the bottle on the desk and slice up Tod's face and walk out, free. Or maybe just walk out, no bottle, no blood, just walk out. "He urged, quote, 'people on both sides of this issue not to exploit it for their political purposes.'"

Paul's ideas, my words. This is the wrong life I'm living.

"Give me the bottle," Tod says.

22

This is the second time I've been in Schecter's limo. The first time wasn't like this. Then we had listened to news, not music. No one sat up front—much less did a duet—with the driver. No one made the bodyguards smile. Calliope wasn't there.

Schecter, Todd, the two bodyguards, and I are listening to Calliope and Roberto power into the second verse of Bread's *I Would Give Everything I Own*. As if that weren't excellent enough, our destination this morning is the Lesbian-Gay-Bisexual and Transgender Community Center. Why do I ever worry about anything?

Because there are bodyguards here, that's why. A month ago Schecter started getting threats that the FBI considered credible. Even if liberals overstate the danger posed by the racist right, it can't be pleasant knowing you've aroused the fury of Neo-Nazis, Christian Nationalists, and assorted other folks who love guns as much as they hate Jews. I used to take great delight in calling Schecter a coward; now the term seems imprecise.

One of the bodyguards, good-looking despite a beard of pockmarks, is facing Schecter, and the other one is sitting on his left. I'm on Schecter's right, so if an attack comes from this direction, I guess I'm taking a bullet. This is as close as I've been to Schecter for an extended period of time. He gives off a sizzle, a nervous energy that people, because of his stature, mistake for charisma. He also gives off a stale odor that reminds me of an airless room. It could be breath or sweat or the fifties-style goop he uses to tame his Brillo-pad hair.

Now Calliope is dancing with her arms, slowly, as though pushing them through water. Like a ballerina. Like a conductor on acid.

Todd, Schecter, and I have been silent since the song began; they're probably doing what I'm doing: enjoying the duet, which actually sounds pretty good, and thinking about having sex with Calliope. She's not Arnie's type, nor is she Tod's, but she's a woman singing and dancing, being free, and what's hotter than that?

It's surprising that Schecter seems comfortable allowing someone else to be the center of attention. But then he probably thinks Calliope is performing for him. And maybe he's not wrong. She can't be as unconcerned as she seems about his opinion of her. Maybe she's trying to impress him with her free-spiritedness. For that matter, isn't there something a tad self-conscious about her lack of self-consciousness? A tad *obvious*? The chick comes into a congressman's car and acts like a freak in a VW bus. And isn't that exactly what it is, an act?

No, she's being herself.

She's cool.

I'm not.

"Bravo," Schecter says when the song ends, leading the cheers. Calliope smiles and blushes, as if she didn't know we were watching.

"Now take off your shirt," Tod whispers.

"Tangyouberymuch," Roberto says. "We here all week."

"You two should perform before my speech," Schecter says.

"We could sing some Bah-bra," Calliope says.

"Maybe the national anthem," Schecter says, missing the joke.

He's not well versed in pop culture. Or in gay people, his avowed and probably genuine tolerance notwithstanding. In writing the speech he's about to deliver, I was able to say what I believed, although I had to avoid one subject: gay marriage, which Schecter opposes. We didn't expect to still be working to shore up this important constituency. Both the local and national gay rights groups have stayed out of the race because Washburn has suddenly become a supporter of gay rights. It's a canny move, making him look like a moderate and forcing us to spend time wooing groups whose support we would have taken for granted. More to the point: in October you want to be talking to steelworkers or seniors, not to a crowd of lefties, especially one that includes more than a few people sporting sexual organs that they picked out of a catalog. We're hoping a twenty-minute in-and-out will secure the endorsements and the checks that come with them.

Calliope turns around and smiles at the sight of me, sitting stiffly. I pretend to strangle myself, bulging out my eyes, and she laughs into her hand.

It was a nice surprise, her joining us. Tod, concerned about the question-and-answer period, wanted at least one friendly person there to raise his hand, so he asked Calliope to produce an articulate and gay-but-not-too-gay Schecter fan. After discovering that none of the volunteers who fit the description were available, Calliope enlisted her friend Donovan, whom I've never met.

"Is Washburn quoted?" Schecter says to Tod, who's reading a piece about Mohammed.

"I don't know," Tod says, not wanting to get him riled up before the speech.

"He must be," Schecter says.

"Here it is," Tod says. "He said, 'There seems to be kind of a campaign to turn this Mohammed character into sort of a radical chic kind of cause, and I'm afraid that my opponent, with his equivocations, is adding fuel to the fire.'"

Schecter says nothing. He takes out his copy of the speech and looks it over.

What Tod didn't tell him was that the quote was the most benign of three from the senator. I doubt Washburn's attacks are having much impact because the Mohammed story hasn't blown up the way I thought it might.

Which is exactly why I wish Schecter would take a stand. It's not as if a statement from a politician (except the governor) could save Mohammed's life, but a strong stand from Schecter might bring the issue into the mainstream. Despite the recent revelations, despite Stein's stance in the Primary, it's still seen as something of a fringe cause, a black issue, a rallying cry for the Loony Left. The cause hasn't been helped by Billy Record, who has unilaterally acquitted not only Mohammed but LaBrie on grounds that a decorated, dead cop shot first. Can of worms, to say the least.

But something more fundamental is at work: the city's millions of so-called liberals, freedom fighters of yesterycar, are complacent and content. Things are going so well. Market's up. Crime's down. Let's not ruin the mood with all this talk about injustice. Besides, it simply couldn't be. An innocent man on death row? In New York? No, it couldn't happen here. Someone needs to wake these fuckheads up.

"Turn that off," Schecter says, meaning the radio. He tucks the speech inside his jacket and closes his eyes. I've heard about this, his silence before speeches. Wes's suspicion is that Schecter thinks about his father, Jacob, who died in 1989, just as Hungary, his native land, was crawling out from under communism. Jacob came to the US in thirty-eight, not a minute too soon, and worked his ass off to become a successful tailor so that his only child could work his ass off to become something more prestigious. Schecter is a member of that famous generation of super-achieving Brooklyn Jews, pushed along by loving, demanding parents. Jacob was, by all accounts, tyrannically supportive. When I imagine Schecter as a child, I scare up some sympathy for the guy. I see little Arnie on report card day, walking around Flatbush as night falls, afraid to go home because of that one A-minus.

It's a strangely hot day, summer's last stand, and Donovan is dressed for the weather, in short shorts and a beaded vest with no shirt underneath. "Good God," Tod says, before leading Schecter into the building.

"*Hey*, girl," Donovan says. Holding his hand-rolled cigarette off to the side, he kisses Calliope's cheeks.

"You must be Ben," he says. He takes my hand and gives it a firm shake. "Cal and I were *so* worried when you were thinking of quitting. We're glad you stuck it out."

"Me, too," I say, enjoying the thought of the two of them talking about me. But why couldn't I hear this from her?

Calliope squeezes his thin, upper arm. "I don't think you'd cut it in Chelsea."

"Girl, don't *even* get me started on that hellhole."

"Here are your lines," she says, handing him a folded note card. "Memorize them and make sure you stand in a place he can see you."

"I love it," he says, flaring his eyes. "It's like so *Saturday Night Live* meets *The Candidate*."

"Vile, isn't it?" Calliope says.

"Disgusting," Donovan says, and the two of them chuckle. I used to hope that Calliope would get angry once she got wise to the game, but I'm afraid she sees politics the same way she sees, say, Martha Stewart, or much of male behavior, as an unfortunate, amusing reality.

When we go inside Schecter is already on stage, greeting the president of the Equal Rights Campaign Fund. Donovan burrows into the crowd while Calliope and I join Tod on the steps that lead up to the stage.

"Does Arnie know who Donovan is?" Calliope says.

"Doesn't have to," Tod says. "I'm going to be passing around the microphone."

"And you saw him?" she says.

"Oh yeah. I got a good look. *Too* good. Didn't I say moderately gay?"

"Like you?" Calliope says.

To open, Schecter tells the joke I wrote for him. After thinking up the joke I decided not to use it because it portrays conservative Christians as stupid—not the kind of better-angels politics I claim to believe in. Then I told myself not to be such a puritan. Then I tried to delete the joke, and Tod wouldn't let me. It's a made-up story about a bible thumper who confronts Schecter.

"This gentleman unleashed a torrent of vitriol," Schecter says. "He said I was, quote, destroying the moral fiber of this nation. He called me a, quote, sodomite-lover. Then in what he imagined to be a final, incisive insult, he said, You, sir, are a Homo . . . Sapiens."

The crowd goes wild, as I knew it would.

Within a minute I realize what I must have already known, that the speech is ordinary, a hodgepodge of truisms about tolerance, dignity, etc. But if the speech fails to rise above the genre, it's not all my fault; a speech, like a song, is as strong as the delivery, and Schecter's is tired at best. But at least he remembers to punch home the applause lines, which is all it takes for a speech to go over fine.

There's one part of the speech I like—I was surprised Tod didn't cut it out—and when Schecter gets to it, I look at a couple in the front row, an old white gent who strikes me as British and an Asian guy who strikes me as teenage. My own little focus group.

"As you know, Senator Washburn is among those who want to impeach the President of the United States. They try to justify it with legalistic mumbo jumbo, but make no mistake: Clinton is being persecuted because of sexual behavior that the country's self-styled arbiters of morality find distasteful. Now I want to be clear: I don't approve of what President Clinton did. Maybe I don't approve of what some people in this room do. But guess what? It's none of my business."

The old guy smiles; his lover claps: not quite the reaction I was looking for. But what did I want them to do? Cry and hug and demand to know who penned such brilliance? Yes, that's exactly what I wanted them to do.

The applause at the end of the speech is long, longer than politeness requires. A success, it appears, but there are questions to get through. Tod, saving Donovan for later in case momentum needs to be reversed, hands the mike to a black guy in a tank top, who asks about AIDS funding. It's the kind of policy question Schecter loves; you can see him relax into the legispeak: dollar amounts and bill names and the funding compromise he hopes will emerge from the conference committee.

Next up is a woman in a business suit, whom Tod probably picked because she's conservative-looking; but I know from the assertive way she grabs the microphone that she's going to ask a tough question. "You could truly set yourself apart from Washburn by supporting our right to marry, but you voted for the Defense of Marriage Act." She pauses while hisses slither through the room. "Do you stand by that vote?"

I do my best not to listen to his answer; it's some nonsense about tradition. This is pure politics. Why is Schecter so Schecter? Thirty years ago, he didn't set out to become a typical shameless pol. No one does. What happens to politicians? It's an all-important question, and there are probably a thousand answers, or maybe just one—power corrupts—but watching Schecter now, I'm struck by the ease with which he offers up his poppycock. Has he absorbed the conventional opinion so thoroughly that he believes it to be true? My guess is no. I suspect that on some not-too-deep level he knows he's making a political play, and that he's at peace with doing so. Big-time politics is a self-selecting business. Those who win tend to be pathologically ambitious and self-important. To them victory itself feels like a moral imperative, the principle that trumps all others.

The irony is that voters as well as the media are often drawn to candidates who take unpopular stands. Most voters base their choice not on issues, but on a general impression of the candidate, and what's more appealing than a maverick? Even on individual issues, candidates have more freedom than polls suggest. It's my belief that enlightened positions, framed the right way by the right people, are salable. So the potential's there for having it all: victory, integrity, the whole shebang. But it's chancy, no question. To defy the evil logic of polls is to take a risk, and risk, for those who fear losing more than they fear hurting people or being ordinary or burning in hell, is unacceptable.

I'm struck also by the reaction of the crowd when Schecter finishes giving his answer, an answer that essentially denied their humanity. They're not clapping; but they're not booing, either. Or laughing. Or throwing pieces of rotten fruit onto the stage. Call it sophistication or jadedness, strength or weakness: they can live with the lies.

Donovan has got the microphone now. "First of all," he says, "I want to tell you, Arnie, that I think you're much better than Washburn, not that that's saying much. I don't know why any queer in her right mind would vote Republican. They must have some kind of persecution fantasy."

"What's he doing?" I say as Tod glares at Calliope.

"I don't know," Calliope says with a cringe.

Donovan's voice has taken on a super-feminine lilt, and his hand, poised next to his head, is flopping at the wrist, as though tossing little balls onto the woman in front of him. He seems to be doing an imitation of a gay person. Whatever he's doing, he's enjoying himself. "Or maybe they just care about money. My friend calls them BBQs, bank balance queers. Isn't that just *fabulous*?"

There are hoots of laughter. This is about seven seconds

away from becoming a disaster. I wouldn't care except that Calliope's ass is on the line.

"Anyway, Arnie," Donovan says, reigning it in, "you've done so much over the years to combat violence against gays and lesbians, but as you know, it continues to be a problem. What more, sweetie pie, do you think can be done?"

"I'm glad you asked that question," Schecter says, unfazed, and then he's off and running, talking about all that he's done and will do to make the world safe for gays, lesbians, and people of all sexual persuasions, paraphrasing the crime section of his stump speech. He talks on this topic for a good five minutes, running out the clock; when he's through Tod signals to him with a tap of the wrist that it's time to go.

As the crowd clears Tod makes a beeline for Calliope. "You should have prepped your witness," he says.

"Sorry," Calliope says.

"I hope you're fucking sorry," Tod says.

"It's not her fault," I say.

"Then whose is it?" Tod says. "Never give a job to a chick who doesn't douche."

I step in front of Calliope and put a finger in Tod's face. "That's wrong."

"This whole event was wrong," Tod says.

"It turned out okay," I say.

"Barely," Tod says. Reporters, the ones not gathered around Schecter, are waiting for Tod. "Schec and I have to get uptown. You two are on your own."

I'm assuming that Calliope and I will have lunch with Donovan, but he has to get to class, he tells us. He's a lounge singer studying to become an X-ray technician.

"Thanks for doing this," Calliope says. "You big ham."

"You wanted a gay boy," he says, "I gave you a gay boy."

"I'd kiss you goodbye," Calliope says, "but we're still on stage."

"All the world's a stage," he says. He winks at me and walks out.

23

The West Village looks brilliant in the sunshine, although there's a haze that makes it seem like August. "It's a shame we have to go back to the office," Calliope says.

I look at her, she looks at me, and we think it at the same time: we don't have to go back, not for a while. "Let's walk," she says, heading west.

A nice turn of events: I was expecting to be trapped in the tight air of the limo, which even Calliope's duet with the driver couldn't quite loosen; instead she and I are strolling in the sun. She's pleased, I think, that I stood up for her.

This is the first time I've been in this neighborhood—I've never been west of Hudson Street—and I like it. The buildings are low, the streets cobblestone, and there seems to be, at first feel, a relatively rage-free vibe emanating from the people we pass. Lots of dogs.

We take a left, half-searching for a deli Calliope went to once. A debate is raging on a stoop we pass, a Latino and a white guy talking over each other, pausing only long enough to suck their cigarettes. They're wearing identical navy-blue getups, plumber's garb; maybe that's why I assume they're talking sports. But then the Latino says something about "the people" and the white guy says something about "America," and then they're both barking and sweating, as if someone were keeping score, as if their discussion were the most important thing in the world. And it is, of course.

"New York," Calliope says.

"Amazing."

"There it is," she says, meaning the deli, a signless little place tucked into the corner of an apartment building.

It's crowded inside, five people plus us filling up the place, and you can tell from the smell—pork, onion, coriander—that there's real food to be had. Authentic Mexican, or Argentinean. Authentic something.

"I love these," she says, pointing at little yellow pastries, empanadas. "Let's share some." Not what I had in mind, veggie pockets. I was envisioning chicken, the dry but delicious kind, or crumbly roast pork. But it wouldn't kill me not to have meat.

"All right," I say, warming to the idea. I tend to get caught up in other people's enthusiasms; it's better, easier, than the reverse, people taking my recommendations, relying on me. "Let's get six."

Her face twists up with concern. "On second thought, it's not good hot-weather food. None of this stuff is."

"Yeah. But what is?"

"I'm not sure."

We're silent, stuck. What's wrong with us?

"Let's just get them," I say.

"Okay. Yeah. Who cares about the weather?"

She orders in Spanish, which surprises me. We eat on a shady stoop down the street from the plumbers, who are still going at it, their voices audible when the traffic isn't. We got four kinds of empanadas, but they all taste the same to me, and not great at that, potato-onion mush. But I like how much Calliope likes them, and I tell her that I love them. It doesn't

— 204 —

seem like a lie because I love the lunch, the idea of it, us, here, now.

"You speak Spanish," I say.

"A little. I spent a semester in Madrid. It was—I was about to say it was great, but it wasn't. It was pretty awful, actually."

"Why?"

"The woman I stayed with was nuts, and I was lonely. It's good for me to remember that. I have this bad habit of thinking my life was peachy-perfect before Ari died. The truth is, the years since have probably been my best."

"*Because* of his death?"

"Yeah, partly. Everything's sharper, or something, and I think it inspired me to take more control of my life. Did you have enough to eat?"

She wants to change the subject, and I need to let her. "Yeah." She reaches into her bag for what I expect to be chocolate, but it's gum, a good idea after potato-onion mush. She gives me a piece. "No chocolate?" I say.

"I'm trying to lose weight."

"You don't need to."

"Let me ask you something." She looks at me, her face tight around the eyes. "Do you think I'm attractive?"

This is unusual, Calliope acting like a girl. I love it. And I know just what to say. "I think you're beautiful."

"That's nice," she says, trying not to smile, then stands up. "Let's move."

We cut west to the path along the river, which is full of bikers, joggers, and Rollerbladers. Nakedness all around: skin, sweat, muscles. Up ahead, going south like us, are two tall women on blades, models, holding hands, giggling, wearing just enough clothing to be legal. They're too skinny. But still. Asses like little helmets.

The asses, Calliope, and my bold little "You're beautiful" have conspired to give me a hard-on. "Just a second," I say, sitting on a bench, giving it a chance to go down, but it won't, not with Calliope sitting next to me now, close, her arms crossed, her smock-shirt split wide at the neck, showing me bulge of breast.

"What's the matter?"

"My shoe," I say. I untie my shoe, and she smiles like she knows.

"It was sweet, you defending me to Tod. But I have to say, it made me really uncomfortable." My temple pulsates—blood shooting straight from hard-on to my head. "He was right. I fucked up."

"Oh come on. It's ridiculous to begin with, scripting a question like that."

"But I agreed to do it, and I had a responsibility to do it well."

"Oh, come on."

"We're part of a team, whether you like it or not."

"Tod didn't have to be an asshole about it."

"No. He's a misogynist pig. But if anybody was going to defend me, it should have been me. I don't like seeming a weak little girl, *especially* in front of the Pod."

"You didn't seem like a weak little girl."

"Well, that's the way I felt, and I thought you should know." She puts her hand on my thigh. "What do you think?"

"What do I *think*?" I take her hand off my leg and set in down on the bench. "I *think* you just went out of your way to find fault with me."

"I was just telling you how I feel."

"Well, let me tell you how *I* feel. Angry, hurt, unperceptive, stupid."

"You always say you want me to be honest with you, and I admit, you seem to like it on one level, but at the same time you want me to think every last thing about you is fabulous, which basically means you want me to lie."

"That's bullshit. It sounds insightful, but it's bullshit."

She slaps my thigh. "Don't just dismiss what I'm saying. *Think* about it."

My dick is soft now, but there's still a hard-on in my head—

the slap felt sexual—so I stand up and walk around the bench, as if I were actually thinking about what she said. And maybe I should. This has the feel of a breakthrough conversation. There's something good on the other side of it. Sex maybe.

I sit back down, ready to be reasonable, my anger fading like a cramp.

Calliope says, "It's like you need me to like you as much as *you* like you, and that's not easy to do."

"Not fair."

"But do you know what I mean?"

"I'm hard on myself, and I don't mind you being hard on me, as long as you think I'm great, and a lot of times it doesn't feel like you do. You're so intent on not being a little lady standing by your man—"

"But you're *not* my man. That's the point. I mean, you're right. I'm too critical sometimes. I know that. But it's not because you're my man; it's because I don't know *what* you are. I'm trying to keep some distance. It feels safer when there's hostility."

"I know. We hide behind the tension."

"I hate it. It's so . . ."

"Stupid."

"Undeveloped."

"Junior High."

She mock-screams, her hands on her head.

"But there's no tension now," I say.

She looks at me. "No."

"And it's nice," I say.

She smiles, and I have to kiss her—it's kill myself or kiss her—so I lean in, telling myself, go slow, slow is better. Her lips are like pillows. It's nice, the kiss, I think it's nice. I put my hand on her cheek, and that's the best part, her soft skin.

When it's over, we both lean back. I should say something. I should look at her and say something. I'm looking at New Jersey.

"I didn't love those empanadas," I say.

"I could tell. But you know what? I didn't care."

We both laugh, the humor elusive and perfect, and then I'm on top of her, kissing her neck, trying not to fall off the bench, people rolling and walking by.

"Imagine if *we* did that," a gay voice says.

We smile with our lips touching, then untangle ourselves and sit up. She buttons her shirt, which I must have unbuttoned. I got lost there for a moment, which is unheard of for me these days, getting lost. Penis, without underwear to impede it, is pushing up painfully against my pants.

"This is a surprise," she says, her chin pink from the scratch of my stubble.

"Yeah, no one could have predicted this." Cool guy, playing it down.

She pokes me in the side. "The bad news is, we need to get back."

"What we need to do is go to my apartment," I say without thinking, and it feels good, as good as anything we just did.

"I've got volunteers coming in."

"They know what to do. You've taught them well."

"All right." She hunches over, her elbows tight to her sides, and rubs her palms together. "Let's do it."

Charles Street is beautiful, so beautiful it makes me want to kiss Calliope. I grab her shirt and she inhales when I pull her toward me. Her body is large and soft, something to get used to. She hooks her leg around me as I grab her ass, and we stumble and fall onto a car, setting off the alarm, which makes us run and laugh and kiss some more.

On the elevator, hugging her from behind, I'm thinking about what I managed not to think about back on the bench: my apartment. I did laundry yesterday, praise Allah, but it's still a stinky mess—more messy than stinky, I hope.

"I'm sorry to do this," I say, unlocking the door, vowing to rip my life up by the roots, "but could you wait out here for just a minute?"

"Come on, Ben. I know what to expect, and I don't care."

"Just give me a minute."

I feel despicable closing the door on her but when I take a look around I'm relieved I did. At least a freshening breeze is coming in through the window. My second good break is the mood-appropriate music in the stereo, Tom Waits's *Closing Time*, which I turn up to conceal the sound of me tossing crap onto a laid-out sheet. I put the bundle of crap in the closet, then spread the comforter on my bed, floating it down nicely.

Opening the door I fear that the hallway will be empty, but there she is, rocking heel to toe, her hands behind her. She kisses my cheek and walks in, going to great lengths, the sweetheart, not to take in her surroundings. But she does look at the clock, which is twenty minutes fast. "Your place," she says, sitting on my bed.

"Yup." I kick a pizza crust under the stove. "Does it smell?"

"Yeah, but not that bad. It smells like you."

"Can I get you anything?" I say, trying not to think about her comment.

"What do you got?"

"Beer, Nutterbutters, and frozen vegetable medley."

"You're a bachelor boy, aren't you," she says in a mock-sultry voice that makes my hard-on harder. "Come here." She lies back with her legs bent and spread. "Come here, you bad, bad bachelor boy."

Our shirts come off quickly, as does her bra, and it's nice, the nicest, that first feel of skin on skin. I love her skin. It occurs to me that I'm with Calliope—Calliope!—and the realization sends my mind racing to bad places, like the office. Like tomorrow. I yell out to my mind as it runs away: get back here, you little bastard! This doesn't work, of course; but kissing her stomach does, hearing her soft moans.

When I reach for her pants, she grabs my wrist, and I assume she's playacting again—first a vamp, now a prude—but no.

"Really?" I say.

"Is that okay?"

"Of course," I say, mostly relieved. I'd be in serious danger of a L'il Abner, Ethan's name for it ever since I told him about the artist's difficulties.

"I want us to go slow," she says.

"Isn't that what we've been doing?"

"Maybe that's why." She rubs me through my pants, the mixed message wishboning my brain. "Slow feels right, don't you think?"

"Yeah," I say, and it does. Calliope is the girlfriend I should have had all along, the sneakily hot girl I should have been making out with on her parents' couch instead of fingering sad girls in cars. It's as though I were starting all over again, doing it better, paying attention, drinking less, falling in love. Yeah, slow feels right.

She grabs the back of my head and kisses me deeply, her breasts hardening against me. Her hand goes down the back of my pants, which seems illegal given the laws she laid down. I pull away and stand up.

"What are you doing?" she says as I take off my pants.

"It's starting to hurt."

"You poor lamb." She looks at the clock.

"You can keep your clothes on. Doesn't mean I have to."

"You're totally naked."

So I am. I'm totally naked and looking down at Calliope Berkowitz. Smallish nipples. I like them, though, them and everything else, all of her.

"I'm in bad shape," I say, sounding more self-conscious that I feel. I squeeze my handle, a good three inches of fat.

"I like your body. And I like that." She points at my penis, which is staying hard. "It's going to feel good when you put it in me."

"You can't do that. That's not fair. If you want to talk like that, you're going to have to help me out here."

"No way. You're not getting that kind of pleasure if I'm not."

"You could be getting all the pleasure you want."

"Oh, is that right, Mister Man?" she says through a giggle. "If I took off my pants I could get *all* the pleasure I want. All my fantasies would come true."

"That's right, woman." I step up onto the bed and straddle her, my feet by her knees.

"What would you do to me?"

"You don't want to know."

"Oh, yes I do."

"I'd do whatever I want. I'd take what I want, because it's mine."

"Oh yeah?" she says, caressing her stomach with one finger.

"You better believe it," I say, deciding to try this for real. I've certainly had enough preparation. "No foreplay. You don't need it. With other guys you needed it. Not with me. Actually, everything is foreplay; it never stops. You get wet when you hear my voice on the phone. I walk in the door, it's trickling down your thigh."

I have to fight off a giggle, but her face is as serious as it gets. She's staring up at me and gently pinching her nipples. "And no talking, not tonight, dear. Talking's fine. We're good at it. But it doesn't satisfy you. Talking is *not* what makes you feel beautiful and talking is *not* what makes you feel understood."

Now she has one hand flat on her stomach and the other clutching her belt. Trying to keep them out of her pants? "I take my time. I have a whisky while you walk around, pretending you're not aching. Always pretending, aren't you? Like an insecure girl. I tell you to take off your clothes and you strip with almost embarrassing speed. I sniff your panties, I put them in my mouth as I circle your beautiful trembling body. You're cold and hot and desperate, and now I'm turned on, now we're in this together."

I start stroking myself, and Calliope's mouth opens, but not in objection. "It's amazing how hard you make me. I can't believe I get to do what I'm about to do. No, actually, I *can* believe it. There's part of me, the best part, that thinks I deserve this . . . I don't kiss you, not once. I bite your neck, then bend you over. I take off my clothes. I sip from my drink. You're leaning against the wall and waiting, the anticipation physically hurting you. You could not be more ready, but still, I'm a little too thick at first—"

Calliope smiles, liking the thought of my girth. Or amused by it. I smile back at her, and she blushes. "You're filled up yet you want more. You're greedy, greedy and spoiled. I know exactly what you want, and I can't resist giving it to you. I confess: I want you to love me. I want it so badly it terrifies us both. I put two fingers right there and my thumb in there and the vibrations start immediately, delicious vibrations emanating from the deepest part of you, the very center. That *feeling*, growing, growing, growing, growing—I pause when you're on the edge and in that moment you'd kill me if you didn't need me . . . then I release you. You're free, you're flying, you're in love."

There's no fantasy in my mind, no image, only Calliope, real, so real, perfect, perfect, perfect as it falls on her neck and chest and stomach and hand and leg.

Then we're silent. The smile I try doesn't get one from her. Her hand creeps up to the side of her breast and with her thumb she rubs a drop, a single drop, into her skin.

"Are you okay?" I say, sitting down, putting my feet on the floor.

"Yeah."

"Really?"

"I think I liked it."

"I got a little carried away."

"Can I have some tissues?"

"Of course."

Of course not, in fact, since I don't have any, and toilet paper seems wrong, so I grab a towel from the bathroom. I'd like to wipe her off myself, but her body language suggests she doesn't want me to touch her, ever again.

"Are you sure you're okay?" I say.

"No," she says, wiping her chin. "That was pretty . . . intense."

"Good intense?"

"Please stop asking me questions."

"Okay. So much for going slow."

"Yeah." She shakes her head, her eyes huge. "We should have just had an anal sex threesome, then moved up to that." She reaches for her bra, her shirt.

"Don't tell me you're leaving."

"It's four o'clock."

"That's twenty minutes fast. It'd be weird if you left this minute."

"I've got to. You do, too."

"I'm not going back there. Fuck that place. I want to stay here and talk to you. I'm sorry if I freaked you out."

"You didn't. Maybe you did, I don't know."

"I got caught up in the moment."

"You think?" She slides to the edge of my ridiculous, collegiate bed. "We can talk about this on the subway if you get dressed."

"How can you go back there? From this to that."

"I've got volunteers."

"Tell them to go home and do something useful."

I stand up too quickly and my head pulsates like a lighthouse light; my vision goes black, then blurry. I want to scream.

"What about that gay speech today?" I say, my sight clearing, but not enough. I guess it's dark in the room. "I wrote that piece of trash."

"I thought it was pretty good."

"Then you weren't listening." She glares at me as she buckles her shoe. I'm standing here: naked, limp, and cold. But my brain is the real problem, as always. Frayed is how I feel, rubbed raw, and I should tell her that. "Do you know what Schecter's doing for Hakim Mohammed? Nothing! He's going to have blood on his hands."

"You're blowing it out of proportion."

"Yeah, it's not a matter of life and death."

"I mean, it's not like Schecter could save him."

"He needs to try. But he's doing nothing because he's afraid. Democrats are so afraid. They're like kids who are bullied so much they become bullies. And you know what? Jews are especially susceptible. Because of our history, we think it's death to not look strong, and we're getting weaker as a result, morally and spiritually weaker."

"I've never heard you talk about Jews as *we*." She walks out of the bathroom, where she was checking herself in the mirror and smelling my stink.

"You've probably never heard me talk about anything as *we*."

She stops moving, looks at me. Now is when she's supposed to say something along the lines of, we could be a we. "Would you mind putting on some clothes?"

"Yeah, sure." I bend over and grab a pair of jeans that somehow avoided both the laundry bag and the giant bundle in the closet. "But please don't go. Give me a minute. Hear me out on this. You think I expect too much from Schecter, and you're right. There are political realities, and the issues are complex. There's grayness and uncertainty and compromise. Of course there is. Welcome to the world, Ben Bergin, right? But there are exceptions, times when the truth is clear and beautiful. We're going to kill a guy who's probably innocent. We all know that's wrong, right? If we agree on nothing else, can't we all agree on that? Can't we? I mean *everyone*, you and I and everyone else?"

"I don't know," she says, the softness of her voice making me realize that I was yelling. "Hakim Mohammed isn't exactly at the top of my mind right now."

"Right," I say, feeling icky and loud, like the TV news.

We walk to the door, taking separate routes. She turns and looks at the kitchen: sink full of dishes, empty cabinets, trashcan surrounded by trash. She's wondering what she's gotten herself into, and if she can get herself out.

"You're really not coming with me?" she says.

"No." I carefully touch her shoulder. When I kiss her, she keeps her arms at her sides and barely moves her lips.

I watch her walk down the hall to the elevator. Before she steps in she looks at me. I can see the pink rawness of her chin, the wound left by my hard mean beard.

"You're not coming back today at all?"

I shake my head. "Tell Tod I got food poisoning from the empanadas."

24

I'm at my desk, waiting for the meeting with the pollster, when it occurs to me, with more force than ever, that my life might not turn out okay. I could end up in a homeless shelter or a mental hospital or a morgue. The net that's supposed to catch me when I fall is gone. It was probably never there. I got up four times to drink Jack, hoping it would dull my thoughts about Calliope. Around four-thirty, on the fire escape, I half-convinced myself that although she was disturbed, she was also moved and turned on; she just needed time to digest her feelings. Or, translated into Tod's brutal wisdom: chicks dig shit like that.

But this morning I stopped by the volunteer room. Despite her best efforts, she wasn't herself. Seeing her that uncomfortable was like seeing an animal in a too-small cage—excruciating, all the more so because I'd put her there. As she crossed her arms over her breasts and struggled through small talk, I feared that I'd lost her.

The meeting, not Calliope, is what should be on my mind. It will determine the course of the rest of the campaign. If I'm going to have any effect on what Schecter does about Mohammed, I need to speak out today.

My plan is to power through the morning with coffee and Jack, the bottle of which is in my bottom drawer. I'll make a stand in the meeting, then make things right with Calliope. Gas dribbles out of me, and the smell is a monstrous caricature of empanadas. I don't have the energy to be embarrassed and besides, Jen and Jenny—my sandwich-mates in those innocent days before the great semen storm of Ninety-eight—will assume that the stench is Gerry's creation.

I pour Jack in my coffee and proceed to the conference room, where Peter Meltzer, the pollster, is walking around the table, handing out copies of the results. These stapled stacks tell our fortune, and we grab them hungrily.

"I'll walk you through," Meltzer says. Well-built in a wiry way and handsome beneath his glasses, Meltzer is one of those nerds that makes you wonder why nerds don't simply choose not to be nerds.

"Forget the walkthrough," Wes says as Paul sits down. "What's the upshot?'"

"Dead even," Meltzer says. "Senator Washburn's picking up white men, age twenty-eight to forty-five. It's difficult to say why."

No one speaks. Everyone is waiting for someone to make a joke about Washburn picking up white men. Too easy, I guess, even for me.

"Here's what I can say," Meltzer says. "Among white men, he's beating us bad on 'shares your values.' He's up eight points to seventy-eight, fourteen better than us."

"It's Clinton, that dog," Tod says, as if he didn't wholeheartedly support the President's policy on cocksucking.

"Unlikely," Meltzer says. "Frankly, gentlemen, there's no obvious explanation."

All of us look down at the numbers, hoping they can tell us how to pick up white men. "Is it Hakim Mohammed?" I say as sweat flows from me in a single pulse, as though I were a squeezed sponge.

"Unlikely," Meltzer says. "It's not a huge issue, and this group doesn't see much of a difference between the candidates on this."

"So Washburn's attacks aren't working?" Tod says.

Melzter shakes his head. "The waters are good and muddy."

"Could it be guns?" Paul says.

"No," Meltzer says.

"Goddamn," Wes says. "I thought I'd seen it all. Is this not New York? I ask you, are we not in New York?"

"The Big Apple," Danny says with a stoner's smile. Maybe it's no surprise that these overworked, self-involved men haven't noticed the change in Danny, but he's a different person now.

"Or are we in Alabama?" Wes says.

"Spit it out," Schecter says. It's the first time I've heard Schecter snap at Wes, and for some reason it encourages me. I take a swig of my drunkard's brew.

"Devin Pierce," Wes says. "Whitey liked the fact that Washburn didn't want his daughter dating a black guy."

"Unlikely," Meltzer says. "This group—"

"Well, what are they going to say?" Wes says. "That it's fine and dandy that Washburn's a racist slob? This is a classic 'shares your values' issue."

"It's also a classic case of backfire," Tod says, taking a shot at his mentor. I ought to be able to use all this tension to my advantage.

"Perhaps," Meltzer says. "There are some things polls can't measure."

Like the darkness of the human heart, is what I want to say. But I don't say anything. No one does. The acknowledgment that polls aren't omnipotent has put us at a loss.

"We can try to win them back," Meltzer says, "or we can go after our base. There's room to move with our core supporters."

"Not with Jews," Schecter says.

"No. We're at fifty-seven and that's as good as it gets with

Washburn doing everything short of buying a summer home in the West Bank."

I give Meltzer the laugh he wants, figuring I'll need a friend once the debate begins. It's close now, just two or three steps away.

"Blacks," Melzter says. "Too many are undecided and the ones we've got aren't committed enough. We need to excite them."

"Let's rub them," I say, trying to get in a rhythm.

Meltzer says, "There was a question asking who people would like on the ballot who isn't. Forty percent of blacks said Billy Record. We could sure use his endorsement."

I revise the first line of my presentation.

"Which brings us back to Mohammed," Tod says.

"No," Paul says. "*God*, no."

My turn. "Record or no Record, we can win on this. We can rally blacks without alienating anyone who might vote for you. We turn it into a discussion about values. We talk in the most basic terms: about fairness, about the importance of getting the guy who did it, about the horror of executing the guy who did-n't. We should *welcome* this."

Silence. A head-scratching kind of lull, as if I had spoken Serbo-Croatian. It's clear that my cute little rise is over, and if you're not gaining power you're losing it. Fine with me. The cheap high of Schecter's approval is one of the things that's kept me here. I've been hanging around this slum, looking for an occasional fix.

"If it were that simple," Tod says, "we wouldn't be having this conversation."

"This is about Record," Wes says. "We need to decide before tomorrow morning."

Everyone except me seems to know what happens tomor-row. I ask Tod with my eyes and he mouths, "Parkside," mean-ing that Schecter's appearing at Parkside Church up near Columbia, which has a big lefty congregation and a black min-ister who's emerged as a leader in the Free-Hakim movement.

Attention focuses on Schecter, even more than it was. He's

rocking and tonguing his teeth, as though trying to free a string of steak.

He leans forward, looks at Tod. "Find out what he wants."

"You cannot do this," Paul says. "It'll look like a pander."

"He's got a point," Tod says.

"We can deal with that," Wes says. "We talk to Record, work out a statement we can both live with. Then I make sure Arnie gets asked about it today, and he just puts it out there, nice and breezy. When reporters call here, y'all play dumb, even act pissed, like Arnie went off half-cocked. Doesn't look like a pander if it's not planned."

"It's wrong," Paul says, a minority of one. But he's had a good run; it's the first time since the Primary that he's found himself on the wrong side of the politics. "Look, I can accept if we change our tone on Mohammed. I'm starting to have doubts about the case myself, but I cannot accept us groveling to Billy Record."

"Easy, Paul," Wes says.

"I won't allow it," Paul says.

Schecter generates a laugh, the one he emits on cable news shows whenever a Republican congressman, always his "good friend," makes a joke about the two of them finally agreeing on something. "You won't allow it?"

"You don't want to give in to that hustler," Paul says, staring at Schecter. Paul's passion is impressive. He's bringing more energy to the debate than I did, and this was supposed to be my great stand. I used to think Paul was a player, but he's more of a dreamer than I am. I wish he'd shut up. "He's bringing you down to his level."

Schecter stands up, his face a quiver of tension, and walks toward Paul. Meltzer flees to a corner of the room, as though fearing schrapnel. Paul's staring straight ahead, past my shoulder. If he'd look at my eyes, I'd try to give him strength, not that I have much to give.

Schecter stands over Paul, looking down at him, his tie lapping his Afro. "I've made my decision," he says, and keeps walking.

"I disagree with your decision," Paul says.

Schecter stops in the doorway, turns. Funny things are happening on his face. When his nostrils aren't flaring, his left eye is almost closing. An alternating double twitch, turning his face into a Picasso painting. Anyone else but Paul would already be unemployed. Schecter doesn't dare rip into his only black advisor this close to an election.

But The Man is nothing if not disciplined. He breathes in and out in a way that reminds me of *her*, the woman I'm not thinking about. Then he walks over to Paul, who's sporting a nostril-flared look of his own. Schecter puts one hand on the table and the other on the back of Paul's chair. "Hey Paul," he says in his impatient-daddy voice. "You're going to be quiet now, okay?"

I'm relieved that Paul doesn't say okay and that Prick doesn't ask him to. Schecter walks away energized, perhaps pleased to discover a politically correct method of exercising power. And it works for Latinos too!

Paul and I are the last ones in the room. He's still looking past me.

I envision myself comforting him, and then I'm doing it: I'm walking around the table and putting my hand on his shoulder. I try to think of something to say, then decide that saying nothing isn't bad at all.

"I'm all right," Paul says, and he seems it, his voice as sturdy as ever. "Apparently he's under the impression he can intimidate me. That man has no idea what I've dealt with in my life."

"He's a jerk."

Paul twists at the waist and looks up at me, making eye contact, not adoring what he sees. "*You* got what you wanted."

"Doesn't make him less of a jerk."

Taking an early lunch break, I go down to the street, and the noise makes me regret not sneaking a hit of Jack. I walk down the block and into the lawyer bar. Ordering a drink, I magnanimously forgive myself for buying something that I have upstairs.

The lawyers are filing in, with their briefcases and plea bargains and jadedness. Chuck Nagorski, the *News* reporter, is here, drinking his whisky. I'm introducing myself before I have a chance to get nervous. "We spoke on the phone a few months ago," I say.

"Okay," he says, pretending to remember. "Right." He gestures to the stool next to him, and I sit down, comforted by his comfort; the man seems to be an adept bar-sitter.

"I was wondering: did you cover the Hakim Mohammed case?"

"Sure did, and I've been covering the latest stuff, too."

"What do you make of it?"

He smiles. His face is lined, but neatly: straight, symmetrical creases. "Is this for your professional or personal interest?"

"Both."

He lights a cigarette and hack-coughs on his first drag; the man is no less interesting for being a type. The only thing that doesn't fit is his voice; it's not the chainsaw you'd expect. "I'm surprised by all the holes. The case seemed pretty solid at the time, although in retrospect, maybe it was a little too solid, a little too neat for a killing that was so messy and chaotic."

"You mean the whole crack house scene?"

"Yeah, you've got all these messed up people lying around, passed out and drugged up and everything else. I wouldn't be surprised if no one, including Mohammed himself, knows exactly what happened. Yet you had this parade of witnesses basically singing the same tune. But maybe it was all kosher, I just don't know."

"This is probably naïve of me, but I have trouble believing the DA would railroad a guy with all that publicity. I mean, it was one of the first capital cases."

"The second, to be exact. I don't know if they *railroaded*

him"—he smiles, making fun, I'm guessing, of my TV-lingo—
"but I do know that all that publicity and scrutiny wouldn't stop
them. Internal pressures take over. They always do. I don't care
if it's small-town Texas or New York. A cop was killed, and they
needed a conviction. They had a guy holding the murder
weapon and a bunch of guys saying he did it. Maybe the case
wasn't strong, but maybe it was the strongest one they had.
Let's just get a conviction, and we'll worry about the indignant
editorials in the *Times* later on."

"Right," I say, wondering why I don't sit here and drink with
this guy every day. "Can I buy you drink?"

"You most certainly can."

"One more question. I guess this one is off the record."

"Uh-oh. Getting serious on me now."

"I'm wondering how much Schecter knew about the case
from the beginning."

"You're asking me questions about *your* boss. And the
answer is, I have no idea. I'm sure he'd want to know what was
going on. Cop was killed in his district."

"And he'd have the means of finding out."

"I imagine so. Politicians have a way of getting what they
want. Of course, the DA's office is supposed to be hush-hush,
but if someone, including Coyne himself, got a call from
Schecter, I don't know how circumspect they'd be."

Michael Coyne, Brooklyn's longtime DA. "Are Coyne and
Schecter friends?"

"Friends, I don't know, but they certainly know each other.
If the world's small for the rest of us, it's a friggin' garbanzo
bean for power people."

★ ★ ★

I usually hit a rut in the middle of the afternoon, a pothole, but
this is a canyon, a cliff, and I'm falling. Lunch was a joke. I
resolved to turn my life around by eating a salad, as if roughage
might compensate for alienating Calliope. But in the deli I got

nervous that I wouldn't enjoy a basic salad, so I loaded up my plastic container with three kinds of animal. And what exactly is Thousand Island? Nothing healthy, I know that much. It's like soft-serve ice cream, spicy soft-serve with lumps. What *are* those lumps? Are they the islands? This country's got problems. So do I. Could I have a plastic container of chewy animal slathered in spicy soft-serve? Because I'm hoping to turn my life around. Five or six bites in, I stuffed the whole nine-dollar tragedy into the trash as vomit rose in my throat, heating up and flavoring my breath.

You'd think I'd be doing better after the victory of sorts in the meeting. But this is about Calliope. I guess it always has been.

I stopped by the volunteer room after lunch. She was divvying up a little box of chocolates with Eileen. I stood there, waiting for her to look up while she waited for me to walk away. Finally, she relented, and the expression on her face made my stomach seize up. I know thousands of her faces; this one was new: pleasant and closed, a face for a non-intriguing acquaintance, maybe your dad's tax guy, someone you don't want to know or be known by.

I should have gone back to the office with her. Rookie mistake, fucking asshole. As for the dirty deed itself? I'm not sure. At least I made a move. Maybe I went too far, but after years of not going far enough, I think I have more pride than regret.

The longer we go without discussing what happened, the larger it will become. But she's obviously not going to initiate a conversation and I'm sitting here, burping up gummy chicken and bits of island.

Tod walks in, and I'm glad to see his shiny happy mug; it allows me to imagine that I'm okay, merely bad, same as always. He sits on my keyboard, and a line of g's goes streaking across my screen. Bony ass.

"Couldn't work it out with Record," he says. "Piece of shit wanted too much."

"So we're doing nothing?"

"Status quo the rest of the way. It's better."

"No, it's not."

"You look awful."

"I'm sick," I say, not lying. Maybe not physically sick but I'm every other kind: heartsick, soul-sick, sick of this smarmy, bony-assed motherfucker smiling at me.

"You stink," he says.

"You suck."

"You need sex."

I consider telling him about yesterday, earning his cheap validation, but that's a line I must, must, must not cross.

"That's horny juice coming out of you," he says. "It's precome."

"That's funny, you're funny."

"I'm serious."

"I hate you."

He walks away laughing and stops to chat up Jen and Jenny: banter that the ladies seem to enjoy even though his "Hey there" is more lurid that anything I've ever said.

This room doesn't have windows. I've worked for a year in a room without windows. The roof is what I need—fresh air and a cigarette—but I'm afraid of running into her.

I kneel down, pull out the Jack, and suck from the bottle for eight seconds. I exhale slowly, the way she taught me.

★

Schecter Will Keep Saying Nothing About Mohammed

Today Congressman Arnie Schecter decided once and for all to say nothing about the case of Hakim Mohammed. For a while today it appeared that Schecter would release a statement in exchange for Billy Record's endorsement, but negotiations fell through. "It's better this way," stated Tod Wilcox, bony-assed commissar and head hard-on.

"No, it's not," replied Ben Bergin, stewing in sweat. But what,

Bergin asks himself, could Schecter say? In the meeting you claimed it wouldn't be political suicide to take a stand; on the contrary, you said we should welcome this. But do you really believe this, or are you just looking for another reason to hate both Schecter and yourself?

No. I think I believe myself. Well, let's see it, then. Let's see what Schecter should say. Put your words where your mouth is, prick. Okay. Here goes:

The murder of Officer Frank Zito has a special significance to me. It happened in the district I have represented for twenty years and Officer Zito worked out of a station house I know well. When doubts were first raised about the guilt of Hakim Mohammed, I was more than skeptical, I was angry. But recent developments have given me no choice but to reconsider. Another man, a convicted killer, has credibly confessed, and four of the five men who identified Mr. Mohammed as the killer have recanted their testimony. As a former assistant district attorney, I know something about prosecuting cases. If I were given this case as it now stands, I couldn't bring charges, much less win a conviction.

The doubt is beyond reasonable. Mr. Mohammed is entitled to a new trial.

I hesitate in releasing this statement only because it might add to the burden of Officer Zito's family. If it does, I'm sorry. But a cloud of doubt already hangs over the conviction. While I wouldn't presume to know how the family members feel, I'm confident that they would want that cloud removed.

If I know my opponent as well as I think I do, he will charge that I'm being soft on crime or coddling a cop-killer or some such nonsense. Let him. Most New Yorkers know that true crime-fighters ensure that the right person is punished. If tough on crime means executing someone who might be innocent, then we need a new definition of tough on crime.

New Yorkers—including this New Yorker—voted to reinstate the death penalty. It's an awesome power we have given the government, and in the sense that the government is all of us, we have given it to ourselves. With that power comes the responsibility to prevent tragic mistakes. Unless new facts come to light, we must not execute this man.

I read it over and over and over. Every time I feel a little calmer, more hopeful, transported. It's like escapist literature. Political Erotica.

The release gives me the strength to venture out into the hallway, which seems strangely short and low-ceilinged, as if I were visiting my old grade school. The coworkers I pass don't seem real. Why did I used to care what these people thought of me? I'm already forgetting them. I'm walking through a fuzzy memory. Only one coworker matters.

And she's not here. The volunteer room is dark, shut down for the evening. Somehow it got to be five forty-five. She left without saying goodbye, which she's never done. I could cry. I could puke.

There's light under Danny's door, and I walk in without knocking. He's smiling and alone. "Never wear a beret, no matter how cute you think it looks," he says, and holds up a magazine: Monica, sweet Monica. "It could come back to haunt you."

"Can you believe what's happening to this country?"

He holds up his hand like a traffic cop and shakes his head. Doesn't want to hear it. "What are you up to on this fine autumn evening?" he says.

"Fuming about our stance on Mohammed."

He raises his hands over his head and stretches, his neck shortening to nothing. "The other day I had pizza with mango on it. You ever heard of that?"

"What's your feeling about Mohammed?"

He smiles. "Float like a butterfly, sting like a bee."

"What are you *on*?"

"What are you talking about?"

"You know what I'm talking about."

"Go away. Go fume somewhere else."

"It's a fake escape, man."

"Yeah, well, it's the best escape I can manage right now."

"I hope you get out, Danny. As soon as the election's over."

He stares at me with those beleaguered eyes, wider than they were a month ago but more vacant. This look is real, though. It's Danny, piercing through the haze. He wants me to leave him alone, and that's what I do.

Everyone is still here, everyone but her. My coworkers are talking and typing, blissfully unaware of their insignificance.

From the research room comes her voice. I can't make out the words, but it's her deep tones, no question.

"There you are," she says when I walk in. Her normalcy makes me want to tilt my head back and laugh like a cartoon villain: Ha Ha Ha Ha Ha! She's sitting in *my* chair with her feet on *my* desk. The researchers, watching me, know something is off-kilter. They've been an attentive audience all these months.

"I thought you left," I say.

"I'm right here," she says with a not-so-normal smile. "Roof?"

We're silent all the way up the stairs and into our corner. The sky is almost dark, which seems wrong, but it's fall, isn't it? Summer gave way to fall and I didn't notice.

"Oh for fuck's sake," she says when my match goes out in the breeze. She pulls the cigarette from my mouth, lights it off hers, and sticks it back in my mouth. "I'm not sure where to begin. Yes, I am. I thought it was really fucked-up that you didn't come back to the office with me."

"I totally agree. I'm sorry. It was wrong."

"That's it?"

"No . . . I mean, what do you want?"

"I want to know why you did it. I was in utter disbelief when I got on the subway."

"Right. Okay. First of all, my hatred for this place is genuine. But that wasn't a big part of it. Forget that. Forget I said that. I got the sense you didn't want me with you."

"That doesn't matter."

"No, it doesn't, in terms of the wrongness of it. Nothing I say here should be taken as a justification, okay? I'm just explaining. Without thinking enough about it, I assumed that you wanted some space. I mean, there's no question that if you had said, Ben, I'd—"

"I shouldn't have to say that."

"No," I say, resisting the urge to say she's being irrational. Has my ugly maleness turned her into a normal woman? But I'm not exactly shining myself, coherence-wise. "I'm trying to explain what bad stuff in my brain might have been at work: callousness or insecurity or whatever. You felt vulnerable and alone, that's my fault, but I felt vulnerable and alone, too. Believe me, I wanted nothing more than to touch you, but you didn't want that."

"That's not true. I think holding your hand on the subway might have been pretty nice. At least I wouldn't have cried the whole way back."

Oh. I made her cry, and she's almost crying now.

This is the part I'm not good at, and it's almost everything: being depended on, feeling for two. Usually I want to run. But I don't now. I want to stay. I want to stay.

"I feel awful," I say. "Really, I'm . . . " She looks at me, seeing, I hope, what I can't seem to put into words. "That's not how I normally am. It was an unusual situation."

"Now there's something we can agree on. At some point I might want to talk about some of the things you said."

"We're going to parse my words?"

"They were revealing."

"I'm already embarrassed."

"Good." I'm hoping this is humor, but when I look at her I have doubts. She's smoking like I've never seen her, furiously, the paper burning like paper. "All I really want to say right now is that I was overwhelmed and freaked-out and I think you should have been more sensitive to that. I made it clear I wanted to go slow, and it felt like you intentionally did the opposite. I felt pretty un-taken care of."

"I didn't *intentionally* do anything. I got caught up and turned-on and everything else. I was just *being*, you know? Expressing myself, and I think that's a good thing."

"What, you want credit?"

"Maybe I do, a little. I think it was basically a healthy, human thing, and I think you felt that, too. You started it and you were with me for at least most of it."

"*Some* of it, yes. It was sexy, I admit. It's confusing. I'm confused. It's hard for me to look at it objectively because I'm pissed about what happened afterwards. Jesus, Ben, you said all these . . . things. After saying next to nothing for months, you said all these amazing, intense things, except you didn't really say them."

"I *did* say them."

"I don't want to talk about that."

"Maybe we should."

"No, not now. I'm too confused and unsure."

"Unsure about what?"

"Everything, us."

"You're saying you don't want us to be anything?"

"I'm saying I don't know."

"Not even friends?"

"Of course we're going to be friends."

"But nothing more?"

"I don't know."

"We have this intense, confusing, and at least partly amazing time together, and now we're just going be nothing?"

"I don't know, I don't know, I don't know. What part of that don't you understand?"

"What part of that expression don't I hate?"

"Fuck you."

"All this time I've been beating myself up for being a pussy. But you're the scared one. You're a fucking coward."

She backs up, hands raised. "I really don't want to be yelled at, and you don't want to be yelling."

"Don't leave," I say, too softly for her to hear.

She walks backwards all the way to the door and when she get there she says, "I need time to think, Ben. Give me that, please."

★ ★ ★

The workers, impossibly, are still working. They're campaigning, politicking, fighting the mediocre fight.

My roommates are talking about somebody's something on the environment. The environment. It's time to stop pretending I care much about it. I'll be maggot-food by the time we really fuck it up.

I poke my spacebar and when my computer wakes up it shows me the dream release. It's still good.

There are more than a hundred reporters on our list. Press releases go straight from my computer to their fax machines. I remove the first three paragraphs, leaving only the statement I wrote for Schecter. It's just a few key-taps away from going out.

My chest tightens at the thought, squeezing my lungs, and I race-walk out of the room. I duck into the kitchen and close the door, hiding from my release.

"There a problem?" Paul says. He's sitting at the table, peeling an orange.

"No," I say, and pull the door open.

"They'll find you eventually." He smiles at this, a little joke with himself. He's peeling the skin off in one thin piece.

"You must be pleased: no Billy Record."

"Yeah, that's good news. I should have known he'd want too much." He finishes peeling, then pulls the orange into halves. "Like I said, I could live with us getting involved in the Mohammed debate, but not for the purpose of kissing up to

Billy Record, no matter how many votes he'd deliver. You can lose by winning." He chews, his lips balled up. "Umm. This is a fine piece of fruit, you want some?"

"No thanks. The meeting doesn't seem to have fazed you."

"Nah, man. I don't have time to be fazed."

"Let me ask you a question." He looks up, flattering me with the intensity of his gaze. "What Schecter did in the meeting, do you think it was racist?"

"Oh, I don't know. I suppose that if I analyzed it I could come to some disturbing conclusions, but I'm not one of those blacks who collect grievances. If you go looking for racism, God knows you'll find it. Like I said, I don't got the time."

"But I imagine that blacks usually aren't looking for it, they just feel it."

"Of course. I've felt it plenty of times and I'll feel it plenty more. I'm a black man in America. But today? No, I didn't feel it. I thought he was condescending. More importantly, I thought he was wrong. And I told him so."

"You sure did. It was impressive."

He brings his head almost to the table in an exaggerated nod. "My preacher always says, 'You are what you believe.'"

"See you, Paul," I say, feeling both emboldened and nervous.

"Be good, Bergin."

I stop by Tod's office and knock on his open door. He looks at me over the sports page. "I'm leaving," I say.

"Tomorrow we start hitting Washburn again; on affirmative action or gun control, something, anything, I don't know. We need to stir things up."

"Sounds good," I say in my best Maine accent.

My computer has gone to sleep again. The dream release is right there, behind the darkness. I put on my jacket. I force myself to think because it's what you're supposed to do at a time like this. This is big, and there's no going back.

I tap my computer awake. Now all I have to do is cue up the release and hit send.

I cue up the release and hit send.

I sit calmly as the release rides invisible wires to newsrooms all over the state. Then I shut down the computer and drift into the hallway, nervous only because I'm not.

25

I burst awake, my mind spinning in search of the reason.

Oh, yeah. *That.*

Sweatpants, boots, a trench coat, and I'm jogging down the stairs, hating myself for half-hoping that the newspapers didn't pick up the story—a possibility given that I didn't hear from anyone last night. I stayed up late, drinking red wine that tasted like salad dressing and waiting for the phone to ring. Some of the reporters who got the release would have called Tod or Danny, and I can't believe my bosses would wait until the morning to fire me. Maybe there was a technical glitch. Maybe no one believed the release was real.

The sidewalk is crowded, morning having already begun. I stayed up *very* late.

Some cock-fucker-prick honks his horn as I jog across the street to the deli. Nothing on the front page of the *Times*—there wouldn't be, though—but there it is, front page of the metro section: "Schecter Calls for New Trial for Death Row Inmate." The story includes meaty chunks of my release and a quote from Danny: "The congressman did a lot of soul searching on this."

Danny's quote turns my thinking around, makes me wonder if they're going to choose to take this in stride. Perhaps they prefer the neatness of a changed position to the sloppiness of a "disgruntled-employee" imbroglio. This, I suppose was my "plan."

The other papers include similar stories, and there are two editorials on the subject, one lauding Schecter's "political courage," the other blasting his "shameless interest group pandering."

The guy in front of me in line buys the *Times*, and the thought of all the people reading my words unleashes a stomach-tingle of excitement.

The afterglow of the excitement shines a new light on my apartment. This is the humble den of an iconoclast, a visionary, a fryer of big fish. I'm engaged in a struggle to save a man's life. I'm supposed to open my mail, too?

Calliope catches up with me in the shower; last night she, not the release, dominated my thoughts, my mind ping-ponging between anger at her and regret.

And now, as news of the release makes its way through the office, she and I have something else to deal with. She does, anyway.

I put on black jeans, black boots, an olive pullover shirt, and an old flannel-lined jean jacket—my most flattering outfit according to the rankings Ethan gave me during one of our teenage-girl-like and/or deeply gay conversations.

Where do I want to get fired? No one with the authority to give me the ax will be in the office this morning; they're all at Parkside Church for the speech, which starts in just a few minutes. I could go into the office and wait for them to come to me. Or I could go listen to Schecter elaborate on my dream release. That's no choice at all. My head feels like a blood blister. Never again with the vinaigrette wine.

★ ★ ★

The crowd on the steps of the church confuses me: am I early or late?

On time, it turns out. This is spillover from the church, and Reverend Coles is still speaking. The crowd is immense and growing, six, seven, eight people pulling up on the sidewalk behind me. I'm reluctant to assume that Schecter's brave stand on Mohammed is solely responsible for the buzz—surely you don't create this just by hitting *send*—but what else could it be? Thousands of people haven't packed into a church on a gray Wednesday morning to hear Schecter enunciate his plan for combating junk e-mail.

I feel self-conscious cutting in front of people, but no one seems to mind, and when I make it inside, a black woman in a hat with flowers growing out of it makes room for me against the back wall. Everyone is so friendly that I entertain the notion that they know I penned the release. Or maybe they just dig the outfit.

"I've known this man for quite some time," Reverend Coles says. "Never have I been more proud to call him my . . ."

I can't see the crew from the office and, assuming they're up front, they can't see me. But just to be safe I hunch down, making myself shorter than my flowered-hat friend. I don't want angry eyes on me during the speech. Afterwards, I'll let myself be seen. Give me the speech, pricks, then do what you want.

"Ladies and gentlemen," Coles says. "It's my pleasure to present to you the next senator from the state . . ."

The applause is thunderous, and it would be even without the organ-music backing. Everyone but the oldest and the youngest is standing and cheering. The crowd is probably two-thirds black and younger than I expected. Parkside is a genuinely mixed-race institution, the kind of place that defies you to be cynical within its walls. You can make fun of their hard-on for Jesus—and their silly hats—but that's about it.

Schecter pushes down on the air around him, pretending to try to quiet the applause. You're welcome, Senator. It was my pleasure. Don't mention it.

"Thank you, thank you, thank you, Parkside," he says, and one loud final cheer goes up before everyone settles down.

Schecter stares out at the crowd and squints. Spotting me? Could this all be an elaborate ploy to punish me? No, crazy thoughts. I need to get food in my system.

"I was planning to talk about my plans for economic development, but I guess y'all want hear about something else, now don't you."

The crowd claps, forgiving Schecter's lapse into black-talk. I'm inclined to forgive him too, since no white politician has ever mounted a pulpit in front of black people and resisted the urge. The first one who does deserves to be president.

"I appreciate your reception and the kind words of Reverend Coles, but all of you are being too generous. I simply did the right thing. And it's something of a sad statement when a politician doing the right thing is big news."

Much nodding and laughter: generous, indeed.

"I acknowledge, however, that it took a while for me to arrive at my decision. I talked it over with my staff and my family and my rabbi." Schecter casts his eyes skyward to let everyone know that his consultant on this matter is high-powered indeed. "It took more than a few late nights of soul-searching. I feared that this issue might divide this city I so dearly love. But the correct course of action became obviously and painfully clear to me one night last week. I was watching the news when my six-year-old granddaughter, Abigail, walked into the room."

Schecter bites his bottom lip while I try not to laugh. "I picked her up and put her on my lap, hoping she wouldn't look at the TV, which was running a piece on a serial killer. But she turned around and saw him before I could change the channel. 'Is he a mean man?' Abigail asked. It dawned on me that if my darling granddaughter had been pointing at Hakim Mohammed I could not have said yes. My decision was made."

"Even a child understands," says Flower Hat, clapping.

"*Especially* a child!" I say.

"Um-hmm, that's right."

"I came to the conclusion, ladies and gentlemen, that there would be nothing more divisive than a wrongful execution. But make no mistake: my opponent will try to use this issue to divide us. He will charge me with being soft on crime or coddling a cop-killer or some such nonsense. Let him. Senator Washburn, if you want to turn this into a debate about which one of us is tougher on crime, here's what I say to you. Bring . . . it . . . on."

The crowd rises to its feet again, clapping in rhythm but staying quiet enough to hear Schecter's words. My words.

"I have faith in New Yorkers. Senator Washburn thinks they're stupid. He thinks they're too stupid to realize that true crime-fighters make sure the right person is punished. He thinks they're too stupid to see that when you punish the wrong person, the real culprit goes free. Ladies and gentlemen, if tough on crime means executing a person who might be innocent, then we need a new definition of tough on crime."

I lead the clapping in my section, excited and chastened to realize that Schecter is improving on my words. The crowd's still standing.

"Now, I support the death penalty. I know a lot of y'all don't, and I respect that. But here's something we can agree on: we need to do everything in our power to ensure that tragic mistakes are not made."

"Amen," I dare to yell, and no one laughs at me.

"There's a chance that a man on death row is not guilty. *Think* about that." Schecter, obviously having a grand time, rubs his chin as if to show people what thinking looks like. Actually, he seems more genuine than usual, despite all the lies. He might just be capable of convincing himself that this was all his idea. "I'm afraid there's a tendency among some to say, 'Well, it's just one man.' Just . . . one . . . man. To those people, I say, what if that one man was your son or brother or husband or father? Unless new facts come to light, ladies and gentlemen, Hakim Mohammed must not, *will* not, be executed."

The cheers are the loudest yet. "Not on my watch!" Schecter says. An awful edit, but it won't sour the moment for me. This churchgoing crowd, accustomed to vocalizing, is generating stadium-like sound. Cupping my mouth with my hands and tilting back my head, I let loose a scream, which I enjoy so much that it turns into a cackle. I'm set to scream again when I realize that Flower Hat has her hands over her ears. "Sorry about that," I say, putting my arm around her.

"That's all right, child. Ain't nothing wrong with getting excited."

Reverend Coles keeps the applause going by pumping his fist. I let my back slide down the wall. I rest my elbows on my knees and close my eyes and just listen.

I try to absorb the applause. I'll need it in the hours and days to come, when fear and regret are trying to spin the story.

"I've got a few other topics I want to touch on," Schecter says as the cheering finally dies down. Using the still-standing crowd for cover, I sneak out the door and cut through the mass of people out front.

I walk toward the river, not knowing where I'm going. Or why I left the church. If I'm going to get fired, I might as well go ahead and get fired.

As I sit down on the bench by the river, I realize what I'm doing: trying to savor the moment, to get as much out of it as I can before other people ruin it. This is mine.

I light a cigarette, thinking it will help the savoring effort, but two puffs make me aware of my heart, that fragile organ, so I put it out. Food.

In a bagel place I get my standard order for special occasions: sesame with whitefish, cream cheese, and onion. The bagel's not just warm but hot, and I eat it walking.

The crowd in front of the church has grown to hundreds. Schecter and Tod are on the top of the steps, surrounded by microphones. "Yes," Schecter says. "I had just about made up my mind, but that moment with Abigail sealed the deal."

I move in close and stand behind a TV camera, not quite hiding. "Isn't this a matter for the courts?" yells a reporter, addressing an issue I should have covered. It might have been my dream release, but it was far from perfect.

"As you know," Schecter says, "the primary mandate of the courts is to address questions of procedure. Indeed, a court has already upheld the verdict because, it said, he got a fair trial. Now, perhaps the revelations about the eyewitness testimony will affect the appeals. But courts are not perfect. More to the point, various political players—from citizens' groups to the Brooklyn DA to policemen's associations to the NAACP—are involved in this debate. And the governor himself has the final word. It would be naïve in the extreme to think this is not a political issue."

Well done, my man. You and I might have made a good team. I finish my bagel and step to an open area of the sidewalk. It takes two seconds for Tod to spot me. I'm expecting him to run his finger across his throat—one of his favorite gestures—but he's just staring at me, looking more excited than angry.

Then Schecter sees me. He's answering a question, so there's not much room for a reaction; his eyes catch mine and widen just a trace.

I walk away, unnerved by their subdued response. It's got to be a power play of some sort; that's what they do, who they are. Maybe they're going to pretend the release was their idea and leave it at that. Maybe they don't want to fire me for fear I'll let the press know that I forced this position on them, and that the Abigail story is bogus.

Holy shit, I've got leverage.

I don't want leverage. I want Calliope.

"Come here, child." It's Mrs. Flower Hat, tearing into a packet of Kleenex. "Let me wipe that cream cheese off that handsome nose of yours." She pulls out a tissue and smiles. "What a glorious day!"

26

Bernice doesn't acknowledge my presence. But that's normal.

"She's at the Manhattan office," George Blue says when I walk into the volunteer room. "Don't look so sad, bro. She'll be back soon."

"How soon?"

"Not sure. You really like her, don't you?"

"Yeah."

"Then love her, bro. Life's a blink. Love that girl like there's no tomorrow."

When Lana says, "Ben Bergin, nice of you to join us today," I know that news of my mutiny has been contained. The higher-ups don't want anyone in the office to know the idea wasn't theirs. There's no proof it wasn't.

Which doesn't mean I'm not going to get fired. But in the short term I'm presented with the surreal option of going about my routine.

Shawn's practicing his thoughtful look, using the microwave as a mirror, or a TV screen. I pretend not to notice, and he

shows me the fruits of his rehearsal. He's pinching his chin, giving it a dimple.

"I've been doing some thinking," he says as I pour coffee
into the glass vase I've just decided to use as a mug.

"I doubt that."

"I've been ruminating and reflecting on Hakim Mohammed.
I've been asking myself some *serious* questions, Bee. And I
keep on ending up where I start out: even if the brother's guilty,
what right do we have to finish him?"

It seems his fake black consciousness has raised his consciousness. "Good question," I say, regretting that my release
didn't take dead aim at the issue.

My roommates are where I left them last night, in the middle
of a discussion about the environment. "That's a flower vase,
dipshit," Jen says.

A comeback's needed, but my brain gives me nothing good.
I settle for: "Then why is there coffee in it, poopdip?"

"Are you just getting here?" Jenny says.

"Yeah, I was at Parkside."

"Pretty amazing, hunh?" Jenny says. "We finally did something unconventional."

"It's risky," Gerry says, and pokes a calculator with his pinky.

"It's *right*," Jenny says, her pretty Asian face exhibiting no
signs of subtext.

"I agree," Jen says.

"Me, too." I take off my jacket, reluctantly breaking up the
outfit. I sit down, put my feet up, slurp coffee. So normal. So
strange.

They're either going to fire me and tell me to be quiet. Or
they're going to keep me on and tell me to be quiet. Either way
I'm quiet.

My phone rings. Something tells me it's a friend, one of the
many I've lost touch with, but it could be Mom or a reporter, so
I let my voicemail handle the call.

"Hey, Ben," Jenny says, and I swivel my chair around to see

her. "I was just out front talking to Danny—"

"Danny's back?"

"He's been here all morning. Anyway, your name came up—
I was making fun of you—and I think he wants to see you."

"You *think*?"

"He was hard to understand. I think he's finally cracking."

I breeze down the hall, relieved that it's happening. But
when I walk into Danny's office, my legs lose their weight; the
muscle and bone, all the hard stuff, it just goes. "Shut the door,"
he says without looking at me, without looking at anything.
Except for the black-red skin pinching his eyes, his face is yel-
lowish and moist, like swiss cheese left out of the fridge. He's
pulled his greasy hair up into an accidental pompadour.

"Are you okay?" I say.

"Okay? Am I okay? No, I am not okay. Okay I am not." From
a teapot he pours black goop into a shot glass. "Coffee?"

"No thanks."

He shoots the shot, then pours another. "I'm not even in the
same galaxy as okay. You want to hear a little story?"

"Yes?"

"Last night I was sitting here, minding my own business. I
was going to get out of here before eleven for a change. But
my phone rings, and it's McGrath from the *News* saying he's
blown away and can I tell him what went into the decision? I
do my best to act casual: 'Yeah, yeah, yeah, get back to you in
a minute.' I call up Tod—"

"Why didn't you call me?"

He looks at me, sort of. "Your phone's been disconnected."

"Oh, yeah." As if knowing about it makes me seem together.
And why do I care about seeming together for *this* guy?

"Tod said he was going to drag you out of bed and pummel
you with his one-iron, but I guess he didn't. Everyone knew it
was you, soon as they heard. Wes, Paul, Tod. All of us were here
last night. Even Schecter for a little while. He was screaming at
me like it was my fault." Danny's voice has gotten strangely

high-pitched, and he's tugging on his pompadour so hard that his eyebrows are bouncing. "Tod gets the release off the system, and we all agree it's best to go with it, since the feedback from reporters is great and backtracking could be fatal. My more immediate problem is that the elephant-dose of Valium and OxyContin I took in anticipation of getting out of here is kicking in, so I go to the bathroom and I make myself puke. It doesn't do any good, so I start in with the caffeine, 'cause Wes and I have to write the speech."

"It was good."

Somehow he makes his eyes narrower.

"I was there," I say. "Best speech in years."

"It gets to be about six-thirty, and we only have a couple sentences. Wes lights up a joint to get his creative juices going, and I have a hit, which doesn't help my head *at all*, but Wes loves it. He takes off his shirt and starts line-dancing or two-stepping or some Southern shit. He dictates to me while he dances."

"Fucking Wes," I say, missing him already. "The Abigail bit was priceless."

"You seem to think I care about the speech. I don't." He stands up, does the shot of mud. "I don't care about anything." He comes toward me in a stumble and puts his hands on my shoulders. "My wife's pregnant, Ben, and I don't care. I've got no feeling about that. None. I don't care. I don't care about anything. But here's what I don't understand, here's the mystery I'd care about if I cared about anything. I'm nervous all the time, scared. I'm so scared. But if I don't care about anything, what am I scared *of?*"

He buckles as tears come; the sob-burst almost knocks him off his feet.

I hug him. Out of love and guilt I hug my friend, holding my breath against his toxic stench. He's soft and warm, a leaking hot water bottle.

When he seems to have stopped crying, I gently push myself away. "Go home," I say. "Get some sleep."

"Sleep! Why don't I just go home and cure cancer?"

"Take a shower, then. Hug your wife. Just leave."

"I can't! I can never leave!" He points at his chest with his thumb. "I'm . . . the campaign . . . manager!" He turns to look at his desk, then looks down at his feet, as if confused about how he got from there to here.

"What are you guys going to do to me, Danny?"

"I don't know. And guess what?"

"You don't care."

He nods with his entire upper body and almost falls. He's gone into a trance. I help him back to his chair, then hustle out the door and down the hall to the volunteer room.

"She's not back yet," Blue says, and pulls down his shades to look at me. Danny did a number on my shirt: tears and mucus. Blue tosses me a bandana, and I wipe up what I can. "Keep the kerchief, bro. And I tell you what: the second she gets back I'll tell her to go see you, and you'll tell her how you feel. I don't think she knows."

"Okay," I say, wondering what I'd say. I'm still angry. I'm angry at her for being angry at me. And for being unsure. And, yes, for not loving our naked time together. I want to yell at her. Argue with her. I want to stay up all night arguing, then apologize and cry and fuck. Then sleep, Jesus fucking yes, sleep.

"Life's a blink, bro. A blink."

Back to my quasi-normal day, with Gerry, Jen, and Jenny speaking in numbers and acronyms. I'm too jittery to sit down, but I go back to my vase nonetheless. I take gulps even as I tell myself not to. Danny's pain has gotten inside me, but I'm not sure if it's making me feel stronger or weaker.

Gerry looks at the door.

I hope it's Calliope. I know it's not: something about the silence.

"Please excuse us, folks," Schecter says. "I'd like to have a chat with Mr. Bergin."

Jenny is lingering in the hallway, peeking in. "Please close that door, Ms. Kim," Schecter says, and when she does, it's the first time I've seen that door closed. I spread my legs, wanting a strong base.

He saunters over to me with his arms folded, looking at the floor. He nods at the couch, meaning for me to sit. I hesitate, not wanting to play the subordinate. But perhaps the decent thing to do at this point is to show a little deference.

I sit down, and he sits down practically on top of me, his elbow jabbing my rib. "You're gone," he says, looking straight ahead. "You're gone inside of fifteen minutes, and I mean gone. I wanted to do this myself, so that there's no misunderstanding. What happened is our secret. If you tell anyone, including anyone in the office, I ruin your life. Other than that, our business is done. Got it?"

I nod, strangely disappointed by the brevity and quiet of the interaction. "It was the right thing to do. And the smart thing."

He shoots me a look: squinty-eyed disgust. "That's not the point. I made a decision, and you betrayed me. You betrayed all of us." Then he's on his feet, walking away.

"You're going to win."

He stops, rubs the side of his neck. "You're damn right I'm going to win, because that's what I do, I win." He turns, his nostrils flared, and walks back. "But your despicable little ploy's made it tougher on me. You might be interested to know that at this very minute Washburn's holding a press conference with the Zitos."

"You don't care about that." I force myself to look at his face. "Didn't you hear what you said today?"

"You have no *fucking* idea what it's like to be me," he yells, spraying saliva into my eyes. But then he regroups, breathes. He's not going to explode because he doesn't want people to hear. And because he knows I want him to. "You think you made a choice, but you didn't. It's not a choice if you don't have to live with the consequences."

"I lost my job," I say to his belly.

"Big shit. *I'm* the one who has go to police funerals and get booed. *I'm* the one who has to question the quality of my police protection. I'm the one who'll get spit on and sworn at in white working-class neighborhoods. *I'm* the one who's going to get death threats. And I'm the one who, despite all this, will keep going, keep fighting, and, yes, win. Do you know how disgustingly easy it is to say the right things, believe the right things when you're holding forth at a fucking cocktail party? Being pure on paper is the easiest thing in the world. But how many people put themselves on the line? Not many, and certainly not you, so fuck you. Fuck you."

When I hear the door open, I look up. Schecter walks out past a cluster of eavesdroppers. "Jesus Christ," he says. "Doesn't anyone have any work to do?"

Time to pack. There's nothing I want to keep, but there's stuff I don't want people to discover. Under my desk I find a plastic bag filled with protein bars, which I bought months ago at my gym, the gym I went to twice. My hands shaking, I empty the bars onto my desk, thinking someone might want them, then rummage through my drawers.

"What are you doing?" Jenny says.

"Leaving."

"Why?"

"Philosophical differences," I say, realizing that there will be no grand exit for me. But there will be an exit, a gauntlet-walk.

I put the bottle of Jack in the bag, along with the remains of a roast chicken I stole from the fridge late Monday night and a pair of underwear, old tighty-whiteys I took off one morning because they were failing to contain my gonads.

I turn off my computer. Now there's nothing to do but leave.

"Did you get fired?" Jenny says, following me down the hall, Jen right behind her.

"I'm resigning."

"What'd you do?" Jen says.

My goal is to make it out the door with my dignity intact—and with the contents of my bag undiscovered. I forgot my jacket, the pillar of my outfit, and I can't go back, not with everyone watching. I thought I'd held up okay under Schecter's barrage, but he broke something, shattered something. There are shards of glass in my chest.

Wes is in the doorway of Tod's office. Behind him Tod is casually swinging a golf club, jolly as ever. Does he respect what I did, the audacity of it? In any case, he's not interested in laying into me. Wes signals for me to come closer so that no one in the crowd will hear. His eyes are bloodshot. "What you did was wrong, Benny. And that is a word that doesn't emerge from my mouth very often."

I manage not to apologize, and keep walking.

Calliope's standing in the doorway of the volunteer room, her workers clustered behind her as if in solidarity. Her face is asking at least three questions. From behind Danny's door comes a thud. He might have dropped dead, yet we're all standing here, waiting for something. For me to speak, I guess. The shards sharpen.

"Go on, boy," Wes says. "Get out of here."

"Good-bye, everyone," I say, turning to the crowd. "It's been great working here. Well, not great, but . . . I hope you win. I think you will. I'm almost sure of it. Thanks." I wave, and then in a tribute to Mona, I flash the peace sign.

A few claps: my sandwich-mates. Behind them, Shawn is raising his arm in what could only be a black-power salute. What the hell: I clench my fist and punch the air.

My arm still raised, I turn toward Calliope, who has both hands on her head, matting down her hair. "Can I talk to you?" I say.

She stares at me with an open mouth.

"Go on," Blue says. "Talk to the guy."

"Quiet, George," she says, and moves her hands to her cheeks, making her eyes sag.

"Please," I say, my voice just about disappearing. "I need to talk to you."

She relents with a sigh and walks out of the office. "God-*damn*," Bernice says as the door closes behind me.

"What'd you do?" she says, standing between the elevators.

"You can't tell anyone. I sent out the release on my own."

"*What?*" She turns almost all the way around. "So the article I read in the paper today. That was all your doing?"

"Yes."

"And you're totally peachy with this?"

"I feel all right"—I try to step into her line of vision—"but ask me tomorrow."

"Who *are* you?"

"Benjamin Ralph Bergin. And I'd like to take you out to dinner."

"Your middle name is Ralph?"

"Not if it's a problem."

"Your timing is almost funny. But that's part of your plan, isn't it? You're trying to fuck things up but make it look like *I'm* fucking things up."

"I'm trying to make things work." I put my hand on her shoulder, and she lets me turn her toward me. "I want us to try."

She laughs a little. "I was just starting to come to grips with the other thing, and then you do this. You do crazy, confusing things."

"Do you have to approve of everything I do?"

"I think you *need* me to. This feels like a test. Is that why you did it?"

"Do you think that poorly of me?"

"You're telling me that I had nothing to do with this?"

"Well, I admit that our conversation last night didn't exactly make me excited to hang around this place for another month. But my reasons went a lot deeper, and you know that. I don't need you to approve of what I did. We can talk about it and argue if we have to. We'll get through it. We'll get through it all, and we'll be fucking great together."

"What if I think what you did is awful?"

"Number one or number two?"

"At the moment we're talking about confusing thing number two."

"*Do* you think it's awful?"

"I don't know. I found out about it two minutes ago. I guess you had good intentions, I *know* you did, but there's other stuff in there, too. There's a selfish quality to it. It seems almost . . . "

"Masturbatory?"

She points at me. "You say things like that but still you're going to be all surprised and sad when this conversation comes to a bad end."

"I'm sorry, I'm sorry." I move closer to her, and she backs away, her face lifting into a wince. "What, I'm repulsive now?"

"No. Your breath: it's alarming."

"Does it smell anything like coffee, whitefish, onion, and cigarette?"

"I wish."

"I have two people's mucus on me, too."

"You trying to win me over?"

"I am, actually. I've been trying to for a year. But I was also hiding from you. Not anymore. I'm right here, and I'm not going away, not unless you want me to."

She closes her eyes and inhales, then exhales slowly through her mouth, her warm breath hitting my chin.

"Let me guess," I say. "You don't know."

She opens her eyes. "Last night I asked you for time, and I would have wanted more than, oh, twenty hours, even if in those twenty hours you hadn't launched your own vigilante political campaign and gotten fired and made an absolutely bizarre exit from the office. So I'm going to try not to feel bad about going back inside."

"I don't want you to feel bad. That's the last thing I want."

She touches my cheek with the back of her hand and walks away from me.

The feel of Calliope's hand gives me a morsel of hope, which I've consumed by the time my feet hit the sidewalk. It occurs to me that I didn't bid farewell to Paul. Just as well; he'd be pissed. Then again, maybe not. I suppose I'll never know.

I imagine myself homeless, my coworkers walking over me on the sidewalk as I babble about human sacrifice. I'll be sucking on chicken bones and drinking Jack and wearing my tighty-whiteys on my head. I set the bag down in a trashcan.

I walk a block, trying to calm myself by thinking about a beach, a white sand beach you have to hike to get to. Then I turn around, my sights set on the bottle of Jack, which was almost half full. I need to save money now.

27

Not until I'm in the diner do I realize that I don't remember much of last night. Leaving the party, walking home, going to bed—it's all lost except for the moment in a pharmacy-bright pizza place when two black girls were laughing at me as I tried to extricate my wallet, which was trapped in my pants pocket beneath my keys. It's my first blackout in years, and the non-memory makes me feel stripped bare. A shiver stiffens my neck as my plate arrives, clanked down by a horse-faced waitress who hates me.

The problem last night was Other People. The people at the party shouldn't have been uninteresting—most were journalists, including my friend Tim, who'd invited me—but the things they said seemed frivolous, even more frivolous than the things I said. Everyone seemed to be talking about air travel, media mergers, and a certain sushi restaurant. Like someone who'd just returned from prison or a third-world country, I had an urge to shake them and yell, "You have no idea what I've been through." I was off. I was awful. Standing in the kitchen, pretending to not mind not talking, I longed for the comfort of the campaign, where people, for all their flaws, at least spoke my language. I tried to drink away my self-consciousness, and it worked, to a degree; I had a conversation with a fat woman whose parents had been murdered when she was five. "You have a good spirit," she told me as I left her in favor of another drink.

A blackout! That's not part of the plan. Nor is greasy food, but the bacon tastes too good to be entirely wrong. And I saved a dollar by coming to this diner in Chelsea, which offers a two-egg special for a dollar-ninety-five. I'm trying.

For a few days after Schecter spit in my face, I made predictable use of my newfound time and freedom: I drank and smoked, slept and didn't sleep, tried to get laid and didn't get laid. I had almost no fun. Flashes of excitement about my wide-open future kept morphing into anxiety.

So three days ago, like a good American, I drew up a self-improvement plan. The goals range from the lofty (tutoring needy children) to the mundane (making sure to shake my dick dry after peeing) to the essential (cleaning my apartment). I've yet to make much headway, although I did get my phone reconnected.

I wipe my plate with my last piece of toast, then leave a three-dollar tip in an attempt to win over horse-face. A not-good memory of last night flashes on the edge of my consciousness. Maybe I'll call Tim.

Hoping to head off the hangover at the pass, I buy a can of Bud, and on my third swig I know my job search will be delayed for at least one more day. To compensate I'll walk a lot. Exercise is part of the plan.

The sky's a deep blue, so deep that New York's a shade darker than it should be. Calliope's right: fall's the best.

Calliope. She really might not call. As crushed as I felt leaving the office, I didn't really think we were done. Arrogant fuck that I am, I doubted that she'd be able to just shake me off. I'd gotten inside her, for better or worse, and she would want more. But she's less self-destructive than most people.

Apparently she's come to the conclusion that I'm bad for her, or just plain bad. So cold turkey it is.

I don't think I'm devastated. I'd know if I were, right? Those last few days in the office, I felt sure that I wanted to be with her, but perhaps I longed more for clarity than for her, certainty for certainty's sake. Aside from a few late-night pangs, I haven't been missing her as intensely as it seems I should. Plus, I'm furious at her.

As I walk up Ninth Ave, I decide that I'm okay, and that I'd be even more okay if I knew I didn't do something horrendous last night, so I stop at a payphone. I get Tim's voicemail, and waiting for the beep I get so bored I put the listening end of the receiver in my mouth. "Just wanted to thank you for the party," I say in my Mr. Mellow voice. "Or blame you. Holy fuck. Did you slip something in my drink?" Yuck. Tim, thankfully, isn't the kind of person to sniff out insecurity.

Passing a newsstand I decide not to get a paper. I don't want to spend money and I don't want to find out about the race. Last time I checked, Schecter was up two points, a statistical tie. Of course, if what I did was right, it was right regardless of its impact on the race. Still, if Schecter loses, I might move to New Zealand.

At a urine-stinky payphone by Port Authority I surprise myself by figuring out how to check my messages. Tim didn't call. No one did.

My pride in the dream release was solidified, at least for a while, by an encounter with Paul. I was sitting in a coffee shop near the office, having abandoned a ridiculous plan to sneak in and grab my jean jacket. (Reassembling the outfit would, I was sure, increase my luck with the ladies.) Paul walked by, and I knocked on the window to get his attention. "It's the saboteur!" he said as he approached my table.

"You're not going to hit me, are you?"

In fact, he gave me a hug, then sat down. "I'm not going to lie to you. I don't like what you did. I think it's going to hurt the campaign. But I also know that there are higher causes than winning. You followed your conscience, and I respect that." Then we shared a rice pudding and argued amiably about The War on Drugs.

I've been milking the memory. I go back to it when I feel alone and regretful. Or when I fear that I've destroyed not only Schecter's campaign, but my relationship with the only woman I've ever loved. Or when I wonder if the loss of Calliope has instilled in me a mind-numbing pain that my mind is too numb to feel.

I stop at a payphone and check my messages: nothing.

I need to let go of last night. Chances are I did nothing wrong, and what if I did? I'll never see those people again. The problem is, rational thoughts like this aren't carrying much weight with my emotions right now. They're correct but they lack clout. They're like leftists. The demagogues are winning, irrationality rules, fear holds sway.

Near Columbus Circle, a power-walking woman, pumping her arms like a soldier, smiles as though she knows me.

At the third payphone I find there's a message; but it's from Ethan, who's been spending every free minute with his new girl-friend. He wants to get together tomorrow night to watch the baseball playoffs. What am I going to do with myself until then?

★　★　★

The ring pulls me out of a shallow sleep, so shallow it takes me a moment to be sure I was asleep. Danny was in my dream. I pick up the phone, hoping for Tim, but it's Ethan. We decide to meet in a bar at eight, twenty-two hours from now.

Stumbling toward the bathroom I step on stuff and some of it sticks. I sit down to pee so as not to touch the stucco-like bumps on my prick—the result, I suspect, of the weirdly dark baby oil I got at the ninety-nine cent store. Or maybe the bumps are reverse VD, what you get from not having sex.

I sit down on the bed and call Tim, whose laughter when he

hears my voice makes me stand up. I trip over something and fall hard on my side, keeping the phone on my ear. It turns out I did nothing terrible last night. In fact I made quite an impression. I gave slurry speeches on everything from the magnificence of black olives to the need to balance chaos and order in one's life. The fat woman wants me to call her.

I hang up and roll onto my back, my upper arm landing on wetness. My kidneys feel like punches. I hear animal movement in the kitchen. The talk with Tim brought not relief but regret, regret that I wasted a day regretting.

When I get into bed, my brain (or Brain, as I've dubbed my spiteful conjoined twin as he asserts his independence) imagines what my day would have felt like had I not lost it to regret. I know my day would have sucked regardless, but Brain doesn't.

I could not be more awake.

I try to think soft thoughts—a cabin in the woods, a woman who loves the shit out of me, a backdoor curve breaking into the strike zone—but Brain pushes them away in favor of the one thought that assures I won't get to sleep. He yells it out with sadistic glee: "We're still awake!"

I put on clothes and go down to the street. One of a group of women comes up to me, says she needs to suck a quarter out of my mouth. She has a black dildo on her head, duct-taped. Her nametag says *Slut*. It's a bachelorette party: young professionals, blond Republicans, feminist anti-feminists. "Here," Slut says, and hands me a quarter. I'd like to kiss her, but there's a film like onion relish in my mouth. She must be drunk to have picked me. Of course she's drunk; she's wearing a dildo. The dildo is realistic, veins and everything. "Come *on*," Slut says, getting close, the dildo grazing my cheek. I scoot away. "Freak stole my quarter," Slut says, and her friends laugh.

I walk west, thinking I might find that block where Calliope and I had lunch that day, and I'll come up with another destination after that. I swing my arms and loosen my calves. Walking is not nothing; I'll just keep walking.

★ ★ ★

I'm on my third Jack when Ethan shows up, half an hour late and unapologetic, his getting-laid great mood annoying me before he even sits down. He seems happy to see me. He seems happy to have been sprung from his mother's womb.

"What's the score?" he says, looking up at the TV, one of about fifteen in the bar. This place used to be a gathering spot for West Village activists and artists. Now it's a sports bar.

"Yankees are up two nothing."

"Fuck."

I want the Rangers to win, but I can't help pulling for Roger Clemens, who's on the mound for the Yankees. He used to pitch for the Red Sox, and Sox fans are supposed to hate him now, but I don't. People think he's a choker, the sports world's word for coward. I want him to lose that reputation, tonight.

"How's it going with Emily?" I ask as if I don't already know.

He pulls his eyes away from the TV. His three-day scruff reminds me of lazy days in college, back when we thought we deserved lazy days. "I'm into her. She's so . . . *cool*. And the sex, it's probably—I don't want to say best ever, but . . . "

"Best ever."

"Yeah."

"That's awesome," I say, and mean it, but he should make an effort to contain his excitement. I would if I was up and he was down. But I haven't given him reason to know I'm down. When I told him what had happened at work, I went out of my way to be excited, and he was supportive. A good move, we agreed. But Ethan knows me; he can tell I'm not good. So probably what he's doing is trying to keep it light. He thinks I should crawl out of my skull for a few hours.

The crowd claps as Pudge Rodriguez strikes out on a splitter from Clemens. "It's the Yankees' year," I say.

Ethan nods, then hears what I said. His mind is elsewhere— at work or, more likely, between Emily's thighs. When you have a new girlfriend, you have a body and brain to explore and you don't want to do anything else, least of all hang out with your depressed friend in a sports bar filled with Yankee fans.

"Want to get out of here?" I say.

"Already?"

"Let's go to a bar-bar. I found a good dive last night in the Thirties."

"That might be tough," he says, squinting to see the clock behind the bar. "I'm supposed to be at Emily's at eleven."

"All right."

"I can go somewhere, just not that far." His eyes are full of apology, which is the worst thing yet.

"Let's just walk."

Sheridan Square is alive, New York seeming very New York, a smorgasbord of humanity. Transvestites walking proud on heels. White-faced black women stepping out of limos. Homeless vet, Chinese nun, greasy man with large ferret.

We walk in silence. I can tell Ethan anything. I have in the past and I will again. But right now I need an invitation. I need him to ask.

"This was too quick," he says when we pull up in front of my building.

"I'd like to meet Emily sometime."

"Yeah, she really wants . . . "

"To meet me?"

He nods, but he's gone away again. Or finally arrived. "Have you spoken to Calliope?"

"No," I say, unsure if this is the invitation I had in mind. "We might really be done."

"She said she wanted time. This is time."

"Two weeks?"

"That's nothing."

I know he's trying to make me feel better, but Brain is angry that he's taking her side. "I thought it was ridiculous, her wanting time. But even if it's legit, even if she's really figuring shit out, she should have called to see how I'm doing."

"You haven't called to see how *she's* doing."

"If it was up to me, we would never have *stopped* talking."

"Right, and I think that's what's going on. You put yourself out there—"

"I *did* put myself out there."

"I know, so you're pissed and hurt, which is understandable, but the problem is, it's the wrong head to have if you want to make it work."

"What, you're the love doctor all of a sudden?"

He makes a serious face and sucks in his cheeks, his mock-stud look. "Excuse me, but have *you* gotten laid today? Because I've already gotten laid three times today. But maybe that's normal for you, I don't know."

"Really? Three times?"

"Twice."

"Once?"

"Yeah."

"Look, there's a real chance, regardless of what *head* I have, that she doesn't want to be with me."

"Not possible." He smiles as he backs away. "You're such a catch."

"Yeah, where else is she going to get a guy so messy, jobless, and gassy?"

"Don't forget self-destructive. Give her a call her, dummy."

The phone's ringing when I walk in. It's got to be Calliope—the perfect coincidence—but it's Mom: "I was beginning to worry. I haven't heard from you in so long."

"Sorry."

"How are you?"

"Well, I've got some news."

"What is it?"

"I quit my job." Saving the full conversation for my next visit to Maine.

"Oh."

"I was miserable."

Her exhalation is loud, like air coming into a car. "Okay," she says, trying to calm herself. "Okay."

"It wasn't easy, Mom. Believe me, I did the hard thing, not the easy thing."

"Are you all right?"

Her concern seems simple, without layers; it makes me want to talk to her. "I'm all right with that, but there's something else. There's . . . a woman."

"And?"

"I don't know, she's just . . . "

"Breaking your heart?"

"No . . . Maybe."

"I'm sorry. This is unusual for you, is it not?"

"Yeah," I say, trying to remember ever talking to her about a woman.

"Unusual as an adult, I mean. You were certainly hurt deeply as a teenager."

"No I wasn't. Was I?"

"Karen Byers?"

"She didn't break my heart."

"I suspect that she did, even if you didn't have the emotional vocabulary to understand it, and the pain she caused made you guarded in subsequent relationships. At least that's what I've always thought."

"Could be," I say, awed by how well she knows me.

"In any case, what are you going to do about—what's her name?'

"Calliope Berkowitz."

Pause. "Why is it that you're never interested in Jewish women?"

I forget that Mom can be funny. With Ethan and Mom backing me, I might just be all right. "Because all their parents are shrinks."

"My funny boy. Is it wrong that I'm pleased you're in love with a Jew?"

"*Maybe* in love, and no. As long as you're angry at her for not loving me back."

"You bet I am. What the hell is wrong with this Calliope Berkowitz?"

28

I see someone who could be Tod, those balding good looks. I dart away, then wish I'd followed him since it's weird for Tod to be in Times Square at this time of night. Not that weird, though, if you consider his wants, but then I'm not sure you can scratch that itch in this new scrubbed-up, mallified (and mollified) Times Square.

A bar is what I need, some dark hole to fall into; but no matter how little I sleep, I can't seem to fall out of time. I know that it's just after one and that it's been sixteen and a half days since Schecter spit in my face and that it's thirty-eight hours before my next scheduled anything, an appointment at a temp agency. That's what I did today, set up the appointment. I work in two minutes spurts. I make one phone call, complete one errand, read one page, then fatigue swallows me up, and I have a drink, drinks, many drinks. The booze brings my brain back together, fills the cracks like sealant.

I'm working on my tiredness, amassing it. Punishment, I guess, though at this point I doubt I could sleep even if I tried. Steve Earle claims to have stayed up for thirteen days, but he

was smoking crack. All I'm doing is drinking and smoking cigarettes, a benign little bender for a benign little Benny.

Commotion: a little crowd forming around a black couple.
She's got a body and so does he, muscles moving under leotard
black shirt. Neck chains hang down, medallions.

"You ain't the boss of me," she says, finger moving like a
windshield wiper, head shifting side to side on a neck of rope.

"You a fucking ho," he says. He grabs her arm and pulls her
toward his spaceship car, rumbling with the door open.

She pulls free and swings her purse, connecting with a
thwack; then she stumbles backward, tits jiggling on the edge
of leather.

He puts his hand to his cheek, checks his fingers: no blood.
"I'm a kill you, ho," he says, everyone looking on. The crowd
is twelve, thirteen: troubled people, all-night people, except for
a cluster of Asian tourists hoping for American violence, the real
thing.

I step inside the circle, getting close but not close enough,
and he goes at her, grabs her by the hair and slaps her face,
forehand then back. She screams into a sob, blood flowing from
her nose, streaming with tears off her chin. He pulls her away
by her hair, and I step forward to not quite block his path.

"The fuck *you* want?" he says to me, her hair stretched out
like a leash.

"You a very bad man," yells an old Asian guy, showing me
up, making me look as weak as I feel. The old guy hammers
the air with a rolled up *Playbill*. "You very bully."

The bully stuffs his bloody ho in the car and slams the door.
Her dead eyes disappear behind tinted glass.

I find myself on Eighth Avenue, walking fast, so fast I trip on
nothing. I stand up and run to catch up with my heart, thumping like a woofer.

The darkness of the bar takes me in, and I feel calmer, just
being in here. It's seedy but not scary, *Country Roads* emanating straight-faced from the juke, people keeping to themselves

except for the pug-faced guy two stools down. He's griping to the bartender, a frosty blonde who was hot a hundred cocks ago.

John Denver gives way to Lynyrd Skynrd, *Tuesday's Gone*, which brings back everything at once, the generic past, time gone by, and the specific past too, Mark's cushy basement, Julia's small cunt, California, roof-time with Calliope. She used to make fun of me for liking Skynrd. The absurd thing, the shameful thing, is that it bothered me as much as it did. Something's seriously wrong with me.

Pug-face is griping about politics now, in response to Schecter, who's on TV. "Hide your money," Pug says. He takes out his wallet, shakes it. "This is mine. It's *my* money. You can't have it, you fucking fucking . . . Schecter."

"How much money you make?" I ask.

He looks at me. More pig than pug. "None of your fucking business."

"You've got nothing to fear from Schecter."

"Let me tell you something." He moves to the next stool, sliding it close to mine, and gets in my face. He's got no smell, oddly. "You see, guy," he says, softening his tone, "the tax burden is destroying this country. I tried going into business for myself, but I couldn't swing it because of all the regulations and taxes. Republicans aren't perfect, believe me, but Democrats, Jesus Christ, they spend our money like drunken sailors."

"So we shouldn't pay taxes at all, right? I mean, it's our money."

"I didn't say that. Don't put words in my mouth or I'll put my fist in yours. I'm just kidding. Jesus Christ, you look like you shit yourself." He puts his arm around me. "What I'm saying is, the government can take the money it needs to provide the basics. Anything more is tyrannical. You see, this country was founded . . . "

It seems crucial to set him straight, but I probably couldn't, not even if I weren't beyond tired. It's a struggle just to pay attention. Boston Tea Party, Patrick Henry, God, Ronald Reagan, God . . .

"You see, guy," he says, putting me in a playful headlock, "it's the American way."

"You're a fucking idiot," I say, being the person I least want to be. He loosens his grip, and I break away. At the door I turn around, half-wanting to get shot, but he's just sitting there, the big sad pig, looking at me as if I'd let him down.

Home, I guess. A generous term for that prison cell, but it's where my bed is, and there's the chance of sleep, pure physical necessity.

I take as direct a route as possible, slanting down north-south streets. I look at the ground as I walk. No more faces. No more people.

A voice I know: Teddy, a homeless guy I chat with sometimes to feel virtuous. I want to protect the sleepy feeling I'm pretending to have, so I ignore Teddy and surge head-down into my building and onto the elevator, which carries me like a parent to my door. I leave the light off and get naked and tiptoe through the minefield, stepping on stickiness, my dick burning-itchy from those bumps. All my bedding is tied up in a dank ball. I try to unravel it with my feet, but then I'm just kicking and punching, Brain being bad bad bad. I stand up to see about a drink and when I turn on the light, roaches go scurrying under the stove. I remember to breathe.

I scratch my dick and take a look around. I'm surprised to discover a tall bookshelf untouched by chaos, full of books I claim to have read. And somewhere on that shelf is a book that I tend to forget I own, *A Country That Works*, by James Palazzo. I've never made it past the dedication: *For my family, of course.* Of course.

I walk over to the shelf and step up into it. Books bending under my feet, I pull on the top of the shelf, rocking it, and on the fourth rock it falls . . . pain clearing my head when my back hits the floor, but I don't like the numbness in my legs when I struggle to stand up. In the corner there's a tall black hateful halogen lamp that's never worked. I pick it up and beat the back of the bookshelf, the fake wood breaking right away, and I move on to the coffee table and the bed and the floor and the walls, whacking everything. I swing the lamp like a bat and I swing the lamp like an ax. It's not a real flip-out, though, because I make sure not to hit the stereo, but I do go at the windows, hitting the glass again and again and again and again and again until my hands are burning and bleeding from splintered lamp plastic.

Lying in bed, catching my breath, I realize that the blood streaked on the floor isn't from my hands but from my feet, all cut up from the glass. I pull the pieces of glass from my feet and place them in an empty bag of Cheetos. Then I put the bag of Cheetos in a half-full bag of Smart Food, which I put in a Duane Reade bag, in which I discover an unopened roll of toilet paper. On stinging feet I walk to the bathroom and put the paper in the holder, the silver spring-rod popping magically into its hole.

Cleaning up, I realize, is something you can do to music. I put on socks to absorb the blood, then study my CDs, needing just the right one. Steve Earle's *I Feel Alright*, his back-from-the-dead album, seems an obvious choice. Too obvious perhaps. I put on Wilco's *Being There*, and its abrasive-then-gentle opening helps me fight through the overwhelming emotion that strikes me when I take in the mess in its entirety.

Standing on top of my refrigerator, amazingly, is a bottle of dish soap, and there are three green inches left. I clear all the dishes out of the sink except for a frying pan. In the cabinet under the sink, next to a pile of mouse turd, is a fresh sponge. I run the water hot, I soap up the sponge, and I start to scrub.

29

Election Day. On my way to work, I stop by the polling place and cast an enthusiastic vote for Congressman Arnold Abraham Schecter. After all, he took a brave stand on the Mohammed case. I'm more nervous than I would be if I were still working for the guy. Fortunately, my shift at the café will kill most of the hours before the polls close. Tonight Ethan and Emily are coming over to watch the returns.

I walk west on Thirteenth, my thighs sore from jogging a week ago. It was after my one "run" that I reentered the work-force. I was sprawled out on the sidewalk off the West Side Highway, wheezing so loudly that a woman came to my aid. As it turned out, she was one of the journalists I'd met at that party, and I pretended to remember her. As she helped me to my feet, she apologized for her "defensive" reaction to my "trenchant" criticism of the media. I assured her that I wasn't offended. We walked and chatted, stopping by a café run by her friend, who was looking for help. The job seemed like a reward for exercising. Or for drinking too much.

I like the simplicity of the job. I fill up cups with coffee. I make sandwiches. I say thank you. The seeds of discontent are there: its smallness, the tweak of guilt I feel when I charge eight dollars for a sandwich, the theatrics of Petra, my annoyingly hot aspiring-actress coworker. But for now it's ideal. I work five-hour shifts four days a week, leaving me time to organize my life and my thoughts. I don't want to kid myself— you can't turn your life around in two weeks—but I've stopped the bleeding.

Victor, my other coworker, is smoking in the alley outside the door that employees use. He smiles when he sees me, and then we shake hands and slap arms like old buds long parted. He's a well-built, good-natured Guatemalan who doesn't speak much English. He takes at least five smoke breaks a shift, much to Petra's elaborate dismay.

"Done almost?" he says, nodding in the direction of the book I'm holding, *Armies of the Night.* It's my third book in two weeks, a clip that's impressed Victor.

"Yup, almost."

He shakes his head and whistles in amazement. "Want a cigarette?"

"No thanks. I better get in there."

"Yeah, man, she's a moody mood, man."

Only one customer is at the counter, but Petra is looking as hassled as ever. She's like Julia Roberts playing a beaten-down girl: you can't take her pain seriously. "*There* you are," she says, implying that I'm late, which I'm not. This job's not completely unlike my old one.

"Please have a seat and we'll bring that out to you," she says to the customer, an elderly woman who seems to be checking out Petra's wiry, small-breasted body. And to me: "I need a turk on a bag, l-t-m."

Petra's shorthand gives Victor and me something concrete to make fun of. I think she's trying to evoke a waitress in a greasy spoon: Frankie in *Frankie and Johnny*. "C-r-u," I say. Against her better judgment she looks at me. "Coming right up!" I say.

She blows out with her bottom lip, making her bangs dance. "Not today, all right? You have no idea how crazy it's been." She pivots like a robot and heads for the espresso machine, moving her arms as though running.

I wash my hands, eager to begin the sandwich-making, an activity that has set up happy camp in my imagination. Often at might, as my thoughts melt into dreams, the image I see is that of the knife going through a sandwich, right down the middle.

I put mayo on both sides of the baguette, making sure to spread to the edge. The turkey was sliced by Victor early this morning. Carefully, but not too carefully, I put the pieces on the bread, overlapping them; then comes one more layer of turkey. I stagger the pieces so that the sandwich has plenty of air. Our gourmetness allows us to charge too much, and I'm always tempted to overstuff. But two layers of turkcy arc all a baguette can accommodate. I have ideas for sandwiches, ideas I'm going to share at the next staff meeting. I've been pondering a sliced pork tenderloin with stewed apple, and a spicy sliced beef with peppers that would be like cold Chinese on bread. I also want to come up with a healthy sandwich, one that fits into my new diet, something with fish and fruit.

I set the sandwich on a plate, which Petra grabs before I have a chance to say, "Pick up." A small crowd has formed near the register, but no one is stepping forward to be heard. "Who's next?" I say. "Can I help someone?"

★ ★ ★

As I buzz open the downstairs door, I take a final look around. Aside from the cardboard windows, the place looks good, borderline immaculate. What it's not is *cool*. Music would help, so I scan my CDs, trying to figure out what might impress Emily, who, from what I gather, is a bit of a hipster. Jazz seems too affected. Beck seems sufficiently downtown but too white-boy ironic. I go with Tom Petty's second album, which is what I actually want to hear. When in doubt, do an impression of yourself.

Emily, striking with buzzed dark hair and much metal in her face, gives me a smile that loosens me like a drug.

"Ben Bergin," she says. "Is it you, is it really you?" I give her a hug and enjoy it a little too much. I give Ethan one too, a heartfelt thing masquerading as a half-joke.

"Great view," Ethan says.

"I've got to call my landlord," I say.

"Land-Lord," Ethan says, amused by the word.

"What happened?" Emily says.

"I flipped out one night and trashed my apartment." The openness is no accident—showing myself, I'm beginning to think, is a big piece of the puzzle—but there's something in Emily that brings it out. She'd be quick to show me her own shit.

While I pour red wine into the glasses I bought yesterday at the Salvation Army for this very purpose, Ethan and Emily settle into the couch, their cuddliness not bothering me as much as I would have expected. She's Jewish, Ethan told me, but looks vaguely Asian. Attractive, I'm glad to see. Not beautiful, I'm equally glad to see.

"Who wants a cookie?" I say.

"Have you been baking again?" Ethan says.

"You bake?" Emily says, not getting our language, and why should she?

"No," I say. "But I'm excellent at buying baked goods."

I set down the plate of cookies on the coffee table, which suffered only a character-enhancing crack during my rampage. Then I bring over the glasses, and we tap them together. "Thanks for having us over," Emily says.

"Thank you for coming," I say, and stop myself from telling them that I love them both. I've been spending way too much time alone.

"Why isn't the TV on?" Ethan says.

"I'm nervous," I say. I finish my wine in a gulp. I've been allowing myself small amounts of wine and beer. Pot and booze are banned until such time that Brain has become sufficiently subservient.

"Schecter's going to win," Ethan says. "Wait a second." He removes his hand from Emily's lap and pulls back his head to look at her. "You didn't vote, did you?"

Cutely sheepish, she bites the tip of her thumb and shakes her head.

"That's not right, Em," he says. "You've got to vote."

"It just doesn't interest me."

"I don't care. You've got to vote."

"I'm *really* not in the mood for a lecture," she says, initiating a tense silence. It's a nice little argument, one that will make their sex better tonight. I'd love all that, sex and little arguments.

"Cookie?" I say, holding up the plate between them.

Ethan grabs a chocolate-chip oatmeal and points it at the TV. "Aren't you're dying to find out what happened?"

"Dying is about right."

Shortly before they arrived I rolled the TV into the corner to give the impression that it wasn't a focal point of my existence. I take my time retrieving it because Ethan and Emily have some making up to do. Their argument seems to have evolved into a gentler disagreement, this one concerning which one of them is more sorry.

With the TV in place, I return to my chair and close my eyes in a sort of prayer.

"Why are you so nervous about this?" Emily asks.

"Ethan didn't tell you?"

She bites the tip of her thumb. "I didn't know if I was supposed to know."

"Turn the fucking TV on!" Ethan yells, and I do.

"The party has just begun," says the reporter, standing in front of a group of arm-wavers who, in their crustiness and hairiness, could only be Democrats. "Senator-Elect Schecter will be out any second."

"He did it," Ethan said. "*You* did it."

"Congratulations!" Emily says.

"You probably can't call eleven points a landslide," the reporter says, "but it's a bigger victory than anyone expected."

I munch on a peanut-butter cookie, tasting it along with my vindication. It's presumptuous of me to take credit—I have no idea what happened on the campaign these last few weeks—but there's no question that with this large a victory, the Free-Hakim base was out in full force.

And there's more good news: Democrats have done well nationwide. It's an anti-impeachment statement, a triumph of reason.

"Trust the people," I say, feeling proud of my country. Yes, patriotic.

"They're wise," Ethan says. "Even if sometimes they seem very, very stupid."

Schecter begins his speech by thanking "the best staff in the world." He turns around to clap for them, and the camera pans across the stage—pausing, I swear, on Calliope, who looks tired and flushed and happy, post-coital.

"You haven't called her yet, have you?" Ethan says.

"Who?" Emily says. "That chick with the groovy hair?"

"She *does* have good hair," I say.

"Story, please," Emily says, moving her fingers as if to say, come closer.

"She needed time to figure things out," I say.

"How much?" Emily says.

"A month and counting," I say.

"It'd be crazy if you and Calliope never see each other again," Ethan says.

"Her name's Calliope?" Emily says. "You must marry her. At least call her."

"You're right. I need to call her. I think I'm afraid."

"Of what?" Emily says.

"What am I afraid of? Getting hurt, maybe? Hurting her. Yes, hurting her, being depended on. Not being free. Freedom, too, I'm definitely scared of that. Doubt. Difficulty. Doubt. Did I mention doubt? Having power. Not having power. Feeling too much. Not feeling enough. Failure. Sex. That's a big one: sex, impotence. Looking stupid. Being boring. Going crazy. Flying. Dying. Living . . . Guns, bombs, war. Arabs. Black people. Gay people. People with deformities. People with tool belts. People. Policemen. Doormen. Identical twins. Teenagers. Kids dressed up like adults, beauty-pageant girls; they really freak me out. Let's see, what else? I'm afraid that none of this is real, this life, that it's just a dream, and not *my* dream. It's an insect's dream, an alien's dream, an alien's nightmare, or if not, if it's real, whatever that means, I'm afraid that it doesn't matter, that there's no point to it."

Emily's laughter, which prompted me on, is now a smile. She puts her arm around Ethan. "He sounds pretty healthy to me."

"That's my friend, Ben."

"Nice to meet you," I say.

★ ★ ★

They take off around three, which is too soon—next month would be too soon—leaving me alone in my clean apartment. My clean, sad apartment.

I didn't try hard enough with Calliope. I had a few spasms of boldness, then went back to running. The campaign's over. The bumps on my penis are gone.

What am I waiting for?

She's probably in a bar or a cab or bed. Bed, most likely. As much as I like the romantic potential of a middle-of-the-night phone call—or, better yet, a middle-of-the night visit—I have to be prepared for the possibility that she won't be excited to see me, even less so if I wake her. Tomorrow.

30

When I come up from the subway at Borough Hall, I'm seven blocks from where I think her apartment is. I feel wrong, and not just because I stayed up all night. I feel . . . empty-handed. The obvious gift is flowers, which, I've been told, no woman doesn't love. But I can picture Calliope implying with a flat "thanks" that giving flowers is easy. It can't be the wrong thing, though, so at a deli I buy a bouquet that seems to suit her, purple irises and small, almost weed-like wildflowers.

Her block, cloaked in the quiet of mid-morning, reminds me of Paris, that year I pissed away. My previous life. I walk into a breeze that makes me aware of my tingling nerves. But I feel strong, considering.

Her building is a red brownstone. In the foyer I find a door-bell labeled Berkowitz. I breathe in and push the button as I breathe out.

There's no response: no buzz of the door, no crackle from the intercom. She's already up and out or she never came home or she's in there, wanting to be left alone. Or she's not alone. I push the button again and prepare for the worst. Victory party, too many drinks, Shawn. Victory party, too many drinks, Tod.

The silence holds so I walk out, considering my options. I could wait here or leave a message on her machine and wait at home.

"Flowers!" says a woman not Calliope.

On the steps I turn toward the voice, which belongs to a pretty face in the second-floor window. "Looking for Calliope?" This woman glowing down on me is young and blonde, smooth and clean. Now *that's* confusing.

"Yeah. Do you know where she is?"

"Yoga."

"Yoga," I say, relaxing as if I were doing it.

"Are you Lorenzo?"

I fall to my knees. My version of the worst was fun by comparison.

"You're not Lorenzo."

"I think I might be the opposite of Lorenzo."

She laughs. "You're funny."

"Thanks?"

"So who *are* you?"

I'm embarrassed to tell her; my name sounds dumb and stumpy. "Ben."

"Oh my God. She'll be surprised to see *you.*" She claps twice, a gesture she picked up from her downstairs neighbor. Unlikely buddies, the two of them, this woman seeming like someone who's shaken pompoms and attended pledge parties. "The yoga place is right up there on the corner. You should go there and surprise her. She'd love it."

"You think?"

"How could she not?"

They're not close; I know that now. They chat about everything, as women do, but Calliope doesn't let her in on the complexities, complexities that would explain why she might not love seeing me burst into her yoga class. Still, it might not be a bad idea, so I say goodbye to this woman, whom I thankfully no longer love, and walk up to the corner, where a cluster of women are sipping healthy hot drinks in front of the yoga place. One of them looks at me—a man with flowers, of mild interest.

Surprising her in yoga class seems beyond me, a power move I'm simply not capable of making. Like a dive off a cliff, or a hunger strike in the street. There are things one just can't do. On the other hand, what better way to leap into my new life?

But putting aside the symbolism, the idea of it, there's the question of effect. Maybe she would be moved and disarmed. Just as likely, she would see it as an unwelcome interruption, a violation of her sanctuary.

All this deliberation is delay; I'm hoping the class ends. And sure enough, by the time I walk into the building and drink from the water fountain and check my fly and go upstairs and sit down in a common area, people are filing out of one of the rooms, the moment upon me, impossibly, too real to be real.

She stops when she sees me, some ten feet away. Her face, usually so expressive, reveals nothing. Other women notice me. They make the connection between the guy with the flowers and Calliope, hugging her rolled-up mat to her chest. The women linger to watch, which strikes me as pretty un-yoga.

I stand up, holding out the flowers. "Congratulations."

"I've got to grab my coat," Calliope says, not quite to me. "Meet me out front."

She walks through a door, leaving me holding the flowers. The women turn away, embarrassed for me, but they don't know what I know, that this is part of it, that this bubble of hurt expanding in my chest is actually what you want.

Calliope, somehow already outside, starts walking as soon as I come out. She's wearing green hospital pants and a fake-fur coat. Her hair is in a tight bun, tighter than I'd have thought possible. "This is quite a surprise," she says, a half step ahead.

"A nice one?"

"*Way* too soon to tell."

"How was yoga?"

"It was good. I'm sorry if I was a little standoffish, but that's my place, you know? I felt kind of invaded."

"And now?"

"I don't know, okay? Jesus, give me a little time."

"I've given you a month."

She pulls up, stares at me. It's not a nice look, not even close, but its directness gives me hope. "Let me take a shower." She starts walking again. "Then we'll talk."

From the window Calliope's friend, positioned so that only I see her, gives me a big round smile and a double thumbs-up. Does she know something I don't?

Calliope pauses at the threshold, unsure if she wants to let me in. She pushes open the door but half-heartedly holds it for me, and I have to raise my forearm to protect the flowers. "Do you want these?" I say.

"Of course," she says, snatching them.

She walks to the right, to the kitchen, the living room beyond that. The bedroom, its door shut, must be to the left. I stand stupidly in the hallway.

"What are you doing?" she says, and I take that as an invitation to walk into the living room, which is full of sunlight from the street. The living room gets light in the morning; her bedroom never gets light. She told me this during our fourth conversation. This place is different from the one I imagined, less busy, less funky, although there's a lime-green sofa with black velvet pillows that I'd think was ugly if I didn't trust her taste on such matters more than my own. The rest of the furniture is rustic—her coffee table is an old bench—and plants are gathered in bunches near the windows.

It's a welcoming room except for the painting above the fireplace. A Daddy original, I suspect, depicting what seems to be the inside of a factory, a mangled human form caught in a conveyor belt, head and limbs stretched out like gum. It's not subtle, but it's not trying to be. The thing stops you cold.

She puts the flowers in a white ceramic vase, and the vase on the mantelpiece. She steps back, then forward to slide the vase an inch to the left.

"I'm going to take a shower," she says. "Don't snoop."

"Who's Lorenzo?"

She looks at me, mouth open, and in her face I see my mistake.

"Your friend upstairs asked if I was Lorenzo."

"Bridget. She's got a big mouth."

"Who is he?"

"He's none of your business."

Something in her tone—a false or soft note—tells me that I need not fear Lorenzo. If this doesn't work, Lorenzo won't be the reason.

When the shower's been going for a few minutes, I walk around the living room, not snooping, just looking. The place is more interesting than it seemed at first. The shelves are filled with stuff: pottery, seashells, incense holders, sculptures, wooden boxes, unidentifiable doodads, and weird things like enormous screws. There are photos too, lots of them, mostly black-and-white. But it's a color print that gets my attention, of Calliope, two women friends, and a handsome black guy who must be Drew, her ex. It's a candid shot at a campsite or an outdoor concert, everyone laughing and looking beautifully grungy, having a better time than I've ever had.

"What do you think?" Calliope says.

I'm standing in the middle of the room, unmoored, having drifted away on a wave of jealousy and self-doubt. It's just a photo.

"Well?" she says. "It's hard to tell because it's wet. I had eight inches taken off."

She's talking about her hair, which is shorter, civilized. "I like it."

"Really? I was nervous about it. It's my first real haircut in five years. I figured it's a good way to start my new life."

"You did it this morning?"

"Yeah, I got up early. After going to bed at five. That's why I'm in my jammies."

So she is: blue-and-black plaid flannel. Not exactly lingerie. Better than lingerie. "So this new life of yours, what is it?"

"I don't know," she says with a mocking, parentlike voice that suggests I was talking about us, which I wasn't.

"You're not going to keep working for Schecter?"

"What do *you* think?"

"Probably not."

"I disliked it almost as much as you did."

"I doubt that."

"Well, I disliked it, but I wanted to see it through."

"Can we not start there?"

"Where do you want to start, Ben? Tell me where you want to start."

I take a step toward her, but she walks away and sits on the couch. If you look at the painting carefully, you see that only the head seems to be caught in the machine; the rest of the body has *become* the machine.

"It's nice to see you," I say.

"It's nice to see you, too. Really nice. Work was weird without you."

"My *life* was weird without you." She looks at me, then looks away. "I'm where I was a month ago. I'm even more there now than I was then, you know?"

"So romantic," she says.

Pretty nasty, I feel, but I forge through. "Have you done your thinking?"

"I've been thinking a ton, but not deeply enough or something. I've been so busy. I guess I viewed this as something I'd deal with now."

"You're not seriously asking for any more time."

"Maybe. I don't know."

"You're stuck, Calliope. I should know: I've been there.

You're trying not to try, and it's stupid and self-destructive. I'm not giving you more time."

"You're just going to make me be with you?"

"Pretty much. You want this as much as I do."

"Don't tell me how I feel."

"Then let me tell you how *I* feel. I want you."

"Why?"

"Why?"

"Yeah, why?"

"Because . . . because I come alive when I'm with you. Because the more I know you, the more I want to know you. Because you're sexy and smart and kind and I love you. That's what I'm saying, I'm in love with you."

Calliope, fighting tears or a smile or both, has her fist over her mouth. I sit down on the couch but keep my distance, confident enough to go slow.

She says, "Now you're not playing fair."

Reuben the Cat, whom I already know from Calliope's reports, saunters into the room, oblivious to the trials of her owner—her friend, she'd say, objecting to the notion of dominion. He's a ginger cat, plump but less plump than he was, having slimmed down in the months since Calliope brought home Mona, a sad-looking Calico, who's nowhere in sight. Reuben plops himself down on the small rug, a piece of maroon shag Calliope bought at a flea market with her little friends in mind.

Reuben stretches out, doubling in length. Above me dust snows in a shaft of sunlight. The sweet smell of old wood sends me back in time to a year I didn't live through, nineteen sixty-something, when we were going to defeat not only political oppression but ordinary unhappiness as well. *Park Slope, Circa 1965. Lovers, talking.* I suppose I'd rather be living inside the moment than regarding it, but at least I like what I see.

"What are you scared of?" I say.

"You make me uneasy," she says.

"Why?"

"I saw something in you, something I guess I'd seen all along, but it was crystallized for me. I guess it was the cumulative effect of our sexual . . ."

"Liaison."

"Is that the name for it? Then you sent out that press release. Neither thing was all bad, or bad at all, so I don't want to call you selfish; that has too negative a spin. Self-centered, I guess. Even all this stuff here this morning, what you've said and done, it feels kind of aggressive. You're really . . . focused on fulfilling your own needs, and that doesn't make you a great candidate for the kind of partnership I want."

"A candidate for a partnership? You want references?"

She glares at me. "Just *don't*, okay?

I slide closer and take her hand. "It sounds like your head is doing too much work."

"Is yours doing any work at all?"

"Not so much, thank God." I kiss her hand. "Have faith in me. You'll be pleasantly surprised. Come on. Hop aboard this crazy train."

"Oh, dear God."

"We can go slow."

"Yeah, right," she says with a giggle, then looks at me.

I kiss her non-aggressively, but then we're stumbling across the room before we have a chance to decide we shouldn't. And we *should*, obviously, the feeling of it quelling doubts. Her largeness I love, but it makes me wish I were nine-feet-tall, and I can feel her feeling her size too, wanting me to be the strong one. Which is confusing because I need to be gentle. In the hallway, with her facing the wall, I carefully take off her pants, then rub her lovely ass. She pulls away, and I lose her in the darkness of her bedroom. My eyes adjust to see her on the bed, naked, very naked. A condom's not needed; neither, apparently, is more foreplay; she takes me in hand then takes me in, and I tighten my ass to prevent a L'il Abner. Her skin I can't believe, the smooth softness, and I put both arms underneath her.

Remembering to be *with* her, I look into her eyes when I'm deep inside, and hold it there. We both grunt-giggle at the strangeness or not-strangeness, and the laughter relaxes me, allows for a flash of perfect hunger. I'm desperate to fuck her, but I already am. "Oh," she says. "*That.*" I fight the orgasm at first, then give in, my closed eyes seeing her in the hallway, that ass. She groans when I slide out and snuggles close when I turn onto my back.

Quick, teenage quick, the quickness defining it possibly. Abner's revenge. I'm going to choose not to care because she seems not to. She's already asleep, my tired girl, and I'll soon join her. For the first time in weeks I don't have to chase sleep, to stalk it, to try to sneak up when it's not looking. It's coming to take me. All I have to do is let it.

I wake to the turn of a page, Calliope reading. With my eyes still closed, my hand finds her knee, then the inside of her thigh, edging upward, and she puts her hand over mine, showing me soft circles. I settle in, my arm relaxed, but she's suddenly straddling me, wedging me in. She leans back, one hand reaching behind, and in the lamplight I see her beautiful realness, freckles, moles dark on fair skin. Wanting her face, I try to push her hair away, but she grabs my wrist and sucks my fingers, one by one. "Jesus!" I venture. "Jesus Fucking Christ." Feeling powerful, powerful and greedy, I push us off the bed and, with one hand on her ass, flip her around, thrusting as we land.

"Oh," she says.

My back hurting from the flip, I grunt as if from pleasure. "You like that?"

"Yeah," she whispers. "Harder."

I put my hands under her ass, and she puts her legs in the air, her muscles tightening against my palms. This, finally.

★ ★ ★

We make it out of bed in the middle of the afternoon, Thursday. I'm free till tomorrow at eleven, when I have to work. Free is the right word. The only thing maybe better than getting laid is having just gotten laid, walking down the street with the woman you got laid with, feeling like a man, sated, hungry, your dick sore but ready to go again, your heart open to whatever other sumptuous pleasures the world has to offer.

Calliope takes me to her brunch place, the kind of expensive-egg, fruit-on-the-side restaurant I normally avoid. I don't care where we go today as long as I can touch her. It's amazing how natural it feels, being with her out in the world.

"Ouch," she says as she sits down. "I might have to ask for a pillow."

My penis hardens, feeling like a bruise, feeling *gigantic*. Of course, insufficient foreplay or simple repetition is responsible for her soreness, but tell that to my cocky cock. "Does that mean we're done for the day?" I ask.

"Probably not."

"I'm starting to like you."

"They use free-range eggs here."

She introduces me to the waiter, a chunky gay guy she first met at her food co-op. He gives me a knowing smile when I shake his hand, suggesting that Calliope told him about me. Or maybe we're giving it off, a smell or a vibe.

She orders an omelet with avocado, and so do I. "That's a rather tame order for you," she says. "Shockingly free of fried pig carcass."

"I've been trying to eat better."

"You look good. Unemployment suits you."

"Actually, I've been working in a café," I say, realizing how little we've actually talked. "It's good for now."

"And then?"

"I don't know. I refuse to do something I don't love. Here's what I'd really like to do: change the world while people clap for me. What job is that?"

"Rock star, maybe? Or president. Benjamin, are you going to be president?"

"Probably. I'll make you my Secretary of Defense."

"I like not knowing what I'm going to do. It's exciting, don't you think? I mean, we could do anything."

She looks down, uncharacteristically unable to hold me gaze. My guess is that she was overcome by a too-soon-to-express thought similar to mine: that we could do something together, make a documentary or travel overseas or move to the mountains.

The food tastes as good as food can taste, both indulgent and deserved, necessary, a resupply of nutrients and vital fluids. Her bare foot finds my hard-on and makes like a hand. It's quite a skill she's got, one that I find a little scary. She sucks on a honeydew chunk and smiles, lips gleaming with melon juice. "This is a nice first date," she says.

★ ★ ★

After a walk in the park and a pit stop in a bar, we get back to her place in the early evening. The walk was good, the stout was good, and the blowjob in the bar was phenomenal, but I'm happy to be on this weird couch in this cozy apartment, with Chinese food and more sex as inevitable as nightfall.

"I've got an idea," Calliope says, and claps twice. "Scotch."

She brings me a glass of Oban along with a wooden box that contains her weed. Banned substances both, but I've earned this little party. Brain, I'm confident, will behave. Safe is how I feel, and it's weird how weird it feels.

Calliope kisses me on the cheek. Hot scotch breath. "Roll a joint," she says.

"I don't know how."

"Big surprise," she says, removing the papers from the box. "I can't believe the man I'm involved with is so not handy. Do you even own a toolbox?"

"Yeah, but it's plastic."

"God help me."

She rolls the joint quickly, a master, and seals it with her saliva, her puckered lips bringing me back to the bar.

"The scotch is great," I say.

"I can't believe you drink it with ice."

"I'm a vulgarian."

"That much I know." She kisses smoke into my mouth, a college-girl trick I'll forgive her for. "Let me ask you something."

"Anything."

"How would you feel if Schecter had lost?"

"Bad. But bad enough to regret what I did? I don't think so."

"More," she says, moving her finger as if twirling. "Tell me more."

"It's strange: on the one hand I think it's one of the best things I've ever done, yet I'm not entirely at peace with it. But is that guilt or the pain of taking a risk, of making a hard choice that pissed people off and made them not like me? I go round and round with it. But then I go round and round with most things."

"You went round and round with us."

"Yes, I did. But not anymore."

"I love you," she says for the first time, relieving me of an anxiety that was just starting to grow teeth. She kisses my neck and stands up.

"Where you going?"

"Putting on music."

My new life: not wanting her to leave my side for a second. The pot hits me quickly, my brain munching on it as if it were a spinach salad. Brain food, mentally delicious. Reuben, I realize, is on my lap, looking up at me like he can't believe I'm not petting him. It figures Calliope's cat would have the softest fur in the land.

"Why does Mona never come out?" I say.

"She's shy. She'll warm up to you."

"You did."

"Ha." She takes the joint from my hand, scratching Reuben's tennis-ball head in the process, and he follows her fingers, leaving my lap for hers. "Hanging with my two guys."

It dawns on me that I need to stop trying to tame Brain. Brain wants to be free, to run with the horses. Stoned, yes. "Heh heh heh heh heh."

The woman singing tells us she's hurting, and she is. "Who's this?"

"Lucinda Williams. I figured you'd like her. She's sufficiently down and dirty. It's beautiful, isn't it?"

Beautiful, I'm not sure. What it is, is real. Pain unfiltered, an emotional strip show, what art should be. Beautiful, I guess so. I'd stopped noticing the painting, the hell-factory, but now it freezes my blood all over again. Dad, I realize, has got big talent.

"That's an amazing painting," I say.

"Um, yeah." I look at her; both she and Reuben look back. "It used to hang in our house. I remember the day Dad put it up. I was in tenth grade. I hated it at first. It was dark, even by Jeremiah's standards. But I grew to like it. It was part of our house, you know? Then a few years ago I came home one day and the painting was on the floor, ready to be taken away. Then it hit me: the painting was of Ari. Or at least Ari inspired it. This was right after he killed himself, and they were getting rid of the reminders. The worst thing was that my parents, *especially* my father, didn't even acknowledge that Ari had problems until he tried to kill himself the first time. He was fifteen. Yet Dad painted that picture when he was in fifth grade. It's, like, wake the fuck up, Pops."

I give her a hug and Reuben, squeezed between us, squirms free and bounds onto the table, knocking over my scotch. He sneaks a peek back at Calliope, as if maybe she didn't notice, and we crack up, our laughter strong because of what came before.

"I'll get a paper towel," I say.

"I'll order food. Should we share?"

"*Got* to."

"Here's what I'm thinking: dumplings, sesame noodles, string beans, and there's this fried tofu dish I love."

"Perfect, but ask if they'll split the dumplings, half meat, half veggie."

In the kitchen Mona is hunched near her food bowl, eating the nibblets that have spilled onto the floor. She looks up at me, her sad little face making me think of her namesake, that party where she wore the cheese, one of the crimes against morality that contributed to my departure. Maybe the way I went about it wasn't the best, but I needed to get out. Had I sucked it up to the end, Calliope and I might have given it a shot; maybe I'd be standing here right now. But I wouldn't be able to stomach the sight of myself through her eyes. We'd be a couple like most couples, imploding from the first second.

It takes me three days to remember why I came into the kitchen, my mind tracking events backwards, from cat to cat. Paper towels.

"Who's the good-looking numbskull in my kitchen?" Calliope says.

I close the door to the freezer, which for some reason I've been searching, and her face is right there, stretched into a smile. "You don't have paper towels," I say.

She points to a roll over the sink, on a steel holder attached to the side of the cabinets, an appliance unto itself.

"Oh," I say.

"I took care of it," she says, handing me a clump of wet tissues that I find oddly titillating. "Trash is under the sink."

"Can they do the dumpling split?"

"Yeah, lucky you. Sometime we're going to talk about your relationship with meat."

"Is it a problem?"

"No," she says in a two-syllabled way that means, sort of. "I don't want to, you know, moralize. Or proselytize. I just want to talk about it. I'll tell you how I feel, and you'll tell me how you feel. 'Cause that's what we do. We *communicate*, right?"

"Right," I say, wanting to ask if she'd marry a meat-eater. I'd do it, too—I'd give up meat. I'd marry her. We'd eat shrubbery and live happily ever after. Down boy, as Wes would say. You're one day in, one five-orgasm day, about as representative as Thanksgiving. I've been here before. No, I haven't.

"What are you thinking about?" she says.

"Good things."

"Do you . . . " She looks down, embarrassed.

"What do you want?"

"How do you know I want something?"

"I can tell."

"I'm not sure how to put this, so I'm just going to say it. The first time we were together, in your apartment, the fantasy—"

"Be quiet."

"Why?"

"No talking."

"Oh." She smiles. "I get it."

★ ★ ★

We're fucking against the living room wall when the food arrives. "So much for the fantasy," she says.

"Speak for yourself. This is an excellent revision."

Staying inside just for the funny of it, I guide her to the buzzer, then to the door. I'd fear for her back if not for her yoga. "I feel like a wheelbarrel," she says.

"It's wheel*barrow*, sweetheart."

"It's so enlightening being with you."

The delivery guy is a girl. She smiles, maybe at the way I'm leaning back, peeking around the door. I hand her two twenties and start thrusting my hips, recharging in response to Calliope's stifled moans and to this Chinese girl's girlness, her cute concentration as she licks her thumb and slides ten singles from her wad.

We stay in the hallway, colliding, Calliope pushing off the door with both hands, her ass jiggling its approval. Faithful to the fantasy, I put my fingers where they belong, and her body responds with a tremble. But then she says, "I don't think I can come like this." She reaches back and pushes me out of her, then heads into the bedroom. When I walk in, she's lying on the bed, waiting.

31

She wakes me up getting out of bed, and when I wake up again, she's still not next to me. It's six-thirty, weirdly early for her to get up after a late night. Once we were all sexed out we sipped scotch and smoked cigarettes and talked till around two.

I sit up to listen for the shower, for any bathroom sounds, but the only thing I hear is Reuben or Mona digging in the litter box. I have a hangover, a slight ache around the eyes that I find almost amusing, like a childhood bully who no longer scares you.

Wanting to give her whatever space she might be carving out, I'm reluctant to get up, but my curiosity pushes me out of bed. I get dressed and go into the living room, which is occupied only by a raised-leg Reuben, licking himself by the window. It might just be the gray weather or the sadness of the dank, morning-after room, but I have a bad feeling.

I don't think I did anything wrong: aside from a moment of excessive honesty when I told her that I didn't love her haircut, I was my best self. Maybe she woke up, saw me lying there, and felt overwhelmed by her new reality. It's amazing *I* don't feel that way, although standing here alone, I could begin to.

I light a cigarette, then remember that last night's indoor smoking was a one-time thing, a celebratory exception. Which makes me think she's on the stoop.

And that's where I find her, hunched against the cold, smoke hovering around her head. It's time for us to stop smoking. "Morning," she says, not looking up.

"Are you crying?"

She rubs beneath her eyes. "It's not because I'm sad. I'm happy."

"Those are tears of joy?"

"No. I don't know." She twists her mouth to the side, unbearably cute. "Sometimes I cry in the morning, especially after I drink."

"Me, too."

She looks up. "Really?"

"No, but I probably should." I sit down next to her, surprisingly unperturbed by this turn of events. "You want to talk about it?"

"No, it's not specific, it's just . . . emotion. Fucked-up, huh?"

"No." I put my arm around her, kiss her head. "Let's get back in bed."

"I can't, unfortunately. Remember: I have to go eat with my grandmother."

"Now?"

"Yeah. In fact I'm already late. Joan gets up at four. This is like lunch for her."

"Your dad's mom?"

"No, mom's. She lives on the Upper East Side. You don't want to come, do you? Joan would love-love-love it. She's always getting on me about not meeting the guys I date. But you don't want to, right?"

I feel her peek at me.

"That's fine," she says in response to my silence.

I'd been looking forward to a peaceful morning. I was going to read the newspapers for the first time in weeks, then head home before work to change these clothes I've worn on and off for two days.

"I'll come," I say.

"That's nice, Ben, but you really don't have to."

"I want to."

"Really?"

"Really."

"Yippee," she says, somehow without irony.

"I don't have to shower, do I?"

"No. You look fine. Just don't tell Joan you're unemployed."

"I'm not. I make sandwiches."

"Yeah, don't tell her that, either. You're going to love Joan." She kisses me on the cheek. "She's awful."

While Calliope gets ready I walk to a deli to buy the papers. In the deli I see Bridget, studying the nutritional information on a breakfast bar. I'm overcome by fondness for her, this woman who urged me to barge into Calliope's yoga class. I can't handle her perkiness right now, but someday I'll thank her. I'll buy her flowers.

Calliope is walking out of the building when I get back. She stops abruptly, looks at the sky. "Do you think it's going to rain?"

"Probably. Maybe not."

She continues to study the sky, something in the moment reminding me of every relationship I've ever had. "I'm going to get an umbrella," she says, and heads back in.

Both Arnie Schecter and Hakim Mohammed are in the paper. A short article says a federal court will hear Mohammed's appeal "amid a firestorm of controversy over his possible innocence." A long article says Schecter won big because he got his "core supporters" to the polls. But where's the article about me, the political guru who masterminded the victory by adding fire to the storm?

I need to *do* something with my life. I don't know if I'm relieved or disappointed that the yearning is right there where I left it, stronger than ever.

Calliope comes out holding not one umbrella, but two. Women are awesome. She hands me the smaller of the umbrellas, which I'll lose, but maybe not today.

"Thanks," I say, looping my arm in hers.

In an attempt to make her appearance somewhat grandma-friendly, Calliope's put on a sweater and a collared blouse. But like most halfway measures, it's backfired, serving only to highlight her scuffed boots and old flowered wool pants.

I pull up, stopping her with me, and kiss her on the lips. She smiles, then we keep walking. She's caught up in her own thoughts. Her quiet comes as a relief; I don't like talking pre-coffee, not even to her.

Rain starts to fall as we turn onto Seventh Avenue, not hard enough for us to open our umbrellas. A black man, shirtless and wasted, is yelling at a young cop, who's standing there calmly, possibly trying to understand. An interesting scene, not least because the guy is spanking his own bottom.

I'll get Calliope's take on what we just saw, later. We'll talk about it on the subway or after breakfast or next week. Right now I want to be silent.